GW01046018

THE LOTUS KEY

AN EDEN BLACK THRILLER

LUKE RICHARDSON

"The lotus cannot be there without the mud.
Likewise, happiness cannot be there without
suffering. Looking deeply into our suffering, we
gain an understanding of it, which gives happiness a chance to blossom. Thus, the lotus does
not have to reject the mud, and the beauty of the
lotus actually gives value to the mud."

Thich Nhất Hạnh

PROLOGUE

The City of Angkor, The Khmer Empire (modern-day Cambodia). 1218.

"MAKE WAY! MAKE WAY!" SOTHEA ROARED, CHARGING through the crowded streets of Angkor. His bare feet slapped against the stones as he accelerated through the marketplace. He jumped over the merchants sitting on the ground, their wares assembled on a cloth laid out before them.

"Get out of the way! Let me pass!" Sothea shouted at a man leading a pair of cows down the lane. He weaved between the beasts, his orange robes billowing out behind him like flames.

The sound of countless voices haggling in Khmer, Chinese, and a dozen other tongues was almost inaudible to him beneath his heavy breathing.

A pair of noblemen stepped around the corner, recognizable in their glittering silk gowns. Sothea hopped to the left, splashing through a puddle and almost losing his footing, before charging on.

The path widened ahead, and Sothea accelerated again. In an attempt to soothe his aching lungs, he drew a greedy gulp of air. The scent of incense drifted from a nearby shrine, blending with the earthy aroma of elephant dung, fermented fish paste, and the sweet perfume of frangipani blossoms.

"Move, please move!" Sothea shouted as a group of young monks bustled out onto the lane. He pushed between the holy men, scattering them like a flock of startled birds. Shouting a hurried apology, he pressed on without looking back.

He veered off the main thoroughfare and into one of the marketplace's narrow passageways. Barreling beneath a line of hanging clothes, he slammed into a portly merchant. The man stumbled, nearly dropping the pole balanced across his shoulders. The chickens tied to it squawked and flapped wildly, feathers flying as they thrashed for freedom.

"Watch where you're going!" the merchant bellowed, his voice barely audible above the sound of the screeching birds.

Sothea hopped around the man and, without losing a moment, weaved on through the crowd. Now away from the market, he passed a quieter residential area. The homes of lesser nobles and wealthy merchants lined the streets on both sides. The air here tasted sweeter, perfumed by carefully tended gardens of jasmine and orchids.

Sothea ran beneath the shade of a broad-leafed banana tree, momentarily disturbing a group of children in the middle of their game. The children paused, watching the unusual spectacle.

He emerged into a wider thoroughfare and slid to a stop. This was one of the broadest streets in the city, and Sothea had hoped that the space here would allow him to make some quick progress.

"Karma is testing me today," he muttered under his breath as he saw that the street was far from empty. A procession of colorfully adorned elephants lumbered down the road, stomping up clouds of dust. The beasts filled the thoroughfare from edge to edge, casting long shadows across the stones. Ornate seats perched on their broad backs glinted in the sunlight, decorated with a dazzling display of gold leaf and precious gems.

"May I find merit in swifter feet—or a clearer path!" Sothea muttered, dancing from foot to foot as he searched for an opening. He spotted a narrow gap between two of the gentle giants. Without hesitation, he sprinted forward. As he approached, one of the elephants trumpeted loudly. With a burst of speed, Sothea dove between the elephants. For a moment, the gap between the gray flesh narrowed, threatening to crush the young monk between tons of shifting muscle and bone. He ran through the gap and stumbled back out into the sunlight.

Without pausing to catch his breath or look back, Sothea charged onwards. He was on the home straight now, and nothing could stand in his way. Rounding the corner, he caught a glimpse of the jewel in their city's crown—the temple of Angkor Wat. Its stone walls shimmered in the late afternoon light. The central lotus tower soared above the city, clawing at the heavens. On any other day, Sothea would have paused to offer a prayer of gratitude for the magnificent temple. Today, however, he barely spared it a glance.

He sprinted around the moat and onto the grand causeway which led to the temple's entrance. Charging down the stone path, he eyed the balustrades on either side, carved in the image of the Naga—an immense, serpent-like being which symbolized both water and fertility.

Sothea weaved through a group of pilgrims, forcing two men to jump out of his way to prevent being knocked flat, and sprinted up the stairs toward the grand entrance. He burst through the gateway and into the vast courtyard beyond. The late afternoon sun cast long shadows across the stones, creating a strange lifelike tapestry of light and dark. He turned his attention to the temple's central structure—the five towers representing the five peaks of Mount Meru, the home of the gods.

Sothea darted through the crowd, eyes locked on the central tower. Reaching the stairs, he launched into his ascent without hesitation. The narrow, sharply angled steps, meant to humble those climbing toward the heavens, did nothing to slow his pace. His legs burned, but he ignored the pain, leaping up two steps at a time. As he climbed, the sounds of the world below faded beneath the whispering wind and the twittering birdsong.

Reaching the top of the stairs, sweating and panting, Sothea straightened and brushed down his robes. He stepped toward the guards stationed on either side of the gateway. The guards, both far larger than Sothea, looked down at his stained and crumpled robes.

"What business have you here, monk?" the taller of the two guards demanded. One of the most sacred places in the kingdom, Sothea had only visited the royal chamber once before.

Sothea gasped for breath, momentarily unable to speak. "Prince Indravarman ... he sent for me ... I was told ... told to attend immediately," Sothea panted. "I must see the prince ... it's a matter of ... utmost urgency."

The guards exchanged wary glances. "The prince is

indisposed," the second guard grunted. "None are to disturb him, by order of the king."

"Go! Ask Prince Indravarman," Sothea shouted, straightening up and drawing upon every ounce of authority he could muster. "I have been summoned here on urgent business. The fate of the empire hangs in the balance. There's not a second to waste."

Something in Sothea's voice—a sense of desperation maybe—forced the guards to take him seriously. They exchanged a look, then, knowing the situation which waited for the monk inside, stepped aside and allowed Sothea to pass.

Not wasting a single moment, Sothea hurried through the gateway and into the chamber. Momentarily disoriented by the transition from the bright sunlight to the dim interior, Sothea paused. His eyes adjusted and the scene before him came into focus. The chamber was vast, its ceiling lost in shadows high above. Stone columns, each as thick as an ancient tree, supported the massive weight of the tower above.

The scent of incense and flowers hung in the air, masking a foul, sickening odor that Sothea recognized immediately. The smell brought with it a wave of nausea, which the young monk pushed away. He stepped forward, moving reverently toward the center of the chamber. The stench grew stronger, leaving Sothea with no doubt about its meaning—death would visit them today.

As he walked around a pair of columns, a raised platform near the center of the chamber came into view. Sothea glanced upwards, thinking about the vast lotus tower somewhere above them. Shafts of light streamed in through narrow windows, washing the platform in a dull golden glow. Upon the platform sat an ornate bed, and on that bed lay the withered form of the most powerful ruler in Southeast Asia.

"My king," Sothea whispered, stepping toward the bed. As he neared, the scent intensified further, clawing the back of his throat and attempting to choke him. Sothea slowed his breathing, locked his hands behind his back, and tensed his now-roiling stomach.

The figure on the bed shuffled and turned toward Sothea. The king's once bright eyes were now faded and dull. Even so, recognition flickered in their depths.

"Venerable Sothea, you have come." The voice boomed through the chamber. Sothea thought it was the king, then realized the tone was far too powerful for the frail man lying before him.

Sothea turned to see another man crossing the chamber. The man moved into the light and Sothea recognized Prince Indravarman's imposing figure. The prince's size and power cut a stark contrast to the frail monarch lying on the bed.

"Prince Indravarman," Sothea said, dropping into a kneeling position and bowing his head to the cool stone floor. "How can I be of service to you?"

Momentarily ignoring the monk's question, the prince walked toward his father. Passing through a shaft of light, the golden threads of his gown glittered like rippling water and the jewels set into his crown glowed.

The prince kneeled beside his father and lifted a cup to the old man's lips. Carefully tilting the cup, the prince poured water into the king's mouth. The old man swallowed feebly, slurping as the water slipped down his throat. The prince straightened up and placed the cup on the nightstand beside an oil lamp, which was already burning. The prince picked up a cloth and wiped the moisture from his father's lips.

"Venerable Sothea, how long have we known each other?" the prince said, placing the cloth beside the water jug and looking at the monk.

"Since we were children, your Highness," Sothea said. "I remember us playing together in the court, long before we even knew—"

"The weight of the crown I would one day bear," Indravarman said, a phantom smile flickering across his face. "Yes, I remember those days well."

The prince turned and stared into the depths of the chamber. Sothea followed the prince's stare but saw nothing beyond the king's bed.

"We were so carefree," Indravarman said, his shoulders drooping. "Of course, you were destined for the monastery, and I for the throne. But neither of us truly understood what that meant."

Sothea rose to his feet, sensing the shift in the prince's mood. "Your Highness, I—"

"Please, old friend," Indravarman said, turning back to face Sothea. "In this moment, let us speak as we once did before titles and ceremonies came between us."

Sothea nodded and met the prince's gaze. Looking into those deep-set eyes, he felt the years peel away. Remembering his old friend's authority, he looked down at the floor.

"Sothea, I called you here because I need your council ... and your help," Indravarman said, his voice hardening to the point of urgency. "My father's condition worsens by the day, and with it, I fear for the future of our empire."

The king stirred in his bed, mumbling incoherently. Noticing a line of drool running from his lips, Sothea averted his eyes. It felt disrespectful to see their once-great leader reduced to this.

The prince fetched the cloth, wiped his father's face, and turned his attention back to Sothea.

"Do you remember what I told you many years ago?" Indravarman said, his gaze once again meeting Sothea's.

A shiver worked its way down Sothea's spine as he latched on to the prince's meaning.

"The Lotus Key," Sothea whispered, awe lacing his voice. "That's why you summoned me?"

Indravarman nodded gravely. "You have always been perceptive, my friend."

Sothea remembered the evening, several years ago, when the prince had turned up at his lodgings and shared the secret of the Lotus Key. The king had told Indravarman of the relic and how one day it would be his cross to bear. Not knowing what do to, Indravarman had sought Sothea's council on the matter.

"The key has allowed my forefathers to achieve greatness, but that has come at a cost," Indravarman said, dragging Sothea back to the present. "The cruelty which my father has had to inflict, and the madness it has generated within him ..." The prince's voice trailed off and he turned to look at his father's feeble outline beneath the sheets.

The sound of birdsong drifted in through the window as parakeets circled the tower.

"I know now, as sure as you stand before me, I cannot and will not let the Lotus Key control my fate, nor the fate of our people," the prince said, turning back toward Sothea.

Sothea knew he was one of the few people outside the royal family to even know about the key's existence. Ever since he had learned of it, curiosity about the relic had gnawed at his stomach. He longed to know more, and understand this powerful object, but he couldn't simply ask.

He had been told about the relic in strict confidence and would take that knowledge to the grave.

"What do you intend to do?" Sothea asked, though he feared he already knew the answer.

Indravarman looked at Sothea. "We must remove it from Angkor and hide it where its power can never be used again. And you, old friend, are the only one I trust to carry out this task."

"It won't be easy," Sothea said, his mind already racing with the implications. "Is it not large and cumbersome?"

"Indeed, it is," Indravarman replied, placing a hand on Sothea's shoulder. The warmth of the gesture reminded Sothea of their shared childhood. "But I know you can do this."

"I will do all I can and more." Sothea stared into the darkness where the shaft led down to the Lotus Key's hidden chamber.

"What's more, I will have men remove the discs and hide them separately in different parts of the kingdom. With all three pieces away from the temple, a new era will be upon us."

"What if these are needed again?" Sothea said.

The prince turned, the slightest smile now flashing across his face. "I have the finest stone masons working on a new carving for the temple as we speak. This will hide the secret, should it ever be needed again."

Sothea nodded deeply, recalling his old friend's explanation of how the key worked all those years ago.

"As for now, you will move it. I have thought long about this, my friend," the prince said, his eyes glowing. "We will provide you with a cart and the finest oxen in the kingdom."

Sothea nodded.

"But that's not all," the prince continued, lowering his

voice even though they were alone in the chamber. "I will assign six of the empire's most fearsome warriors to accompany you. They will be disguised as merchants, blending in with the common folk on the roads."

"Merchants?" Sothea raised an eyebrow.

"Yes." Indravarman nodded. "You'll pose as a trading caravan. The Lotus Key will be hidden among ordinary goods—spices, silks, and pottery. No one will suspect that you carry the fate of the empire."

"And our destination?" Sothea said, stroking his chin.

"The sea," Indravarman said, his voice turning hard. "You will take the key to the sea. There you will find a ship waiting. Once the key is on board, you will sail for seven days before completing my final command."

"Your final command?" Sothea said, once again locking eyes with the prince.

As if on cue, a cool breeze swept through the chamber, causing the oil lamp on the king's nightstand to flicker. Shadows danced across the walls, bringing the figures in the bas-reliefs to life.

"Yes, no one else but you must know the final command—"

The prince's words were cut short by a sudden, rasping gasp from the bed. Monk and prince spun around to see the king's body convulsing, his eyes wide and unseeing.

"Father!" Indravarman cried, rushing to the bedside. He grasped the king's trembling hand, his own fingers white with the force of his grip.

The king's body arched. A gurgling sound escaped his throat. With a long, shuddering exhale, the old man fell still. The hand in Indravarman's grasp went limp.

The chamber fell into an eerie silence. The flickering oil lamp cast dancing shadows on the walls, as if the spirits of the ancestors were gathering to witness this momentous passing.

Indravarman bowed his head, still clutching his father's lifeless hand. When he looked up at Sothea, his eyes were bright with unshed tears, but his jaw was set with grim determination.

"You must go," he said, his voice now hardened by the weight of the empire. "May the gods watch over you, old friend. Listen now as I give you the final command."

THE GULF OF THAILAND. ONE MONTH LATER.

SOTHEA STOOD AT THE BOW OF THE SHIP, THE GENTLE creaking of the wooden planks and the rhythmic slapping of waves against the hull the only sound. He looked out across the inky black water, moonlight shimmering on the surface, and thought about their perilous journey from Angkor.

Sothea and the warriors had traveled mostly under the cover of night, winding their way through jungle paths and small villages. Every moment he had been alert, fearing discovery by those who might seek to keep their secret load within the empire.

They had faced challenges—a wheel stuck in mud during a torrential downpour, a close encounter with a patrolling group of soldiers, and tense negotiations with a local warlord who demanded an exorbitant toll. Through it all, though, Sothea's six warrior companions had proved their worth, negotiating when possible and fighting when not.

On reaching the coast, Sothea had met the arranged contact—a trusted ally of Prince, now King, Indravarman II. Under the cover of a moonless night, seven days ago, they had transferred the Lotus Key onto the ship, hiding it among crates of spices and silk.

The vessel itself had proven to be robust and versatile. Made from teak which had been especially reenforced to cope with the weight of their cargo, the ship had sped them away from land and to the location of the king's final command.

Sothea turned and glanced at the men sleeping at the vessel's stern. The sleeping draught Sothea had slipped into their drinks would ensure they remained unconscious throughout the whole ordeal. He envied them in a way as their work was done. They had served their king and would slide painlessly into the afterlife. Sothea, on the other hand, still had work to do.

With a trembling hand, he reached for the dagger hidden beneath his robes. He had agonized over this moment for seven long days and nights—thinking over the king's final command.

With silent steps, he made his way to the center of the vessel. He placed his palm against the large stone casket containing the Lotus Key, strapped into place in the base of the craft. He eyed the heavy stone box, wondering about its powerful and illusive contents. Since learning of the Key all those years ago, Sothea had longed to see it, to understand its power. He leaned in close to the stone, which was designed in such a way to seal the artifact hermetically inside. For a second, he considered shoving off the lid and taking a look. With the men asleep, there was no one here to stop him.

Recalling Indravarman's instructions, Sothea shook his head and stepped away from the crate. He kneeled and ran his fingers along the hull. Finding a spot where the wood had started to splinter, he worked the blade of the knife between two planks. The teak was strong, but he managed to work the blade between the planks. He heaved back on the knife handle, prying the plank out of place. Water bubbled in through the crack like blood from a wound.

Sothea steeled himself, gritted his teeth, and pushed all his weight against the knife. The wood groaned as though battling against his intrusion. With a crack, the plank relented, splitting in two. Water gushed through the opening, lapping over Sothea's feet in seconds.

A loud creak reverberated through the craft, forcing Sothea to stand upright. For a moment, he feared that one of his companions had woken from their slumber and seen what he was doing. The noise came again, and he realized it was the boat's hull, twisting under the strain of incoming water.

Sothea dropped to his knees, the water now splashing up and over his chest. With the bottom of the boat now obscured, he worked by touch and slid the knife beneath the next plank. Galvanized by his determination that whatever was about to happen would be over quickly, he pried the knife up, forcing another plank from its position. Memories flashed through his mind as he worked. He heard the laughter of children playing in the streets of Angkor, blending with the solemn chants of monks in the temple. He recalled the weight of Indravarman's hand on his shoulder as he was entrusted with this mission.

The second plank came away easier than the first,

widening the breach. Water bubbled through, soaking Sothea's robes. He moved to a third plank, and then a fourth, working methodically, ensuring that the damage was beyond repair in case one of his comrades should wake at the last moment.

Abandoning the knife, Sothea grabbed at the fourth plank with his hands. Splinters dug into his palms as he tore it free. He released the plank and let it float away on the rising water. He stood, the chill of the sea now reaching his waist. The ship groaned as it listed to one side, the masts swaying precariously.

Sothea half-walked, half-swam up to the bow, swirling currents tugging at his robes. As he scrambled up onto the bow, the boat slipped lower and lower. He glanced down at the figurehead—the Naga, the spirit of the water, now riding above the deep blue. He looked behind him and watched the stern drop out of sight, water creeping towards the bow like a predator. The ship's hull, which had sheltered them on their long journey, was now being dragged down by their powerful cargo.

Sothea settled himself into a cross-legged pose atop the Naga figurehead, his back straight, his hands resting lightly in his lap. His eyes lost focus as he slipped into meditation, as he had thousands of times before. He closed his eyes and pictured himself back in the tranquil gardens of Angkor Wat, surrounded by the gentle rustling of lotus leaves in the temple ponds.

The sea's icy embrace crept up his legs, but Sothea remained still. His breathing slowed. The physical world faded. The creaking of the sinking ship, the lapping of waves against his body, even the weight of his sodden robes, all receded into nothing.

1

Qincheng Prison, Beijing. Five years ago.

THE METALLIC CLANG OF THE BOLT SCRAPING OPEN DRAGGED Raven Mo back into consciousness. She rolled over on the lumpy mattress, regretting the movement as pain surged through her body.

The door screeched open, casting a square of light into the room. The silhouette of a man filled the square, watching her from the doorway. Although just an outline from where Raven lay, she recognized Dr. Shimo immediately.

"Sorry, we have no burgers and fries," Shimo said in a mocking American accent. "I'm sure that's what you would have wanted as your last meal on earth."

Raven ignored him and placed her head against the stained pillow. With the mattress feeling as though it was stuffed with rocks, and the countless injuries she'd sustained from Dr. Shimo and the prison guards, she had given up trying to find a comfortable position a long time ago.

Shimo placed his briefcase on the floor by the door, strode into the cell, and dropped a tray on the small metal table. The smell of steamed rice and boiled vegetables cut through the stench of the prison—stale sweat and over-flowing toilets—and elicited a rumble from Raven's stomach. She forced herself to sit, her muscles aching.

Shimo back stepped and leaned on the doorjamb.

Peering through her unkempt hair, Raven eyed the man. The usual immaculate gray suit covered his trim figure, and the usual smirk played across his lips. Raven didn't think she'd seen anyone in the world who enjoyed their job quite as much as Dr. Shimo.

"I don't know why you're smiling," Raven groaned, struggling to her feet. "You have to come to this place every day. I'm getting out of here soon."

Shimo tilted his head back and laughed. The sound echoed out into the corridor and elicited a string of grumbled profanities from the poor soul in the cell next door.

Raven padded across the cell, trying to ignore the pain that jarred through her ankle as she placed weight on it. She wouldn't allow Shimo the pleasure of seeing her suffering. Although it hurt, the swelling had gone down and she could now walk, albeit painfully. She slumped into the seat and looked down at the meal.

"When I heard you were joining us, I expected more," Shimo said, switching to his native Mandarin, just one of the languages in which Raven was fluent. Although growing up in the United States, Raven's Chinese-born mother refused to speak to her in any other language.

"The infamous Raven Mo, coming here, to our little facility." Shimo puffed out his chest as though taking personal pride in caring for her. "The woman who tried to take on the People's Republic of China. One woman against our country. Imagine!"

Raven ignored the man's jibes. Since her arrest in China's Xinjiang region several months ago, she'd been taunted, bullied, and hurt by the people who were supposed—she thought at least—to look after her. In all honestly, she didn't know how long she'd been in captivity. She'd tried to remember the days, but without a window in her cell, she had no way of knowing when one day ended and the next began.

"Tell me again what you were doing in Xinjiang?" Shimo said, leaning casually as though simply passing the time.

"We've discussed this already," Raven said, holding her face an inch from the plate. At this distance, the food's aroma almost masked the stench of the prison. Her stomach rumbled in response to the thought of getting a meal.

"Ha! Just to think, tomorrow it will be you who is food. Food for the worms!" Shimo said, banging the door to illustrate how amusing he thought he was. The noise rebounded down the corridor, eliciting more shouts from the prisoners in the neighboring cells.

Raven clenched her jaw and forced herself to relax. With a shaking hand, she picked up the chopsticks and shoveled some rice into her mouth.

"Yes, I am aware we have discussed this before," Shimo said, his tone once again all business. "It's incredible that you thought you could come here and get away with it."

Raven ignored the man and focused on finding a place to chew that didn't aggravate any of her broken teeth.

"You know, if you told me who you were working with, maybe we could buy you some more time," Shimo said, his tone softening. "We know you couldn't have done that alone."

Raven stopped chewing and eyeballed Shimo. Although physically beaten, the fire burned in her eyes like always. "I did it alone," she said. Her voice was so sharp it could cut steel. "It's disgusting what you do there, and even if you kill me, I won't regret it."

When her mother disappeared, Raven assumed she'd returned to her country of birth. After six months of silence, fed up with waiting, Raven went to find out. She traveled to the Xinjiang province, where her mother was born. Though the trail quickly grew cold, what Raven found was far more sinister than she could have ever imagined: a sprawling network of detention camps, the systematic oppression of the Uyghur people, and a community being erased with chilling efficiency.

She swallowed, the rice moving down her dry throat with difficulty. Even now, in her mind's eye, she could picture the faces of those she'd rescued, running from the blazing detention camp.

"You'll never understand," Raven said, her voice low but steady. She set down the chopsticks and looked up at Shimo. "This was never me against China. I was making a stand for basic human rights."

Shimo's smirk faltered, replaced by a flicker of something—confusion, perhaps, or a shadow of doubt.

"Human rights?" he scoffed. "You think you're some kind of savior now? This is about a foreigner meddling in affairs she doesn't understand."

"I saw the camps, I spoke to the people, and I made sure the world knows what's happening there," Raven said, the fire burning even more brightly in her eyes.

It was true her actions had not only frustrated the government—she had broken people out of the detention camp—but also embarrassed them by exposing the camp's conditions to the world.

"And what good did that do you?" Shimo said, anger crossing his face for the first time. He stepped into the room and loomed over Raven. "You're here, and tomorrow, you'll be executed. No one will even remember your name."

"That's where you're wrong," Raven said, leaning back in her chair. A small smile crept across her bruised cheeks. "The information is out there now. What happens to me doesn't matter."

"You had a comfortable life in America. Instead, you chose this. For what? For people you don't even know?" Shimo's hand twitched, as if he was considering striking her. Instead, he took a deep breath, visibly composing himself.

"I did it for my mother," Raven said softly. "And for the millions like her. And yes, for people I don't know. Because someone has to."

A long silence stretched between them. Shimo's eyes narrowed, studying Raven as if trying to see the cogs of her mind whirl.

"I've seen hundreds of prisoners face their last day." Shimo pointed at Raven. "However confident they are at the start, it always ends the same. Once they realize no one's coming to save them, they cower like a naughty child." He chuckled, forcing humor into his tone.

Raven's fingers tensed, longing to clench into a fist. She resisted, forcing herself to take a deep breath. She snatched up the chopsticks and shoveled another clump of rice into her mouth.

"I can picture the moment now," Shimo continued. "When they strap you down. It won't matter what you've done, or who you are, or what you believe—you'll beg and cry like the rest of them."

Raven still didn't respond, focusing on her food.

"Maybe you came here thinking you could change our country, but now look at you. You're rotting in a cell. Your father has abandoned you, and so has the rest of the world."

Raven tensed at the mention of her father. It was true that since her arrest, he hadn't once reached out.

Clearly not getting the reaction he wanted, Shimo crashed his fist into the table. The noise boomed through the cell, causing Raven to drop a mouthful of rice. She glanced up, immediately regretting the movement as pain shot through her body.

Shimo fetched his briefcase and sunk into the seat opposite. He opened the case and pulled out a small wad of papers.

"Anyway, this is not a social call. We have documents to complete. I am required to make you aware of your rights and all that nonsense." Shimo placed the papers on the table between them and returned the briefcase to the floor.

"My rights?" Raven said, an eyebrow raised.

"Yes, we may be misunderstood by our brothers and sisters in the West, but we are not animals. The People's Republic has many rules and guidelines, just like everywhere else."

It was Raven's turn to laugh. It started in her throat, like a strange gurgling noise, and when the sensation passed her lips, it felt as though it had come from someone else entirely.

Dr. Shimo reacted with such speed, Raven didn't even see it coming. He swung out and smashed the bowl from the table. Rice and vegetables splattered across filth-covered concrete.

"You do not disrespect the People's Republic," he snarled, his eyes burning. He pointed at her, wielding his finger as though it were a weapon. "This is why someone like you can never be free. You are a scourge to be wiped out." Shimo drew a pen from inside his jacket. "Is the patient in full health and of sound mind?" he said, reading from the document. A grin lit his face, and his voice took on a mocking, singsong quality. "The problem is that despite what I can see before me, anything other than *yes* will delay tomorrow's..." he paused, choosing the words carefully, "... event." He made a show of scribbling on the paper. "Yes, the patient is in full health and has been looked after with the utmost care." He pursed his lips and turned to the next page. "Has the patient been informed of the method of execution?" Dr. Shimo continued, his tone as casual as someone discussing a ball game. "Oh yes, I believe we've covered that quite thoroughly. You will be administered with a lethal injection. It will be quick, and painless, or so I've been told. Of course, we can't know for sure as we've never had the opportunity to ask anyone afterward." He glowered at Raven, the light from the corridor glinting in his eyes.

Raven's jaw clenched, but she remained silent.

Shimo looked down at the document. "Has the patient been given the opportunity to make final arrangements?" He looked up again. "Do you have any last wishes, any family you want informed? Oh, wait, your father hasn't spoken to you since you left. It's not surprising, really. Imagine the damage you could do to the share price of his business. He might be forced to sell one of his yachts. Now for my favorite question," Shimo said, a smile of pure enjoyment lighting his face. "Has the patient been offered spiritual counseling? I could arrange for a monk to visit you. He could help you with a few moments of inner peace before ... well, you know."

Raven didn't move, her stare silently burning a hole in the man across the table.

"I'll take your silence as a no." Shimo ticked a box and straightened up. "Well, I think that covers everything. A few signatures here and there, and we'll be all set." He signed the papers with a flourish and tucked them back into his briefcase. He stood, brushed the folds from his suit, and crossed to the door.

Raven didn't move as the door swung shut and the bolt clunked back into place.

2

Chaoyang District, Beijing. Five years ago.

POWERING HIS HONGQI H9 UP THE FREEWAY EXIT RAMP, DR. Shimo breathed a sigh of relief that soon he would be done with the infuriating Raven Mo. He'd known when she'd arrived that she would be trouble—she was a high-profile foreigner, meaning she had to be handled carefully. He preferred the prisoners no one missed, because when no one missed them, there was no one to complain.

Shimo recalled the circumstances surrounding Raven's arrest had been problematic, too. Before she'd interfered, governments around the world had been unaware of the scale of the internment camps in Xinjiang. Now with the eyes of other countries, potential business partners, and allies questioning their every move, the Peoples' Republic needed the whole situation dealt with quickly and quietly.

Shimo slowed as he reached the main gate of his secure community. He flashed his lights at the guard lounging behind bulletproof glass. The guard sat upright as though he'd been caught doing something he shouldn't. The gate rolled open, revealing the manicured lawns and curving avenues that Shimo and the other residents called home.

Shimo eased through the gate, the headlights of the Chinese-made luxury car sweeping across the impressive facades of the surrounding mansions.

Fortunately, Shimo reassured himself, this time tomorrow, Raven Mo would be nothing but a memory, and this whole messy business would be over. Passing the lake in the center of the community, Shimo wondered whether he should have administered a lethal dose tonight, just to get it over and done with. He shook his head. It paid to do things by the book, where possible.

Shimo crested an artificial hill, designed to make the estate look more picturesque, bringing his house into view. Although he lived alone, the house had multiple bedrooms, a bathroom for every day of the week, a gym, and a swimming pool. Other than his own private security detail, chef, and fitness coach, who all lived off-site, Shimo had the place to himself. The isolation suited him perfectly.

He pulled up outside his private gate and clicked the button on the car's central console. Although the gate and perimeter wall around his property wasn't necessary with the security measures the entire community enjoyed, he had decided that it paid to be careful. The gate slid open and Shimo pulled inside. Lights automatically illuminated the driveway, the immaculately landscaped front lawn, and the Grecian-inspired fountain which burbled softly.

He pulled up beside the front door and stepped out of the car. He fished his keys out of his pocket and entered the building. With his mind still working through the events of the day, he tossed his keys onto a Qing dynasty table by the door and navigated through the darkened living room and into the kitchen.

He ran his hand across the wall and flicked the switch. Light blazed, illuminating sleek marble countertops and state-of-the-art appliances, and something else—something Shimo had not been expecting.

He gasped, took a step back, and crashed into the wall. He blinked, expecting the image to change, but it didn't. Two men lounged against his custom-designed cabinetry, watching him with cool, unwavering eyes.

"What ... what's going on?" Shimo said, his voice a hiss of air. He looked from one man to the next, expecting an explanation. To Shimo, the men looked American, or maybe European. Both wore black suits, which were pulled tight against bulging muscles. He saw something that turned his nerves to ice—each man held a pistol, barrels pointed directly at his chest.

Shimo backed toward the door, but as he neared it another man stepped through, cutting off his exit route. He turned one way and the next, realizing he must have walked straight past the stranger waiting in the darkened living room. Shimo looked at the newcomer. He was older than the pair of brutes and dressed like a businessman. Also, as far as Shimo could see, he wasn't armed.

The older man strolled into the kitchen, deliberately scanning the room as if inspecting it. For several seconds the only sound in the house was the older man's shoes squeaking on the tiles.

"It's a wonderful place you have here, Dr. Shimo," the visitor said, turning his attention to Shimo. He spoke in English, with what Shimo recognized as a British accent.

"What ... what are you doing here? Who are you?" Shimo said, looking from the visitor to the pair of gun-wielding brutes. Although the pair lounged against the counters, their eyes were hard and focused.

"I'm here to have a conversation, nothing more," the visitor said. He stepped up to the kitchen's island counter and nodded once. The brutes lowered their weapons but didn't holster them. "If you do exactly as I tell you, this will be over in a few minutes."

Shimo tried to swallow, but a lump now blocked his throat. He glanced up at the ceiling, where he knew a hidden security camera—one of many positioned around the house—recorded every movement.

"Your security system has been disabled," the visitor said. "Along with that of the entire estate. There will be no record of us being here." The man glanced around the room as though the whole process was boring him. "So, let us not waste any more time. Take a seat and we'll get down to business." The visitor pointed at one of the stools which surrounded the island counter.

Shimo glanced at the two brutes. Catching their icy stares, he thought it was best to do what his visitor asked. He shuffled across the room and slid onto the indicated seat.

Remaining standing on the other side of the counter, the visitor drew an envelope from the inside of his jacket. He flipped open the flap, drew out a handful of photographs, and placed them on the counter. He swept his hand across the pile like a casino dealer, spreading the photographs so Shimo could see each one.

Shimo felt as though all the air had suddenly left the room. He tried to take a breath, but his lungs didn't want to obey.

The visitor stood in silence for what felt like a very long time, clearly giving Shimo time to absorb what he saw.

The pictures had been taken inside the prison, but were not the sanitized images Shimo would allow to leave the facility. These images revealed the grim reality of what happened behind closed doors.

The first photo showed a prisoner strapped to a chair, with electrodes attached to various parts of their body. Bruises bloomed across their exposed skin, and their face was contorted in a grimace of pain.

Another image depicted a small, windowless cell. The occupant was huddled in the corner, their skin gaunt and papery. The prisoner's face was partially obscured, but one eye was visible—drooping and unfocused. A portion of their scalp was bare, revealing a neat surgical scar that hadn't quite healed properly.

Shimo's stomach churned. Ice moved up his spine, locking each of his vertebrae in place, one after another. These weren't random shots—whoever had taken them knew what they were doing and had been watching for some time.

He looked at the next photograph and felt a wave of dizziness. This picture showed Shimo himself, administering an injection to a prone figure.

"I think you've seen enough," the visitor said, shuffling the pictures together and slipping them back inside the envelope. "Now, allow me to tell you what might happen if these pictures found their way to the President of the People's Republic, followed by the international press."

Shimo stared at the envelope in the same way a person might look at an unexploded bomb. He tried to answer, but little more than a gurgling sound escaped his throat. He finally looked up and saw the visitor silently challenging him to deny what was plainly evident.

"First, let's address an important point," the visitor said, holding up a finger. "It doesn't matter whether your work is officially sanctioned. Although, I would bet that it's not. I suspect, having got to know you and the abhorrent way your mind works, you think these experiments are somehow within your job description."

Shimo attempted to stutter an answer, but the visitor silenced him with a look.

"Allow me to lead a brief thought experiment and consider what might happen if these images, and the video footage from which they're taken, should come to light."

Shimo slumped further into his seat, his hands hanging at his sides.

"First, there would be the public outcry. Your name and face would be plastered across every news outlet in China, perhaps even internationally. Imagine the headline—*Rogue Doctor Conducts Illegal Experiments on Prisoners.*"

The blood drained from Shimo's face, and the room tilted from side to side.

"Your colleagues would distance themselves immediately. That prestigious position at the university? Gone. Your medical license? Revoked. Every award, every accolade you've ever received? Stripped away."

The visitor's eyes bored into Shimo's. "But that's merely the beginning. The party would need to save face. They'd deny all knowledge of your activities, of course. You'd be branded a traitor, acting against the interests of the People's Republic."

Shimo's mind raced, trying to keep up with the unfolding scenario.

"You'd be arrested, publicly. Perhaps they'd parade you in front of the cameras, to make a point on the international scene. I suspect your trial would be swift—no one would want to risk you saying too much in open court." The visitor's voice dropped even lower. "And then, Dr. Shimo, you'd find yourself on the other side of those prison bars. Perhaps even in the very facility where you now work. Poetic justice, some might say. Imagine ... you might even get to share a cell with one of your old *friends*."

"What ... what do you want?" Shimo stuttered, his voice almost inaudible.

The visitor paused like a master showman, letting Shimo's utter defeat hang in the air.

"Now that is the correct question to ask," the visitor said. "Let me explain ..."

3

Qincheng Prison, Beijing. Five years ago.

KNOWING SHE WAS GOING TO DIE TODAY, SLEEPING FELT pointless. With no natural light in the cell, Raven had no idea what time it was. As the hours stretched on and on, she thought through the events that had led her to this cell and would, most likely, lead to her death. Strangely, she didn't fear death but was frustrated to meet it on someone else's terms. If she'd died in a blaze of gunfire while rescuing the persecuted from the burning internment camps in Xinjiang, that would have seemed fair. But to meet it here, in a grim, stinking prison, administered by the cold and calculated prick of a needle, seemed wrong.

Somewhere on the block, another inmate howled with a pain so raw the noise didn't even sound human. It was as though they had lost all other forms of communication, leaving only that pained, beastly screech.

Raven thought of the woman for whom she had come to China in the first place—her mother. Even during the months she spent in the country, planning her attack on the internment camp and scheming with others to get the prisoners to safety, she'd heard nothing. It was as though her mother had disappeared into the air like incense smoke from a mountain temple.

Raven exhaled, emotion threatening to overwhelm her. She had no regrets about what she'd done, although still had no answers. If she'd found her mother, or found out what had happened to her, then the trade might have felt fair.

Somewhere outside her cell, a door screeched open, and footsteps approached. Remembering Shimo's words from the day before—*once they realize no one's coming, they all cower like a naughty child*—she steeled herself. She would certainly not hand the power of her emotions over to her tormentor. Rubbing a hand across her face, she was surprised to feel tears. After all this time, she hadn't expected to feel anything this raw. Maybe Shimo was right, maybe facing death did funny things to people. Either way, her time was up.

Raven focused on the footsteps and identified at least three people approaching her cell. Dr. Shimo clearly wasn't taking any chances.

The footsteps drew near and stopped right outside her door. Keys jangled and scratched around inside the lock before the mechanism disengaged.

Raven sat up slowly as the cell door creaked open. She squinted and rubbed her eyes. Her body ached as usual, but today, faced with the thought of eternal oblivion, the pain didn't bother her. At least if she was in pain, she was still alive.

The door swung wide, and light from the corridor cast its angular glow into the cell. Three figures stood in the doorway—Shimo in the center, with a guard on either side.

"It's time," Shimo said.

Raven looked at Shimo, but he looked away before she could catch his eye. The gesture wasn't what Raven had expected, after all the gloating and teasing he'd inflicted over the previous months.

"Get up now," Shimo barked, his attention fixed somewhere on the floor. "Let's get this over with."

Raven rose unsteadily to her feet. Moving her weight from foot to foot, she considered making a last-ditch attempt at an attack. At least that way she would go out fighting. As though sensing her intention, the guards seized her arms and led her out of the cell. As they marched her down the corridor, the howling from the neighboring cells intensified. It was as though, through some spiritual connection, the poor souls trapped inside those concrete cubes felt what was taking place close by.

Shimo led the way down a dim corridor. The guards followed, dragging Raven along with them. They reached a stairwell and descended—flickering light casting eerie shadows across the walls.

As they descended, Raven thought it appropriate that their destination was buried deep underground—as though the earth could hide the sins inflicted on the unfortunate.

At the base of the stairwell, they passed through a series of metal doors. They reached a door at the end of the corridor and Shimo paused.

"What are we waiting for?" Raven said. "Have you grown a conscience all of a sudden?"

Shimo didn't turn, but Raven noticed something in his posture. There was something less confident, less self-assured than the day before. Physically shaking himself into action, he removed a key, unlocked the door, and led them into a brightly lit room. The chamber was square with stark white walls that seemed to amplify the harsh fluorescent lighting. In the center of the room stood a single chair, a monstrous thing of stainless steel with thick leather straps. To the right, two syringes waited on a small metal trolley.

"If you're watching this, you're sick," Raven said, looking into a large mirror which she suspected was a one-way window, allowing people to watch the proceedings.

The hands around her arms tightened as the guards shuffled her toward the chair.

Her chest tightening, Raven realized that once she was trapped in that chair, her fate was sealed. She let the men move her across the room and place her in the chair. Then, as expected, their grip loosened as their focus shifted to the straps.

She kicked forward as powerfully and suddenly as she could. The move caught the men off guard, and their grip slipped. She twisted, wrenching free and leaping from the chair.

Now on her feet, she spun around and drove an elbow into the stomach of the guard on her right. He let out a whoosh of air and stumbled backward. She pivoted and smashed her fist into the second guard's jaw.

"Stop her!" Shimo yelled, sprinting across the room and hitting a button. An alarm sounded and a red light mounted on the ceiling strobed.

The first guard, recovering from the blow, lunged at Raven. She sidestepped, grabbed his arm, and twisted it up behind his back, forcing him to his knees. She brought her knee up, connecting with his face with a crack. He crumpled to the ground, unconscious.

The second guard, blood streaming from his split lip, pulled out his baton. He swung it in a wide arc, aiming for Raven's head. She ducked under the swing and struck the guard in the nose. He staggered back, blood exploding from his face.

Raven took the baton from his loosened grip and swung it hard, catching him on the side of the head. He went down, joining his companion on the floor.

Panting, Raven turned to face Shimo. He stood frozen by the door, his eyes wide with a mix of fear and disbelief.

"I'm not dying today," Raven said, pacing toward the doctor.

Shimo backed away like a cornered animal, his eyes wide with fear. The door burst open, and four more guards rushed in. The men fanned out, blocking Raven on all sides. She paused, eyeing the wall of muscle and bone, waiting to see what would happen next.

"Stop wasting time!" Shimo shouted. "Get her and let's get this done."

Raven hurled the baton at the guard on the far left, catching him by surprise. She spun around and snagged one of the syringes from the trolley. She used her teeth to pull off the cap, then pointed the needle at the guards. Clearly knowing what the chemical inside would do to them, the guards slowed their approach.

"Stop wasting time, get her!" Shimo shouted, from the relative safety of the doorway.

The guards took another step forward, although their confidence had diminished.

With time against her, Raven hurled the syringe at the guard in the center. The men sprang aside, flattening themselves against the floor.

Raven grabbed the trolley, spun around, and hurled it at the observation window. The glass smashed, revealing the observation room. Through the fractured glass, Raven saw men in expensive suits, watching the action as though it were a reality TV show. The men jumped to the feet and charged for the exit.

"You think this is entertaining? You people are sick!" Raven shouted, launching through the window, glass cutting her hands and face. Falling to the floor on the other side, she wasted no time climbing to her feet. The spectators charged for the exit, slamming the door as they passed.

Raven glanced toward the far side of the room, surprised to see one person remained in position. A woman sat calmly, her arms folded.

Then, with a feeling akin to a punch in the face, Raven recognized the woman. Her knees shook and the air left her lungs. The room spun around her.

"Mother? What ... what are you doing here?" Raven stuttered, her voice not even sounding like her own.

The guards were at the window now. They pushed the remaining shards of glass aside and reached into the observation room.

Strong hands closed around Raven's shoulders, but she was too stunned to move. The door flew open, and two more guards charged in.

Raven barely even noticed, her eyes locked on the woman she'd followed, quite literally, to the end of the earth. Dressed in a trouser suit, with her black hair tied in a ponytail, her mother looked exactly like she'd remembered. The woman sat up straight, her knees crossed, watching the events play out.

"You shouldn't have come," Raven's mother said, her voice a monotone. "You should have stayed in America. You have no business over here."

Three or maybe four guards—Raven couldn't be sure— surrounded her now. They gripped her arms and legs and dragged her back through the window.

"What? Where?" The questions bubbled and swirled through Raven's mind as she was pulled back toward the chair.

"I didn't want you to come, Raven," her mother said, still sitting motionless. Her gaze was hard and cool, showing no emotion.

"Wait ... wait ... I need to know. Where have you been?" Raven said. Thick leather straps closed and locked around her wrists and ankles. More straps were then looped around her stomach and chest before they were pulled tighter still.

"You don't need to know anything," her mother said. "You should never have gotten involved."

Shimo plucked a syringe from the wreckage, his hands visibly shaking. He moved toward Raven, although to her he was invisible.

"But ... I don't ..." Raven stuttered as all the strength and bravado left her like a reverse tidal wave. "I need to—" Raven tried to speak, but then Shimo interrupted.

"Raven Mo, by order of the People's Republic of China, your sentence is to be carried out." Shimo inserted the needle into Raven's arm and pressed down on the plunger. "May your..." He faltered for a moment, then continued. "May your soul find peace."

A cold sensation spread through Raven's arm where the needle had pierced her skin. Her vision blurred, the bright lights of the execution chamber smeared and ran together. She watched her mother's emotionless face as it melted into a haze of shapes and colors. Then, like a candle being snuffed out, Raven's world descended into darkness.

Unknown Location. Five years ago.

For an indeterminate time, Raven floated through the darkness, as though she were traveling through an endless void. Fragments of memories and sensations flashed into her mind's eye—the cold steel of the chair, the sharp pinch of the needle, the emotionless face of the woman she had come to save. Time seemed to stretch and compress. Minutes grew into hours and snapped back to seconds again.

Suddenly, a burst of light exploded behind her eyelids, momentarily blinding her even through closed eyes. Colors swirled and danced, forming patterns that seemed to hold meaning beyond her grasp. The sensation of falling gave way to a gentle rocking, as if she were adrift on a calm sea. She took a deep breath, suddenly aware that for the first time in a long time, it felt real.

Confusion overwhelming her, she opened her eyes. She struggled for a few seconds against the brightness, then she picked out shapes of light and dark moving around her. Soon, reality solidified, appearing as she had remembered before her time in the hell-hole prison. She found herself staring at a pristine white ceiling, so different from the grimy concrete of her cell.

Confusion washed over her as she raked her memories for an explanation as to what had happened. The execution chamber flashed through her mind, causing her heart to race. Now, instead of cold steel and leather straps, she was lying on a comfortable mattress beneath soft sheets.

She moved her eyelids, first both together, then each one separately. Satisfied she was in control of her movements, she tried to tilt her head to get a better view of the room. A large window dominated the wall in front of her. Beyond the glass stretched an expanse of brilliant blue ocean, its surface shimmering in bright sunlight. White-capped waves rolled gently towards a distant shoreline, and seabirds wheeled lazily in the cloudless sky.

"Of course, this makes sense. I'm dead," she said, her dry throat hinting otherwise.

The room itself was spacious and airy, more like a high-end hotel than a hospital. Soft beeping from nearby monitors provided a subtle reminder of her medical status, but otherwise, the atmosphere was calm and comfortable.

The door opened and Raven tensed, half-expecting to see Dr. Shimo. Instead, she saw a man in his late middle age. He was followed by a woman who crossed to the medical equipment beside the bed.

"What's ... what's going on?" Raven said, her voice croaking. "Am I dead?"

"Oh no, you're not dead," the man said, placing his hands on the foot of Raven's bed. His voice was sonorous and authoritative, although kind.

The woman checked the medical equipment, entered some information into a tablet computer and nodded at the man. She put the device down, poured a glass of water, and helped Raven sit up and take a sip. The cooling liquid felt better than anything she'd ever tasted before.

"Then ... what ..." Raven said.

The man stopped her with a raised hand. "I understand you have many questions, and the answers will come in time. For now, all you need to know is that you're safe."

"Where am I?" Raven said.

"This is your new home, it's a ship," the man said, turning to glance out of the window. "Exactly where we are on the globe, no one knows, but we call this place the *Balonia*."

4

Koh Rong Island, Cambodia. Present day.

"Are you sure it's here?" Eden Black said, looking out at the dense mangrove forest surrounding them on all sides. She dipped her paddle in the mud-colored water and heaved the kayak forward.

"There is much here," Vireak, their guide and a direct descendent of the island's first inhabitants, said from the bow. He gestured, pointing vaguely at the surrounding trees. "Just because mangroves are all you can see, doesn't mean we are alone here. Powerful forces work on this island."

Vireak dipped his paddle and navigated them effortlessly around a thick root, which reached across the waterway like a skeletal hand. The kayak moved through a shaft of sunlight which dappled the water in alternate shades of light and dark.

Watching the ease with which Vireak navigated the kayak, the muscles of arms bulging beneath sun-darkened skin, Eden once again tried to calculate his age. Although sprightly and clearly strong, his eyes wore the deep lines of a long and well-lived life. The closest estimation she could come up with was somewhere between fifty and seventy years old.

"The spirits of our ancestors are strong here," Vireak said, inhaling deeply.

"Nowhere near as strong as my desire to turn around and get out of here," Athena grumbled from the seat behind Eden. "You told me we were going sightseeing. A nice tourist day on a tropical island is what you—"

"The spirit of the trees and water are one," Vireak continued, sweeping a flat palm from right to left. "They guard the secrets of our past, reveal them only to those deemed worthy."

Eden flashed her friend a look which was a cross between amusement and admonishment. Athena huffed out a breath and wiped her hand across her brow in an obvious attempt to stop the sweat running into her eyes.

"I didn't actually use the term *sightseeing*, did I?" Eden said, grinning.

"Well, maybe not, but I'm pretty sure the word *fun* passed your lips."

"That's true." Eden nodded sagely. "But then, after so many council meetings, anything outside is *fun*."

"On what planet is paddling through a dense forest of mangroves, in one-hundred-percent humidity, in the midday heat, fun?" Athena groaned through gritted teeth. "You're clearly a very disturbed young woman."

"Look at this nature. Un-spoiled nature." Eden swept her paddle back too quickly, splashing water up at Athena.

"You've got to be joking me," Athena said, wiping the water from her face.

"Just trying to cool you down." Eden shrugged.

"In the last two hours, we've seen nothing but

mangroves, a few monkeys, birds, and lots and lots of water," Athena said.

"Have patience," Eden replied, keeping her voice low and cupping a hand around her mouth so that Vireak wouldn't hear their complaints. "Vireak is certain the old settlement is around here somewhere. Anyway, the whole point of looking is—"

"Yeah, I understand." Athena groaned. "The whole point of looking is that we're not sure what we're going to find." Athena dipped her paddle again.

"You understand well," Vireak said, clearly having heard the entire exchange. "It is the search itself that is sacred. Our ancestors do not reveal their presence to every traveler."

Eden flashed Athena a smirk and got a raised eyebrow in return. Behind them a pair of long-tailed macaques skipped through the tightly woven branches, following the kayak's progress with curiosity.

Vireak straightened up and inhaled. He held the breath for a few seconds and let it go slowly. "Do not fear, we are close now."

Based on a private island off the coast of Koh Rong for a council meeting, Eden had been told it was customary to pay respects to the island's original inhabitants and their ancestors before conducting business here. Although she knew several members of the council, including Athena and Baxter, thought such things were mumbo jumbo, she decided that, if nothing else, it would be an interesting experience. As such, she'd spent their first day on the island searching for someone who could conduct such a ceremony. That led her to Vireak and his family, who were said to be direct descendants of one of the earliest settlements on the island.

"In order to ask for permission, we must visit the old

settlement," Vireak had said, looking at Eden as though he'd been waiting for her arrival. "There is something you must do." Without another word, they set off on what turned out to be over two very sweaty hours, and counting, in the kayak.

"The spirits of my ancestors' flow through these waters. They whisper through these leaves." Vireak leaned forward at such an angle, Eden feared he might fall out of the kayak. As though in reply, a gust of wind rustled through the mangroves, sending ripples across the water. Vireak closed his eyes, listening intently.

"The spirits speak," he said, sitting motionless. "They say we must proceed with caution. Not all who dwell in these waters are friendly."

Although Eden didn't turn to see it, she knew Athena was rolling her eyes. Eden dipped her paddle again as they slipped around a bend in the water.

As another unbroken wall of mangroves came into view, Vireak stiffened.

Eden was about to ask what he had seen, but Vireak raised his hand in a gesture of silence. They slid further around the bend and Eden saw it for herself. Amid the tangled maze of mangrove roots stood a row of massive stone blocks. As they drew closer, she realized the stones were in fact a vast set of crumbling steps, leading up from the water's edge. At the top of the steps, two columns marked what would once have been a grand entrance. She twisted around and shot Athena her trademark *told you so* look.

"The dwelling place of the old ones," Vireak whispered, pointing at the structure. "Many centuries ago, a great storm wore away the land here, then the mangroves spread.

Unable to live here, my people moved to the hill." He pointed vaguely in the direction of their village.

"This is incredible," Eden said. As they got closer, she saw that the structure was not just a single wall, but a temple rising from the ground like a pyramid. "And no one knows this place exists?" She noticed that Athena had gone silent, clearly as enraptured as she was.

"Other than my family, you are the first people to visit this place for as long as I can remember."

Vireak instructed them to paddle around the side of the structure and down a narrow channel a few inches wider than the kayak. Once inside the channel, they dropped the paddles inside the boat and pulled themselves along by grabbing the overhanging branches. After a few feet, they slipped alongside a stone platform. Once part of the grand temple, the platform sat half submerged in the water, providing the perfect place to scramble on to land.

"This place is sacred to my people," Vireak said, pulling the kayak in close to the platform. He hopped out without causing so much as a ripple. He lashed the kayak to one of the trees and held out a hand to help Eden and Athena out.

"How did they build this place?" Eden said, stepping up to one of the giant stones. The blocks were so well joined that they remained in place, even though the wall leaned at an angle.

"Legends speak of a man who was not of our tribe," Vireak said. He gestured they should follow and stepped through an opening into what would have been the temple's central chamber. Although, in most places, the roof had collapsed, the walls remained in remarkable condition. "The elders told me that the outsider was washed ashore here, long ago. He was incredibly strong, unlike any man my people had seen before. He was a man of peace, too. Having no desire to return to wherever he came from, he was accepted by our tribe. He taught them much, including how to build this place."

Eden crossed the chamber, scrambled over fallen chunks of roof and examined a section of the wall. Although now slightly out of place, the structure's survival was a testament to its construction.

"Do the elders know where he came from?" Athena said.

"The elders speak of a ship wrecked in a storm, which washed the stranger ashore here."

"That explains the architectural style of this place," Eden said, running her finger across the joint between two stones.

Vireak opened his mouth as though to speak but froze.

Noticing their guide had stopped his explanation, Eden turned away from the wall.

Vireak stood in the center of the temple, his finger raised. All color had drained from his expression, and he stood rigid, as though ready to run or fight.

"What is...?" Eden started to speak, then noticed the sound too. The noise cut through the air like an assassin's knife. It was the unmistakable roar of an outboard engine, and it was getting close.

"Someone comes this way," Vireak said, his expression darkening. "The spirits told of danger. This is not good."

"Tourists taking a wrong turn?" Athena said, peering back toward the kayak. "It would be really easy to get lost out here."

"This far from the sea, not possible," Vireak said. "No one comes this way."

Eden scrambled up a section of wall and peered out across the canopy. A motorboat sped in their direction. As the boat neared, the engine slowed, eventually dropping to an idle gurgle. Through a thin section of the trees, she saw the boat turn from the main channel and into a narrower one. From her vantage point, she could see the channel ran to a sand bank behind the temple.

"Whoever they are, they're heading that way," Eden said, pointing to the temple's far side. She scrambled back down and joined the others as the motorboat slipped out of sight.

"The spirits here are bad. We must go," Vireak said, indicating the direction from which they'd come.

The motorboat chugged on, then the engine died completely.

Eden strained her ears, catching the faintest sound of movement filtering through the ancient walls. Then a frantic squawking, cawing sound disturbed the stillness.

"I don't know what that sound is," Eden said, "but it doesn't sound good."

"This is sacred ground," Vireak hissed. "Nobody should be..." He stopped talking as Eden approached the sound.

Athena rolled her eyes and followed. "I knew a day of sightseeing was too much to ask," she said.

5

Angkor Wat, Cambodia. Present day.

THE JEWEL IN CAMBODIA'S CROWN, THE TEMPLE OF ANGKOR Wat, stood silent against the moonlit sky. A gentle breeze whispered through the surrounding forests, rustling leaves and spreading ripples across the temple's wide moat. In the gnarled branches of a nearby tree, a troop of macaques nestled together, their furry bodies intertwined in sleep. Insects provided a subtle backdrop of sound—the rhythmic chirping of crickets, and the occasional buzz of a night-flying beetle. A lone gecko called out with its distinctive *tzzzuk tzzzuk* from somewhere within the temple's vast galleries.

From the east, a new sound drifted through the tranquil scene. Beginning as a faint thrumming, it rumbled through the air like the mating call of some nocturnal beast not from this world. Gradually, it grew louder—a steady, mechanical pulse, jarring against the stone. The noise rose—reverberating across the forest canopy and skimming over the moat

—now recognizable as the distinctive thrum of an incoming helicopter.

In the trees, the macaques stirred, blinking and gazing up at the sky for the source of the noise. Birds erupted from their roosts in a flutter of wings, their cries of protest drowned out by the approaching helicopter.

From the east, a Sikorsky S-92 burst into view. It thundered low across the forest, whipping the highest branches into a chaotic dance. A shadow, like a rogue chunk of night, the chopper flew without a single light marking its position. Making a beeline for the temple, the craft swept out across the moat, churning water into foam.

From the chopper, Mei-Ling Zhao peered out at the temple below as they banked, slowing above the grand western entrance. Although their approach would not have gone unnoticed, she was confident they would be back on board before any reinforcements could be called.

The chopper dropped in close to the ground; the downdraft sending the dust into swirling eddies that whipped around the walls like ghosts.

"Twenty feet," the pilot said, his voice gruff through the comms system.

"Ready," Zhao said, climbing to her feet and sliding open the chopper's rear door. Wind whipped into the cabin, roaring in Zhao's ears. She glanced at Gui, her second in command. Gui climbed to his feet, the interior of the craft forcing his massive frame to remain hunched. He instinctively checked his weapon and joined Zhao at the door.

Zhao clipped a rope onto the anchor point above the door and swung out, lowering herself quickly to the ground below. Gui followed a moment later, a bulky pack hanging from his back. He made light work of the descent down the rope, dropping the last few feet and landing with a thud beside Zhao.

"Clear," Zhao said, tapping the comms device in her ear. The pair turned and set off at a run toward the temple entrance.

The whirring of the Sikorsky's rotor blades increased in volume as the craft powered away, spinning around to head back the way they'd come.

Zhao paused at the base of the stairs and glanced up at the chopper, the rotor blades shimmering in the moonlight. She sprinted up the staircase and into the main entrance with Gui a step behind.

"We've got company." Gui pointed at the causeway, which was the only way into and out of the temple. A pair of flashlight beams swung from right to left as the security guards, alerted by the chopper, charged in their direction.

"We'll deal with them," Zhao said, snagging the pistol holstered at her thigh. Gui did the same, and the pair opened fire.

Two soft *phuts* pierced the air, barely audible above the guards' shouts. Despite the distance, the first shot hit home, smashing the guard in the shoulder. His legs in full motion, the guard continued running for three further steps before slamming to the ground. His flashlight beam swung wildly before falling to the stone, coming to rest on the multiple heads of the Naga balustrade.

The second guard spun around to face his fallen colleague. He fumbled for his radio, fingers slipping on the smooth plastic in the humid night air. Before he could reach the transmission button, Zhao and Gui fired again. Now stationary, the guard offered an easier target, and both rounds slammed him in the back. He swayed for a moment, confusion flashing across his face before his knees buckled. He slumped against a pillar and rolled to the ground.

"We'll be out of here before the next patrol notices they're gone. This way," Zhao said, running through the entrance.

Working by the moonlight filtering through the gallery windows, they weaved their way through the structure. Reaching the inner sanctuary, Zhao paused to look up at the central lotus tower. Its tiered spires stretched toward the star-filled sky like a mountain of stone.

"The whole structure represents Mount Meru, the center of all creation in Hindu and Buddhist beliefs," Zhao said, uncharacteristically thoughtful. "Climbing the stairs symbolizes the ascent toward enlightenment."

"What would you know about enlightenment?" Gui replied, glancing at his boss.

"I've read about it," Zhao said, her frosty exterior momentarily thawing. Shifting her attention to the steep staircase, her expression hardened once again. "Time to move."

Zhao led the way up the staircase, breathing deeply. She paused at the top and looked back at the causeway. Seeing approaching flashlight beams, she strode into the central gallery. She led the way through the royal chamber and turned into a narrow corridor on the structure's far side. They and stepped out into a courtyard on the building's opposite side and stood beside a large carved section of wall. Zhao switched on her flashlight.

"This is it," she said, her voice barely audible above the jungle sounds which drifted in across the rooftops.

"You're sure?" Gui asked, hands on his hips. He leaned back and looked at the carvings, which showed a procession of devas, their bodies twisted in dance. A towering Vishnu figure stood in the center, poised in mid-battle with a chaotic array of demon figures around.

"Yes, see how the joins between the stones are rougher here?" Zhao said, running her finger over one such section. "In the rest of the temple, they're perfect. You'd struggle to even notice that two stones were joined together."

"It's as though someone did it in a hurry," Gui said, catching his superior's meaning.

"Exactly. Why would the whole temple be completed in such perfection, except for this carving?"

"I suppose you know the answer," Gui said, shrugging.

"It's simple. This section wasn't created along with the rest of the temple. This is the work of Indravarman the Second."

"But why? Why mess with something after it's finished?" Gui said, his arms outstretched to indicate the expanse of the temple.

"Isn't it obvious?" Zhao said, her eyes boring into Vishnu as though he could reveal the secrets through a look alone. "It's here to cover something up."

"But what?" Gui said, turning his head to look at Zhao.

"That's what we're here to find out. Whatever Indravarman was hiding, it's beneath this carving. Set up the scanner."

Gui swung the bag from his shoulder and placed it carefully on the ground. He unzipped the bag and pulled out a portable x-ray scanner. He clamped the machine to a tripod and powered it up. The scanner hummed to life, several lights blinking. He connected a tablet computer to the scanner and loaded the program, which would allow them to see what the machine picked up in real time.

"Start at the bottom and work upwards," Zhao whispered.

Gui nodded and adjusted the scanner's position. The device got to work, emitting a low, pulsing sound. Ghostly images formed on the tablet computer, revealing the hidden layers beneath the visible carving.

"There," Zhao said suddenly, pointing at a faint anomaly on the screen. "Do you see that?"

Gui leaned in, squinting at the image. "It looks like ... a cavity? No, wait ..." He adjusted the scanner's settings, enhancing the resolution. "It's more than that. There's something inside."

"Just as I thought," Zhao said, her eyes locked on the screen. "There is a message carved on the inside. A secret diagram, waiting to be discovered."

"Do you know what this means?" Gui said, focusing the scanner on three shapes at the center of the hidden carving.

"Not yet, but we will soon," Zhao said, her eyes wide.

Gui worked the controls of the scanner again. "And behind the carving, there's a big open space."

A faint sound drifted from the courtyard below, snapping the pair from the excitement of their discovery.

"Have you got it?" Zhao said, looking toward the noise.

"All saved," Gui said, already packing down the scanner.

"Excellent," Zhao replied, killing the light. "Then we've got everything we need. Let's get out of here. For now."

6

Koh Rong Island, Cambodia. Present day.

REMAINING OUT OF SIGHT, EDEN AND ATHENA DROPPED INTO a crawling position. They moved toward the sound, using the crumbling walls for cover. Nearing the back of the structure, Eden held her finger in the air as an instruction to stop and listen. Still out of sight behind one of the walls, she could now hear the voices clearly, followed by the clanking of metal on metal.

"This is no good, no good at all," Vireak hissed, scurrying up beside her.

Eden peered over a pile of fallen stone which many years ago had probably made up part of the temple's roof. Still unable to get a visual on the men, she scrambled over the pile. She stopped at the once-grand archway, now little more than a pair of jagged columns, and looked across the sandbank behind the temple. What she saw made her drop into a fighting stance through sheer anger.

Three men, each wearing worn jungle-colored fatigues, moved across the sandbank. It wasn't the presence of the men, however, that made Eden's blood boil. It was what they were doing.

In the center of the sand bank sat a metal cage. The object was about ten feet square and disguised with leaves and branches. Several monkeys trapped inside the cage howled and smashed their tiny fists against the bars.

"This is a terrible thing," Vireak whispered, popping up beside Eden. "Those creatures ... they're part of this forest, and part of our heritage. They must not be removed."

"Why would they do that?" Athena said, appearing a moment later.

"There's a thriving illegal market for them," Vireak said, shaking his head. "Traditional medicine, mostly."

One of the men emptied a bag of bananas, mangoes, and jackfruit on to the ground. He then set about chopping the fruit with the hunting knife, clearly preparing the next round of bait. The other two men unfurled a large sack and stepped toward the cage. The trapped monkeys screeched and howled, rattling the bars in a desperate bid to escape.

"For many years we have known that this goes on," Vireak said. "They should be stopped, but the police force here is too small to catch them."

"Do people still think that eating monkey meat has healing properties?" Athena said, glancing at Vireak. "I thought that was a dark ages kinda thing."

"Sadly, it is true. Most people know better now, but some are still stuck in the old ways. These animals are part of the sacred balance of our forests," Vireak said.

Of the two men working on the cage, one held the sack open while the second removed a padlock and prepared to open the trapdoor.

"They're not getting away with it today," Eden said, straightening up, her muscles immediately tense and ready.

"Wait!" Vireak said. "Those men have knives, and maybe guns." He reached out to grab Eden's arm, but she'd already stepped through the opening.

"She gets like this when something isn't right," Athena said, flashing Vireak a look. "Don't worry, she's tougher than old boots."

"Afternoon, gentlemen," Eden said, striding onto the sandbank with her hands planted on her hips. "I'm afraid this is a protected archaeological site. I'm going to have to ask you to leave."

The men froze, one with the blade in mid strike, one held the bag ready to secure their catch. The largest, poised to open the cage door, turned to look at Eden.

Eden cocked her head to the side and waited for the man's stare to finally meander its way to her eyes. She read the simple gesture of the man stepping forward as an indication that he was in charge. She would take him down quickly and hope that discouraged the other two.

"This not an archaeological site," the leader said, his English broken. His tongue darted out between his lips, as though preparing to eat something delicious.

Eden remained stationary, eyeing her foe. The brute had bulging forearms and various scars, which she doubted were the results of medical procedures. She thought the men looked like locals, although why someone would treat their own island with this much disrespect, she couldn't figure.

The leader stepped toward Eden, rolling his shoulders forward and back. The other two men followed suit, flanking their leader on both sides. One dropped the sack, while the second swished the knife through the air.

"Pretty lady thinks this place is some archaeological site," the leader said, addressing his cronies. The three laughed, emitting the same deranged cackle as a pack of hyenas. "This is just some useless piles of rock." The leader pointed at one of the walls. "No one cares about this place. But now you've walked into something you shouldn't have. That's a big problem."

"Big problem," one of the other men parroted.

Eden shifted her stance, bending her knees and positioning one foot slightly in front of the other.

"I'll ask you one more time," she said, folding her arms. "Get out of here now, or you'll regret it."

The men laughed again, glancing at each other in shared amusement. When the laugher died out, having lasted far longer than appropriate, the leader cleared his throat.

"I think we should show you how we not like people who mess with our business."

"Yeah," the man with the knife said, swishing the blade from side to side again.

"Okay," Eden said, exhaling as though thoroughly frustrated. "But don't say I didn't warn you."

The men shared a glance, clearly confused by Eden's nonchalance.

Although the gesture was fleeting, it was the moment she needed. She bolted forward, reaching the leader before he could react, and drove her knee up hard, connecting solidly with his groin. The man doubled over in pain and surprise, opening himself up for her next attack—a swift elbow to the back of his head. With a crack like a breaking egg, the man slumped forward, crashing face first into the sand.

"Now you've got a golden opportunity," Eden said, her fists raised. She nodded down at the prone figure lying on the sand. "This will happen to you if you stick around. Be sensible and get out of here now."

The men shared a look, clearly seriously considering Eden's suggestion.

"Come on, what's it gonna be?" Eden said, growing impatient at the idiots' warring brain cells. She glanced to the side and saw Athena, still obscured behind the temple wall. Athena nodded once, indicating she was ready whenever Eden needed assistance.

Finally reaching a decision, the remaining thugs advanced. The man with the knife broke into a run, wildly swinging the blade in Eden's direction.

"I was really hoping we wouldn't have to do this," Eden said, ducking. The blade sailed inches over her head as the man ran past her. The thug took another step and spun around. But Eden had already turned to face him.

Although she was now fighting men in two directions, which made it even more challenging, she didn't expect this conflict to last long.

The man with the blade grinned. A giggle escaped his lips as he misread the situation entirely. He stepped forward, moving the knife in line with Eden's throat.

Then, exactly as she'd expected, Eden felt the other man grip her from behind.

"This be your biggest mistake, little lady," the man behind her said, his stinking breath tickling her neck.

"I don't think so," Eden said, remaining stationary.

Athena burst out from the temple entrance, a large rock held high. She swung the rock into the back of the knife-wielder's skull with a crunch that sent the man slumping into the sand.

With the man behind her momentarily distracted by his comrade's demise, Eden took the opportunity to drive her heel into his shin. He grunted in pain and loosened his grip enough to allow Eden's elbow to smash him in the stomach. The breath whooshed from his lungs like a deflating balloon, and he staggered backward.

Eden spun on her toes and delivered a swift kick to the side of the man's knee, buckling his leg, followed up by a powerful right hook to his jaw. The man fell backwards, crashing into the cage and knocking the door open. The trapped monkeys seized their opportunity for freedom, bursting out in a chaotic mass of fur and shrieks. They ran across the fallen thug, three of them pausing to bite him on the face and neck, before disappearing into the safety of the mangroves.

Howling from his human and monkey inflicted injuries, the man who was now the only one conscious, struggled into a crawling position and attempted to drag himself toward the motorboat.

Athena snagged up the knife and threw it to Eden, who marched across the sand and held the blade against the guy's neck.

"Get into the cage," Eden said, nodding toward the open door.

"What? No!" the guy said, looking up at Eden.

"You're not in a position to say no," Eden replied, pushing the blade further into his skin.

Reluctantly. the thug crawled forward and slumped in the back corner of the enclosure.

Working together, Eden and Athena picked up the two unconscious men and folded them inside. Eden then secured the catch and clicked the padlock into place. Then the two women stood, hands on their hips, as the leader's eyes blinked open.

"I think you should have listened to her," Athena said, nodding toward Eden.

"You little..." the leader groaned, struggling across the enclosure and pulling on the bolt. The locking mechanism jarred as the padlock did its job.

"Well, that isn't very nice," Eden said, holding up the key for the thug to see. "Don't worry, we'll give this to the police chief back in town and see what he wants to do with you."

"Although it'll probably take us a couple of days to remember," Athena added, grinning.

The caged thugs shouted and banged on the bars as Eden and Athena turned around and strode back into the temple. Vireak sat in the center of the structure, watching them calmly.

"That was impressive," he said, grinning knowingly. "It seems you have passed the test my ancestors sent for you. They say you are welcome on our island any time you please."

7

Paris, France. Three days later.

MEI-LING ZHAO SWEPT HER FINGERS THROUGH HER LONG, black hair and fastened it into a tight ponytail. She doubled the band over again, making sure it wouldn't come loose, then pulled open the twin doors and stepped on to the third-floor balcony. For a second, she thought back over the last few days, which had led her from Angkor Wat in Cambodia to this apartment in the center of Paris.

She looked down at the traffic passing several stories below. While the number and intensity of the cars had reduced with the sinking sun, then decreased further once the theaters and cocktail bars closed, early morning deliveries and taxis on the airport run still passed with surprising regularity.

"Looking good," came the voice in her earpiece.

She glanced at a rust-colored RV parked on the street opposite. Complete with several parking tickets, the vehicle looked as if it had been dumped there weeks ago. By the morning it would be gone.

"Keep your eyes on the screen," Zhao replied, rubbing her hands together. "And don't distract me."

"Roger that," Gui said. Stationed in the RV, it was his job to watch her back from afar and get her out when this was done. Eyeing the vehicle, she considered how crucial Gui would be in the weeks to come. Although, of course, she would never tell him that.

Zhao stepped to the stone balustrade, turned and looked up at the wall of the apartment building. On the top floor of the building, offering views of the streets below, the apartment spoke of old money and refined taste. She ran her hands down across her belt, checking once again that she had everything she needed. She tightened the straps on her custom-built backpack and, satisfied everything was ready, she pushed the balcony doors closed. The lock snicked into place, indicating that there was no way back.

Zhao rubbed her hands together and hoisted herself onto the balustrade. She gripped the decorative stonework and scrambled up to the top of the door.

A delivery truck rumbled down the street below, but Zhao didn't even notice. Dressed in black, and far beyond the streetlight's glare, she was as good as invisible to anyone who didn't know she was there. She shimmied up the ornate molding and grasped a decorative cornice set just beneath the roof. She drew her legs up beneath her, leaned out at an almost impossible angle, and gripped hold of the roof's edge. She then pulled herself up and rolled onto the roof.

"Twenty-five seconds, not bad," came Gui's voice through the comms system.

Without reply, Zhao stood and took a moment to survey her surroundings. The Parisian skyline spread out before her in a glittering tapestry of lights and shadows. The Eiffel Tower's silhouette dominated the view to her left, now dark against the night sky. The Seine's glittering ribbon curved out of sight in the other direction, and, in the distance, the Sacré-Cœur glowed pearly white.

Zhao turned away from the view. She was no tourist and certainly not here to enjoy the sights. She stalked across the rooftop, rounded a stack of chimneys, and scrambled over a waist-high wall and on to the roof of the adjoining building. She crossed two more buildings and peered across the narrow gap at the Musée Guimet.

She checked the alley between the buildings for movement but saw only a row of bikes and stacked bags of trash. Satisfied that she had the place to herself, Zhao backed up a few paces then sprinted across the tiles. Accelerating past the point of no return, she launched into the air. For a long moment she was airborne, before touching down on the museum's roof and dropping smoothly into an impact-absorbing roll.

"I'm on the roof," she said.

"Got you. I'm inside the system, ready and waiting," Gui replied.

Zhao rose into a crawling position and darted across the building. Reaching the front, she paused, taking a moment to look for any security cameras or motion detectors which hadn't come up in their search. Seeing none, she scurried across to the building's far side.

She approached the skylight which they'd identified on the blueprint and leaned in close to the glass. As she'd expected, the room on the other side of the pane was completely dark.

The burst of a siren howled from the street below, causing Zhao to freeze.

"Don't worry, they're not coming for you," Gui said, his voice calm. "Just passing by."

Zhao turned back to the window as the police car sped away. She removed a small hydraulic device from her belt and slipped it between the window and the jamb. She pumped the device, forcing the pane open. The hinges creaked, straining against the mounting pressure. She gave the device three more pumps and heard a subtle pop as the seal finally gave way. Slipping a small pry bar through the gap, she disengaged the locks and turned her attention to the alarm sensors mounted on the window's edge. As expected, they were the typical magnetic type—when the window opened, the circuit was broken, and the alarm triggered.

Zhao reached into her bag and extracted a pair of coin-sized magnets. She eased the window up enough to get her fingers inside and slipped the magnets onto each of the sensors. Confident that the alarm was now taken care of, she eased the window open. When the glass was an inch or two out of position, she paused, listening carefully. Satisfied that no alarm had sounded, she opened the window completely.

"I'm in," she said. "Waiting for confirmation."

"I'm looking at the system's dashboard now," Gui replied. "No alarms have been triggered. You're clear."

"Wěn zhā wěn dǎ," Zhao said, repeating one of her often-said Chinese proverbs. *Go steady and strike hard.*

"You're so old school," Gui said.

Zhao set a timer on her watch and sat back, listening for approaching sirens. It was true she couldn't hear any alarms, but that didn't mean her approach had gone unnoticed. From here, if the police came, she could head straight to the extraction point and *strike hard* another day. If she got inside and the police arrived, it was game over.

Zhao took the time to put on her gloves, making sure

each finger was fitted perfectly, then checked and rechecked her equipment.

"Time's up," Zhao said, her watch vibrating. "Still clear down there?"

"Of course," Gui said. "Like I said it would be."

"An impatient thief is a dead one," Zhao replied.

"That's not an ancient proverb."

"It might be one day." Zhao fished out a length of rope, anchored it to a pipe which ran across the roof, and dropped it through the window. She slipped inside and lowered herself, hand over hand, until she reached the floor.

The faint outlines of crates and shelving units surrounded her on all sides. Using her tiny flashlight, Zhao made her way to the door and paused.

"I'm ready to go in," she whispered, tapping her earpiece.

"About time," Gui said, the line crackling slightly. "I'm inside the security system. Ready on your mark." Gui had worked for forty-eight hours straight to hack into the museum's network. Despite his efforts, he could only pause the system for three minutes before an alarm was raised.

"Ready?" Zhao said, clasping the door handle.

"One hundred and eighty seconds starting now," Gui said.

Zhao tapped her watch, activating the timer.

She depressed the handle, swung the door open and stepped through into the gallery. The large room stretched before her in both directions, lit in the dull green hue designed to protect the artifacts. She set off, moving swiftly and silently, her path committed to memory.

"Unexpected heat signature coming your way," Gui said.

Zhao pressed herself against a wall and heard footsteps trudging her way. Glancing around the room, she searched for a hiding spot. She spotted a massive brass pot, part of an ancient Asian collection, sitting in the corner.

The footsteps grew ever louder, ever closer.

Zhao darted for the pot. Reaching the potential hiding place, she hoisted herself up and dropped inside. Careful not to clang against the brass, she ducked out of sight the moment before a flashlight beam swept through the room.

Slowing her breathing right down, she listened closely as the footsteps neared her position. The beam played across the pot, glittering across the carved exterior. Now holding her breath, Zhao heard the soft crackle of the guard's radio, and the rustle of his uniform. The footsteps drew close and stopped.

Zhao tensed, ready to spring into action if discovered. She counted the seconds to reassure herself she had time. Although she could hold her breath for well over a minute, her lungs started aching after half that time. Eventually, the footsteps trundled away, reverberating back into silence.

Zhao let her breath go slowly, waited another ten seconds, and peered over the rim. The guard turned into the next room, his light sweeping from side to side as it probably did every night.

"Heat signature has gone. You're clear," Gui said.

8

Paris, France. Present day.

MEI-LING ZHAO EXTRICATED HERSELF FROM THE POT AND stepped down onto the floor. She took a moment to calm her breathing and checked her watch—she had a little over two minutes before the alarm would sound. She set off at a run, charging through two galleries without glancing at a single thing.

"You're clear," Gui said, watching her progress on the screens back in the RV.

She rounded a corner and, for the first time, saw the glass case that contained the target of her efforts.

"I've got eyes on it," she said, her voice no louder than an exhale.

"Good," Gui replied. "Now bring it home."

Zhao covered the distance in a flat-out sprint, sliding to a stop inches from the glass. She peered through the glass at the object inside.

"The Ta Prohm Stele," she said.

Through the glass, the stele's sandstone surface seemed

to absorb the dim light of the gallery. At the top of the small sandstone tablet, a group of carved celestial figures stood frozen in a dance. Decorative borders adorned the stele's edges, featuring the lotus motifs and geometric patterns typical of the period.

Dating back to the early thirteenth century, the Ta Prohm Stele was a crucial artifact from the reign of King Indravarman II. Although originally positioned in the temple of Ta Prohm, the fact that the stele was younger than the temple itself proved a constant source of debate. Different academics posited a range of theories as to why Indravarman might have added the stele to a temple his father built. For Zhao, it was the text written on the stele that piqued her interest.

"You have ninety seconds," Gui said, snapping Zhao back to the present.

"Understood."

Zhao removed a small device from her belt and placed it against the glass. The device emitted an electromagnetic pulse, disabling the case's electronic locks with a click. Taking the utmost care, Zhao lifted the glass case and placed it on the floor beside the stele. Without the protective glass, the stele seemed to glow with renewed vigor.

Acting on instinct, Zhao reached out and felt the surface, imagining all the people who had touched it in the past. She slipped off the specially designed backpack and laid it flat on the floor beside the stele. Unzipping the pack, she flipped open the front, ready to receive the stele. Then, she turned back toward the artifact. Taking a deep breath, she leaned in, placed her hands beneath the stone, and lifted it from its cradle. She stood motionless for a second, half expecting arrows to shoot from hidden sconces in the walls, or a giant boulder to roll her way, but nothing happened.

"That only happens in the movies," she whispered, her jaw clenched. She turned carefully, dropped into a crouch, and shuffled the stele inside the bag. Checking it was properly ensconced in the protective lining; she zipped up the bag and hefted it onto her back. She tightened the straps and tested the weight. The additional weight would make the climb back up to the roof more difficult, but she was trained and ready.

"We have a problem," Gui said, his voice now edged with steel. "Security protocols are resetting faster than anticipated."

"How long?" Zhao said, breaking into a run.

"Thirty seconds."

Zhao accelerated, entering a flat-out sprint. The Khmer deities and ancient artifacts became a blur as she approached the corner. She tugged on the straps of the backpack, pulling them tighter still to reduce the bag's bouncing. Rounding the corner, she almost lost her footing on the highly polished floor.

"Twenty seconds," Gui said, his voice raised.

Zhao sprinted through the gallery, racing past the pot she had hidden inside less than two minutes earlier. She rounded the final corner, and the storeroom came into view.

"Two heat signatures coming your way," Gui said, his voice cutting through her heavy breathing.

"Give me some good news, please," Zhao replied, grinding her teeth.

"Your team is going to win the league," Gui said flatly.

"You know nothing about sports," Zhao snapped back, making a dash for the storeroom.

When she was still a few paces from the door, two

guards stepped into the gallery. Without time to hide and wait for them to pass, Zhao swung into action. She changed her course and rounded on the men.

The first guard barely had time to register her presence before Zhao was upon him. She kicked high, bouncing up on her left leg and whipping her right into an arc. Even with the additional weight of the stele strapped to her back, she easily reached the man's neck. She struck hard, knocking him unconscious before he hit the ground.

The second guard, startled by the sudden attack, fumbled for his radio. Zhao didn't give him the chance to use it. She pivoted on her heel, her leg sweeping out and catching the guard behind his knees. As he stumbled, off balance, Zhao grabbed his arm and swung him into the wall. He smashed into the stone and flopped backwards, landing hard against the floor. Before he could recover, Zhao delivered a precise strike to a pressure point on his neck. His eyes rolled back and he went limp.

"Nicely done," Gui said. "You have two se—"

Gui's voice cut out as an almighty screech roared through the museum.

"Correction, security is back online, and the alarms are activated."

"You don't say," Zhao said, running for the storeroom. She threw open the door and ran inside as the beams of several more flashlights swept through the gallery. The sound of raised voices cut through the shrieking alarms.

Zhao reached the rope and climbed frantically back up onto the roof.

"Coming out now," Zhao said, running to the line positioned at the front of the building. "Are you in position?"

"Give me ten seconds," Gui said, his voice now backed by the sound of an engine.

Zhao reached the edge of the roof and paused. The sirens of approaching police cut through the screaming alarm. She ran across the rooftop and found the wire which they'd installed two days before. Looking to the casual observer like a telecommunications cable, the wire stretched across the street to the building opposite. Without hesitation, Zhao clipped herself onto the wire.

"Status?" she said, spinning around to see the first guard scramble through the skylight and out onto the roof.

"Ten seconds!" Gui shouted, his voice distorting.

"Don't hang about ..." Zhao saw the RV speeding toward the roundabout directly in front of the museum. Without a backward glance, she leaped from the rooftop. For a heart-stopping moment, she plummeted toward the street below. Then the wire snapped taut, and she zipped out across the street.

The RV accelerated out and onto the roundabout.

Behind her, Zhao heard angry shouts erupting from the rooftop. Already off the rooftop, she allowed herself a grim smile. As the RV sped up beneath her, Zhao unclipped the line. She half jumped, and half fell, crashing onto the RV's roof. She grabbed the roof rack as they veered off the round-about and accelerated away from the museum. Swinging open a hatch cut into the RV's roof, she climbed inside. She shrugged off the backpack and slipped into the passenger seat beside Gui. Gui slowed the van as a pair of police cruisers sped in the other direction.

"Nice work," Gui said, handing her a bottle of water. "That was close."

Zhao nodded. "Package secured. Now let's go and see the professor."

9

Paris, France. Present day.

On hearing the noise, Professor Etienne Lavigne opened his eyes. He looked up at his bedroom ceiling. The lights of a car moving down the street outside swept around the curtains. He jolted up an inch as the light washed over a reproduction Khmer statue, creating a menacing projection on the wall.

"What ... what?" he moaned, reaching out and grabbing his spectacles from the nightstand. He slid them into place, and the blurry shapes twisted into sharp focus, revealing nothing more sinister than his bedroom furniture and Khmer collectibles.

"Incroyable, you fool," he berated himself, now fully awake. He sat up straight, listening to the silence. Another car passed, its headlights sending the shadows into a frenzy. The Khmer statue seemed to shuffle closer, its elongated silhouette stretching across the wall like a grasping hand.

"It's nothing," Lavigne muttered to himself, slipping his spectacles off in preparation to bed down again. "Just the—"

Another dull thud reverberated through the house. Although little more a muffled echo which seemed to crawl up through the walls, to Lavigne, it sounded like a gunshot.

He jolted upright again and planted his spectacles back in place. Constantly anxious about intruders trying to steal his collections, he had installed museum-grade locks on the doors and windows, along with a top of the range alarm system.

He swung his legs over the side of his antique rosewood bed, a piece he'd imported from Cambodia, and placed his bare feet on the cool marble floor. A shiver worked its way through his body, which was nothing to do with the cold stone beneath his feet. He reached across to the nightstand and clicked on the light. Looking around the room, everything appeared normal. The bronze statue, which had been responsible for the strange shadows, stood like a sentinel by his wardrobe. Several large photographs and schematics of various Cambodian temples covered the room's walls.

Another thud reverberated through the house.

Lavigne spun to face the door so quickly he almost slipped from the bed. His finger lurched toward the panic button which was mounted on the underside of the nightstand. He thought for a second about dragging the security operatives out here in the middle of the night unnecessarily.

"For once in your life, maybe you shouldn't be so damned scared of everything," he muttered to himself. "Probably a window left open or ..." Lavigne scoffed at the thought. He would never leave a window open. To do so was an open invitation to feral animals, burglars, or even killer bees. He recalled a story of a burglar who had learned to dislocate his shoulder joints to get in through gaps that were just inches wide. There really was no telling the lengths people would go to steal. No, Lavigne would never be stupid enough to invite such danger inside his home.

"Non merci," he muttered to himself, pressing the panic button with a firm and decisive thumb. He sat back in bed, folded his arms, and thought about the amount of money he paid the security company to come at his beck and call. This was what they were for, so he refused to feel bad about calling them out in the middle of the night.

He lifted his watch from the nightstand and checked the time. The security guards would be onsite within five minutes—or so they promised. He would wait in bed until they had entered using their allocated keys, disabled the alarm system, and checked the ground floor for intruders. Only then would he put himself at risk by getting up.

Watching the hands sweep around the watch face, he counted off the next five minutes. The house remained frustratingly silent. He waited five minutes more, but still heard nothing.

"Ridiculous," he said, turning around and hitting the button three more times. It was obvious that he wouldn't get to sleep again now, not until the house had been checked from basement to attic.

He waited another ten minutes, hearing nothing but the silence of a most-likely empty house and the whisper of traffic through the glass.

"Une mascarade!" he barked, making a mental note to drag the security company over metaphorical hot coals until they got it fixed. With a groan of effort, he got out of bed, padded across the bedroom and out onto the landing.

Wall-mounted lights washed the interior in a sepia-toned glow. The dull light was good for his artifacts and prevented the house from ever being totally dark. The dark, amongst many other things, Lavigne simply couldn't abide.

Why anyone would choose to allow darkness in their home, in this day and age, he could not fathom.

He reached the top of the grand staircase and peered down into the foyer. Silvery moonlight streamed in, illuminating the tapestries hanging on the walls, but nothing else. So far, the place appeared to be as it always was—empty.

Lavigne's house, a stunning example of Haussmannian architecture, had been his sanctuary for almost half his life. The house sat conveniently near the university where he lectured, offered plenty of room for his collections, and was just steps away from the arrondissement's shops and other amenities. For a man who never traveled more than a few hundred steps from his home, such things were essential. Over the years, many people had questioned how Lavigne could be such an expert on ancient Khmer civilizations, while having never visited Cambodia. In fact, in all his nearly fifty years of life, Lavigne had only left Paris on two occasions.

Reassured that no killer monkeys, mad dogs, or anything else that may cause him unnecessary harm were lurking in the foyer, Lavigne padded down the stairs.

When he was halfway down, the noise came again. He froze, one foot in mid stride. Gripping hold of the balustrade, he listened. The noise was clearer from here. It was not a bang as he'd first thought, but a soft scraping, as though someone was shoving an item of furniture across the floor. Whatever it was, it sounded as though it was coming from the ground floor.

"Mon Dieu!" he groaned, glancing back at his bedroom and considering the pointless panic button. Heads would certainly roll in the morning. He steeled himself, adjusted his spectacles, which had the annoying habit of always sliding down his nose, and continued down the stairs.

He reached the bottom and stepped across the foyer. He glanced at a collection of Angkorian bronze figurines in a cabinet beside the door, then up at a plaster molding from a lintel at the Bayon temple—one of the few examples in existence.

Another scraping sound emanated from the direction of his study, causing him to freeze. He spun to face the noise but couldn't see anything.

"C'est un scandale!" he hissed, passing beneath a crystal chandelier which, of course, was an original Haussmannian feature.

Reaching the dining room, he paused and peered inside. Eight place settings gleamed in the dim light. Years ago, Lavigne had set the room ready for guests, although he never actually considered inviting them. A centerpiece of exquisite Khmer silverwork—a miniature representation of Angkor Wat—stood proudly amidst the unlit candles.

The noise came again, louder this time. He spun around and saw that the door to his study was partially open. Golden light spilled through the gap.

"Incroyable," Lavigne muttered, a flicker of unease creeping into his voice. "I would never ..." He racked his memory, trying to recall if he'd left an appliance powered up before retiring to bed. A slave to routine, Lavigne was obsessive with turning off everything—just in case something should inexplicably burst into flames during the night.

Lavigne crept down the hallway, each step slower than the last, his fingers trembling as he reached for the door. With a hesitant push, he swung the door open, revealing the familiar sight of his study. He eyed the crowded shelves of books, the glass cases filled with ancient artifacts and delicate jewelry. He turned and looked around the room, his attention finally settling on his desk.

"What ... who ...?" he stuttered, his breath catching in his throat. He staggered back, heart pounding. A woman sat at his desk, staring up at him with unnerving calm.

"Good evening, Professor Lavigne," she said. "I'm sorry to interrupt you like this."

Lavigne spun around, ready to run back upstairs, or out through the front door, when a firm hand gripped his shoulder from behind. Another figure moved in close behind him, shoving him roughly into the room.

"I don't ... what are you ...?" Lavigne stumbled forward, nearly colliding with a bronze statue on top of a pedestal.

He caught his balance, then adjusted his spectacles and looked at the woman seated at the desk. She had delicate features and the unmistakable hint of East Asian ancestry. Chinese, he thought. She exuded a calm confidence, so much so that, for a moment, it seemed as if this were her study and not his. She leaned back in the chair, her hands resting casually on the desktop.

"This is great work," she said, picking up the neat stack of papers which Lavigne had been working on before bed— his latest translation of an ancient Khmer inscription. The passage was particularly complex and detailed various royal decrees from the early Angkor period.

"I can see why you were up so late," she said, flicking through the pages.

"Who ... who are you? What do you want?" Lavigne stammered, his voice little more than a dry croak.

The intruder's lips curled into a smile. But before she could answer, Lavigne felt a sharp prick in his neck.

"What ... what have you ...?" Lavigne's words slurred as a wave of dizziness washed over him. The last thing Lavigne saw before darkness claimed him was the woman rising from his chair, then, the world faded to black.

10

Oil Corporation Rig 5, Gulf of Thailand. Present day.

Supervisor Wu looked back in the direction of the Cambodian Mainland, over one hundred miles across the sea. He wiped a hand across his forehead, flicking the sweat away. It was just his luck to be sent somewhere inhospitable like this. He glanced over his shoulder, then, confident that no one was nearby, lifted the cigarette to his lips and inhaled. Although smoking on the oil rig was strictly forbidden, Wu's superiors were back on the mainland. Plus, Wu looked around scornfully, he would gladly quit the cigarettes if they actually found some oil.

He peered down at the water as a wave slammed into the support columns, sending a fine spray of salty mist into the air. Wu grimaced, the water now running with the sweat from his face.

The constant drone of machinery drifted up from the drill floor below, punctuated by the occasional shouts from the workers. They had been at it for almost six months now, boring relentlessly into the seabed. Initial surveys had promised a substantial find—estimates ranging from one hundred to one hundred and fifty million barrels. It was supposed to be a game-changer, a new jewel in China's energy crown. As the days turned into weeks, and then into months, they'd found rocks, endless layers of sediment and more rocks, but not a single drop of the promised Black Gold.

Wu finished the cigarette, burning it right down so that he could feel the pinch of heat between his fingers, then flicked the end into the water. He turned away from the railing, stomped down a metal staircase, and strode onto the drilling floor. The space was a hive of activity as the men went through the motions, just as they had every day of the last six months. It reminded Wu of an American film he'd once watched where the guy lived the same day over and over again—*Pig Day*, or something like that.

He paused to watch a group of men connecting a new length of drill pipe to the string. One man maneuvered the massive tube into position with a remote control, while others used wrenches to secure the connection. He watched the derrickman, clinging on to the ladder high above them, guiding the next section of pipe into place. The men clicked the pipe into place and re-started the system, sending a shudder through the entire platform.

Wu looked up at the motor that powered the drill, hanging from the derrick high above the platform. The system howled as it powered up the entire drill string, ready to once again breach the seabed in search of their fabled payload.

The system was now back online. Wu turned and strode toward the control room. On the way, he paused to eye the mud return line. This was the same tube that had told the same story for weeks on end—rock, sediment, and mud, but no oil.

Wu pushed, strode inside, and wound his way through the rig's internal corridors to the control center. He entered the room, immediately hit by the heat of all the computer and electrical equipment they ran in here. Crossing to the bank of screens, he looked up at the dizzying array of data. A team of men huddled around the console, their voices carrying a note of frustration that Wu knew all too well.

"Liang, tell me there's something new?" Wu said, stepping up to the technician, who was young enough to be Wu's son.

"We're about to drop the new drill line. Let's hope this one gets the—"

A piercing alarm shredded Liang's words. Red lights blazed across the control panels and chaos exploded throughout the room. Technicians leaped from their seats, scrambling for their stations as a violent tremor rocked the entire platform, sending two men crashing to the floor.

"What's happening?" Wu demanded, his eyes darting between the screens.

Liang's fingers flew across the keyboard, pulling up data streams and readouts. "We've hit something on the seabed! Something dense ... incredibly dense. The strain on the drill string is off the charts."

The vibrations intensified, rattling equipment and sending loose items clattering to the floor. Coffee mugs shattered, spilling their contents across consoles. A monitor displayed live footage from the platform, on which men grappled to keep their balance as the rig lurched back and forth.

"We need to shut it down! Now!" Wu bellowed, leaning

in to get a closer look at the readings. "We'll lose the whole string!"

"I'm trying!" Liang shouted. He thumped several more keys. "The emergency stop isn't responding!"

Wu checked a different monitor and saw what he feared most—the massive drill shaft buckling and twisting like a crazy serpent. Then, with a deafening roar, the drill string snapped.

A geyser of high-pressure seawater shot high into the air before raining down on the deck. Men scattered, running for cover as the internal pressure sent the pipes into a mad, whipping dance. The torrent caught one man in the chest, sending him head over heels into a wall.

"Evacuate the drill floor immediately!" Wu shouted into the radio.

The broken drill string slammed into an electrical transformer, sending sparks flying. Two workers threw themselves down a stairwell, narrowly avoiding the wildly swinging pipe. Alarms blared and the whole rig tilted precariously.

"The pressure's still climbing!" Liang shouted over the cacophony. "If we don't relieve it soon, the system's gonna blow!"

Wu's mind raced, thinking through their options. Although policy dictated that they should test the drill shut down systems on a weekly basis, Wu had decided against it because restarting the system lost hours of drilling time. Now, whatever fault was stopping the system shutdown threatened to sink the whole rig. As far as Wu could see, there was only one solution.

"Cut the power!" he bellowed. "Shut down everything!"

Liang looked at him, aghast with disbelief. "But sir, that'll—"

"Do it now!" Wu snapped.

Liang leaped from his seat and charged for the main circuit breaker. With a grunt, he threw the lever into the off position. The control room plunged into darkness and the alarms ceased, replaced by an eerie silence, backed only by the distant sounds of chaos from the drill floor. Emergency lights strained to life.

For a moment, nothing changed. Then, gradually, the violent motions subsided. The whipping drill string slowed its frantic dance, before slamming down onto the deck. The geyser of water slowed and sputtered to a stop as the pressure finally equalized. In the sudden quiet, Wu could hear the heavy breathing of his crew and the distant shouts of the men on the drill floor.

"Manually disconnect the drill head and then power up again," he said, turning to the crew. Two technicians rushed out onto the drill floor.

"Disconnection complete, sir!" came the crackled report over the emergency radio several tense minutes later.

Wu nodded to Liang. "Alright, let's bring her back online. Start the reboot sequence."

Liang heaved the breaker back into position, restoring power to the rig's systems. The main generator hummed to life, and, one by one, the screens flickered back into service. Lights throughout the rig blazed, revealing the full extent of the chaos.

"Primary systems are back online," Liang reported. "We've got multiple failures across the board. Pumps are offline, top drive system is reporting critical damage, and we're showing a significant list to one side."

"I want eyes on whatever we hit down there. Prepare the sub for deployment," Wu said, scanning the readouts on the nearest screen. He turned his attention to the camera feed and saw men emerging from their shelters, shell-shocked but alive. Two men picked their way toward the broken drill string, lying across the deck like a giant dead snake.

Half an hour later, Wu and his team huddled around a screen, all attention fixed on the grainy feed from the remote-controlled submarine's cameras. The underwater vehicle descended through the depths, its powerful lights cutting through the gloom.

"We're approaching the drill site now," Liang announced.

The feed showed twisted metal and debris from their shattered drill scattered across the seabed. As the sub inched around the wreckage, something else emerged from the darkness.

"What in the name of ..." Wu muttered, leaning in closer.

An object sat on the seabed; half submerged in the silt. One end stuck out at an angle, as though it had been dropped there moments before.

"It looks like ... like a sarcophagus," Liang said, his face pale in the monitor's glow.

"That ... that can't be possible," another man said. "Not this far from land."

Liang worked the controls, and the sub circled the object, giving the men a better view.

"The lid's smashed in, look," Liang said, pointing at the object.

"That must be where our drill hit," Wu said. "Take us closer."

Liang adjusted the controls, and the submarine inched toward a jagged hole in the casket's lid. As they approached, Wu saw that his initial assessment was correct—the drill had penetrated the top.

"Can we look inside?" Wu asked, curiosity overriding his caution.

With careful maneuvering, Liang took the sub in closer still. For several seconds, swirling clouds of disturbed sediment covered the camera. The control room fell silent, every eye fixed on the monitor, every breath held in anticipation.

As the silt settled, the sub's lights revealed something that made everyone in the control room gasp. Within the casket, partially obscured by the swirling sediment, was an object. Glowing in the sub's light, Wu recognized the shape of the object inside the casket.

"It looks like a lotus," he said.

11

Sok San Private Island, Cambodia. Present day.

EDEN BLACK SAT UPRIGHT IN HER CHAIR AND LOOKED AT THE assembled council members. Now, without the need for anonymity, the group sat in a luxurious conference room. She looked beyond the assembled council and through the floor-to-ceiling window where the *Balonia*, sitting at anchor several hundred feet away, rose and fell as though resting on a giant's chest.

Richard Beaumont cleared his throat, the noise pulling Eden back into focus. She noticed that everyone in the room was looking at her, waiting for her to begin.

"Thank you for joining me," Eden said, looking around the room. Some council members, like Beaumont and DeLuca, she knew well, others she had only met once before. She had been pleased to learn that there were some familiar faces in the council. Although her surprise had been eclipsed by that of Beaumont and DeLuca, learning that they had both been in the council for two decades, and not knowing that the other was there.

"I realize a lot has already changed under my short stewardship, and this is only the start," Eden said, looking from one person to the next.

In the past, all council meetings had been held in total darkness so that the members couldn't identify one another. That was the first thing Eden had changed when she'd taken over, believing that people in power should be accountable to their actions.

"Although much has changed, the role of The Council of Selene remains the same. We are as vital as ever to surf the wave of this changing world."

"Here, here," Beaumont muttered, flashing Eden a smile.

"To begin our proceedings today, Vittoria DeLuca has a report to share." Eden smiled at DeLuca, whose no-nononsense style she'd grown fond of.

DeLuca stood, smoothed down her dress, and stepped up to the table in the center of the room. She activated a holographic display, and a shimmering ball of light appeared above the table. The particles of light swirled, coalescing into a three-dimensional, slowly rotating globe. Various crosses and lines dotted the globe.

"We've been tracking a pattern of unusual satellite activity," DeLuca said, pointing at the illuminated patches on the globe. "Someone is using very advanced imaging technology to scan for underground anomalies all around the world. We've analyzed the data and have found a surprising commonality." Deluca flicked her wrist. The globe disappeared, replaced by several ancient buildings. "This person is interested in key archaeological sites." She spooled through various images of pyramids, temples, and statues.

"Do we know who's behind this?" asked a council member from the far end of the table.

DeLuca shook her head. "Not yet. But they're using some serious technology. This isn't stuff you can buy online."

"That suggests that they're government, or a very well-funded private organization," another council member interrupted.

"Exactly that," DeLuca said, pointing at the speaker. "We've tried tracing their location, but that's got us nowhere."

"Do they know their activity's been noticed?" Eden asked, leaning back in her chair as her mind ran through the implications. For millennia, the council had protected the existence of ancient civilizations, only making very specific things public knowledge. Although Eden favored the truth, she understood that letting the cat out of the bag all at once was not a good idea.

"I don't believe so," DeLuca replied, meeting Eden's eyes. "But there's no way to know for sure."

"Give me an example of one of the places they're looking into," Eden said, leaning forward. "What level of detail are they going to?"

DeLuca's fingers danced through the air, and the holographic display shifted, zooming in on a dense section of the Amazon rainforest. The lush green canopy gave way to a detailed topographical map, revealing the hidden contours beneath.

"This is the Javari Valley region," DeLuca said, her voice tense.

Eden sat up straight, knowing exactly what was hidden beneath the rainforest in that region. The hologram pulsed with a network of lines and geometric shapes that shouldn't exist in nature.

Deluca rotated her hand, and the hologram moved, offering a three-dimensional view of an enormous underground complex with vast chambers and long corridors sprawling beneath the jungle. "Of course, we've known about this place for centuries, but there's an arrangement to leave them in place," DeLuca continued. "We even have a channel open to speak to the leader of the civilization, should we need to."

"What's stopped them from being discovered for all this time?" Eden asked.

"We have a team of highly trained operatives disguised as an indigenous tribe. They've managed to keep explorers and loggers at bay for decades, but against this level of technology ..." DeLuca trailed off, the implication clear. "And this is one such example. They're also taking an interest in the deserts of North Africa, the Antarctic and several sites in the Pacific Ocean, and Angkor Wat, not far from us now."

"How much do they know?" Eden said. "Their scans are not as detailed as ours, right?"

DeLuca shook her head, her expression serious. "No, their scans aren't this detailed yet." She pointed at the holographic image. "This is generated from our own knowledge of the region, but it's only a matter of time before they catch up."

"We need to stay on top of this," Eden said. "Keep monitoring the situation and let's find out who they are and what they want."

"I think we need to intervene," Dr. Marcus Okonjo said. "We could cover the site with something to throw off their scans."

Everyone turned to look at Dr. Okonjo, a tall, broad-shouldered man with dark skin and closely cropped gray hair.

"We've used similar techniques before, albeit on a smaller scale," he continued. "A layer of magnetized material, perhaps, or a mesh designed to scatter electromagnetic waves."

Beaumont stroked his chin thoughtfully. "It's risky. Any major construction could draw unwanted attention."

"How would that work?" Eden asked. "Is this something you've done before?"

"More than you know," Dr. Okonjo said, laughing. "You think the only ancient sites are the ones listed in guidebooks?"

"It works by using metamaterials," DeLuca said, her tone far kinder than Okonjo's. "These absorb or redirect the scanning waves, essentially cloaking the site."

"What's the environmental impact?" Eden said.

"Minimal, if we do it right," Okonjo said. "We've been developing biodegradable metamaterials for such a purpose."

"Alright," Eden said. "Thank you, Vittoria. Marcus, please work on a proposal for the metamaterial solution. Vittoria, I want to know all we can about the party behind this, and why they're taking such an interest."

The council members nodded. DeLuca switched off the hologram and returned to her seat.

"One last thing," Eden added, her voice serious. "We must consider the possibility that we'll have to reveal some of our knowledge to prevent a greater exposure. I want everyone to start thinking about what we could safely release to the scientific community. We want to satisfy curiosity without compromising something crucial."

Eden remained in her seat as the council members left the room. When the others had gone, she rose and wandered out onto the terrace. Slipping through the door, the heat hit her like a physical blow. She crossed to the railing and stared down at the gently lapping water.

"How was it?" Athena said, joining Eden at the railing.

"These people know so much," Eden said, glancing at her friend. "I'm supposed to be leading this council, and yet I always feel as though I'm several steps behind."

"You might feel that way, but it doesn't look like it," Athena said, turning and looking out at the water. "For what it's worth, Beaumont says they respect you. People like that respect decisiveness, and that's exactly what you've given them."

Eden smiled at Athena's words. She took a deep breath of the salty air, letting it calm her nerves.

"Thanks," she said softly. "It's just ... the weight of it all, you know? The secrets we're guarding, the potential consequences if we fail. It's ..." Eden searched for the word. "It's a lot."

Athena laughed. "That's the understatement of the century. It's more than a lot."

In a swift move, Athena stepped out behind Eden and placed her hands across her shoulders.

"What are you—"

"You need to loosen up," Athena said, her hands tightening. "You're carrying so much tension here, it's not good for you. You really should join us for lunchtime yoga. We've got loads of people coming now."

Since they'd been on the island, Athena and several members of the council had attended a yoga class on the beach run by a local teacher. Eden had staunchly refused, claiming she had too much to do to laze about in the sun.

"There's absolutely no way you're getting me—"

"Carrying around this much tension isn't good for you," Athena said, her fingers digging into Eden's muscles. "It'll find its way out in the end. Plus, it might be fun."

"Listen," Eden said, shrugging Athena's hands away and

turning around to look at her friend. "Do you really think my ability to do a downward dog will help me when we're face to face with the next psychopath hell-bent on world domination?"

"See, you already know some of the terms, that's impressive," Athena teased.

"Well, do you?"

"Probably not a downward dog, no," Athena said. "But yoga is so much more than that, it's a—"

"Don't you dare say it." Eden pointed a finger at her friend.

"It's a—"

"No. We've got threats coming left, right, and center. Rolling around on the sand is not going to—"

"Yoga is a mindset which I really think will help you," Athena said, finally talking over her friend.

"Listen," Eden said, raising an eyebrow. "The day I show up to your beach yoga session is the day the world really is ending."

"Let's hope not," Athena retorted, as a cold breeze drifted in across the sea.

12

41,000 feet above the Arabian Sea. Present day.

MEI-LING ZHAO GLANCED OUT THE WINDOW OF THE Gulfstream G650. Far beneath them, the clouds formed a thick, white carpet, racing by as the Gulfstream tore through the atmosphere at Mach 0.925—just shy of the speed of sound.

Zhao's stark reflection stared back at her from the window: sharp cheekbones, almond-shaped eyes, and jet-black hair pulled back in a tight ponytail. The tailored black suit she wore could easily pass in any corporate boardroom across the globe, but Zhao was no mere corporate bean counter.

She looked again at her wristwatch. Despite the Gulfstream's reputation as one of the fastest and most luxurious private jets in the world, cutting across continents in mere hours, the journey from Paris to Phnom Penh, Cambodia, was taking far too long for Zhao's liking.

She looked down at her half-finished meal. Whilst the scent was tantalizing, Zhao's appetite still lagged somewhere back over central Europe. She knew she should rest because there would be precious little time for that once they landed. As though encouraging her to close her eyes, the cabin lights glowed dimly, casting a warm, muted light throughout the cabin. Despite all this, Zhao's mind refused to slow—swirling with calculations, strategies, and contingencies. It was as though her brain constantly ran in hyperdrive, calculating every potential obstacle, every possible threat, every unknown variable.

A whimpering sound filled the cabin, interrupting Zhao's internal monologue. She leaned out from her seat and peered toward the front of the aircraft. As usual, Zhao had positioned herself at the back, meaning she could see what everyone was doing at all times. It was a practice that had saved her life on many occasions.

Splayed out on the front seat, Professor Etienne Lavigne sobbed again. Since regaining consciousness about two hours into the flight, he had done nothing but moan. As Zhao watched, he writhed from side to side. When he first started making a fuss, Zhao had considered giving him another dose of the tranquilizer, but she didn't want anything to affect his mental capacities later. She needed him thinking clearly and couldn't spare the time for drugs to leave his system.

Zhao rose from her seat and strolled through the cabin. Gui sat in the row behind Lavigne, tapping away on a laptop computer which looked tiny in contrast to his bear-sized hands.

"Anything?" Zhao said, pausing to speak with her second in command.

"I've run the images of the stele through the encryption software, but still can't find anything," Gui said, looking up from the screen. "It all looks ... normal."

"Keep at it," Zhao snapped, as Lavigne whined again. "We need answers as soon as possible." She strode on and dropped into the seat beside Lavigne. Although the man wasn't restrained, with Gui sitting right behind him and Zhao not far away, he wasn't at risk of causing any trouble.

"Can I get you something, professor?" Zhao said, her voice dripping in faux sweetness. "A glass of champagne, or a whiskey, something to calm your nerves."

Lavigne's tear-stained face turned towards Zhao, his eyes wide with terror. He shrank back in his seat as though trying to put as much distance between himself and his captor as possible.

"S'il vous plaît, let me go," he whimpered, voice trembling. "Just let me go. I won't tell anyone, I swear!"

"That's not an option, I'm afraid, professor. We're forty thousand feet above the ocean."

"Forty thousand feet!" Lavigne squealed, clutching at his cheeks. "It's not natural! Not possible!"

"I can assure you, it is possible," Zhao said calmly. "You really calm yourself. This constant whimpering is not becoming, especially for a man of your stature."

Lavigne's head snapped up, his eyes wild with fear. "C-calm myself?" he sputtered. "You've kidnapped me! Taken me from my home! And now we're ... we're aboard one of these death traps!" His voice rose to a near-shriek at the last word.

Lavigne gripped onto the armrests as the Gulfstream bumped slightly.

"Professor, try to relax." For the first time in as long as she could remember, Zhao attempted to sound kind. Then, feeling uncomfortable, she changed her mind. "You are perfectly safe. As I've already explained, we're going to Cambodia where your expertise is required for a matter of great importance. I'm afraid that on this occasion, your lifelong reluctance to travel is an inconvenience we can't accommodate."

Lavigne's face contorted with a mixture of fear and indignation. He blinked several times, his eyes large behind his spectacles which sat askew on his nose. "Do you have any idea how dangerous these flying machines are?" He looked around the cabin as though it were about to disintegrate before his eyes. "We're not even on a commercial flight. Private aircraft are even more dangerous! Consider the things that could go wrong—engine failure, bird strikes, pilot error, extreme weather..."

As if on cue, the plane encountered a small pocket of turbulence. Lavigne yelped, whipping his head from side to side. He turned from white to green, and his spectacles slipped further down his nose.

"Professor Lavigne, I do not have time for your nonsense," Zhao said, her normal frosty tone now back in full effect. "You are in no danger from this machine. However, if you continue to moan, you will be in danger from me."

Lavigne shook his head and swallowed. "But you don't—"

"Consider this the trip of a lifetime," Zhao said, placing her hand on the professor's forearm. Although the touch wasn't hard, it was firm enough to make her point. "You'll finally get to visit Cambodia, the country you clearly love so much."

"No!" Lavigne said, his eyes darting between Zhao and the sky through the oval-shaped window. "I can't go there. Do you have any idea of the diseases? The dangers? I've read about them all! Malaria, dengue fever, poisonous snakes, not to mention the political instability! Have you not heard of Henri Mouhot?"

"Yes, of course I have," Zhao said, sighing loudly.

Gui shifted in his seat behind the professor, clearly frustrated by the constant noise.

"Imbécile! Then I can't believe you are doing this!" Lavigne screamed. "Henri Mouhot, after rediscovering Angkor Wat, ventured into the jungle and what happened to him? Dead! Struck down in his prime by a mosquito!" Lavigne inhaled with the fervor of a man saved from drowning, and then adjusted his spectacles.

Zhao sighed, pinching the bridge of her nose. "Professor, that was almost two hundred years ago. Medical science has advanced considerably since then."

"Medical science! You know how many people die from adverse reactions to modern pharmaceuticals? Plus, mosquitoes still carry malaria, dengue fever is still rampant, and let's not forget about the other insects! Centipedes, scorpions, giant hornets ... The outside world is a death trap!"

"We've taken all necessary—"

"It's not enough! C'est pas possible! You can't account for every danger. What about the unstable political situation? Landmines? The—"

Zhao cut him off, sweeping her hand through the air. "Enough! Professor Lavigne, I understand your concerns, but they are misplaced and, quite frankly, tiresome. I need your expertise, and you will provide it. Your comfort and safety are secondary concerns."

"What about my medication? My special diet? My daily routines?" Lavigne said. "How can I possibly survive in such conditions?"

The plane bounced a little, causing Lavigne to yelp and curl even tighter into his seat.

"Professor, let me be clear. You will survive because I need you to survive. Your knowledge of ancient Khmer scripts is unparalleled, and there's an artifact that requires your unique interpretation."

Zhao and Lavigne locked eyes for a moment. Finally, the professor looked away and straightened his spectacles.

"Tell you what," Zhao said, her tone softening. "To help facilitate your best work, I am willing to aid your comfort."

Lavigne looked up at Zhao with the hopeful look of a young puppy. Zhao shoved a notepad and a pen across to him.

"Make a list of medications and things you need for your allergies. If we don't hear any more moaning from you, I'll get someone to go and fetch them when we land."

Lavigne blinked several times, then nodded. A piercing ring filled the cabin, causing Lavigne to let out an involuntary whimper. Remembering Zhao's offer, he clamped his hand over his mouth.

"Relax, Professor, it's just my phone," Zhao said, rising smoothly to her feet. "After you've made your list, you might like to consider getting dressed." She pointed at Lavigne's portly stomach, which was barely contained inside a pair of silken pajamas. Without the time to dress the comatose professor, they'd simply draped a coat around him and carried him to the car.

"Ça ne va pas du tout!" Lavigne cried, looking down at his attire and shrieking as though seeing it for the first time.

"Before we left your house, Gui packed a selection of your clothes and toiletries. As promised, anything else you might need we can send out for when we arrive. The bathroom at the rear of the cabin is spacious enough for you to get changed."

The phone continued ringing insistently.

"I think you'll agree that, despite the situation, it's preferable to be presentable," Zhao said, returning to her seat.

Lavigne snatched up the bag and scurried down the aisle to the bathroom.

Zhao sat sideways in the seat, one eye on the bathroom door, and snagged up the satellite phone. The screen flashed with an encrypted number.

"This is Zhao," she said, hitting the answer button.

"It's Wu," a rough voice came down the line. In the background, the chaotic noise was unmistakable—the clatter of equipment, muffled shouting, and the distant roar of machinery.

"You have a development?" Zhao said, her voice dropping to an excited whisper.

"Yes, we've found something," Wu said, before describing the artifact.

Zhao listened in silence, a grin spreading across her face. "You are equipped to bring it to the surface?"

"Yes, although it'll take some time," Wu said. "It's a large object. We don't know how heavy it is."

"Don't waste my time," Zhao said. "You are prepared for this. I will be with you in twelve hours, and I expect to see the object on deck. And Wu, keep the men away from it." Without giving the foreman time to reply, Zhao ended the call.

13

Oil Corporation Rig 5, Gulf of Thailand. Present day.

TWELVE HOURS LATER, WU STOOD AT THE RAILING LOOKING up at the crane. Slowly, the thick steel cable wound upward, lifting the mysterious object from the seabed. Powerful motors groaned under the immense strain, sending vibrations through the platform.

The last few hours had been a complex and dangerous procedure as the sub's hydraulic arms attached reinforced harnesses to the object and hooked it on to the cable. They had then faced the long process of hauling the object through ocean currents, watched closely by the sub's various cameras.

"One hundred feet." The crane operator's voice came through the radio. The crane's motor dropped into a lower register as the operator slowed the climb in preparation for the object to break the surface.

Wu gripped the railing and looked at the point where the cable met the water.

Although the rig was set up to remove broken equipment from the seabed, this casket was something entirely different. First, they didn't know how heavy it was, and if it was even possible for their crane to haul it up. Attempting to lift something beyond the crane's capabilities would not just risk damaging the equipment but could destabilize the whole rig. Second, they had no idea if the object was wedged into the silt on the seabed. Even if they could lift it, suction buildup over centuries could hold it in position. And finally, they had no idea if the object was strong enough to stay in one piece during the turbulent journey to the surface. But, Wu thought, watching the cable drag the mysterious object closer, he had been given instructions and he would do all he could to follow them.

"Fifty feet." The crane operator's voice came again.

Word had spread throughout the rig at the news of their unfortunate afternoon and the subsequent find. Now every crew member was on deck, leaning out over the railings as they tried to catch the first glimpse of the object.

"Twenty-five feet," the crane operator said, his voice tense.

Wu saw a shape as the object neared the surface.

"Steady!" Wu shouted, lifting the radio to his mouth. "Bring her up slow and easy!"

The crane groaned under the weight, the cable visibly straining. Wu's heart raced as he considered the dangers of the cable snapping. Not only would they lose this incredible find, but the backlash could potentially damage the rig or injure crew members.

"It's coming! I can see it!" one man yelled, pointing down at the water.

The water beneath the platform roared and frothed. Bubbles broke the surface, followed by a surge of displaced water. Then, inch by agonizing inch, a shadowy shape broke through the churning depths.

Wu held his breath as the mysterious object emerged from the depths, water cascading from the top in shimmering sheets.

A collective gasp rose from the crew. Even Wu, who had seen the thing on the monitors, felt his breath catch in his throat.

Now that the object was out of the water, the crane strained against the weight. The motors groaned, their vibrations moving through the structure. Metal creaked and popped as the machinery approached its limit. The entire platform tilted and rocked as the heavy object swung from side to side. Men stumbled, grabbing onto railings and equipment to steady themselves. The vibrations intensified, traveling through the metal like a low-frequency earthquake.

"Ease off!" Wu shouted into the radio. "Slowly."

The operator reduced pressure, and the shaking subsided.

Wu leaned over the railing and watched the object swinging on its cable, threatening to hit one of the supports. Ideally, they would attach additional lines once the object broke the surface, but they weren't equipped for such things.

With the ascent now slowed to a crawl, the swinging subsided. When the casket hung like a dead weight, the crane operator once again worked the controls, bringing the object up and over the platform.

"Get back! Get back!" Wu roared, signaling for his men to step aside.

As though in a trance, the men retreated, watching the object swing overhead. For almost a minute, the casket hovered over the deck. The men formed a circle, into which the crane operator lowered the casket.

A ghostly silence settled over the rig as the object touched down with a gentle thud. Two men stepped forward and unhooked the crane's cable, letting the straps in which the casket had rested drop to the deck.

Wu leaned over the railing of the upper deck and peered down at the object. Although still quite a distance away, he realized he had never seen anything quite like it before. The men crowded around the object, reaching out to touch the smooth stone sides.

"Don't touch it, step away!" Wu roared, gesticulating wildly. A strong wind whipped through the platform and carried his voice away. Recalling Zhao's strict instructions not to let anyone near the thing, Wu set off at a run toward the stairs. He was about to leap down the first flight when an agonized scream split the air. He turned to see what was going on down below as a second and third scream joined the first.

A man recoiled from the object, thrashing and clawing at his face, as though suffering a burn. The two men beside him did the same, flopping to the ground like fish out of water. Another man, clearly now unable to see, tripped over one of his colleagues. He writhed and twisted, his screams becoming more of a senseless gurgle than a human noise. As he turned, Wu saw his face. His skin was blotchy and discolored, bubbling like wax. His eyes bulged grotesquely, swiveling from side to side.

The deck below erupted into panic as men scrambled away, pushing and shoving in their desperation. One man hurdled the railing, his terrified scream cut short as he hit the water.

"Get back! Everyone, get back!" Wu roared, his voice lost in the madness.

A group of men that were still unaffected by the object turned and ran back inside the rig. In an effort to save themselves, they swung the bulkhead door closed and locked it, trapping several men outside. The trapped men crowded around the door, slamming their fists against the steel.

Wu heard another noise rising above the uproar. He glanced away from the nightmarish scene and saw a chopper flying in their direction. Thoughts of his own survival winning out, he spun on his heel and charged for the helipad.

Taking the metal staircase two steps at a time, Wu swung around a corner and charged out on to one of the suspended walkways. He reached the next flight of stairs and sprinted, his breath coming in ragged gasps. He burst onto the next gangway and looked up at the helipad which extended out the side of the platform. The chopper, a Sikorsky twin engine, slowed as it neared the pad.

With a final burst of speed, Wu vaulted up the staircase and out onto the edge of the helipad. Then, with a bone-jarring thud, the Sikorsky touched down.

Wu wasted no time charging toward the chopper as the door slid open.

"Thank heaven and earth that you're here," Wu yelled. "Don't stop the engines. We can't stay here. Something has—"

Two sharp cracks pierced the air, barely audible over the roar of the rotors. The first bullet slammed through Wu's chest and came straight out the other side. The other smashed him in the shoulder, spinning him around. For a moment, he looked down at the spreading pool of blood in shock and disbelief. His knees folded and he collapsed onto the helipad.

As his vision blurred, Wu saw several figures all dressed in anti-radiation suits step out from the chopper. They walked around Wu without a single glance. Before blacking out, Wu heard a voice. With his last conscious thought, Wu recognized the voice as Zhao's.

"Secure the artifact. No survivors."

14

"WE'LL SECURE THE ARTIFACT," ZHAO SAID, POINTING AT GUI, his bulky figure straining against the hazmat suit. She indicated the two men at the rear of their group. "You two set the explosive charges at the points we discussed." The men nodded, then turned to collect the kit bags, which contained the explosive charges and detonators.

"How long do you want on the timer?" one of the men asked, swinging the bag on his shoulder with ease.

Zhao paused and thought. "Thirty minutes. We'll be long gone by then." She led the group across the gangway that connected the helipad to the rig. They descended two flights of stairs and paused for Zhao to check the rig's schematic on a tablet computer.

"This way to the control room," she said to Gui, pointing at a set of double doors. "You two continue down to the lower levels." The men with the explosive charges nodded and continued on down the stairs.

Zhao and Gui pushed through the doors and into the rig's interior. Zhao led the way, searching for indications that something wasn't right. Gui followed, panning his rifle from right to left, ready to shoot first and ask questions later.

White-painted metal walls lined both sides of the corridor. Bundles of thick cables snaked along the ceiling. Fluorescent lights bathed everything in a dazzling white glow, occasionally flickering. As they moved deeper through the structure, signs of panic became more obvious.

Zhao paused to look at a bloody handprint smeared on the walls and a tattered high-visibility jacket lying on the floor.

"Signs of infection," Zhao said, speaking for the benefit of the voice recorder mounted in her suit. "This is an indication that the Lotus Key's protective casket has been damaged. Radiation levels are so far unknown."

Zhao led them further through the structure, passing storage areas, maintenance bays and crew quarters—all eerily vacant. Reaching a bend in the passageway, Zhao heard voices. She stopped and glanced at Gui, who had his rifle raised and his gaze focused on the passageway ahead.

Listening closely, Zhao heard shuffling from around the corner. She peered around the corner and saw a rig worker at the end of the next passage, struggling to stay upright on his shaking feet. Zhao raised a hand, indicating for Gui to stop.

Clearly hearing movement, the worker turned toward them. His face was blistered and raw.

"Interesting," Zhao said, assessing the man with the quiet detachment of a scientist analyzing the results of an experiment. "It's clear that the artifact is active. Either the protective shield has been damaged or is no longer effective after years of submersion."

"Hello ... someone there?" the rig worker said, taking an unsteady step toward Zhao and Gui. He reached out, his hand more raw flesh than skin, and steadied himself against the wall. His hand slid downward, leaving a bloody smear.

"The artifact's power doesn't seem to have diminished," Zhao said. "These men can't have been subjected for long, but the effects are ... powerful."

The rig worker took another step, his eyes milky white and unfocused. He opened his blistered lips to speak.

"Help ... please ..." he wheezed. He took another unsteady step toward Zhao and Gui.

"It appears as though, without regulation, the artifact's power is causing people to break down at a cellular level," Zhao dictated, watching the man with clinical interest.

"Is ... is someone there? I can ..." the man croaked, taking another step.

"The radiation, or whatever it is, seems to affect soft tissue first, including the eyes and the skin. It also seems to have damaged hearing, but not completely."

The man stretched his arms out, feeling his way along the corridor.

"Movement is stunted too, suggesting muscle tissue has been affected. One thing is for sure, the Lotus Key is as powerful as expected."

Her observation at an end, Zhao flicked her wrist toward the rig worker. Gui squeezed off several controlled shots, the bark of the rifle reverberating through the passageway. When the sound had echoed into silence, Zhao continued down the corridor, skirting the man, who now lay splayed across the floor.

"We head to the control room," she said, not even looking at the fallen man. "We need to see who's still alive, and then secure the artifact."

"THEY ... THEY SHOT HIM!" LIANG EXCLAIMED, HIS VOICE A MIX of disbelief and terror. "Why would they ...?"

Liang watched alone in the control center as chaos raged throughout the rig. In all his twenty-one years, he had never seen anything as abhorrent as what played out on the screens.

Liang had watched as the chopper arrived, assuming they were here to help. When the figures climbed out and shot Supervisor Wu in cold blood, it became clear he was wrong.

Liang now watched the screen as the figures passed through the rig, getting closer and closer to the control center with each turn.

"I need to get help," he muttered, reaching for the phone. His hand froze in midair as a suspicion crept in. "How did they know about the artifact?" he said, once again looking at the figures. "And how did they know to bring radiation suits?"

Realizing that what he really needed was a way off the rig, he looked at the radio system mounted on the wall. Although the radio was old and outdated, it remained a vital part of the rig's safety protocol. Maritime law required that all sea vessels, including oil rigs, maintain a functional long-range radio system specifically for use in emergencies. It wasn't simply a formality—the system was a critical lifeline, linking the rig to nearby ships, emergency services, and coast guards.

Liang ran across the room, knocking over his chair, and grabbed the receiver. He spun the large dial, shifting to the international distress and calling frequency—Channel Sixteen. He thumbed the button on the receiver. The radio crackled to life with a sharp burst of static.

"Mayday, mayday!" Liang said, turning back to the monitor with the receiver still clamped to his mouth. The hazmat-wearing figures paused at a junction. The smaller of the two checked their location on a tablet and turned, leading them in his direction.

"This is the Oil Corporation Rig Five," Liang said, giving their location as the figures approached the door. "We are under attack and require immediate assistance. They're coming for me now. I don't have much time."

Liang watched as the leading figure stepped up to the control room door. The handle clicked down, and the door started to swing open. He dropped the radio and, keeping low, ran for a hatch that allowed access to the rack mounted computer systems. He silently worked the hatch from its position, revealing a cramped space on the other side. He slipped inside, pulling the hatch closed as the door swung open.

ZHAO SHOVED THE DOOR OPEN AND LED THE WAY INTO THE control room. She moved into the center of the room and looked around. With no windows, the only light in the room came from a row of monitors fixed to one wall, and a red light which pulsed on and off in the far corner. Some of the screens appeared to be working, showing data from around the rig, others flickered with ghostly error messages. She stepped up to one of the desks and placed her finger against a mug of tea.

"It's still warm," she said for the benefit of her voice recorder. "Someone's been here recently."

She took a step back and looked at two tattered office chairs, the filling spewing out through threadbare upholstery. One more lay on its side, behind one of the desks.

"Three people work in here," she said. "And it looks as though one of them left in a hurry. The question is, where are they now?"

Gui dropped into a crouch and checked beneath the desks. He clicked on a flashlight and swept the beam through the gloom.

"No one here," he said, rising to his feet and studying a screen which displayed camera footage from around the rig. Tapping the console, he flicked through the various camera positions. No one spoke for several seconds. The soft crackle of their respirators and the occasional beep from the still-functioning equipment were the only sounds in the deathly quiet.

"This is interesting," Zhao said, approaching an old-fashioned radio system. "It's set to the emergency channel." She picked up the receiver, which was hanging on its wire. She thumbed the button, and a bolt of static came through the speaker.

"Think someone tried to call for help?" Gui said.

Zhao thought about it for a second before yanking the receiver from the radio and dropping it to the floor. She raised her boot and stamped on the device until the brittle plastic shattered into countless pieces.

"It doesn't matter," Zhao said, looking down at shards of plastic and exposed wiring. "By the time anyone gets here, this whole rig will be underwater."

"I've found the artifact," Gui said, pointing at the monitor.

Zhao strode over and leaned across the desk, looking closely at the screen he indicated.

Gui tapped the console, and the camera zoomed in on an object in the center of the deck. Several rig workers lay around the object, their bodies twisted and splayed out in unnatural positions.

"Hold on, is that movement?" Zhao said, pointing at something at the edge of the screen.

Gui panned the camera to the side, bringing a group of men into view. They hammered against a door, their movements jerky and uncoordinated.

"These people are close to the relic," Zhao said, looking from the men to the casket. "It looks as though they've survived for some time and still have use of their—" Zhao stopped talking as the screen caught her eye. On the monitor, one man dropped to the floor, clearly succumbing to whatever power the object possessed.

"It seems as though it's only a matter of time," Zhao said, narrating some details about what she saw.

"Some go quickly, others take longer," Gui said.

"What's the status with the explosives?" Zhao said, activating her comms unit.

A crackle of static came first, followed by a response: "Almost done. We're setting the last charges now."

"Good. When you're finished, meet us on the main deck. We've located the artifact and will need some help to get it out of here."

Gui eyed a pair of large computer racks built into the wall at the back of the room. Various modules within the racks blinked and flickered. "What about the systems in here?" Gui said, looking at a small service hatch. "We should shut them down."

He stepped toward the hatch and dropped into a crouch. He reached out and grabbed the handle, ready to pull the hatch away from the wall.

"Leave it," Zhao snapped. "When the charges blow, this is all going to the bottom of the sea. The relic is our priority."

Zhao stepped out into the corridor and strode away. Gui followed a step behind.

15

Sok San Private Island, Cambodia. Present day.

EDEN HAD KNOWN, PROBABLY SINCE BIRTH, THAT LIFE WAS divided into two categories: the difficult and the impossible. Tackling the difficult built courage, success, and resilience. But attempting the impossible—like finding inner peace while her muscles screamed and sweat dripped onto an overheated bamboo mat—was pure foolishness.

"Let your thoughts drift away, like leaves on a stream ..." came the soothing voice of the so-called expert.

Looking around at almost every member of the council, all seemingly at ease and focused, Eden couldn't believe Athena had talked her into this. The whole scene would have been almost comical if it weren't so frustrating. Here she was, when there was so much to do, flopping around on the beach just because Athena thought it was a good idea. "Come once," she'd said, handing Eden the stupid multicolored leggings she now wore. "You never know, you might even enjoy it."

"Move up on to your hands and knees and into the cat-cow pose," the instructor said, her voice backed by the sea, whispering against the sand.

Eden watched Vittoria DeLuca, positioned directly in front of her, move into the pose with an impressive fluidity. Even her father and Beaumont were making a good go of it.

"Inhale, drop your belly, lift your heart to the ceiling. Exhale, round your spine like an angry cat," the instructor continued.

Eden tried to replicate the motion, arching her back as muscles she didn't know existed pulled taut. In front of her, DeLuca moved with the elegance of a dancer, while Eden wobbled like a newborn giraffe.

"Now, lower down into Child's Pose," the instructor coaxed. "Let your forehead rest on the mat and stretch your arms forward. Sink into the earth."

Eden followed the instruction, placing her forehead against the mat. Her thighs burned as if punishing her for every life decision leading to this moment. Although she was fit, training regularly, this felt like a whole new world.

"Now roll onto your back for Supine Twist," came the next instruction.

Eden watched DeLuca draw her knee up to her chest, then twist it across her body as directed. She couldn't help but glance at Athena, who was serene with her face the picture of bliss and her leg at an impossible angle.

"Now, as we move toward the end of the session, watch your thoughts drop like leaves in the fall ..." the soothing voice came again.

A bead of sweat slithering down her neck, Eden tried to picture her thoughts as leaves, although they felt more like piranhas, circling and snapping.

"Now, let's end in Savasana," the instructor whispered.

"Lie flat, arms relaxed by your sides. Close your eyes. Feel the support of the mat beneath you."

Eden collapsed into the pose; her body finally stilled. The bamboo mat, clearly now unhappy that she was relaxing, poked her in the thigh.

"Notice any tension in your body," the instructor continued, her voice carrying the serene confidence that came from never having to do anything dangerous in your life. "Release it with each exhale ..."

Eden shifted, grimacing as another piece of bamboo dug into the other leg. The only tension she wanted to release right now was the growing urge to throw her mat into the sea.

"Focus on the present moment ... Focus on your breathing ..."

"Present moment ..." Eden groaned through clenched teeth. "Which bit of the present moment should I focus on ... the sweat, the mosquitoes or this bamboo mat poking me in the—"

A sudden tap on the shoulder pulled Eden from her pathetic attempt at meditation. She opened her eyes and looked up to see Baxter standing over her.

Baxter signaled that he needed to speak with her, his body language suggesting it was urgent.

Trying not to show her total relief, Eden reached across and tapped Athena, then climbed to her feet. Her legs protested after being stretched in ways they'd never experienced before. She waved an apology to the instructor and followed Baxter back inside the hotel.

"It's not like you to interrupt," Eden said, placing a hand on Baxter's shoulder. "But thank you so much."

"Didn't you feel your thoughts floating away?" Athena

said, her voice uncannily mirroring the tone of the instructor.

"I felt something slipping away, but it wasn't my thoughts," Eden said, brushing sand from the brightly colored yoga pants she couldn't wait to take off.

"It was great, wasn't it?" Athena said, rolling her shoulders.

"Look, if I ever need yoga skills to save the world, then I'll do it. Until then, give me combat training any day," Eden said, turning to Baxter. "What's up?"

Baxter gestured that they should step inside the conference room, which was secure from prying ears. Seeing the seriousness with which he moved, Eden hurried in behind.

"The *Balonia* has received a message from an oil rig," Baxter said, not speaking until the door clicked closed behind them. He stepped up to his laptop and entered the passcode.

"Right?" Eden said, flashing Athena a sideways glance. "And that's important because ...?"

"The message came on Channel Sixteen," Baxter said, looking up at Eden and Athena as though this news was deathly serious.

"Isn't that a shopping channel?" Eden said, arms folded.

"I thought it was one of those channels that showed Christmas movies in August," Athena said.

Baxter looked from Eden to Athena and back again, clearly not quite understanding why they didn't know this key piece of information.

"Please remember you're talking to normal people here," Eden said when Baxter didn't reply. "What is Channel Sixteen, and why is that important? Although I am super grateful to have escaped pretending my thoughts were leaves."

"It's such a powerful image," Athena said. "Be like nature, and let it go."

Eden looked at her friend, not sure if she was being serious or not.

"Channel Sixteen, 156.8 MHz, is the international distress frequency," Baxter said, talking quickly, as though the process of explanation was an unfortunate hurdle he shouldn't have to jump through. "It's monitored constantly by the coastguards, naval vessels and any other ship at sea. Using this channel is ... well, it means that whatever's going on is serious."

"Someone's in trouble?" Athena said.

"In short, yes. Any self-respecting mariner would never use Channel Sixteen if it wasn't crucial," Baxter said.

"And you have a recording of the call?" Eden nodded at the laptop.

"Yes, fortunately, our system logs and records all communications on that frequency." Baxter hit a key and a young man's voice boomed from the laptop.

"Mayday, mayday!" The man spoke in English with a Chinese accent. "We are under attack and require immediate—" the voice stopped, and another sound interrupted the recording.

"That's gunfire," Eden said, looking at the laptop where a wave form jumped up and down.

Baxter nodded.

"Lots of gunfire," Athena added.

The speaker gave their location in hushed tones, and the recording ended.

Eden, Athena, and Baxter glanced at each other.

"How far away is this rig?" Eden said, her voice now devoid of all humor.

Baxter loaded a map and quickly calculated their route.

"It's about fifty nautical miles from here." He pointed out toward the *Balonia*, on the back of which their trusty helicopter sat. "That's no time in the chopper."

"Before we go charging in there, do we have any idea what they're being attacked by?" Athena said. "We've come under fire in that chopper before, and it's not something I'm keen to repeat."

"All we know is what's on that recording," Baxter said, pointing at the laptop. "But, given the location and the nature of the facility, this is highly unusual. Oil rigs rarely face this kind of threat, especially not one that would prompt an emergency broadcast."

"Are there any other ships nearby?" Eden asked.

"The nearest is over sixty miles away. That's a freighter, so it'll take them almost six hours to change course and attend."

The three exchanged silent glances.

"Then we've got to go," Eden said, her hands on her hips. "We'll be there in a few minutes. Check the place out and advise the emergency services if we need to."

"Agreed," Athena said, looking out at the chopper. "Come on, Captain, let's make like a tree and leaf."

"This way, not far," Zhao said, leading them toward the deck using the schematic on the screen of her tablet computer. The sound of movement was clearly audible now, reverberating through the structure from somewhere ahead.

They rounded a corner, Gui going first with his rifle raised. He indicated the coast was clear, and Zhao followed.

Up ahead, the passageway terminated in a bulkhead door, through which the sound of thumping fists and muffled cries reverberated.

"This is it," she said, remembering the group of rig workers she'd seen on the screen. Zhao approached the door and saw that a metal bar had been wedged through the door's locking wheel, sealing it shut. The wheel juddered from side to side, clanging the bar against the wall as someone from the outside tried to get through.

"Ready?" Zhao said, stepping to one side and indicating that Gui should go first.

Without a word, Gui approached the door, yanked the bar from its position and spun the locking wheel. The bolts clanged back and Gui swung the door open. Not giving the men a moment to react, Gui pushed through, spraying bullets as he advanced.

Zhao stood motionless, listening to the rifle's report combined with the groans of the infected rig-workers.

"Clear," Gui shouted back a few seconds later.

Zhao paced out through the door, placed her hands on her hips and looked at her prize.

"We shouldn't stay long," Gui said, looking at one of the rig workers, his skin blistered and red. "We don't know how strong this is, or if our suits can take it. We don't know what the effects are."

"I have waited years for this," Zhao said, stepping entranced toward the object. "I must see it with my own eyes."

"I don't think that's a good idea," Gui replied, his voice tight. "We'll have time to run tests—"

"No," Zhao snapped, spinning around to shoot a look at her second in command. "I will not delay." She stepped up to the casket and ran a gloved finger across the stone.

"It seems to be in good condition. It's thick, as we'd predicted."

Gui stood riveted to the spot, watching his superior closely.

"Get me that ladder," Zhao said, pointing at a ladder lying across the deck behind them. The placement of the ladder suggested that some men had tried to climb to one of the upper decks, before falling foul to the strange illness.

"We really shouldn't be—" Gui said.

"Just do it," Zhao snapped. "I need to see inside now. The quicker I do, the quicker we get out of here."

Gui swung his rifle over his back and hurried across the deck to retrieve the ladder. Following Zhao's directions, he placed it against the casket, then held it in position as Zhao climbed.

"I'm now performing a visual inspection of the upper section," Zhao said, reaching the top of the ladder. "That makes sense," she said, her voice barely audible through the hazmat suit. "The casket is in perfect condition, even after all these years. As suspected, it appears as though the lid has been penetrated by the drill."

"Are you feeling that?" Gui said from beneath her. "I feel a strange tingling sensation. I really think we should—"

"Silence," Zhao snapped. "It's nothing. That's your mind playing tricks on you. I need to look inside." She climbed on to the top of the casket and crawled towards the damaged section. As she moved, a strange prickly sensation moved its way up her arms, as Gui had reported. She ignored it, focusing on the task at hand. She leaned across the top of the casket and peered in through the hole.

"Amazing," she breathed, her voice hushed. Inside sat an object unlike anything Zhao had ever seen. The object was made from some kind of metal, formed in the shape of a lotus flower. Mounted in the center of the object, a crystal glowed with some otherworldly light.

As Zhao leaned closer, she felt the prickling sensation intensify, spreading across her entire body. The crystal's glow seemed to respond to her presence, pulsing more rapidly. Despite the protection of her hazmat suit, Zhao felt an overwhelming energy tingling her skin.

Zhao pulled herself away from the hypnotic pulsating and straightened up.

"I want the artifact secured and ready—"

"What about these?" Gui interrupted, pointing at the bodies of the unfortunate men.

"You're right, we can't risk them washing up on a beach somewhere," Zhao said. "Take them to the lower levels and lock them inside. They'll go to the seabed with the rest of this place. I want us out of here in ten."

16

"VISUAL ON THE RIG, DEAD AHEAD," BAXTER SAID, ADJUSTING their trajectory toward the structure on the horizon.

Eden squinted into the sunlight and saw their destination, a block against the shining water. They'd been airborne only a few minutes and already left Sok San and the Cambodian coastline far behind.

"I've been going through the data we have on the rig," Athena said, speaking through the comms system from the cabin behind. "It's a relatively new operation, only been active for about six months. No reported issues until now."

"Any chatter on Chinese military channels? Could this be some kind of territorial dispute gone wrong?" Eden said.

"Nothing," Athena said. "It's all quiet. Too quiet, if you ask me."

As they approached the rig, the sheer size of the structure became clear. Towering steel legs plunged into the sea, supporting the massive structure. Multiple levels of decks, walkways, and equipment sprawled out from all sides with the lattice frame of the drilling derrick reaching high into the sky.

"We're going to need to know where we're going," Eden said, checking out the structure's multiple levels through the binoculars. "Any chance we can get a schematic?"

Athena tapped away on her tablet computer for a few seconds. "Got it here. I just hope it's up to date."

They neared the structure, and Baxter swung the chopper around to perform a circuit. As they tilted, Eden raised the binoculars to her eyes and looked for signs of life.

"It's all quiet," she said, eyeing one of the walkways that clung to the structure's exterior. "No signs of distress, no people at all."

"That's got to be weird, right?" Athena said, turning away from her research to check it out herself.

"Yeah, although it's a mess down there," Eden said, pointing toward one of the main decks. Broken equipment lay abandoned on the floor.

Baxter nodded. "Definitely weird. Operational rigs run twenty-four hours a day. There should always be people visible, even from this distance." He reached for the radio controls, flipping switches to change the frequency. "Oil Corporation Rig Five. We received your distress call and are incoming to offer assistance. Please respond, over."

They waited, the only sound the steady thrum of the helicopter's rotors. Seconds ticked by with no response.

Baxter tried again, this time more urgently. "Oil Corporation Rig Five, we are on the final approach to your helipad. Please acknowledge and confirm landing clearance. Over."

Again, silence.

"We'll land anyway," Eden said. "Be ready for anything."

Baxter nodded and made another call to the rig. "We are approaching the helipad. We're here to help."

"It's even stranger that there's no one on the radio,"

Athena said. "They would man communications at all times."

"I know," Eden said, her feeling of disquietude growing as they approached the helipad.

Baxter swung the Eurocopter around the platform and hovered in close to the helipad. He carefully adjusted the controls, compensating for the side winds, and touched down with a gentle thud.

Eden was about to swing open the door when Baxter placed a hand on her forearm.

"Give it a minute and see what happens," he said, making no move to shut down the rotors.

"You think they'll have a welcoming committee?" Eden said.

"I've no idea, but something here doesn't stack up."

Eden let go of the handle and watched the staircase for movement. After a minute, satisfied that no one was racing their way, Baxter powered down the craft.

"Hold on, check that," Eden said, pointing at the radiation detector they had installed in the chopper. "The radiation here is higher than usual."

Baxter leaned over to examine the dial. "You're right. It's only slight, but it's far above normal levels. And the signature ... it's unlike anything I've seen before."

"Gear up with the radiation suits," Eden said, throwing Athena a glance. "I told you this wasn't a time to pack light. You're staying with the chopper," she said, turning to Baxter. "The last thing we need is someone messing with our ride out of here."

Eden scrambled into the back of the chopper as Athena dug out the radiation suits they kept in the chopper in case of emergency. They slipped into the suits and checked each other to ensure all the seals were secure.

"Comms check," Eden said, her voice muffled by the visor.

"Reading you loud and clear. Take this, just to be sure," Athena said, holding a handgun out to Eden.

They both slipped the weapons into specially designed pockets in the rad suits.

"Ready?" Eden said, glancing at Baxter.

"Be careful," Baxter said, nodding, and fetching a handgun for himself.

"It's my middle name," Eden said, sliding open the door and dropping to the helipad. Athena stepped down a second later, and swung the door shut, sealing Baxter inside.

Eden led the way around the helipad, a strange eerie silence surrounding her. The only audible sounds inside the suit were the rustling of the fabric, the distant crash of the waves, and her breathing. Approaching the stairs, she stopped and pointed up at a security camera mounted high above them. Spinning around, she saw another on the other side.

"There are cameras all over this place," Eden said, looking at Athena. "If we can find a recording system, then maybe we'll get our answers."

"Eden, look at that," Athena said, her voice cold.

Eden turned and saw what her friend was looking at. A few steps away, liquid pooled across the yellow circle which marked the outer edge of the helipad.

Eden stepped across, crouched down beside the liquid, and touched it with the tip of her gloved finger. "It's still wet," she said, holding up the finger. "That's blood. It's got to be."

"There's a lot of it, too," Athena said. "Whoever that came from isn't walking around any longer."

"And that suggests that wherever they are, they didn't

walk there," Eden said, eyeing a streak of blood that led toward the stairs. "Someone's done this."

Athena glanced at the schematic on the screen of the tablet computer. "First stop, the control room. From there we can look at the camera footage and get answers."

"Or survivors," Eden said, the sick feeling in her stomach already telling her that wasn't likely.

Following the schematic, Athena led the way down the stairs and into the rig's main structure.

Feeling more uneasy with each step, Eden drew out her weapon and walked behind Athena's right shoulder, ready to fire if necessary. They pushed through a set of double doors and into a corridor, passing various storage areas, living quarters, and equipment rooms. They paused to look into each room, but all were deserted, many showing signs of destruction—overturned chairs and scattered belongings. They turned a corner and saw another stain spreading down the wall and across the floor.

"We need to keep moving," Athena said. She turned sideways, passing the puddle without stepping in it. "Whoever did this might still be here."

Ahead, the corridor stretched into the gloom. Lights flickered ominously, plunging their destination into darkness before washing it with bright light again. The rig creaked and groaned as though it were a living thing.

Reaching a junction, Athena checked the schematic. They turned right and started down a long corridor which looked almost the same as the previous one. Silence hung all around them like a physical weight. The breathing inside their suits was the only sound.

About halfway down the corridor, Athena stopped and pointed at a door. "That's it."

They approached the door, weapons ready. Eden leveled her weapon at the door while Athena tried the handle. The door clicked and swung open.

17

THE OPENING DOOR REVEALED A SPACIOUS ROOM WITH BANKS of monitors, control panels, and computer stations. The room was dimly lit by flickering screens and pulsing warning lights.

"Right behind you," Eden whispered as Athena stepped through.

"What's going on down there?" Baxter's voice came through the comms system, surprisingly loud in Eden's ear.

"We've found the control room," Eden said, sweeping the room to check for hostiles. Overturned chairs and papers scattered across the floor suggested a struggle had taken place here.

"It's clear, there's no one here," Athena said, her weapon dropping to her side. She stepped toward one of the large central monitors, the screen smashed into a spider's web.

"Look," Eden said, pointing at a radio system fitted to the wall on the far side of the room. The wire to the receiver hung down to the floor, although the device itself had been smashed. She leaned in and looked at the dial. "It's set to 156.8 MHz."

"Channel Sixteen," Baxter said, his voice like some omnipotent being in Eden's head.

"We need to find the security camera controls," Athena said, searching the various control consoles. "If we can access the footage, then we can piece this thing—"

Her words were cut short by a sudden, muffled thump. Both women froze, listening intently.

"Did you hear that?" Athena whispered.

Eden nodded, raising her gun again. "It was close. We're not alone here."

They both stood stationary, listening to the room. After a few seconds, another thump, louder this time, came from the back of the control room.

Eden spun around, raising her weapon toward the sound. Athena mirrored the movement, both women now facing a closed hatch in the rear wall.

Using hand gestures, Eden communicated she would open the hatch while Athena trained her gun through the opening. Athena nodded in understanding. Eden slid her firearm away and stepped up to the hatch, which was little more than a metal plate allowing access to whatever systems were back there. If it hadn't been for the noise, Eden didn't think they would have even noticed the opening was there.

Eden crouched and seized the handles.

Athena produced a flashlight and held it alongside the weapon.

Eden counted down from three and tore the hatch from its mounting.

"Identify yourself!" Athena called out, shouting into the opening. "We are armed, but we don't intend to shoot."

Eden threw the hatch to one side, removed her gun, and peered inside.

A man crouched at the back of the crawl space. His

clothes were tattered, and his pale face was streaked with sweat. Seeing Eden and Athena in their radiation suit, his eyes bulged with terror, as though witnessing something from outer space. He held his hands up in front of him, shaking uncontrollably.

"Don't shoot, don't shoot!" he croaked in accented English. "I'm not armed."

"We're not going to," Eden said, lowering her weapon. "We're here to help." She slid her weapon away and helped the man out of the crawl space.

Athena lowered her weapon too, although she kept it in hand should the situation change.

Reluctantly, the man crawled out, allowing Eden to help him to his feet. She held on to him as he shook uncontrollably, his breath coming in ragged gasps.

"Who are you?" Eden said. "We're responding to an emergency call that came from here."

"I am Liang," the man said, his eyes filling with tears. "They killed everyone," he sobbed. "I saw it. They killed everyone."

"Who killed them?" Eden said, realizing how young the man was.

His words dissolved into incoherent mumbling, punctuated by fearful glances over his shoulder, as though expecting something to follow him out of the hatch.

"Who killed everyone? We need to know what we're dealing with here," Eden said, attempting to sound calm, although aware that time was running away with them. "Are they still here?"

"I ... I don't think so ... I knew it was bad news ever since we found that ..." Liang's voice descended into a series of erratic gasps.

Eden and Athena exchanged a glance.

"What did you find?" Eden said.

"Eden," Athena whispered, laying a hand on her friend's arm. "He's in shock. You won't get anything from him yet." She stepped forward. "Liang, listen to me. We need your help with something."

Liang looked at Athena as though seeing her for the first time.

"We need to access the security camera footage to find out who did this. Do you know how it works?"

Liang swallowed, his Adam's apple bobbing behind a stubble-free throat. He nodded. "Yes, I can do that. It's on this terminal right here." The words came more quickly now, as though talking about a familiar topic was soothing.

"Show me," Athena said, finally comfortable enough to slide her weapon away.

Liang moved towards the terminal, his movements becoming more purposeful as he focused on the task at hand. He sat down and his fingers danced across the keys.

"Here's the footage from earlier today," he said, his voice steadier.

The main screen flickered to life, displaying a grid of camera feeds from various parts of the rig. He selected one feed and expanded it to fill the screen.

Eden and Athena leaned in, watching intently as the footage began to play. The timestamp in the corner indicated it happened less than an hour ago.

The video showed the arrival of a helicopter. The craft touched down and figures in white hazmat suits emerged. They strode up to a man on the helipad and fired.

Eden pulled out her phone and snapped a picture of the helicopter and the figures.

Liang cycled through the various cameras, following the intruders through the rig.

"You mentioned that you'd found something," Eden said, distracting Liang from the assassination of his colleagues. "Show me that."

Liang nodded, switching to another camera. This one showed a large object being brought up from the depths.

"That's what we found," Liang said, his voice barely audible. "That's what started all this."

"Where is that now?" Eden asked.

Liang clicked to the live feed and brought up a view of the lower deck. "It's gone. I don't—"

An explosion ripped through the rig, cutting Liang off in the middle of his sentence. The control room shook, the floor that had once been solid now twisting and buckling beneath their feet.

"Move! Get down!" Eden shouted, dragging Liang to the floor as a blast followed. The door flew from its hinges, slamming against the wall. Even down low, the blast hit them like a physical force, slamming them across the room and showering them with debris. Sparks rained down from ruptured electrical conduits, smoke caused by burning plastic, twisted through the air. As the sound of the explosion died away, the rig's main support beams groaned.

"We need to get out of here!" Baxter's voice cut through the comms. "This place is going to blow."

"It must have been rigged," Eden said, scrambling up and using the desk for support. "Whoever did this, plans to send the whole rig to the bottom of the sea."

"That way they get to blame it on some industrial accident," Athena said, standing and helping Liang to his feet.

The structure groaned and tilted, as though one of the legs had been ripped out of position.

"Get the chopper started!" Athena shouted. "We're on the way."

"We need to save this footage," Eden said, racing toward the console. "This is evidence of who has done this. Help me with this!"

"There's no time," Athena said, grabbing her friend's shoulder.

Another explosion ripped through the structure. This one felt deeper, more structural. The entire platform lurched, sending unsecured equipment smashing on to the floor. Chunks of the ceiling smashed down, followed by a cloud of dust.

"We need to go, now!" Athena said, dragging Liang toward the door.

A steel beam fell through the ceiling, crashing into one of the consoles in a shower of dust and sparks. The structure groaned, deep and guttural, and slipped another few degrees off center.

"Alright," Eden said, turning away from the control room and hurrying toward the door. "We're outta here!"

18

"Come on, come on!" Baxter shouted, flicking the switches to power up the Eurocopter's engines. He once again looked at the walkway which connected the helipad to the rig, hoping to see Eden and Athena appear. The sound of twisted metal vibrated through the chopper and the helipad tilted. The chopper slipped toward the sea.

"Get this up into the air and come back for them," Baxter said to himself, realizing that if the chopper went down there were all stuck. He snapped the last switch into the on position and the rotors began to spin, thronging through the air with a languorous *thwup-thwup*.

The chopper slid further toward the precipice. Baxter gripped the controls, preparing himself to lurch out if the craft fell sideways into the sea. The skid gripped on the edge of the pad and the chopper stopped, its nose now hanging out over the edge.

Baxter turned and looked back at the drilling platform, several stories below. If he didn't get these engines started in time, they would all go down with the rig.

Another explosion ripped through the platform,

sending a cloud of thick black smoke up into the sky. The rig groaned and shuddered, metal screaming as it twisted under the immense stress. The helipad inched another few degrees to the side. The Eurocopter slid a little further, its whole front end now teetering off the pad.

"Why didn't you leave the engines running?" Baxter said, cursing himself. But with the Eurocopter drinking fuel like Hemingway guzzled whisky, he knew that powering it down was the only option.

The rotors spun, blurring into one. The rhythmic *thwup-thwup-thwup* just about drowning out the cacophony of destruction coming from all around.

The helipad bucked a little more, causing the Eurocopter to slide again, gouging two furrows in the surface. Nearly half the aircraft now hung off the pad.

Looking away from the drop, Baxter checked the gauges. They were nearing the level of power required to get airborne but hadn't reached it yet.

The rig shuddered violently once more. The Eurocopter lurched again.

Baxter's stomach dropped as he looked out and saw the drilling platform below. He didn't know how much of the chopper was still on the helipad, but it wouldn't stay that way for long. The engine whine increased in pitch as it neared full power.

A loud crack resonated through the air. Baxter spun around to see a massive crane, destabilized by the rig's movements, twist, buckle, and fall in his direction. The crane swung toward him, as though in slow motion. The splitting, crunching sound of failing steel somehow cut through the whirring rotors.

Adrenaline surging, Baxter made a split-second decision. With a silent prayer, he yanked on the controls, urging the Eurocopter to lift with all the power it had.

The aircraft shuddered, threatening to stall completely. For a beat, it appeared the engine would fail and the whole machine would topple forward, followed by the crane. Then, with a groan and a shudder, the chopper lurched into the air.

Baxter's relief was short-lived as he realized the Eurocopter was now in a nose-down position, barely clearing the edge of the rig. Alarms sounded through the craft. He fought with the controls, willing the aircraft to gain altitude.

The crane slammed down into the helipad where the chopper had been moments ago. The impact sheered the helipad in two, smashing half of it down into the lower deck, and half into the sea.

The Eurocopter spun, dropping dangerously close to the waves. Baxter leveled it out, the rotor wash spraying seawater across the windshield.

He gained some altitude and pulled away from the falling rig, allowing himself a brief sigh of relief.

"Eden, Athena, do you copy?" he called into his headset. "I've got the chopper in the air. Where are you? We need to get you out of there now!"

EDEN AND ATHENA RAN OUT OF THE CONTROL ROOM, dragging Liang between them. The technician had sunk into a confused silence now, completely disorientated, looking around as though he didn't really understand what was happening or where he was.

They moved as fast as they could along the corridor. The rig shook again, slamming them into the walls and against each other. They reached the junction they had passed minutes before and froze. The corridor through which they'd arrived was now like the slope of a mountain, rising at forty-five degrees.

"Baxter, we can't get back to the helipad," Eden said, watching the wall at the far end of the corridor split and fall away, daylight now shining in.

"Don't come to the helipad, it's already in the sea," Baxter said, the chopper's rotors whirring in the background.

"You left without us, typical," Eden said.

"That ... that way!"

At first Eden didn't know where the voice was coming from. She turned to see Liang pointing down the corridor.

"Emergency evacuation point," Athena said, pointing at a sign which was now hanging on the wall by one screw.

Athena grabbed Liang by the arm and together they raced down the corridor.

"How far?" Eden shouted to Liang, who seemed to have regained some of his senses in the face of imminent danger.

"Just ... just ahead!" he yelled back, his voice half lost in the disharmony of twisting metal and distant explosions.

They rounded a corner and stopped at a sealed bulkhead door. Above it, a flashing red light indicated it was locked down.

"No!" Athena exclaimed, slamming her palm against the unyielding metal.

Liang pushed forward, his fingers flying over a nearby keypad. "I can override it," he said, his voice shaking, but determined. "Just need to—"

Another violent tremor rocked the rig. The floor

beneath them buckled, throwing them off balance. Eden grabbed a railing to steady herself, her other hand still gripping Liang's arm.

"Hurry!" she said, as a crack split the wall beside them. A giant boom shook the floor as another part of the rig fell into the sea.

With a final keystroke, the bulkhead door hissed and slid open, revealing a small passageway. The three rushed through and came face to face with three bright orange lifeboats suspended in launch cradles.

"This'll do," Eden said, rushing toward the nearest boat. She yanked open the watertight door. "Inside! Now!"

"I ... I ..." Liang shook his head. "I don't know how to work this. I've only been here six weeks. We haven't had—"

A section of the roof collapsed, bringing with it a steel beam at least a foot thick.

"We'll work it out. Get in!" Athena shouted, shoving the technician inside.

Eden and Athena followed, before sealing up the door. Eden did a quick check of the craft's layout. With around twenty seats, and a fully enclosed top, it was probably their best chance of getting out of here. She scrambled down to the seats at the front and secured Liang's harness, before clicking her own into position.

The craft groaned and clanged as another shock wave rolled through the rig.

Now secured in place, Eden turned her attention to the control panel. She hit the power button, and the system flickered to life—GPS, radio, and emergency beacons came online.

"Release mechanism engaged," Eden said, thumping a button. "Everyone ready for this?"

"No! I want to get off," Athena shouted, gripping the harness.

"That's not an option," Eden said, as the klaxon sounded.

The boat shuddered as the hydraulic release mechanism engaged.

"Brace!" Eden yanked the launch handle. For a heartbeat, nothing happened. Then the cradle tilted, and the lifeboat dropped into free fall. Eden's stomach lurched as they plunged toward the churning water.

The impact, when it came, felt like hitting concrete. Water sprayed across the reinforced windows as they plunged beneath the surface. For a terrible moment, they were submerged in darkness. Then the boat's buoyancy took over, and they bobbed back to the surface like a cork.

The engine coughed to life. Athena leaned forward and shoved the throttle to full. The powerful engine tore through the water, now forcing all the occupants back against their seats. They bounced for several seconds, hitting each wave like a boxer on a losing streak.

A low, ominous groan echoed from behind them. The sound quickly escalated into a series of sharp, staccato cracks.

Eden unbuckled and staggered to the small porthole at the back. She peered through as a thunderous boom reverberated across the water.

The oil rig, standing several stories above the water, now twisted and gnarled, finally collapsed in on itself. The support beams snapped like twigs, sending steel splinters lancing into the air. Then, like a falling tree, the rig bent and slammed down. With the sound of thunder, jets of water whipped high in the air and a wave raced outwards.

Athena kept the pressure on the throttle as the upsurge roared up behind them.

"Hold on," Eden said, a giant wall of water now obscuring her view. The lifeboat rode up the face of the wave, teetering precariously at its peak before plunging down the other side.

As they stabilized, the roar of the collapsing rig faded, replaced by the steady hum of the boat's engine and the lapping of waves against the hull.

"That was probably your best escape yet." Baxter's voice came through the comms system, which was miraculously still working.

"It wasn't bad, I have to admit," Eden said, striding to the door and throwing it open. She looked up and saw the Eurocopter above them.

"I'm here on my own," Baxter said. "Getting a rope to you is going to be tricky."

Eden turned and looked at Liang, quivering and cold, on the front seat. "I've definitely had enough danger for one day. We've got a full tank, we'll see you back at the *Balonia*."

"Roger that," came Baxter's reply, as the Eurocopter roared away.

19

Bokor Hill, near Kampot, Cambodia. Present day.

MEI-LING ZHAO STOOD ON THE BALCONY AND LOOKED OUT AT the surrounding landscape. Once a private villa for high-ranking French officials, the building had fallen into a state of disrepair until Zhao had taken it over as a base for her operations. They had kept the exterior's crumbling concrete and the cloaking vines to match the rest of the derelict colonial buildings which dotted the area. The inside, however, had been gutted of its old fixtures and refitted as living quarters and a large mission control center. Although basic, Zhao and her team didn't need luxury. In fact, Zhao reflected, glancing at the helicopter sitting in a patch of cleared forest beside the building, comfort made people weak, and weak people were no good to Zhao.

Her patience reaching an end, Zhao turned from the view and marched back inside. The area that would once have been a luxurious living space for the officials who stayed here now housed several high-spec computers.

"What's the status on the Lotus Key?" Zhao said, striding

toward Gui, hunched over a keyboard on the far side of the room.

On arrival back from the rig a few hours ago, Zhao's team had extracted the key from its protective casket and had scanned it with a high-powered laser. They had then placed it in a specially made crate. Far lighter than the old stone casket, the crate would allow a team of men to move the key without falling foul of its strange radiation.

"The digital renders are almost complete," Gui said without looking up. "We've scanned it at an unprecedented level of detail. We're talking about a resolution of less than a micron. That's about a hundredth of the width of a human hair. We can see details on this artifact that would be invisible even under most microscopes."

"How long until it's complete?" Zhao said, stepping close to the screen. The partial render rotated on the screen, its lotus petals shimmering in green and black. The crystal at the center of the artifact pulsed with light, as it had when Zhao had looked back on the rig. Seeing the object on the screen, Zhao recalled the strange energy she had felt pulsing through her body when she'd been close to the key. The feeling had buzzed through her like an energy she couldn't explain, making her long for more.

"At this resolution, we'll be able to analyze the material composition with incredible accuracy," Gui continued. "We'll see microscopic engravings too—anything from the signatures of the ancient craftsmen to hidden messages. If they're here, we'll see them."

"Fine, how long?" Zhao said, straightening up.

"Another hour, maybe two," Gui replied. "But trust me, it'll be worth it."

Zhao marched across the room to where Professor Lavigne sat hunched over the Ta Prohm Stele. His spectacles balanced wonkily on his nose, Lavigne studied the stele, scribbling notes as he did so.

"What have you got for me, professor?" Zhao asked.

"I can't believe you're making me do this!" Lavigne hissed, casting Zhao a disapproving look. His voice dropped to a whisper, as though someone might be listening in. "This artifact is *stolen*. It's supposed to be in the Musée Guimet. How did you—"

"Don't you worry about that," Zhao snapped. "You just need to tell me what it says."

"What if the authorities come in here now? They'll think I'm responsible for removing this from the museum! They'll send me to ... I really wouldn't do well in jail. My allergies—"

"Professor Lavigne," Zhao said, leaning over the professor and meeting his gaze with a hard look. "Right now, going to jail is the least of your worries. Tell me what the inscription on that stele says, or ..." Zhao pointed at one of the guards who stood at the door, a rifle clutched across his chest.

"I've completed part of it already," Lavigne said, nodding jerkily and sliding his spectacles back into position. He turned his attention back to the stele and indicated the lines of characters at the top. "This section here ... it's a standard royal inscription. It talks about King Indravarman II and his bravery in battle, his divine right to rule, the thousands of temples he built. It's all very ... self-important."

"It doesn't mention the Lotus Key?" Zhao said, looking hard at the stele as though she might understand it by concentration alone.

"No, nothing like that." Lavigne pointed at the stele. "This has been in the gallery for decades; it's been translated countless times. If it had a secret meaning, someone would have—" Lavigne yelped as Zhao slapped him around the back of his head.

"Do what you're told and maybe, just maybe, you will survive this," Zhao said.

"Yes ... yes ... of course," Lavigne stuttered, aligning his spectacles again. "One thing I don't understand. If you can answer, it might help—"

"What?" Zhao's stare bored into the professor.

Lavigne took the scarf which he had insisted on wearing and dabbed it across his brow. "As artifacts from the Khmer period go, this is like many others." Lavigne pointed at the stele. "What makes you think it's connected to the Lotus Key?"

Zhao considered Lavigne's question for a moment, her eyes narrowing. Finally, she spoke, her voice low and measured.

"We have discovered something which has got us closer than ever before. We recently completed a high-resolution x-ray of one of the carvings at Angkor Wat. What we found hidden beneath the surface ... it changes everything."

"I must see it." Lavigne stopped what he was doing and looked up at his captor.

Zhao considered the Frenchman for a long moment. "Fine, show him," she said, rising to her feet.

"Are you sure?" Gui said, turning away from the screen for the first time.

"Do it," Zhao snapped.

Gui tapped a few keys, and the scan of the carving replaced the Lotus Key on the screen.

Lavigne rose to his feet, gasping as he saw the ghostly outline of the carving he knew so well.

Gui made an adjustment, and the image of the carving merged into something else entirely.

Lavigne crossed the room as though in a trance, his eyes locked on the image. As the image solidified, he recognized a lotus shape in the center, with two circular objects on either side. Beneath each of the objects was a line of script.

"We believe the symbol represents the Lotus Key," Zhao said, pointing at the object in the center of the image. "And these two circular shapes are some kind of discs, which are crucial in harnessing its power."

"How did you link this to the stele?" Lavigne asked, leaning in. "Une minute! Hold on!" he exclaimed, pointing at one of the lines of symbols visible on the carving before Zhao could answer. "That line appears on the stele."

"Exactly," Zhao said. "We don't yet know what it means, but we ran a comparison of the symbols and found that they also appeared on the stele."

"Koun sao nov krom kar ko-hok robsa sdach," Lavigne said.

Zhao raised an eyebrow.

"That's my best translation of it." Lavigne paused to think for a moment. "It ... it doesn't make a lot of sense."

"What does it say?" Zhao snapped.

"The key rests beneath the king's gilded words," Lavigne said. "And this other one on the left ..."

"Wait," Zhao said, snapping her fingers. "One at a time. What did you say?"

"The key rests beneath the king's gilded words." Lavigne pushed his spectacles up his nose again. "But that doesn't say anything more than I've told you before. It's about the king winning battles and building temples. There's no ..." Lavigne froze.

"What is it?" Zhao said, spinning to see the professor now lost in thought.

Lavigne turned and raced back across the room, the scarf billowing out behind him.

"Incroyable! I'm such an idiot! I don't know why I didn't see this before. It's right there and I ..." Lavigne pulled off his spectacles and pressed the heels of his hands into his eyes. "This is what happens when I'm away from my routines. I miss the most obvious things ... I ... I ..."

Zhao stalked across the room, grabbed the professor by the shoulders, and spun him around.

"What is it?" she shouted, shaking Lavigne with enough ferocity to rattle his teeth.

"It's so obvious. As plain as day. As clear as the nose on my face!"

"What is?" Zhao roared.

Lavigne sucked in a deep breath, shook himself from Zhao's clutches and turned back to the stele. Then, taking a good amount of time over it, he adjusted his spectacles.

"You're quite correct that the text is the same on your hidden carving as on the stele." Lavigne leaned across the table and read from his notes. "King Indravarman II, blessed by the gods, vanquisher of enemies, builder of a thousand—"

"Yes, you read this to me before. Don't waste my time," Zhao said. "What's ..." Her voice died in her throat as she too realized what Lavigne had. "Wait a minute, you said King Indravarman II?"

"That's what it says here." Lavigne turned to look at Zhao.

"Can someone tell me what's going on?" Gui said, looking from Zhao to Lavigne as though he was watching a tennis match.

"The professor has realized that we've been incredibly

foolish. We have missed something obvious that has been in front of our faces this whole time."

"And that is?" Gui said, his expression blank.

"Indravarman II was not the brave vanquisher of enemies. In fact, he was quite the opposite." Lavigne took over the narrative with the confidence of a seasoned lecturer. "He was the king under whose reign the Khmer Empire began to fall."

"What's written on the stele is wrong. It's fake," Zhao said, stepping up to the table and looking down at the object.

"You mean we broke into the museum to get something worthless?" Gui said.

"What I mean," Lavigne said, "it's not what's on the surface of the tablet that's important. I think we'll need to use that x-ray scanner of yours."

20

The *Balonia*, Cambodia. Present day.

EDEN WALKED UP TO THE SCREEN IN HER OFFICE ON THE TOP floor of the *Balonia*. She looked closely at the image, which showed three figures in radiation suits crossing the helipad toward the rig.

"Is this all we've got?" Eden said, pointing at the screen.

"I'm afraid so," Baxter replied. He tapped at the laptop, trying to enhance the image, but not getting anywhere.

"We shouldn't have left without the computer system. We needed that footage," Eden said, crashing a fist into the desk. "This image is useless."

"Then you wouldn't have got out at all," Baxter replied, tapping at the keys. The image lightened slightly but didn't offer any new information about the people, or their arrival, on the rig. "I'm not sure you understand quite how close that all was. The whole thing went under—"

"Alright," Athena said, raising a hand to Baxter. "I know it was close, and we were lucky to get out."

"I'm just saying it was *too* close, that's all." Baxter looked up and his stare lingering on Eden. "That rig was, well ... rigged."

"Someone didn't want us, or anyone, poking around on there," Athena said, taking a step toward the screen. "My guessing is, it's the Ghostbuster lookalikes we see here." She flicked a thumb toward the screen.

"Yeah, I agree, but that image's no help at all," Eden said, looking disdainfully at the screen.

"Maybe we could put a call out to our contacts in the area," Athena said, tilting her head to the side as she scrutinized the image.

"What, ask if they've seen Egon, Slimer and Gozer?" Eden said.

"Ask them if there's something wrong in the neighborhood," Athena said.

"Sometimes I think you kids speak a different language altogether," Winslow said, stepping up to the screen.

Eden threw her father a grin and her frustration thawed for just a moment.

"I agree that the radiation suits do make identification difficult, but that doesn't mean we know nothing," Winslow said, interlocking his hands and leaning back on his heels.

Eden glanced at her father, knowing exactly what he was about to say before he said it.

"We need to turn this around and focus on what we do know," Winslow said, pointing at the screen.

Eden mouthed the words silently, earning a giggle from Athena. She was about to remark on her father's annoying positivity when she realized he had a point, sort of.

"The person at the front of the group is smaller and slighter than the others." Athena stepped up to the screen and pointed at the leader. "You can see how the suit is loose around their ankles and wrists, whereas it's a tighter fit on the others."

"That's right," Winslow said, grinning at Athena with pride. "We'll make an archaeologist of you yet, my dear. And what might those observations mean?"

"It's a woman," Eden said, answering before Athena had the chance. "The person at the front is a woman, and I get the impression from the fact she's leading, that she's in charge."

"Exactly," Winslow said, pointing at his daughter. "Of course, you could be wrong. People come in all shapes and sizes, but as a theory, it stacks up."

"Then there's the helicopter," Winslow said, pointing at the aircraft which appeared out of focus beside the trio. "Although we can't see any registration numbers, I expect if we were to find an expert on aircraft, they could tell us the make and model."

Winslow looked at Eden and then Athena, issuing a subtle nod.

"Hmmm," Eden said, thoughtfully. "Where might we find such an expert on all things flying machines?"

Baxter sat at the computer; his eyes locked on the screen. He tapped away, still working on enhancing the image.

"I don't expect there are any aircraft experts within a thousand miles of here," Athena said, looking around dramatically.

"Such a shame," Winslow said, fake frowning. "It appears we really have hit a dead end then."

"What?" Baxter said, finally noticing that the other three were looking at him.

"That chopper," Eden said, pointing at the screen.

"Ahh, why didn't you say something? I assumed you already knew. That's a Sikorsky S-92," Baxter said. "That's a top-of-the-line machine. It's got a maximum takeoff weight of about twenty-six thousand, five hundred pounds and can carry up to nineteen passengers, which explains how it was able to lift the artifact. It can fly for about five hundred miles—"

"I've often wondered what it would be like to talk to Wikipedia," Eden said, shooting Athena an amused glance. "Now I know."

"For aircraft, yes. Don't bet on me for other topics."

"That means they would have had to land within five hundred miles of the rig, yes?" Athena said. "That's a massive area to search."

"No, because they didn't take on fuel on the platform, so their fuel would have to get them there and back. Plus, the extra weight of the object would reduce their range." Baxter tapped on the keyboard and a map filled the screen. "They would have to land somewhere around the Gulf of Thailand. Somewhere in Cambodia, Thailand, Vietnam, or possibly Malaysia."

"That's still a large area," Eden said. "But we're getting closer. Who can fly a chopper like this?"

"These birds typically need a two-person crew to fly. Then there's the ground crew. The S-92 has a rotor diameter of about fifty-six feet, so you need a lot of space for takeoff and landing. Plus, you'd need proper fueling facilities—this guzzles jet fuel like you wouldn't believe. Then, there's all the paperwork. Everyone needs flight plans, maintenance logs, cargo manifests—especially if they're hauling mysterious artifacts. Someone's keeping records, even if they're trying to stay off the radar."

"Let's look into that," Eden said. "There must be some kind of paper trail, even if they're keeping their real intentions off the books."

"I'll get on to it," Baxter said, turning back toward the screen.

A knock sounded on the door. They all turned as Giulia, one of the research team, walked in. With everyone on the *Balonia* performing two and sometimes three roles, Giulia was also one of the medics.

Liang followed her, dressed in a fresh set of clothes. Although cleaned up, the guy still looked exhausted.

"Considering what he's been through, he's holding up well," Giulia said. "He's showing low radiation, which we're treating with potassium iodide tablets. We've done a full body decontamination using specialized soaps and repeated washing to remove any external contamination. We've also taken blood samples to check for internal radiation exposure."

"Thank you," Eden said, directing Liang toward the sofa. "We have a few questions to try and understand what happened today, then you can rest."

"Take this," Giulia said, handing Liang a bottle of water. "Drink as much as you can. It'll help to flush out your system."

"Do we know what sort of radiation it was?" Eden said.

"That's the strange part. The radiation signature doesn't match anything we typically see. We're still analyzing it, but it's ... unusual, to say the least."

"Thanks," Eden said. "We won't keep him long, I promise."

Liang slumped onto the sofa, then took a long sip from the bottle.

"Anything you can tell us about what happened on the rig would be so helpful," Athena said, stepping toward the technician.

"Do you remember what time the people arrived?" Eden asked.

"I'm not sure, exactly, there was a lot going on," Liang said, giving the impression of a deer in the headlights of a speeding truck.

"I know you've been through a lot in the last few hours," Eden said, softening her tone. "I can't even imagine how stressful it must all be, but I'm worried that whoever has taken that object will use it to do something terrible."

Liang nodded, sweat puckering his forehead. He explained slowly and in broken English the events of the previous day, pausing to answer questions when they were asked.

"It's surprising that they were able to turn up so quickly," Athena said, thinking out loud. "You say you reported the find, and these guys arrived within a few hours?" She pointed at the screen.

Liang nodded.

"It's as though they knew what you'd find," Eden said, tapping her chin. They all stood silent for a moment, thinking through the events as they understood them.

"Tell me about the object," Winslow said, stepping toward Liang. "Could you describe it?"

"Yes, actually," Liang said, looking up for the first time in several minutes. "It looked like one of those flowers."

"What do you mean?" Winslow said, standing up straight, an urgent edge lacing his voice.

"The object was like a box, a casket, but our drill had hit the top and damaged it. The rock was thick, maybe a foot," Liang said, illustrating the width with his hands. "We got a look at what was inside with the camera on the submarine. It was a flower ... a lotus flower."

21

The *Balonia,* **Cambodia. Present day.**

"WHAT DO YOU MEAN IT WAS LIKE A LOTUS FLOWER?" EDEN said.

"I didn't see it clearly. It was deep under the sea at that time," Liang said. "But what I saw looked like a lotus. You know, one of those flowers that grows in the lakes all around Cambodia and other places."

"Yes, the lotus flower holds an important place in Khmer culture." Winslow nodded at Baxter. "Bring up a picture of Angkor Wat, please."

Baxter tapped at the keyboard, and an image of the world-famous temple filled the screen.

"The lotus motif appears extensively throughout Khmer architecture—at Banteay Srei, Preah Khan, even the smaller temples at Roluos. But Angkor Wat ..." Winslow gestured at the image, his finger tracing the temple's iconic silhouette. "It's notably different."

"How so?" Eden asked, studying the image.

"The whole temple, the towers here," Winslow said,

stepping up to the screen and tracing the temple's iconic silhouette. "Each one is designed to look like a lotus bud, rising toward the heavens. It's one of Angkor Wat's most distinctive features."

"Yes, that's it!" Liang said, lifting himself from the chair. "There was something in the middle that looked like a crystal, and it was that shape." He pointed at the tower. "It was surrounded by petals, laid flat like this." He gestured the shape with his hands.

"The lotus imagery isn't simply decorative here—it's fundamental to the entire structure," Winslow continued. "Angkor Wat itself emerges from the earth like a lotus rising from the water. The moat surrounding it, the graduated levels of the temple—it's all part of that symbolism."

"Okay, okay," Eden said, taking a step backward. "But what does that tell us? What does that mean?"

"Angkor Wat is the largest and most renowned temple in Cambodia, maybe the world," Winslow said.

Eden glanced at Athena and exhaled slowly. She knew that once her father started to explain something, you were in it for the long haul.

"Supposedly it was built in the twelfth century, but ..." Winslow said, doing something that surprised everyone in the room. For the first time, possibly ever, Alexander Winslow didn't say anything.

Eden looked from her father to the screen and back again, both shocked by what he said and that he'd finished talking.

"Okay," she said, after a few seconds of silence had passed. "Let me guess, you know something different?"

Winslow nodded. "I do. The official history is that the temple, along with the whole Angkor complex, was built around the twelfth century. And to be honest, it suits the needs of the Council to have people believe that, so we've never revealed anything different. When you think about it, though, it's ridiculous, right? How could a population without machinery have moved thousands of tons of rock over fifty miles, fitted and carved it all in just a few decades?"

"People will believe all sorts of things," Eden said, urging her father toward the point. "What is the truth?"

"Even we don't know for certain," Winslow said. "But we believe, based on some very compelling evidence, that the whole complex is much, much older than this. Perhaps even millions of years old."

"Millions?!" Eden said, not quite believing her father's words.

Alexander Winslow turned to look at his daughter. "Yes, it's hard to believe because the carvings are all so well preserved. But you've got to remember that before the late nineteenth century, the temples were surrounded by the jungle. Many were under thick layers of moss and under-growth, which has protected them remarkably well."

"But even so," Eden said, her hands on her hips. "What makes you think they're so old?"

"There are several clues throughout the site. You just have to know where to look. Such as the Ta Prohm Stegosaurus."

Baxter's fingers flashed over the keys, and another picture appeared on the screen. The image showed a section of intricately carved stone. Among the various animal and plant motifs, there was a distinct figure that stood out—a creature with a rounded back adorned with a row of plates.

"This, my dear, is one of the most controversial carvings in all of Angkor. It's located on a pillar in Ta Prohm, another temple in the complex. At first glance, it looks like an ordinary decorative element, until you look closer."

Eden took a step forward and saw exactly what she was looking at. "That's a dinosaur," she said, pointing at the screen.

"Exactly that. The rounded back, the distinctive row of plates, it's even got the spikes on the tail. This is a creature that's supposed to have been extinct sixty-five million years before humans evolved."

"And yet ... there it is," Athena said.

"It's impossible for the Khmer people to have known what a stegosaurus looked like," Eden said.

"Exactly," Winslow nodded. "That's the mystery. Of course, mainstream archaeology suggests it's just a—"

"Funky looking rhino?" Eden interjected.

"We know that this carving is the result of two factors," Winslow continued without missing a beat. "We know that dinosaurs survived much longer than most people think, and Angkor Wat was not built by the Khmer people."

"Can't carbon dating give us the true age?" Athena said.

Winslow shook his head. "No. Carbon dating is impossible with stone structures." He turned back to the screen, his voice lowering slightly. "But we know that these structures are incredibly old—"

"What exactly are you saying?" Eden said.

"We believe the Khmer didn't build these temples. They were passed down to them from a far older civilization." Winslow turned to face the group, his hands clasped behind his back. "What we're dealing with here is an artifact of immense historical and potentially spiritual significance."

"But how did it end up at the bottom of the sea, a hundred miles from Cambodia?" Eden asked.

Winslow nodded, his expression growing serious. "This is where the mainstream history actually has it right."

"History lesson incoming," Athena said, perching on the arm of the sofa as Winslow paced across the room as though he were on stage.

"Jayavarman VII was one of the most powerful and influential kings of the Khmer Empire, ruling from 1181 to 1218 common era. We know he existed because he's pictured in carvings across the empire. He was responsible for the upkeep of the temples at Angkor. He's the king that most mainstream historians credit with building these temples. He did, as far as we can tell, do a great job of maintaining and restoring them."

"Right?" Eden said, looking at the others, who were all listening closely.

"Jayavarman VII was a devout Mahayana Buddhist, which was a significant shift from the Hindu traditions of his predecessors. Copying the style of the temples at Angkor, he constructed hospitals, rest houses, and numerous new temples across the empire—although none of these were anywhere near as grand as what we see at Angkor."

Eden leaned forward, intrigued. "And how does this relate to our underwater artifact?"

Winslow's tone dropped as though he were sharing a profound secret. "What most people don't realize is that Jayavarman VII wasn't simply revered as a king—people believed he was a God on earth."

"But ... how?" Eden said, returning to silence after a glare from her father.

"This wasn't political posturing or religious fervor. There was a very tangible reason for this belief." Winslow paused for effect, looking at each of the room's occupants in turn.

"We know that this was because of a relic housed beneath the central lotus tower at Angkor Wat. Powered by the sun, the relic had been inherited from the previous civilization that built the temple originally. Jayavarman used this power to expand his empire."

Eden's eyes widened. "And you think that's what Liang and his team found on the seabed?"

"It certainly was a powerful thing," Liang said. "The people nearby went ... they went crazy."

"And that explains the strange radiation," Athena added.

"Exactly. When correctly housed inside the lotus tower, the key is controlled. It's activated by the sun, you see, and inside the lotus tower it only receives direct sunlight for a few minutes each day." Winslow turned to face Liang. "When your team pulled it to the surface, with the lid of the casket damaged, the power would have been far too great for anyone to stand."

Liang swallowed nervously, clearly remembering the horrific scenes he had endured just hours ago.

"Our research suggests that this is some form of advanced technology, far beyond anything known to mainstream science. The radiation, when emitted at the correct frequency, gave the rulers abilities that seemed, well, godlike to their subjects."

"That sort of makes sense," Athena said, looking at Winslow. "I remember reading a legend that said the Khmer king got his power because he stayed in the lotus tower each night. The Khmer people believed he went to the tower to commune with the other gods, but what you're saying here makes more sense."

"Every legend is based on some kind of truth," Winslow said, tapping his chin.

"The king wasn't communing with the gods in that

tower, but using the energy of the Lotus Key to broadcast his wishes," Athena said.

"In the wrong hands, this could be disastrous." Baxter's voice cut through the room like an icy wind. "If someone figures out how to use this, they could make the people of the world do whatever they wanted."

The small group exchanged a glance as the gravity of the situation became crystal clear.

"Okay, but how did the Khmer people know how to work this?" Eden said. "You said they weren't as advanced as people suspect, but they knew about this complicated science that we don't truly understand."

"You travel on a plane, but do you truly understand how it works?" Winslow retorted.

"Yes, of course," Baxter said, leaning forward. "It's a simple balance of four forces: lift, thrust, drag, and—"

"Alright, thanks," Eden said, raising her hand to halt the explanation. "What you're telling me is that the Khmer kings didn't know *how* it worked, they just knew *that* it worked."

"Exactly!" Winslow said. "And so, for hundreds of years, they ruled over one of the largest and most successful empires the world has ever seen. And that's what makes this discovery so exciting ... and so dangerous. We're dealing with technology so advanced it might as well be magic to us. And somewhere out there, someone has gotten their hands on it."

22

"OKAY, THAT SORT OF MAKES SENSE," EDEN SAID, CROSSING TO the door and looking out at the water. "But I still don't understand how this relic ended up right out here at the bottom of the sea. The ancient city of Angkor is hundreds of miles away."

Winslow's expression turned grave. "Ah, well, that's where the story takes a sinister turn. You see, power like this comes at a price. It is suggested that, over time, exposure to the relic begins to have negative effects. The later kings of the Khmer Empire were said to be increasingly unstable, prone to fits of madness and cruelty." He paused, letting the implications sink in. "It's possible that they became addicted to the power, and that addiction drove them crazy. What I believe is that the king to follow Jayavarman, his son Indravarman II, recognized this failing and decided that it was no longer worth the risk."

"So, he had it removed from Angkor?" Eden said.

"Exactly." Winslow paced back across the office, every pair of eyes following him. "Indravarman II ascended to the throne in 1218, following his father's long and prosperous reign. Having witnessed his father's decline firsthand, I believe Indravarman made the difficult decision to remove the Lotus Key from Angkor Wat. But he couldn't simply smash it to pieces—he didn't understand the power and there were still those in the court who believed in its divine nature. Instead, he devised a plan to hide it."

"At the bottom of the sea," Athena said. "He had someone sail away with it and throw it overboard."

"Exactly right," Winslow said. "Although, I think if we were to look in the location where the casket was found, I believe we would find the remains of the ship, too."

"They sunk their own ship, just to make sure it went down," Athena said.

"They gave their lives to make sure the key was out of harm's way," Eden said.

They exchanged glances before Athena took over the narrative. "Then, without the relic, the Khmer Empire fell to the Siamese in 1431."

"Exactly. The Siamese sacked the city, looting its treasures and destroying much of its infrastructure." Winslow looked around at the group, his expression grave. "If what Liang saw is indeed the Lotus Key, we're not simply dealing with an archaeological find. We're looking at an artifact that, if used correctly, would give the holder incredible powers."

A chime sounded from the computer, attracting the attention of everyone in the room. They all turned to look at Baxter, who tapped the keyboard and read the message which had just arrived. His face paled.

"What is it?" Eden said, noticing her friend's change in demeanor.

"Come on, the suspense is killing me," Athena said, crossing the room and leaning against the desk.

"We've got a situation," Baxter said, his voice tense.

"Forty-eight hours ago, there was a break-in at the Musée Guimet in Paris."

Eden furrowed her brow. "Surely that's a matter for the police? We've got far bigger things to worry about than someone breaking into a museum."

"I suppose that depends on what they've stolen," Athena said, folding her arms.

Baxter hit a key, and an artifact appeared on the screen. The image showed a small, intricately carved stone tablet. Although the tablet's surface was weathered, it still bore clear inscriptions.

"That's a Khmer relic, right?" Eden said, pointing at the screen.

"Yes, I'm afraid so," Winslow said. "That's the Ta Prohm Stele."

"And it can't be a coincidence that ..." Athena said, her words trailing off to nothing.

"Very unlikely," Winslow said.

Eden swallowed, trying to remove the ball of dread which had taken root in her throat. She stepped forward and studied the image. The stone tablet was about a foot tall and covered in rows of Khmer script. The edges were adorned with intricate lotus motifs and geometric patterns.

"Do they have any leads on their thieves?" Winslow said. "That could lead us to the people who sunk the rig."

"Whoever did this was good," Baxter said, tapping at the laptop. "All the security footage is down. We've got nothing."

"What about the guards?" Eden asked.

Baxter pulled up a police report. "Two were found unconscious. They described a blur of movement, then nothing. Whoever this was, they're not just tech-savvy— they're highly trained."

"Have we got access to the security footage from the

museum?" Eden said. "We might see something the authorities have missed."

"I can get that." Baxter tapped frantically at the keyboard. A few seconds later, a series of video feeds appeared on the screen. He selected one of the cameras, showing a view of a gallery.

"That's the Ta Prohm Stele," Eden said, striding up to the screen and pointing at the glass case in the center of the room.

For several seconds, the picture was motionless, and then it changed. The top of the glass case now sat on the floor and the stele was gone. A pair of security guards rushed through the gallery, the beams of their flashlights whipping from side to side.

"Whoever stole this hacked into the system and stopped the video," Baxter said. "There's a three-minute update window built into the system, which means they had three minutes before anyone raised the alarm."

"They got in and out again in three minutes?" Eden said.

"That is impressive," Athena added.

"Let's look at all the cameras at the end of that three-minute period," Eden said. "Maybe they weren't as lucky as they hoped."

The group watched intently as Baxter cycled through the feeds.

"Wait, go back!" Eden leaned forward, her eyes narrowing. "There, in the corner of that frame."

Baxter rewound the footage, slowing it down frame by frame. For a split second, a figure appeared at the edge of the screen.

"There!" Eden pointed. "Can you enhance that?"

Baxter zoomed in and sharpened the image as much as possible. The blurry figure merged into a clearer shape—a woman with black hair, dressed in form-fitting clothes. She took down one of the guards, then spun around and disappeared through a door.

"Wow, she's quick," Eden said, pointing at the figure. "What's through that door?"

"It's a storeroom. According to the report, they got in and out through a rooftop window in there," Baxter said.

"And let me guess, there are no cameras in the storeroom," Athena said.

"Correct," Baxter said. "Let me see if I can enhance the image."

As Baxter worked, Athena leaned in closer to the screen. "Look at her posture, the way she moves. She's not some amateur thief. She's trained. I'd say military or special forces."

The image on the screen began to sharpen, pixel by pixel, bringing the woman's features into focus.

"And look at the backpack," Eden said. "It's oddly shaped, probably custom-designed to carry the tablet."

Winslow's brow furrowed. "This was a highly planned operation. She knew exactly what she was after and how to get it."

The image sharpened further, bringing into focus the woman's high cheekbones, almond-shaped eyes, and a determined set to her jaw.

Athena's gasp cut through the room like shattered glass. The color didn't just drain from her face—it fled, leaving her skin so pale that the freckles across her nose stood out like ink spots.

Everyone whipped around to see her breathing in short, shallow gasps.

She staggered backward until her shoulders hit the wall. Her eyes, wide with shock, darted around the room as if searching for something—anything—that might make what she'd just learned untrue.

Eden rushed across and helped Athena onto the sofa. She gripped her knees with shaking hands.

On the screen, the final touches of enhancement settled into place. The woman's face was now crystal clear.

Athena stuttered; her voice laced with pain. "That's ... that's my mother."

23

ZHAO PACED TO THE WINDOW AND LOOKED OUT AT THE surrounding forest. Behind her, Gui and a pair of technicians pieced together the x-ray scanner. As her impatience reached boiling point, Zhao caught sight of herself in the window's reflection. The face that stared back at her was set with an expression of pure determination. Then, for a reason she couldn't fathom, her mind drifted back to that day at the prison in Beijing.

Once the memory sunk its claws into her mind's eye, Zhao couldn't stop it. The image spilled forth unbidden, surfacing as sharp and clear as sunlight. She saw the stark concrete walls and smelled the oppressive tang of the chemical-cleaning agents. As though it were a movie replaying, she saw the moment Raven had broken through into the observation gallery and met her gaze. Zhao saw in her daughter's eyes the look of confusion, followed a moment later by something she now knew to be a betrayal.

Of course, Zhao hadn't wanted to send her daughter to death—her own flesh and blood—the thought still sent a pang of ... something ... through her chest. But it had been necessary. Raven had been snooping around—her curiosity, ability and desire a dangerous combination. She was getting far too close for comfort, threatening more than she understood.

Zhao had faced a choice, revealing who she really was and undoing the work of several years, or saving her daughter. Ultimately, as always, the job won.

The reflection in the glass distorted, superimposing itself with the image of a younger Zhao, sealing her daughter's fate. She blinked and the illusion vanished, leaving only the hard-eyed woman she had become staring back at her.

"We're ready," Gui said, followed by a soft hum of the x-ray machine powering up.

Zhao shook her head, banishing the ghosts of the past. Regret was a luxury she had no time for—that was a pursuit for weaker people. She focused on the tingle of unbridled power she had felt as she got close to the Lotus Key. That intoxicating sensation was the feeling of a supremacy that would soon be hers. She turned away from the window, her grimace of cool determination as hard as ever.

Gui ran a series of final checks on the x-ray scanner, which was mounted on the table in the center of the room. He pressed a button on the machine's beam generator, which hung on an articulated arm. He checked the thick cables which connected the scanner to the computer, and, clearly satisfied that the machine was operating as expected, nodded at Zhao.

"Bring the stele," Zhao said, crossing her arms.

Gui marched across to the stele.

"Non! Not without gloves!" Lavigne shouted with surprising aggression.

Throwing the professor a look of pure contempt, Gui

snatched up the stele with his bear-like paws. He paced back across the room and thumped the artifact into position beneath the x-ray's beam generator.

"That is a sacred relic!" Lavigne said. "It's not a mass-produced plastic toy. To damage it is to damage history."

"Run the scan," Zhao said, ignoring Lavigne's comments.

Gui crossed back to the desk and tapped the keyboard. The scanner issued a series of chirps, followed by a low hum. Various indicator lights blinked red, then amber, then green.

Lavigne wrung his hands nervously, his eyes darting between the precious artifact and the scanner now trained on it

"Initiating scan," Gui said.

"Wait ... wait!" Lavigne said, his lips wobbling. "Aren't x-rays dangerous? How do you know it won't cause—"

A sharp crack filled the air as the scanner burst into life. Lavigne whimpered and backed into the far corner, putting as much distance between himself and the machine as possible. The humming increased, and the machine cracked again. Ghostly images formed on the screen.

"What's happening?" Zhao said, crossing the room and leaning in close to the screen.

"This is the initial scan," Gui said.

The image on the screen coalesced into something that looked like the stele from the outside.

"After I've adjusted the beam's intensity, we'll see what's inside."

Gui tapped at the keyboard and the scanner's articulated arm slid toward the relic. When it was about half an inch from the stele, another crack cut through the room.

Lavigne whimpered and retreated another step, his back

pressed into the flaking plaster. He shoved his spectacles up his nose and blinked several times.

The swirling colors on the screen changed into something solid.

"There's something here," Gui said, pointing at the image where the color palette was darker than the rest. He tapped the keyboard, and the image enlarged. The x-ray continued whirring.

"What is it?" Zhao said, her attention locked on the screen.

Curiosity clearly overcoming his fear, Lavigne shuffled across the room. "That's ... that's ..." he stuttered, adjusting his spectacles.

"There's a pattern," Gui said, zooming in on something which seemed to be right inside the stele.

"Bring up the scan from the carving," Zhao commanded.

Gui did what he was told, displaying the scan they'd found from inside the famous carvings at Angkor Wat.

"This, look," Zhao said, indicating the discs at either side of the carving, then the shape inside the stele. "The shapes are the same."

"They're certainly ... Mon Dieu!" Lavigne's hands flew to his face. He looked from one screen to the next with wide eyes.

"Can you enhance it further?" Zhao said, studying the image so closely she hadn't seen Lavigne's reaction.

"I'll increase the resolution and apply some filtering algorithms," Gui said, tapping away. "That should give us a clearer—"

"The key rests beneath the king's gilded words," Lavigne shouted across the sound of the machine. "C'est impossible! Something has been hidden beneath that self-obsessed nonsense for all these centuries."

Zhao turned around, looked at the professor, and suddenly realized what he was talking about. She smiled triumphantly.

"Not impossible, professor. Inevitable."

"Whatever it is, it appears to be made of metal, possibly gold or a gold alloy," Gui continued, still absorbed by the dancing colors on the screen. "The surface, it's covered in carvings, some kind of text."

"Removing it from within the stele, that's going to be the challenge," Lavigne said, wringing his hands.

"I don't think so, professor," Zhao said, throwing another malevolent smile at him. "The simple solutions are always the best. Turn off the x-ray."

"Given time, I can bring this text to a greater level of detail," Gui said, pointing at the screen. "We might even be able to read it. I can try a variety of—"

"Turn it off now!" Zhao snapped, shooting a fiery stare at Gui.

Gui pressed a few keys and the x-ray's humming dropped to silence. The lights on the beam generator blinked three times, then faded out.

Zhao marched across the room and snatched the stele from the table. "Just to think, the secret has been here all these years. Hiding in plain sight." She turned the tablet over in her hands, looking closely at the stone.

"Please be careful with that," Lavigne said, dabbing at his cheeks with his scarf. "It's incredibly old and a great example of—"

"A moment ago, you said it was self-obsessed nonsense," Zhao said.

"What's written on it is certainly self-obsessed," Lavigne said, leveling his spectacles. "But that doesn't make it any less important. So many ancient Khmer artifacts have been lost. We must treat everyone with ..." Lavigne's voice died in his throat as Zhao raised the stele above her head.

"No!" Lavigne roared, charging across the room as quickly as he was able. "We don't know what damage that could do to the—"

Before Lavigne had the chance to cross the room, Zhao flung the stele. The relic sailed through the air in a slow arc, turning over, before gravity did its work. The stele crashed to the floor, shattering and scattering fragments across the room.

"Oh non! I can't believe ... How could you?" Lavigne roared. Overcome with rage, he leaped toward Zhao his hand raised.

Zhao saw him coming, ducked out of the way, and caught his arm.

"That was a piece of ..." the professor whined, sobbing like a child in meltdown.

Zhao swung a punch which connected with the professor's jaw and jarred him into silence.

Gui charged across the room, grabbed the professor from behind and dragged him away from Zhao. Lavigne writhed for a second, before realizing fighting against the giant was futile. He straightened up, expelled a whole lungful of air, and set about straightening his scarf and spectacles.

Totally unfazed by the pathetic attack, Zhao stepped forward and kicked shards of the stele around with her toe. Seeing something amid the wreckage, she froze.

"This ..." she breathed, her voice barely above a whisper. "This is what we've been searching for."

Zhao kneeled, her fingers trembling slightly as she reached for the artifact. She lifted it carefully, cradling it in her palms as if it was now the most precious thing in the world. The edges of the disc were gold in color and covered with the intricate markings they'd seen on the x-ray. The center, however, was highly reflective, like a mirror.

Zhao ran her fingers over the ridges of the disc's outer rim and the smooth surface of the mirrored center. She carried the golden disc across the room and placed it on the table. She adjusted a magnifying lamp above the object and looked closely.

"Gentlemen, we have the first disc," Zhao said, awe lacing her tone.

"I need to see," Lavigne said, still trying to move away from Gui's giant hands, which remained clamped over his shoulders. "I might be able to read it."

Zhao flicked her wrist and Gui released the professor. Lavigne approached, got his spectacles in the right place, and looked down at the disc in astonishment.

"The first disc?" Lavigne said, looking from the object to Zhao. "You believe that the legends of the Lotus Key are real?"

"I don't believe it," Zhao said, casting a maniacal glance at Lavigne. "I know it. This is one of the discs which will allow us to control the most powerful relic of all time."

Lavigne unwrapped the green scarf from around his neck. He wrapped the material across his hand and leaned in to pick up the disc.

"What do you think you're doing?" Zhao snapped, grabbing the professor by the wrist.

"Trying to understand the writing, of course," Lavigne said. "I need to wipe away the dust and then see both sides."

"Fine," Zhao said, releasing the professor. She watched closely as he cleaned one side of the disc, starting with the reflective surface in the center and working his way out to the outer edge. Then, using only the scarf to touch the object, he turned the disc over and did the same on the other side.

"I have never seen markings quite like this," Lavigne said. "I will need some time to consider them."

"You have done enough, for now," Zhao said, a cruel twist to her smile. She turned from Lavigne to Gui. "Take the professor to his room," she said, an unbridled sense of menace in her voice. "We will give him some time to cool off and think about controlling his temper." She swung around and grabbed Lavigne by the neck with a shocking force. "And professor, if you ever touch me again, you will die. Do you understand?"

Lavigne nodded, sniveling, and let Gui drag him away.

24

With tears in her eyes, Athena slumped forward on the sofa as though all the energy had left her body. Eden sat beside her and placed her arms around her shoulders.

"No wonder you kept your birth identity a secret," Eden said, breaking the silence after almost a minute.

Athena took a deep and labored breath and started to speak. "When I was twenty, my mother disappeared. She left and never came back. I'd always known that she had family in China. Her father was from there, although I'd never met him. Anyway, when she didn't come back, I did some digging. I found she had flown to China and traveled to the disputed Xinjiang region."

She paused, her eyes distant, as if seeing something far away. "What I discovered there ... I've never seen such awful things. The local Uyghur population were being systematically oppressed. There were 're-education' camps, forced labor, constant surveillance. It was like stepping into a dystopian nightmare."

"It's a terrible situation," Winslow said, shaking his head. "One of the worst in our modern times."

"I immediately feared that she was in danger, so went to help," Athena said, her voice growing stronger.

"What did you think you'd find?" Eden asked.

"I ... I really didn't know," Athena said, her eyes unfocused. "Maybe my mother had been imprisoned in one of the camps, or maybe she'd been arrested for trying to help. Either way, I needed answers. I couldn't rest until I got answers."

Eden nodded and looked out at the sea glittering through the window. Although her experience was different from Athena's, she understood what it was like to lose a parent—or at least think they were gone.

"I started asking around, looking for my mother, but no one would talk," Athena continued. "Everyone I spoke to treated me with suspicion. They saw me as an outsider, someone who couldn't be trusted. Really, I was there to help."

"That's what regimes like that do," Winslow said. "They breed fear, and fear stops people from even trying to escape."

"Everyone was worried they would be next," Athena continued. "They were afraid to talk, to even look at me. The moment I appeared, people would stop their conversations and walk away." Athena leaned forward, her hands clasped tightly in her lap. "I remember this one elderly woman I met. She was selling spices in a small market. I showed her a picture of my mother and she practically shoved me away."

"Did you ever find her?" Eden asked.

"No, after months, the trail went cold. But by then I'd realized I had to *do something*. I'd finally found some people to help me, so ..." Athena's voice trailed off.

"What did you do?" Eden asked.

"Some sterling work, that's what," Winslow said, crossing the room and placing a hand on Athena's shoulder.

"Hold on, you knew about this," Eden said, looking at her father.

Winslow nodded in a way that said, *I'll explain later.*

"During my time there I had met some others who wanted to fight back. We decided that we had to do something. So, we broke into one of the camps, freed a load of people, and told the world about the conditions they were kept in."

"It caused an international outcry," Winslow said. "Until then, no one outside the area even knew this was happening."

"I was arrested and dragged into an interrogation room," Athena said, her expression replaying the fear. "I had no lawyer, no call home, no trial. They sent me to death row."

A gasp rose from everyone in the room, except Winslow, who clearly knew what was coming next.

"That's how I ended up here," Athena said, looking up at Winslow and taking his hand.

"I'd heard what Athena had done," Winslow said, continuing the story. "Such bravery! I wanted her on my team. So, I pulled some strings."

"I put that old life behind me and never looked back," Athena said. "Until now." Her tone hardening, she explained how at the last minute she'd realized her mother was involved in the coverup.

Eden pulled her friend in close for a moment, then rose to her feet. "And, unfortunately, we're going to have to go back there."

For a moment, Eden thought Athena might argue, but then something shifted in her friend's demeanor.

Athena climbed to her feet and crossed to the screen.

Her fingers traced the outline of Zhao's face on the screen. Although the resemblance between mother and daughter wasn't striking, it was clear when they were side by side.

"You're right," Athena said, her voice low and controlled. "She needs to be stopped, and I'm the one to do it."

LAVIGNE DIDN'T STRUGGLE AS GUI DRAGGED HIM BY THE shoulder toward the room—or rather the cell—he'd been kept in when not tasked with translating something.

"Okay, okay, I'm going," Lavigne said, glancing up at Gui but seeing little more than his barrel chest. The brute continued digging his fingers into Lavigne's shoulders, suggesting he was unconvinced by Lavigne's claims he would play ball. Or maybe, Lavigne thought, the thug just liked to cause pain.

They reached the door at the end of the passageway and Gui stopped, jerking Lavigne to a halt. Lavigne stumbled against the doorjamb.

Releasing one of Lavigne's shoulders, Gui dug out a set of keys and shoved one into the lock.

"Get some rest," Gui barked, opening the door and shoving the professor inside.

Lavigne stumbled across the room, clanging his knee against the frame of a camping cot. He sprawled forward onto the thin mattress, the bed creaking in protest.

Gui giggled, the sound reverberating through the small room, until the slamming door cut it short. The key crunched in the lock, signaling that Lavigne was sealed inside.

As Gui's footsteps faded back toward the other side of the building, Lavigne sat up. With trembling hands, he got to work quickly, first removing the bottle of sunscreen from his pocket and placing it on the nightstand with the other salves and potions Zhao had allowed him. Requesting the sunscreen had been a stroke of genius, Lavigne thought, although it was one he would hope he didn't need.

He then pulled Gui's cell phone from beneath his waistband. Lavigne had removed the phone from Gui's pocket as the brute manhandled him through the building.

"I did tell him I was fine on my own," Lavigne murmured, thumbing the unlock button. He glanced at the screen and tapped the unlock code.

Lavigne had watched closely as Gui punched in the code several times earlier that day.

Now, Lavigne's incredible memory—the same gift that had helped him decode ancient texts with an ease that seemed inhuman—might have saved his life.

The phone unlocked, the screen glowing with the standard background. Lavigne scrolled through the device for a second and found no saved numbers, no photographs or messages. The phone was clearly new or recently wiped, with no identifying content.

"Damn it," Lavigne whispered, noticing the phone had no signal. Hardly surprising, he thought, out here in the middle of the Cambodian forest. He paced the cell, holding the phone at different angles, searching for a flicker of connectivity.

Approaching the boarded-up window, a bar flashed on the screen. Lavigne froze, holding the phone in position. The bar disappeared, then reappeared a moment later.

He extended his arm up toward the ceiling. And the bar appeared again. He dragged the room's only chair up to the window and stood on it. The little icon flickered again, but this time it stayed in position.

Fingers trembling, Lavigne dialed the emergency number. Not willing to risk the speaker phone, nor wanting to move the phone, he rose on to his toes and placed an ear against the device. The speaker buzzed three times, then connected. Hearing the operator's voice, Lavigne felt a wave of relief. When the voice broke up into a wall of hissing static, his relief turned into despair.

"Hello ... Bonjour ... Hello," Lavigne said, hoping the operator's voice would return. He stopped speaking and listened for a response. When none came, he removed the phone from his ear and looked at the screen. Although he couldn't hear anything, the call looked as though it was still connected.

"My name is Professor Etienne Lavigne," he said, figuring that if his voice was getting out there, then maybe someone would come to his rescue. "Some time ago ... I'm not exactly sure ... I've been kidnapped from my house in Paris. Zhao ... that's who took me. I don't know who she is or what she plans ... Oh non, j'ai peur!"

The phone hissed, followed by the operator's distant voice.

Lavigne stopped talking, listening, trying to make out what the operator was saying. Then he heard footsteps pounding down the passageway toward his room.

"But that's not all," Lavigne continued, suddenly aware that this may be his only chance to get help. "Zhao has a relic. I am an expert in Khmer history, up until now I thought this relic was just a ... a legend." Lavigne stopped, forcing himself to get to the point. "I have no idea how Zhao found the relic, but ..."

The signal crackled, and the voice came again. Although

Lavigne couldn't clearly make out the words, he thought the person told him to repeat himself.

"The relic is incredibly dangerous ..."

The footsteps drew closer, leaving no doubt that someone was coming his way.

"I have no time," he said, hurriedly. "Zhao has the Lotus Key. I don't know what she's planning to do with it, but she must be stopped."

Lavigne ended the call and slipped the phone out of sight. He climbed down from the chair, tiptoed across the room as silently as he was able, and sat on the bed, wincing as the old springs creaked.

The footsteps stopped right outside the door and the key grated in the lock. The lock finally disengaged, before the door swung open.

Gui peered through the narrow gap.

Lavigne slumped over, affecting his best defeated posture.

"What's all that noise, Professor?" Gui said.

"Do you know how many bugs could be in this mattress?" Lavigne said, his voice quivering. "My skin is itching at the thought of it." Lavigne scratched his leg and banged his foot against the floor.

"Keep at it and I'll put you out of your misery," Gui grunted. He slammed the door shut and stomped back down the hallway.

25

EDEN AND ATHENA SPENT THE NEXT HOUR COMPILING ALL THE information they could on Mei-Ling Zhao. Athena spoke with detachment as they pulled together the profile of a woman who had been working for mysterious criminal organizations for years. It seemed that even her relationship with Athena's father, an American businessman, was a sham designed to obtain information for her employer. Exactly who that employer was, though, continued to remain a mystery.

"None of this leads us to where she is now," Athena said, perching dejectedly on the arm of the sofa.

"You're right," Eden said. "But at least we now know who we're up against. That's something." She turned to look at the place where Liang had sat and imagined the horrors the technician had seen as Zhao moved through the rig, assassinating his colleagues and friends. Liang had since returned to a cabin to rest and recuperate from his ordeal.

A chime echoed through the room, signifying they had a notification on one of their searches.

"A phone call to the Cambodian Police mentioning the

Lotus Key," Baxter said, reading the text. As soon as they'd known what they were up against, Baxter had used the Council's call monitoring software to track calls to emergency services in the surrounding countries. "And it's close by too."

Baxter zoomed in on the map, revealing a mountainous region dotted with dense forest.

"What is that place?" Eden asked.

"Bokor Hill, near Kampot in Cambodia. The call originated from somewhere in that area," Baxter said.

Athena leaned in, her eyes scanning the terrain. "I know Bokor Hill ... It's an abandoned French colonial hill station. Lots of old, crumbling buildings. It's the perfect place to set up a hidden base."

Eden nodded, her mind already racing with possibilities.

"Listen to this," Baxter said, pressing a key.

"My name is Professor Etienne Lavigne..." A French-accented voice filled the office. The voice cut out, replaced by a burst of static.

"I can't hear you," the operator said. "Please repeat, sir."

"I was kidnapped from ..." Lavigne's voice cut in again, obviously unable to hear the operator. It sounded as though someone was physically jangling a bunch of frayed wires. "Zhao is the ..."

At the mention of Zhao's name, the three of them shared a glance.

"... she's ruthless and I am in danger ..."

"No kidding," Eden said as the call once again faded into a storm of static.

"But that's not all ..." Lavigne continued "... Zhao has an object ... legend ..." The signal dropped out completely now, a soft buzz the only indication that it was connected at all.

"Sir, are you there? I'm struggling to hear you," the operator said. "If you can't hear me, I'll disconnect the line. Try to call again—"

"... have the Lotus Key." Lavigne's hushed tones cut through the white noise, now clearer than before. "I don't know what they're planning to do. We must stop them." A beep sounded, signaling that the recording had ended.

Baxter's fingers flashed over the keys. "Professor Etienne Lavigne lives in Paris's fifth arrondissement," he said, loading a profile of the professor. "He was last seen four days ago when he presented a lecture on Angkorian temple inscriptions at Sorbonne University in Paris. According to a press release, he'd spent weeks working on a particularly complex translation of early Angkor period texts."

"Sounds like a fun guy to be around," Eden said.

"What's interesting is that Lavigne has never been to Cambodia," Baxter continued, flicking between articles. "The guy's nearly fifty years old and has only left Paris twice."

"Yet he's a world class expert in Angkorian history?" Athena said, an eyebrow raised.

"I guess you can learn anything online these days," Eden replied.

"According to this article, he's a highly anxious person," Baxter continued. "He spends a lot of time and money on his personal security and safety. His apartment is fitted with top of the range locks and has a high-tech security system."

"Which didn't seem to work this time," Eden said, pacing toward the screen to check out the article Baxter was reading.

"Someone like that certainly doesn't make an impromptu trip," Athena said, straightening up, "especially not to Cambodia."

"Exactly," Baxter agreed, scrolling through the information. "When he didn't show up to a meeting the next day, his colleagues raised the alarm. Police went to his house and found that the security system had been deactivated. The panic button beside his bed looked as though it had been activated, but the security company never got the call."

"Zhao must have jammed the signal, somehow," Athena said. "She clearly knows her tech."

"Hold on a second," Eden said, pointing at the screen. "That was the same night Zhao broke into the museum, right?"

"Correct. The museum is a few minutes' drive from Lavigne's house. She could have stolen the stele, picked up Lavigne, and boarded a private plane to Cambodia within the hour."

"Busy lady," Athena said.

"What else do we know about Lavigne's home?" Eden asked.

Baxter tapped the keys and brought up an article showing pictures of the reclusive professor taken inside his house.

"It looks like a museum," Eden said, as Baxter scrolled through various images.

"He has replica statues, temple rubbings, ancient jewelry, plaster moldings from the temples," Baxter said, listing various items.

"No wonder he hasn't felt the need to come to Cambodia," Athena said. "He's got it all there."

"Well, only replicas," Baxter said. "He's actually advocating the return of any missing Khmer pieces in this article. But his study is full of translations and research papers, many of which are one of a kind," Baxter said.

"He's certainly a useful guy if you need something translated," Eden said, folding her arms. "But what?"

"Whatever it is, it has something to do with that Lotus Key," Athena said. "We need to move fast. If Zhao gets what she needs from him ..."

Athena didn't finish the sentences, as they all knew what Zhao was capable of.

"How long will it take us to get to Bokor Hill?" Eden said.

"About an hour in the chopper," Baxter replied, already working on flight plans.

"Then we need to move," Eden said. "If Zhao's there, this might be our only chance to catch her off guard."

True to Baxter's word, less than an hour later the Eurocopter pounded over the treetops which lined Bokor Hill. Below them, the dense canopy of the rainforest stretched beneath them, an emerald ocean broken only by jagged rocky outcroppings. As they neared the summit, the trees thinned out around several crumbling buildings.

The remains of the once-grand structures loomed like broken teeth, their facades eroded by decades of rain and wind. Roofs sagged or had collapsed entirely, exposing their skeletal beams. In the center of the site, the old casino, once a symbol of colonial opulence, stood ghostly and weather-beaten.

"This place looks like something out of a zombie apoca-lypse," Eden said, eyeing the towering spire of an old church which pointed at the sky like a crooked finger. "Why has it been left like this?"

"It was built in the 1920s by the French as a luxury retreat. Important people would come here to escape the sweltering heat of Phnom Penh," Baxter said, his voice coming through Eden's headset.

"As to why you think it looks like a zombie apocalypse, I think that shows you've watched too many scary films," Athena added, tapping her temple. "Films like that get in your mind."

"You're a psychologist now too, are you?" Eden said, throwing her friend a look.

The Eurocopter banked, giving them a better view of a massive, dilapidated building looming on the horizon.

"That's the Bokor Palace Hotel," Baxter said, pointing at the giant crumbling concrete structure. The large windows, clearly designed to take in un-spoiled views across the forest and toward the sea, now looked like the hollow eyes of a skull.

"Why was it abandoned?" Athena said, cupping a hand above her eyes.

"It was abandoned several times. First during the Indochina War, then again in the 1970s when the Khmer Rouge took over," Baxter said, leveling out the chopper and guiding them over the dense forest canopy. "Since then, it's been left to the jungle."

"The call came from somewhere around here," Eden said, looking down at one of the screens on the chopper's console.

"If I was an evil villain, that is exactly where I would hide out," Athena said, glancing back at the ghostly shell of the once luxurious hotel.

"I've always favored the volcano lair idea," Eden said.

"I'm not sure I could face the air conditioning bills," Athena replied.

"Ladies, concentrate, please," Baxter said, his grin hidden by the headset. "We're looking for somewhere small enough not to attract attention, but big enough to run an operation."

"Zhao's not working alone on this. She'll need space for a team to live and work," Eden said, looking across the treetops.

"There's another building further down the hill to the east," Athena said, scanning the map on a tablet computer. "It's very isolated, looks like the sort of place I think Zhao might choose."

Baxter worked the controls, and the chopper dipped forward, sending the treetops below into a frantic dance.

"Hold on," Baxter warned, taking the chopper down low to mask their approach. He weaved around a jutting rock face, and up across a dense patch of forest.

"There." Athena pointed, her finger pressed against the glass. Through a break in the foliage, the outline of a building, smaller than the hotel but still substantial, emerged.

Baxter adjusted their course and banked around the structure, offering a full view of an old colonial mansion. The building's once-grand facade was now weathered and partially reclaimed by the jungle. The two-story structure was built in the classic French colonial style, with wide verandas, and large shuttered windows. The paint had long since faded and peeled, revealing patches of weathered wood and stone underneath.

Eden focused on the wraparound porch encircling the first floor, its ornate balustrades now choked with creeping vines. She grabbed a pair of binoculars and examined the structure closely.

"Hold on, we've got movement," she said, noticing something or someone moving in the shadows. She adjusted the focus and saw two men standing at either end of the building, assault rifles clutched across their chests. Although their postures were casual, they were clearly ready to strike at a moment's notice.

"Nothing says welcome like a Kalashnikov," Athena muttered.

"And look at that," Baxter said, pointing at the ground as they roared almost directly across the structure. Beside the building, obscured from every angle but directly above, sat a large helicopter.

"I'm no expert, but I'd bet that's a Sikorsky," Athena said.

"You'd be correct," Baxter said. "A Sikorsky S-92, to be precise, you can tell by the—"

"That's enough, Captain Info," Eden said, eyeing the aircraft. "Surely people would see them taking off and landing?"

"Not with the angle of the hillside," Baxter said, pointing behind them. "They'd be away from the building by the time anyone noticed, so wouldn't give away their location. It's the perfect spot."

Eden watched the guards step out of the shadows and look up at them. "We'd better get out of here," she said. "The last thing we want is a welcome gift."

Baxter nodded, his hands steady on the controls. "They're probably waiting for orders. The last thing they want is to fire on a sightseeing trip."

"Let's play on that," Eden said, looking back toward the once grand structures. "Take us back that way. We'll head through the jungle on foot."

26

"WE'RE CLOSE, I CAN FEEL IT," ZHAO SAID, LOOKING FROM THE disc on the table to the digital rendering of the Lotus Key, which continued its hypnotic rotation on the screen. "Soon, the most powerful artifact in all of history will be ours."

She clutched her hands across her chest and inhaled. Excitement whirled inside her like a fire as she remembered the feeling of power that had warmed her skin as she approached the Lotus Key. The sensation coursed through her veins like a drug, forcing her to close her eyes.

"... well?" Gui's voice pulled her back to the present. Zhao shook herself back into focus and spun around to face her second in command.

"I have the map," he repeated, holding up a rolled-up map. "What would you—"

"Roll it out there," Zhao snapped, pointing at the table in the center of the room. She strode up to the table and shuffled the disc to one side, creating enough space to study the entire map.

Gui unfurled the map and placed two spare magazines

on one side, and a pair of combat knives on the other to prevent it rolling closed again.

"The second disc will be somewhere in the old Khmer Kingdom," Zhao said, running her finger across the map. "The problem is that the kingdom stretched from modern-day Cambodia all the way into Thailand and Vietnam."

"That's a lot of places to look." Gui shrugged. "Where do we even start?"

"Luckily we're not working on this alone," Zhao said, glancing up at Gui. "Go and fetch the professor. I expect he will point us in the right direction."

Gui straightened up and lumbered away.

Zhao once again turned to look at the image of the Lotus Key. The cravings returned—the unbridled power inching through her bones. Her fingers twitched involuntarily, desperate to experience it again. Watching the digital render of the artifact, its surface pulsing as though it had a heartbeat, Zhao thought about when she had last slept. The days had begun to blur, marked only by their progress toward her endgame.

The sound of footsteps in the hallway snapped her back to reality. The door swung open, and footsteps shuffled into the room.

"Professor Lavigne," Zhao said, still studying the map. "I trust you have had some time to rest and think about your actions."

Gui shoved Lavigne forward, sending the professor stumbling across the room. Lavigne caught himself on the side of the table and looked down at the map, interest lighting his gaze. He opened his mouth to say something, then clearly thought better of it. He shoved his spectacles into place and adjusted the scarf which still hung around his shoulders.

"Now, Professor, I have one more problem I need your help with," Zhao said, smiling at the Frenchman with all the faux sweetness she could muster. His silver hair was matted, his loose cotton shirt wrinkled and stained with coffee, blood, or both.

"Then what, you'll kill me?" Lavigne said.

Zhao's lips curled into a smile, and then she laughed. Gui joined in, cackling awkwardly.

"Oh professor, this is not the movies," Zhao said, turning serious so quickly Gui continued laughing alone. Zhao glared at the brute, and he gurgled into silence.

Lavigne swallowed, his Adam's apple bobbing up and down.

"I have never liked the movies, professor. Do you know why?" Zhao looked at Lavigne, unblinking.

Lavigne nodded, eventually.

"You know, do you?" Zhao said, looking at the Frenchman with a mixture of pity and frustration.

"Non, I mean no," Lavigne stuttered.

"In the films, they make killing people look easy," Zhao said, pleased to take charge of the conversation again. "In movies, it's as easy as this." She snapped her fingers. "Of course, the killing is easy. It's the rest that's the problem."

Lavigne blinked slowly; his eyes shadowed from not enough sleep.

"The mess, professor. The cleanup. The questions. The endless, tedious loose ends that need tying up." Zhao approached the screen on which the Lotus Key continued to rotate. "What do you do with the body? Some people bury it, others feed it to pigs, some dissolve it in acid. Whatever you do, your work must be perfect as there are dental records, DNA, fingerprints. Then there are the digital traces, like cell phones, or security cameras. It's a complicated and frustrating process, professor. Do you understand?"

Lavigne nodded frantically, his spectacles sliding down his nose.

"Put it this way," Zhao said, clasping her hands together. "If I tell Gui here to kill you." She nodded toward Gui, who flexed his shoulders, muscles clicking on cue. "Before I know it, I have police investigators, the embassy, journalists from your country, friends and colleagues ... so many people on my tail. I don't want that, professor, nor do you. So, here's my solution. I have one more task with which I need your help. You provide me with the information I require, and you'll be back on that private jet to Paris before dinnertime. What do you say?"

Lavigne swallowed and then nodded.

"Good," Zhao said, her voice now soft and tuneful. "I'm glad we've found an understanding." Zhao stepped up to the table and placed a finger on the map. Lavigne looked obediently down at the map.

"I need the second disc, professor, and I know it's somewhere here." Zhao spread her arms wide to show the breadth of the ancient Khmer Kingdom.

"Are you sure you know what you're doing?" Lavigne said, his voice weak. "The Lotus Key is—"

"Do not question me!" Zhao roared, her fist crashing into the table. "You tell me where to find that disc, or you will never get back to Paris. Comprendre?"

Lavigne flinched at her outburst. He remained stationary for a few moments before nodding.

"Oui... je comprends," he said quietly, once again adjusting his spectacles, now with shaking hands. He leaned over and studied the map, running a finger across the surface.

"I believe the text on the carving will give you a clue, as it did for the first disc," Zhao said. She snapped her fingers, an indication for Gui to load the image.

"No need," Lavigne said. "I remember the words. Search for the temple where Naga guards the lotus throne."

"Impressive, professor," Zhao said, dipping her head to the side. "Now, where does that lead us?" She once again swept a hand across the map.

Lavigne looked down at the map carefully, his lips pursed. "That doesn't mean much on its own, as both lotus and Naga imagery are common in temple architecture. But it's likely the disc was hidden somewhere significant." Lavigne's eyes narrowed as he searched the map. "The Khmer weren't simply builders—they were astronomers, mathematicians. Every temple was aligned with celestial bodies, every measurement calculated to—"

"Get. To. The. Point." Zhao's fingers drummed against the tabletop, each tap making Lavigne jump. Behind her, the digital render of the key pulsed with an almost synchronized rhythm.

"The lotus reference ... it's not about decoration. It's about geography." Lavigne's finger shook as he traced a path northward on the map. "That's perfect," he said, his voice like air hissing from a tire.

"What's that, professor?" Zhao said. "Do not waste my time."

Lavigne cleared his throat, looked from Zhao to Gui, then back to the map. "Legend has it that there's a temple here, near the village of O'Smach, Northern Cambodia. The locals call it Prasat Lotus Neak—the Snake Temple of the Lotus."

Zhao's breath quickened, that familiar electric sensation crawling beneath her skin. "Go on."

"Many believe that the temple was built during the reign of Jayavarman VII, but it differed from his other works. More ... secretive. The architecture is unique. There are no face towers like Bayon, no grand galleries like Angkor Wat. Just a single tower, shaped like a lotus bud."

"Sounds like the perfect spot for hiding something precious," Zhao whispered, her eyes taking on that strange iridescent sheen again.

"But this is a legend," Lavigne said. "The temple has not been seen in hundreds of years. If it did ever exist, it'll now be lost to the—"

"We will search the landscape inch by inch." Zhao cut him off. "The disc is at Prasat Lotus Neak. I can feel it." Her fingers twitched involuntarily toward the first disc, as though craving its touch. "Gui, make the arrangements. We leave for—"

A mechanical drumbeat thundered into the mansion. It was the kind of sound that vibrated the floor before hitting the ear.

Zhao straightened up, listening closely.

The sound grew from a distant hum to the clear *whump-whump-whump* of an incoming chopper.

"Report," Zhao said, snatching her handheld radio.

"Chopper coming in from the east," came the reply a moment later. "Doesn't look military or police, but they're coming in low."

"Could it be a tourist flight?" Gui said.

Zhao silenced her second in command with a look and stalked to the window. The helicopter's shadow passed over the windows, bringing with it a wind that sent the plastic covering the windows flapping in a frenzy. The chopper powered out across the clearing and banked to the side.

"Shall we fire?" one of the guards said.

"Negative," Zhao said. "But they may be on to us." She turned back and looked at Lavigne. One side of her mouth rose as though she were about to say something before thinking better of it.

"We move out now. Everyone in the chopper. We leave in five minutes."

27

EDEN SHOVED PAST A BUSH, THE SPIKED FRONDS SCRATCHING against her face. She held it to one side, sweat trickling down her neck, for Athena to slip through. The sweet-rotting smell of decaying vegetation mixed with the metallic tang of wet earth filled the air. Somewhere above, the call of a hornbill drifted through the canopy, answered by cries of macaques.

Athena pushed ahead, shoving through a stand of broad-leafed cardamom plants, their crushed stems releasing a sharp, spicy scent. She glanced at the compass strapped to her wrist and adjusted their course toward the mansion. The foliage was so dense here that they could easily miss the mansion all together.

"That way," Athena said, leading them up the incline.

Eden nodded, stepping up to the next tangle of vegetation. She drew out a machete and sliced through the fronds. A red-headed centipede, disturbed from its hiding place, writhed away into the undergrowth.

A distant crash echoed through the trees, probably a branch falling. The sound sent a flock of green birds thundering into the air. Both women froze, listening intently through the constant background hum of insects. When nothing followed, they pressed on, moving more carefully now.

The gradient was getting steeper, and thick lianas snaked down from the canopy, creating natural handholds as they climbed. Occasionally, they passed the crumbling remains of paths or structures, now almost completely reclaimed by creeping vines and orchids. The air grew noticeably cooler as they gained altitude, fingers of mist drifting between the trees.

Eden touched the rifle hanging at her back. Expecting there to be trouble and having been caught out many times in the past, they had both come prepared. She paused, listening to the symphony of jungle sounds which surrounded them.

Athena pushed ahead, slicing through a clump of ferns. The thick stems resisted for a moment before giving way with a wet snap. She ditched the leaves on the ground and stepped through the gap.

Eden shuffled through after her friend and froze. Athena stood motionless, a closed fist held skyward—the signal to halt. Eden's hand moved instinctively to the rifle. She moved the gun around to her chest and raised it at their unseen enemy.

Slowly and deliberately, Athena pushed aside a large, waxy leaf. The dense green wall of the jungle suddenly gave way to a clearing, and there, sitting on the ground before them, was the Sikorsky S-92.

Seeing the size of the craft up close, Eden understood how Zhao could have used it to take over the oil rig and remove the artifact. The chopper was big enough to transport half an army.

"Eyes on," Eden said. She thumbed the comms unit to open a line of communication with Baxter, waiting in their smaller Eurocopter nearby.

"Roger that," Baxter said, sounding relaxed.

"Don't you stress about it," Athena added, shuffling in close to a tree trunk. "You sit there in comfort and wait for us to do the hard work."

"Happy to trade places if you fancy flying the chopper," Baxter retorted.

Eden and Athena rolled their eyes, then turned their attention to the scene through the trees. Eden slipped out her binoculars and scanned the scene.

"Something's different," she said, holding up a finger to silence the no doubt sarcastic comment Athena was about to make. The structure looked almost the same as it had from the air, except for one thing.

Athena gestured, and Eden passed the binoculars across. "The guards on the porch, they're gone," Athena said, noticing that the terrace which wrapped around the entire first floor was now empty.

"That's it," Eden said, cupping a hand across her eyes. "That's strange. You'd think having seen us go past, they'd be extra vigilant."

"Unless they've got other plans," Athena said, sweeping the binoculars towards the mansion's once-grand entrance. "Look at that. They're coming this way."

Eden took the binoculars back and focused on the entrance. Footsteps, grunts of exertion and shouted orders drifted their way. She spun the focus wheel and saw a group of men shuffling out of the entrance and down a staircase. The men took another step, showing Eden the cause of their efforts: an enormous crate.

"They're bringing something out," Eden said, glancing at Athena. "My guess, they're on the move."

"Agreed," Athena said, watching the men shuffle down the stairs. "Eight men in total, and whatever they're carrying is heavy."

"What is it?" Baxter asked, now sounding much more interested.

"It's about the size of a small car," Eden said, sizing the thing up. "It looks like it's made from some kind of metal. It's securely locked with straps around it."

"That's got to be the Lotus Key," Athena said, eyeing the box. "Whatever that box is made from, it's designed to stop the key's radiation from getting out. Otherwise, the men wouldn't be able to carry it. We can't let them get away."

"Zhao was clearly well prepared," Eden said. "My guess is, with the help of the knowledgeable Professor Lavigne, they've worked out what to do with it." Eden removed the binoculars from her eyes and looked at her friend. "You're right," she said, her voice hard. "They're not leaving."

"Do not go in there," Baxter said, his voice cutting down the line like an arctic wind. "We have no idea how many men, or what weapons Zhao has access to. She's clearly armed and dangerous. It's a potential suicide mission."

The men reached the base of the staircase and shuffled across the open ground toward the Sikorsky. Now in clear view, Eden could see how the weight of the object caused each of them to strain, muscles and veins standing out like pistons.

"We don't have a choice," Eden said. "We can't let them get the Lotus Key out of ..." Eden's voice dried up in her throat as she saw Athena's expression melt from one of focused tension to a mask of shock. Athena lifted her shaking hands to her mouth and gasped, her body sagging against a tree.

Eden followed her friend's stare. Four more men stood at the top of the staircase, assault rifles clutched to their chests. They scanned the scene, clearly ready to fire at a moment's notice. Between the men stood a woman. In contrast to the muscle-bound brutes, she was slender and moved with the fluid grace of a viper. Something in her posture, the way she held herself, the calculated stillness of her movements, told Eden she was dangerous.

"Mei-Ling Zhao," Eden said, tapping the comms system. "We've got a visual."

28

LAVIGNE'S HEART FELT LIKE IT WAS FIGHTING ITS WAY OUT OF his chest as he watched Zhao, and her men prepare to leave their hillside hideout. A pair of technicians packed computer equipment into boxes while eight guards moved the Lotus Key's crate down the stairs toward the chopper. Although the crate wasn't especially large, maybe the size of a compact car, it was clearly very heavy. Taking each step slowly, the men cursed and strained against the weight.

"Start the chopper," Zhao said, following the men through the wide doorway and out onto the porch. "As soon as the key is in position, we're out of here." She turned to assess the work of the technicians. "Just take what we need, leave the rest."

Gui elbowed his way through the technicians, paced out on to the porch and spoke with Zhao in whispers. Although no one was watching over Lavigne, he figured there was no point running. There was nowhere he could go, plus Zhao had promised—convincingly, he thought—that he would be sent home. He drew a deep breath of the strange smelling air and thought about how in all the textbooks he'd read, not one of them mentioned that the air in Cambodia would smell different to that in Paris. To Lavigne, it smelled like danger. To calm his nerves, he thought about the first thing he would do when he arrived back in Paris. In his mind, he pushed open the door of his local café and inhaled the bitter richness of the properly made café crème, and the buttery flake of a fresh pastry.

The fantasy shattered as powerful hands gripped Lavigne and dragged him onto the porch.

"Professor, this is disappointing," Zhao said, striding into his vision and forcing the warmth of the daydream away.

"What ... I ..." Lavigne saw the object in Zhao's hand and his voice dried up. She held Gui's cellphone, presenting it to Lavigne like some kind of trophy.

"I assume there's a perfectly reasonable explanation as to why this was hidden beneath the mattress in your room?" Zhao said, her eyes locked on his.

Lavigne stuttered over an answer, but none came forth. A bead of sweat ran down his neck and slipped beneath his shirt. He tried to adjust his spectacles, but his hands trembled uncontrollably.

"After all we've been through together. It's disappointing that you should do this," Zhao said, the sing-song quality returning to her voice. She turned the phone over in her hands. "We were getting on so well. I was looking forward to wishing you bon voyage."

"Non ... non ... I ... I didn't ... I don't ..." Lavigne stuttered.

"Do not lie to me," Zhao roared. "I know you tried to call for help. You cannot be blamed, I suppose. Anyone in your position would. It's impressive that you got hold of the phone." Zhao glared at Gui, clearly blaming him for allowing Lavigne to steal the phone in the first place. "That showed guts," she said, thoughtfully. "Perhaps I underestimated you."

One man carrying the crate tripped, sending the rest of the group into a panic. A groan rose from them, and the crate wobbled from side to side.

"You drop that, and we are all dead!" Zhao yelled, turning away from Lavigne.

The men wrestled the crate back into position and picked their way across the uneven ground toward the chopper.

"I wonder," Zhao said, her attention now back on Lavigne, "who did you call? The authorities?" A brittle laugh escaped her throat. "Or maybe a friend?"

The chopper began to whine as the pilots started the engines.

"Please," Lavigne whispered, "I didn't—"

"Did you tell anyone anything important?" Zhao interrupted, stepping closer. "No, you didn't." She reached out and patted Lavigne on the cheek. Although the gesture looked soft, Zhao's touch sent a bolt of ice through him.

"I didn't ... I couldn't ..." Lavigne stuttered again.

"I know professor, I know. You couldn't get through because there's no phone signal here," Zhao said, as though talking to a child. "Luckily, that means no harm has been done."

The helicopter whined more loudly now, its rotors building from a distant thrum to a thunderous beat. Dead leaves and loose dirt spiraled into cyclones.

Lavigne nodded, the smallest sensation of relief washing through him.

"But professor, I'm afraid you have betrayed me," Zhao said, her voice now ice cold. "And that, I cannot forgive." Zhao looked at Gui. "Kill him."

Gui slid out a gun and pointed it at Lavigne. Although the gun looked incongruously small in the big man's grasp, the sight of it sent a physical shockwave through Lavigne's body. He tried to speak, to beg for his life, but all he achieved was uselessly wobbling from side to side. The world narrowed to that small black circle at the end of Gui's pistol.

The helicopter's rotors continued their thunderous symphony, muted beneath the roar of Lavigne's heart, preparing for its final beats.

"Wait!" Lavigne croaked, finally managing to get his voice to work. He held up his hands, which shook visibly. "You need me to find the temple where the lotus grows. You need me. Don't shoot!"

"Do I?" Zhao said. "You've already told me where the temple is. I know exactly where to look."

"What ... what if I was wrong?" Lavigne said, clutching at straws. "Or, what if I lied?"

Zhao turned around and focused her whole attention on Lavigne. Rather than just looking at him, it felt as though she were looking through him.

"As you're not long for this world, I'll share an observation with you," Zhao said, raising her voice above the whir of the rotors. "Everyone, professor—everyone—is fundamentally selfish. Don't deny it. It's human nature. Those who claim to serve their God, hunger to be recognized as doing it. Aid workers, they crave praise." Zhao's broken-glass laugh cut through the helicopter's roar. "Even the monks in their temples, they meditate on enlightenment while counting their donations." Zhao's laser-sharp gaze returned to Lavigne. "You are no different. You believe that what I'm doing is dangerous. You don't know my intentions, and you don't trust me."

Lavigne started to speak, but Zhao raised a hand.

"Despite that, when your life was on the line, you told me what you needed to do to save your own skin. You are like me, except I don't claim to be anything else."

Lavigne tried to counter Zhao's argument but came up blank.

"I am honest about my selfishness. I embrace it all in the pursuit of my cause. The Khmer kings understood this— ultimate power comes to those who acknowledge their true nature." Zhao turned to watch the men with the crate closing in on the chopper.

"P-p-please," Lavigne stuttered in panic. "You still need me. I assure you."

"How so, professor?" Zhao said, looking at the Frenchman in the manner of an eagle assessing a mouse. "We already have the first disc. And, thanks to you, we know where the second one is."

"But ... but ... you will need me to translate ..." Lavigne stammered.

Zhao shook her head. "In your final moments, you prove my point. Bargaining, lying, begging—all to save yourself." Her smile was razor-sharp. "How ... predictably human." Her voice, although barely louder than a whisper, was ice cold. "Kill him and leave his body in the forest."

Gui clicked off the safety. The sound sent a jolt through Lavigne's body.

"No, please!" Lavigne shouted, his eyes wide. "I've done everything you've asked! I won't tell a soul! I'll take this to my grave."

"Yes, professor, that's exactly what you'll do." Zhao said. "No more whining. Do it now." Zhao flicked a wrist as though dismissing a naughty child. She turned away from the professor and strode down the stairs.

"No ... No please!" Lavigne whined. "I beg ... "

Lavigne's voice was cut short by the sharp crack of a gunshot. The noise wasn't coming from directly in front of him. The shot boomed from somewhere deeper in the forest.

Lavigne looked up and saw Gui's expression change from one of menace to a mix of fear and confusion. Acting on instinct, the big man dropped to the floor and rolled back inside.

Another gunshot boomed, and a bullet thwacked into the stairs, inches from Zhao's foot. For a split second, everyone froze. Then chaos erupted.

29

ATHENA POINTED UP AT ZHAO, HATRED BUBBLING INSIDE HER as she remembered how her mother had set up her execution, then watched the whole thing with indifference. Without another thought, Athena dropped to one knee, grabbed her rifle, and fired.

"No!" Eden shouted, her hand clamping down on Athena's shoulder a moment too late.

The crack of Athena's rifle split the air, even audible over the sounds of the chopper powering up. The bullet sailed through the air, smashing into the stairs where Zhao had stood a moment before. Although hitting nothing, chaos erupted in an instant. She fired again and one of the guards fell to the ground.

Zhao spun around. Registering that they were under fire, she dove behind a pillar and drew her sidearm with lightning-fast reactions. The giant man who had been holding the professor dropped to the ground, saving himself, and rolled back inside the mansion.

Athena swung the gun toward another of Zhao's men and fired. This time the bullet found its target, jerking the man backward as though hit by an invisible freight train. The man crumpled to the ground, his weapon clattering beside him.

The men carrying the crate abandoned their load and vaulted for cover. The crate containing the Lotus Key crashed to the ground, thudding into the soft earth.

For a heart-stopping moment, Eden watched the crate, fearing the impact would split it open and release the poisonous radiation. Miraculously, the crate remained intact— the soft earth absorbing the shock.

The sound of the chopper increased as the pilots rushed through the take-off procedure. Eddies of dust and leaves spiraled away, and loose plastic flapped from the mansion's missing windows.

"Secure the package," Zhao's voice cut through the din. "We can't lose the Lotus Key."

The men who had been carrying the crate positioned themselves around it, while the others turned their attention to the source of the attack. Bullets whizzed through the air, peppering the tree line in which Eden and Athena sheltered.

Eden grabbed Athena by the shoulder and pulled her down behind a twisted root as bark exploded around them.

"We need to move!" Eden shouted over the gunfire. "They've got us locked down."

Athena swung her rifle around the tree and fired blindly. Although the bullets slammed uselessly into the mansion and a few pinged off the crate, the barrage forced Zhao and her men to dive for cover. Athena ejected one magazine and slammed a fresh one into place.

"This way," Eden said, belly-crawling through the undergrowth. A safe distance away, she shuffled in behind a giant tree and looked back at the mansion.

"Report," Baxter said. "What's the situation?"

"We're having a lovely day," Eden said, swinging around with her back to the tree. "Maybe we'll stop for ice cream on the way home."

"Definitely not the time for jokes," Baxter said. "I heard gunfire and what's that in the background ... Don't tell me ... It's a Sikorsky S-92 preparing for take-off."

"Correct and thanks to Ms. Trigger-Happy, we've now got the full works welcome party," Eden said, peering around the root again.

Zhao and her men moved into a defensive formation around the crate, all watching the tree line for any movement.

"We're going to have to pull back," Athena said, shuffling to a tree and a few feet away that afforded her a better view. Two of the guards ran for the chopper and returned with straps and cables.

"In short, we're outnumbered, outgunned, and in unfamiliar territory," Eden said. "Other than that, all's rosy."

"I've got a plan," Athena said.

"Let me guess ... it's so crazy, it might just work," Baxter interjected.

"Hey, that's my line," Eden said.

"We need to split up," Athena said, having released the anger that caused her to fire on a veritable hornet's nest. "If we fire from different positions, they'll be forced to divide firepower. Plus, if we keep moving, it'll look like there's more than two of us."

"Agreed," Eden said. "I wish we'd thought about that before advertising the fact we're here."

"Yeah, I think I've got a bit of pent-up anger over this," Athena said.

"You don't say," Eden said. "It's going to take a lot of yoga and deep breathing to get that out."

"Or maybe a bit of this," Athena said, swinging around and sending a tattoo of bullets toward the mansion. One of Zhao's men fell from his feet in a spray of crimson.

Eden nodded, impressed at her friend's aim, then turned and pushed away through the undergrowth. After several feet, she positioned herself behind a large fern. She parted the fronds and took aim, hitting one of Zhao's men in the shoulder. She didn't pause to watch him fall, already adjusting her aim. Her second shot found its mark on another operative's leg, eliciting a guttural howl of pain.

Athena moved in the opposite direction and ducked in behind a fallen tree. She belly-crawled across the forest floor and took aim beneath the chopper's stomach. Her rifle barked twice in quick succession. Two men fell, their bodies thudding to the ground. She fired again, but the men had now registered her new position and moved to safety behind the crate.

She adjusted her aim, but the bullets pinged off the chopper's hardened fuselage with metallic clangs.

Now working in formation, a group of men laid down covering fire while two of them attached the cable to the crate. They then ran it back to the chopper and secured it to an anchor point on the bottom of the fuselage.

When the firing stopped, Eden and Athena looked out to see the men pulling back toward the craft.

"We can't let them get out of here." Eden pushed back into the jungle and found a position which offered her a clear view of the pilot. She took aim and fired. The bullets ricocheted from the windshield with a ping. She fired again, and again, emptying half her magazine into the glass. Each bullet bounced harmlessly away, leaving only small white marks on the reinforced glass.

"It's bulletproof!" Eden shouted into the comms. "The chopper's bulletproof."

"Yes, I told you this," Baxter replied, sounding genuinely frustrated.

"No, you—"

"Actually, I was about to tell you, but you yawned and said, 'thanks for the lecture, Mr. Boring', or something like that."

"No, it was that comment about talking to Wikipedia," Athena added over the comms system.

"That's the one," Baxter added with finality.

Eden was about to offer a sarcastic reply when a hail of bullets tore through the surrounding foliage. Leaves and bark exploded above her head. She crawled in behind a fallen tree trunk as another volley of gunfire splintered bark all around her.

"Exactly, so the word *bulletproof* did not pass your lips," Eden said, feeling the vibrations of bullets thudding into the other side of her makeshift shelter.

"That bird is not just bulletproof," Baxter said. "It's got a reinforced hull, ballistic protection on all vital components, even an advanced countermeasure system—"

"Focus," Athena said, cutting through the noise. "They've got a—"

Athena's warning was cut short by a deafening whoosh, followed by an earth-shattering explosion. The jungle around Eden erupted in a blinding flash of light and a thunderous roar.

"RPG!" Athena screamed through the comms, her voice barely audible over the ringing in Eden's ears.

The rocket-propelled grenade had slammed into a large

tree some distance from Eden's position. The massive trunk splintered and groaned, toppling over with a cacophony of snapping branches and rustling leaves. The ground shook as the tree crashed down, sending a shockwave through the forest floor. Debris rained down around her—leaves, twigs, and chunks of bark falling all around.

Eden peered out of her makeshift cover and saw one of the Zhao's men with the launcher on his shoulder, scanning the tree line for targets.

"They're trying to flush us out," Eden shouted, her voice barely registering over the whining in her ears. "Athena, do you have eyes on the RPG guy?"

"Negative. He's behind the chopper. And they're making a run for it," Athena yelled back.

As the dust settled further, Eden saw Zhao, flanked by her remaining men, pace toward the chopper.

Eden risked a shot. The rounds whistled past Zhao, missing their mark as the woman ducked and rolled with surprising agility. The RPG-wielding guy, now alerted to Eden's position, swung the weapon in her direction.

"Eden, move!" Athena's urgent voice crackled through the comm.

Eden launched herself from behind her cover, as the distinctive whoosh filled the air. The grenade streaked overhead and detonated against a cluster of trees behind her former position. The explosion sent a shockwave through the clearing, the heat searing her back as she tumbled across the mud. Ears ringing and vision blurred, she scrambled to her feet and pulled herself further into the forest.

"I'm good," Eden said, her ears whining. "What's your status Athena?"

The chopper's engines increased in pitch. Spinning spirals of dust whirled around the clearing.

Eden waited for a response, but the comms remained silent. She tapped her earpiece, hoping to hear even a crackle of static. Nothing came.

"Athena?" she called out, her voice barely audible over the roar of the helicopter's engines. Still no response.

The pitch of the engines increased again, the sound becoming a deafening whine vibrating through the ground. The downdraft intensified, creating a maelstrom of leaves and debris.

Eden turned back toward the clearing, knowing that if she couldn't get eyes on the situation, she was desperately alone. She crept forward, using the chaos of the windswept foliage as cover. She reached the edge of the clearing and peered around a tree.

The Sikorsky was already several feet off the ground. All of Zhao's surviving men had climbed into the chopper. Three of them stood at the open door, their weapons aimed at the surrounding trees.

The cable connecting the crate to the helicopter pulled taut, groaning under the strain. For a moment, it seemed as if the extra weight might be too much for the aircraft to bear. The engines whined louder as the craft strained against the load. The chopper's nose dipped as the pilot fought with the herculean lift. Then, with a speed that bordered on agonizing, the crate lifted from the ground. At first, it was just a few inches, the mud beneath it stretching like thick syrup. Within a few seconds, it was swaying gently, pendulum-like beneath the chopper.

As Eden watched the crate swing beneath the ascending helicopter, movement caught her eye from the opposite side of the clearing.

Athena burst from the tree line and ran toward the chopper.

"Athena, stop!" Eden shouted, her voice hoarse and barely audible over the thunderous roar of the twin-turbines.

"No, no, no," Eden muttered, raising her voice again. "Athena, don't!"

As the crate swung a few feet off the ground, Athena made a desperate leap. Her hands gripped the edge of the container, and, with impressive strength, she pulled herself up.

Eden watched in a mixture of horror and awe as Athena, staying on the far side of the crate to remain out of sight of Zhao's men, climbed up its side.

Athena reached the top of the crate as it cleared the tree line. She flattened herself against its surface, becoming nearly invisible from the ground and from the open door of the chopper above.

Eden shielded her eyes against the downdraft as the Sikorsky banked to the north, taking the crate and Athena out of sight.

30

As the sound of the chopper faded, Eden leaped out through the trees toward the mansion. She crossed the patch of rough ground where the chopper had been and ducked behind a tree trunk, one of many standing out of the ground like stubble. The color of the wood, and the lack of regrowth in such fertile land, indicated that the tree hadn't been felled that long ago.

She looked up at the sky as the thrumming of helicopter blades disappeared into the sound of the jungle. A soft wind rolled in from the sea, dragging with it the smell of smoke from the grenade detonations.

"This woman has caused enough destruction already," Eden said, suddenly feeling very alone. "Baxter, can you hear me?" She tapped the comms device. The tiny speaker buzzed and clicked, but no response came. Just in case Baxter could hear her, she summarized the situation.

She waited behind the tree for two minutes, watching the structure for movement. Seeing no evidence of guards left behind, she approached the building.

Gripping the rifle closely, Eden approached one of the

operatives who had been hit during the gunfight. Walking between the fallen men, she felt her usual welling of frustration at the loss of life. Sure, these men had knowingly entered the fray, but that didn't mean they deserved to die.

She crouched beside the first body, checking for a pulse she knew wouldn't be there. The man was young, probably no more than thirty. He was of Chinese origin and wore black tactical gear and combat boots. Scowling at the grim task, she searched the man's pockets and belt. She found several spare magazines, zip-ties, a few energy bar wrappers, but no dog tags, wallet or phone. She repeated the process with the other fallen men but found nothing to identify any of them. Zhao clearly wanted her people to be like ghosts—leaving no trace of who they were in life.

"It's just too clean," Eden said, turning and crossing to the building's once grand entrance.

Pausing on the bottom step, she listened intently for any sign of movement from within. Hearing nothing but the gentle hiss of the wind through the glassless windows, she climbed, her weapon at the ready.

She stepped onto the porch and paused, tuning in to the sound of the old building. Hearing nothing threatening, she glanced over her shoulder at the sweeping vista out across the forest. She turned, pushed aside a thick plastic sheet which hung across the door, and stepped inside. She paused, listening as her eyes adjusted to the gloom. The room took up at least half of the level, with windows on three sides. Thick plastic sheets fastened across the glassless windows cast the room in a sepia-toned dusk.

Seeing the destruction, Eden grinned. Although Zhao had probably planned to move on from this base at some point, it appeared Eden and Athena's arrival had sped up the process. She stepped further into the room and saw shards of rock and documents strewn across the floor. She shoved a bunch of the papers aside with her toe, but didn't see anything she recognized.

She advanced another few steps and eyed several abandoned computer terminals. The systems in here, and the size of the room, suggested that this had been Zhao's makeshift operations center.

"What's the chance of this working?" Eden said, approaching one of the computers. She tapped a keyboard, but the screen remained black, suggesting the power had been cut.

A soft shuffling noise moved through the room like an icy draft. Eden froze and listened. The noise continued for a second before stopping.

Eden straightened up as slowly and silently as she could. She pivoted toward the sound, her rifle pressed into her shoulder, finger resting just outside the trigger guard. The plastic which covered the window on the other side of the room flapped in the breeze, although that wasn't the sound Eden had heard.

The sound came again—the subtle scrape of something moving. It was the kind of sound someone makes when they're trying their hardest not to make any noise at all. The plastic sheet fluttered again, as the wind broke through and swept a bunch of papers across the floor.

Moving as carefully as she could, Eden made her way toward the noise. She stepped around a computer system which had crashed to the floor and skirted around a pile of paper. She closed in on the door, which led deeper into the building, and paused.

She waited for a strong gust of breeze to aggravate the plastic and swung open the door. A hallway led through the building, lined by doors on both sides. She stepped into the hallway, a board creaking beneath her boots. The sound was impossibly loud in the tense silence. She winced, expecting an attack at any moment, but none came.

As her eyes adjusted further, she saw the outline of a window at the end of the corridor. The rear of the building had been overtaken by the jungle to an extent that no light could penetrate the glass.

She took another step and heard the shuffling noise again. She paused, homing in on the sound as best she could. It sounded as though the movement came from the room at the far end of the corridor. With her rifle raised and ready, she advanced, each step measured and silent.

Suddenly, a loud crash echoed from behind the door, followed by a muffled cry of pain.

Eden paused, listening as someone on the other side of the door gasped for breath.

She stepped in close to the wall and drew out a flashlight. She swung open the door, snapped on the flashlight and raised the rifle all at once. The beam of light swept into the room, which looked as though it had been used as a makeshift bedroom. A small camp-bed sat against one wall, with a chair and few personal effects beside.

As Eden took a step further into the room, she sensed movement in her peripheral vision. She attempted to swing toward the movement, but a figure slammed into her from the side, knocking the barrel of her rifle in the opposite direction. The flashlight flew from her hand, clattering to the floor and sending shadows dancing across the walls.

The figure shoved Eden to the side and bolted through the open door.

Eden spun around, steadying herself on the doorjamb. The flashlight revolved around on the floor, momentarily illuminating the fleeing figure as he raced away. In that instant, Eden saw a man, his eyes wide with terror and his clothes disheveled and torn. The panic with which he ran proved that this was not one of Zhao's highly trained men.

"Professor Lavigne," Eden called out, her voice soft as she recovered from the impact. She scooped up the flashlight and sprinted back the way she'd come.

Hearing his name, Lavigne froze. Slowly, he turned.

"Professor Lavigne," Eden said again, more calmly this time. "I'm not here to hurt you. I'm here to help. We've been tracking Zhao, and I heard your call." She kept her voice low and calm.

Lavigne looked as though he was dressed for an afternoon at the university, as opposed to a mission in the Cambodian jungle. He wore a loose-fitting white shirt, with a green and yellow scarf draped around his shoulders.

Lavigne's gaze dropped from Eden's eyes to the rifle which remained in her hands. He shuffled from foot to foot, as though ready to bolt at any moment.

Eden lowered the weapon, dropping it to its strap. She raised her hands and palms, facing Lavigne.

"I came here to stop Zhao," she said. "I'm afraid she's planning something terrible."

Lavigne nodded, swallowed, and adjusted his spectacles. He blinked several times but still said nothing.

"I'm going to help you get to safety," Eden said, taking another step forward.

"How ... how do I know I can trust you?" the professor said, retreating half a step.

"We intercepted your call," Eden said. "We've been tracking Zhao's activities and plan to stop her."

"I ... I don't ..." Lavigne stuttered.

"There's no one else here," Eden said, taking half a step forward. "It's just you and me."

"They were about to kill me and then ..." Lavigne said, looking around as though noticing the bad guys weren't here for the first time.

"Then we arrived," Eden said. "We forced them to leave in a hurry, although I fear Zhao already has their next move planned out."

"Yes, she has," Lavigne said, nodding. "She's gone, and she has taken ... taken something very important with her."

"The Lotus Key," Eden said.

At the mention of the Lotus Key, the professor's eyes widened. "Incroyable," Lavigne said. "You know about that?"

31

ATHENA CLUNG TO THE TOP OF THE CRATE, THE WIND whipping around her as the chopper gained altitude. The thunderous roar of the rotors engulfed her, the relentless downdraft slamming her against the container. They swayed and jerked unpredictably as the chopper accelerated, each movement threatening to send her tumbling to the jungle below.

After a minute or two, her hands already burning, Athena groaned with relief as the chopper settled into a constant forward motion. She removed one of her hands and flexed her fingers to get the blood flowing, then repeated the motion with the other hand. Satisfied that she could feel her fingers, she shuffled to the edge of the crate and peered over. They were now powering high above the forest, the dense canopy only broken by winding rivers that cut through the landscape like bulging veins.

Worried someone might spot her, Athena turned and glanced up at the chopper. The Sikorsky was so large that she didn't think anyone could see directly beneath them. Then, for a moment, she considered the dangerous artifact which sat just a few inches from her body. She hoped that the crate's protective shielding did the job. She shuffled back to the center of the crate and tried to settle as much as she could, knowing she might be in for a long ride.

After about thirty minutes, the chopper banked sharply to the east. Athena once again shimmied across and peered over the side. The landscape beneath them had transformed from unspoiled jungle to a sprawling urban expanse. Through the hazy veil of golden light, a city skyline emerged, shimmering like a mirage.

"Phnom Penh," Athena said under the breath, figuring that the Cambodian capital was the only city of its size within their flight time.

Night was coming now too, the sun setting behind them and casting the city in a warm, amber glow. With the skyscrapers of the city center still a couple of miles away, the chopper began to descend.

Athena peered down and saw they were heading toward an industrial zone on the city's outskirts.

The chopper slowed, causing the crate to swing forward and back. They hovered above several large and dilapidated structures. The pilot adjusted their position, inching them to the center of a yard, which lay between an old factory with a sawtooth roof and several smaller structures.

As the crate descended past the roof of the main factory building, Athena slipped down the side of the crate. She held on to the top edge and waited as they dropped closer and closer to the ground. Dust and debris swirled in clouds as they neared touchdown.

Athena waited until a moment before the crate landed and jumped. She rolled across the yard and broke into a sprint.

The crate kissed the concrete with a thump, then the chopper shifted its position and descended to the side.

Athena ducked behind a large rusting tank and looked back at the helicopter. The cabin door slid open as the rotors slowed. Zhao's men streamed from the chopper, fanning out around the crate with their guns raised. It surprised Athena that even here, supposedly miles away from any threat, they were cautious.

After the men had secured the area, Zhao climbed out of the chopper. She surveyed her surroundings, barking a series of orders which Athena couldn't hear from her position. Zhao turned and started toward one of the buildings, with the large man who always seemed to be at her side in tow. Two other men followed, weapons raised.

Zhao strode up to one of the buildings, then punched a code into an electronic keypad beside the door. There was a loud click, followed by the groan of rusted metal as the warehouse door slid open.

"Tight security for a run-down place like this," Athena whispered to herself.

Zhao disappeared inside the building, closely followed by her small entourage.

Of the men who remained outside, two set about detaching the crate from the chopper's underbelly, while the others formed a protective circle around it.

Watching the action from her hiding place, Athena assessed her options. To find out what Zhao was planning to do with the Lotus Key, she needed to get inside. She ducked in behind the tank and pulled out her phone. She poked at the device, but it remained lifeless. She lifted it into the light and saw that cracks webbed across the screen.

"Damn it," she muttered, trying the power button again. The device remained stubbornly dark.

The low-pitched grumbling of an engine roused to life within the warehouse. The sound was joined a moment later by a whirring electric motor.

Athena peered out and saw one of the large warehouse doors slide open. Lights flickered on, casting long shadows across the yard as a massive flatbed truck emerged from the gloom. The vehicle rumbled slowly out of the warehouse and stopped beside the crate. Two more vehicles followed, a black Land Cruiser and a military style troop carrier with canvas sides. Two men climbed down from the truck and powered up a hydraulic lift that was mounted on the flatbed.

To Athena, ducking into the shadows to remain out of sight, it looked as though they had only stopped here to mount the Lotus Key onto the truck before continuing by road. It was a good move on Zhao's part, she thought grudgingly. Helicopters attracted attention, but trucks wound their way unnoticed through the Cambodian countryside all day and night. Whatever Athena did next, she didn't have time to waste. Sliding her useless phone away, she turned and stalked off through the gloom.

Nearing the edge of the compound, a small, nondescript building caught her attention. With windows overlooking the yard, the structure looked like it might have once served as an office. Keeping to the shadows which now cloaked most of the yard, she approached the door and tried the handle. To her surprise, it swung open. With one last glance over her shoulder to ensure she wasn't being watched, she slipped inside, easing the door closed behind her.

The interior was dark and musty, years of abandonment evident in the thick layer of dust covering every surface. Despite its condition, the room appeared to have been deserted halfway through a shift, with desks and a filing cabinet languishing in the gloom.

A pair of voices drifted from outside and a flashlight beam moved across the glass, momentarily illuminating the interior.

Athena dropped to the floor and crawled beneath the window. She listened as two men passed, their flashlight beams swinging from side to side. When they'd gone, she crossed to the nearest desk and was surprised to find an old, corded telephone sitting amid the dust and debris. She lifted the receiver, hardly daring to hope.

"No way," Athena said. The dull, crackly dial tone hummed in her ear. She reached for the rotary dial and began to enter the number she knew by heart. The soft, rhythmic clicks of the dial echoed in the office.

As she entered the third number, she heard the thump of boots on concrete right outside. Then came the unmistakable sound of the door flying open. A bright light cut into the room. Heavy footsteps thumped inside, and Athena found herself staring down the barrel of an assault rifle.

32

"THE SECOND DISC IS HERE," ZHAO SAID, POINTING AT THE
map, which she'd unrolled across a steel table at the back of
the warehouse.

She looked up at Gui standing opposite her, then at the
two guards stationed by the door. In the glow from a battery-
powered floodlight, she could just make out the lines of
ancient meat hooks hanging from rails like a row of hang-
man's nooses. She'd bought the facility, an old meat-
processing plant on the outskirts of Phnom Penh, several
years ago. Only needing the place to store the vehicles and
some other supplies, she'd left the meat processing
machines and vast freezers in position.

"You think the professor told the truth?" Gui said, spitting the words with venom.

"I think the professor did everything he could to save his
life," Zhao said, eyeing her second in command. "Although
it was impressive that such a measly man he managed to
steal your cellphone."

One of the guards standing in the shadows made a noise

that could have been a laugh. Gui whirled around and was about to go head-to-head when Zhao stopped him.

"Get over it," Zhao said, her tone mocking. "Get back here. We don't have time for you boys to play."

Gui clenched his fists, clearly imagining driving them into Professor Lavigne and the guard who he thought had mocked him. He groaned and returned to the table. A long moment of silence followed, backed by the distant drone of motorcycles on the highway.

"They do say everyone has a match," Zhao continued. "I just didn't expect yours to be a five-foot-tall, middle-aged professor."

"If I ever see him again," Gui growled, his teeth grinding. He forced one fist into the palm of the other hand.

In a flash, Zhao surged forward. She stretched across the table and slapped Gui around the face. The sound of the slap reverberated through the empty warehouse like a gunshot. The guards standing in the shadows snapped to attention, wincing.

Gui's hand flew to his face and his eyes watered. A red patch bloomed across his cheek. He looked up and met Zhao's stare, sweat beading on his forehead.

"You will do no such thing. You will focus on the mission at hand," Zhao snapped. "This is not about you, and this is not about revenge." She leaned across the table, which would once have been used to strip the meat from a carcass. The steel creaked, and the map crinkled beneath her splayed fingers.

Gui shifted an inch backward in the way a Great Dane might retreat from a raging alley cat.

"No one here is more important than the Lotus Key, do you understand?" Zhao said, her tone making up for her voice's lack of volume. "The professor has got us this far, and we can do the rest alone." Zhao straightened up and shot Gui a menacing glare. "This is the most important task of our lives. I need you to focus."

Her point made, Zhao returned her focus to the map. "Lavigne told us the temple is here." She drove a finger into the map. "It's several hours by road, but if we leave now, we will be there by the morning."

"One question," Gui said, nervously rubbing his hand across his face.

Zhao looked at him, a challenge in her eyes. The floodlight caught a silver streak in her hair, making it gleam like a knife's edge.

"Why has this temple never been explored? Tourists love these temples. Why would they not have clambered over every inch of the place?"

Zhao pursed her lips, thinking for a moment. The rumble of the truck's engine muted as the men finished loading the Lotus Key on to the flatbed.

"It's obvious," Zhao snapped. "This part of the country has been ignored since the war. No one goes there. No one cares. Now, stop wasting time."

A breeze drifted in through a hole in the roof, clanging the meat hooks together, the sound reverberating ominously.

Gui studied the map to avoid Zhao's gaze. He traced out the route they'd need to take with a finger.

Outside, the loader's engine cut out, plunging them into a silence broken only by the distant groan of traffic.

"The words on the hidden carving were clear," Zhao said. "The disc is hidden in the temple where Naga guards the lotus throne. Thanks to our professor, we know where that leads us." She rolled up the map. "Go and tell the men to finish loading. I want to leave in ten minutes."

A commotion erupted from the yard outside the warehouse. First came the sound of shuffling boots on concrete, then a crash of something metal hitting the ground. Shouts echoed through the door.

"Over here!"

"Got her!"

"Watch the—" The warning was cut off by another crash and the distinctive sound of a body slamming against a wall.

Zhao glanced at Gui, and the pair pulled out their weapons.

Footsteps and the sounds of a scuffle followed. Then a woman's voice cried out—not in fear, but in frustration. A chain clanked as something, or someone, collided with the row of meat hooks. A flashlight beam appeared, joined a moment later by a second.

Zhao saw two guards muscling their way across the warehouse, dragging a figure between them. The woman's head drooped forward; her face obscured by hair. The men wrestled their way forward, clearly struggling with the woman. She swung an elbow, cracking one of the men on the nose. The men dragged her onward, only just managing to keep her contained.

"What is the meaning of this?" Zhao said as the prisoner continued to writhe and kick.

"Caught her snooping around in one of the buildings," one guard reported, blood streaming from his nose where he'd clearly taken a blow. His grip tightened on the prisoner's arm as she attempted to drive an elbow into his ribs. "She won't tell us what she's—"

The prisoner thrashed again with the desperate strength of a cornered animal. She twisted one arm free, and swung a punch, connecting with the guard's face.

Gui lumbered forward, his meaty hands seizing the prisoner's arm. He yanked it behind her back, causing her to hiss and grunt in pain. The woman writhed and kicked, but Gui's immense strength held her firm. Realizing she was beaten, for now at least, the woman stopped struggling. She leaned forward, breathing heavily.

Zhao approached the woman, reached out and grabbed her chin. She forced the woman's face upward to get a good look at her. Then, in the harsh light, Zhao recognized a face that she had seen thousands of times in her mind's eye. A face that had haunted her, tormented her, and kept her awake at night.

She gasped, trying to speak, but the words caught in her throat like broken glass. Her jaw dropped. She staggered backward, colliding with the table as though suffering the effects of a physical blow.

"You," Zhao said, the word barely more than a whisper. She staggered forwards and touched Athena's face with a trembling hand.

"Surprise," Athena said.

33

"Look at this," Lavigne said, leading Eden into the large room at the front of the building. He searched through the debris and dragged out a map. Flattening the map on the table, he ran his finger across it, tracing their current location in the south of the country to the site of Angkor Wat in the north.

Eden walked around the table and illuminated the map with her flashlight.

"Zhao found a carving at Angkor Wat which tells of the Lotus Key," Lavigne said, easily dropping into the tone of a seasoned lecturer. He adjusted his scarf, and then fiddled with his spectacles.

"How has no one realized that before?" Eden said.

"The carving was on the reverse of a wall, on the inside," Lavigne said. "It's been hidden for centuries, just inches from the millions of people who visit that temple every year. Even I have missed it when studying many of the—"

"And what was in the carving?" Eden said.

"It's a diagram of sorts." Lavigne snatched up another piece of paper and flattened it onto the table. He tapped down each pocket before turning to Eden. "Do you have a pen?"

Eden crossed the room, grabbed one from a table, and threw it to the professor. He swung his hand through the air a full second before the pen reached him. The pen hit him on the chest and clattered to the table.

"Slick move," Eden said.

Refusing to be distracted, Lavigne set about drawing out the carving, his tongue poking between his lips in concentration. He worked quickly, moving the pen in sharp and accurate strokes. First, he drew two circular objects at either side of the page, then added a lotus shape in the middle.

Eden looked over the professor's shoulder, impressed by the accuracy.

"I believe this is a schematic, detailing the activation setup for the Lotus Key," Lavigne said, adding detail to the central lotus shape. "The geometric arrangement suggests a specific spatial configuration. Incroyable, non?"

"How do you know this?" Eden said, looking from the diagram to the professor.

"I suspect that when Indravarman ordered the Lotus Key to be removed from the temple, he left this hidden, should someone need to reactivate it."

"But how does this tell us where to look for the discs?" Eden said, squinting at the picture.

"There's a cryptic sentence written in ancient Khmer beneath each object. These give us clues about the object's locations." Lavigne wrote out a series of characters beneath the disc on the left. He wrote with speed, clearly not needing to even think about it.

"You remember every word?" she said, looking at the man.

"Oh, I remember everything," Lavigne said. "Phone

numbers going back decades, every restaurant meal, including the price, every street and car in my neighborhood." Eden held the professor's gaze for a second. "It's both a blessing and a curse," Lavigne said, his attention returning to the paper.

"What does that say?" Eden asked, pointing at what Lavigne had just written.

"Koun sao nov krom kar ko-hok robsa sdach," the professor said.

"And in English, that means?"

"This key rests beneath the king's gilded words," Lavigne said. "And the disc was found beneath the Ta Prohm Stele, which I have often found confusing. But now, finally, it makes perfect sense!" Lavigne clapped his hands joyfully.

Eden shot him a confused glance, and the professor huffed out a breath of air.

"The Ta Prohm Stele details all the victories of King Indravarman II."

"Okay, and?" Eden said.

"King Indravarman II didn't have any victories," Lavigne said, exasperated. "Everything on the stele was a lie. For years I just thought it was Indravarman trying to make himself seem more victorious, but it all makes sense now."

"And this one," Eden said, pointing to the image which represented the Lotus Key in the center.

"Kroy pi tngai pram-pil ning yub pram-pil, keu-chea vathu daw sak-se-set bom-pot," Lavigne said, this time offering the translation before being prompted. "After the sun and moon pass seven times, there lies the greatest power."

"Hold on a moment," Eden said. "The Lotus Key was found around a hundred nautical miles off the coast of

Cambodia. That could easily have taken seven days and seven nights in a boat eight hundred years ago."

Lavigne nodded, flashing Eden something of an impressed look.

"And this one," Eden said, as Lavigne scribbled down the third sentence. "Skip to English, please."

"Search for the temple where Naga guards the lotus throne," Lavigne said.

"And that takes us where?" Eden lifted the flashlight beam back to the map.

"It's important to note that the lotus image is incredibly common in temple architecture," Lavigne started, clearly enjoying the attention. "So, we have much to—"

"Professor." Eden placed a hand on Lavigne's arm. "We have a madwoman with a powerful relic, whose intentions we don't yet understand. To make matters worse, she's kidnapped my friend. So please, spare the explanation, and just point to the temple."

Lavigne sighed, his shoulders drooping. "You young people just want everything right now. I blame Google. Many years ago, when I needed an answer, I couldn't just—"

"Professor," Eden said, the hand on Lavigne's arm now squeezing.

Lavigne leaned across the map and pointed to a village on Cambodia's northern periphery. "There," he said reluctantly.

"The Oddar Meanchey Province," Eden said, reading from the map.

"Yes, as it's called today. I've often suspected that this area holds many more secrets than we've uncovered so far." Lavigne pointed at the village of O'Smach. "This place has a complex and troubled history."

Eden leaned in, her flashlight illuminating the area Lavigne indicated.

"O'Smach is a small border town, right on the Thai-Cambodian border," the professor continued. "It's about thirty-five kilometers west of Anlong Veng. The entire region was a Khmer Rouge stronghold until the late 1990s."

"And where exactly might this temple be hidden?"

Lavigne moved his finger to a spot southeast of O'Smach. "I've heard rumors of a temple located around here. It's a heavily forested area with some isolated hills— the perfect environment for a structure like this to lie out of sight."

"And you sent Zhao and her team right there?" Eden said, her tone incredulous.

"I had no choice." Lavigne's balled fists dropped to his sides. "They were going to—"

"Yes, I understand. You did what you had to, this isn't your—" She stopped talking as the distant thrumming of an incoming helicopter drifted through the air.

"They're coming back," Lavigne said, his voice tense and panicked. He glanced from side to side as though searching for a place to hide.

Eden ran to the porch and peered out, searching the sky for the noise. Seeing the lights of the smaller Eurocopter, she turned and threw the professor a grin.

"It's not Zhao." She marched into the room and rolled up the map along with Lavigne's drawing. "Come on, we're getting out of here."

"What ... what are we going to do?"

"We're going after them, of course. Hopefully we'll get there first."

"We?" Lavigne said, weakly. "I... I... really would much rather just go back to Paris."

Eden turned and looked at the professor. "This could be the discovery of a lifetime. We're hunting for a temple that hasn't been seen in decades, if not hundreds of years."

The *whump-whump* increased in volume as the chopper hovered above the building, its powerful lights sweeping the ground and mansion. Baxter, clearly seeing no threats, landed where the Sikorsky had been.

"Yes... an undiscovered temple in the Cambodian Jungle. This could be the discovery of a lifetime," Lavigne repeated, shouting over the noise. His mouth moved as he thought through the options. "I can't be this close and not... but then returning to Paris, that does sound—"

Baxter swung the chopper's door open, a rifle at the ready. Seeing Eden run down the stairs, he visibly relaxed. Eden darted for the chopper, dragging Lavigne by the arm.

"You took your time," Eden said, pushing Lavigne into the cabin and then scrambling in.

"I ... when the comms went down I ... where's Athena?" Baxter asked.

"With Zhao," Eden said. "This is the esteemed Professor Etienne Lavigne, who's going to show us where Zhao's going."

"I... I really would rather just go back to the airport now. Taking on a group of armed mercenaries really isn't one of my skills." Lavigne slid on the headset which Eden offered.

Eden looked at the professor and was about to tell him to get a grip when

Baxter interrupted. "You read ancient Khmer don't you professor?"

"Of course," Lavigne said.

"We need to get our friend Athena back," Baxter continued. "So if you can help, it's really important that you come."

"Also, even if we find the temple, we won't understand

what the runes are telling us," Eden added, joining Baxter's persuasion.

"Yes, this certainly isn't something you can ask Google," Lavigne said.

"Ask Google?" Eden replied, an eyebrow raised.

"Yes, as I said, it seems that internet searches have replaced quality research in the modern age." Lavigne's hands dropped into his lap. "These runes will warn of traps, point to hidden entrances, or even reveal the temple's true purpose. Without the ability to decipher them on the spot, you're walking blind into who knows what."

"Yes, exactly," Baxter said. "Also you know the landscape, I heard that you are one of the world's foremost experts on this place."

"Well ... I wouldn't say ..." Lavigne muttered, his shoulders rising a few inches. "But I have committed every undulation of the ground to memory. Fine, I'll come," he said, so quietly it was barely even audible.

"You'll be able to point out the areas which are more likely to hide ancient constructions," Eden said. "These things are probably invisible to unstrained eyes like ours."

"And you can communicate with the local people," Baxter continued. "In a situation where every second counts, that could make all—"

"I said fine!" Lavigne huffed. "I'm coming, but you're doing all the dangerous stuff, okay?"

"Agreed," Eden said, settling into the co-pilot's seat and nodding at Baxter.

"Excellent, bien sûr." The professor said, smiling weakly.

"And, by the way," Eden said as they lifted off, "Google's now officially a verb. You don't need to ask it; you just *Google* it."

34

Zhao leaned into the center and looked out through the windshield of the Toyota Land Cruiser. The headlights cut through the darkness, illuminating the narrow road which wound between dense jungle on one side and rice paddies on the other.

She glanced at the clock on the dashboard and calculated that, while they'd already been on the road four hours, they weren't even halfway through their journey. She exhaled, frustrated that they could have done the same journey in a fraction of the time using the chopper.

With the Lotus Key already in her possession, and the ability to control it tantalizingly close, Zhao felt the electricity yet again spark through her body. She closed her eyes for a moment and imagined the feeling of unbridled power that would soon be hers.

With the urgency of a mother searching for a lost child, she opened her eyes and looked at the flatbed truck, which swung from side to side a few car lengths ahead. Beneath the discolored tarpaulin, strapped across the back of that flatbed, was the most powerful relic known to humankind.

Forget the invention of the atom bomb, electricity, or even modern advances in artificial intelligence—what was inside that crate would prove more powerful than them all. Thinking about the power, she remembered why it was important they made this journey overland. Right now, it was crucial that they made the journey quietly. They needed to stay beneath the radar until it was too late for anyone to intervene.

The truck's taillights swung from side to side as they navigated around a particularly deep hole in the road.

Gui groaned to himself, gripping the steering wheel as he concentrated on their progress. One of Zhao's guards sat in the passenger seat, his rifle at the ready should anyone interfere with their precious cargo. Four more men rode in the truck ahead and the rest of the unit travelled in the following troop carrier.

Pushing her frustration to one side, Zhao turned her attention to the woman sitting beside her in the rear of the Land Cruiser.

"I never expected to see you again." Although Zhao's tone was flat and emotionless, speaking the sentence brought a strange sensation to her chest. The feeling seemed to radiate within her, as though warming her from the inside. She tried to cast the feeling away, focusing on the truck as it worked its way around another set of potholes.

"That was the idea, wasn't it?" Athena said, looking out through the window. "Watching someone's execution is usually a pretty final goodbye."

"You don't understand the position I was in," Zhao said, her tone hardening. "You were interfering in things you didn't understand. There was nothing I could do."

"Rubbish," Athena said, giving her mother a look with radioactive intent.

"To help you would have ..." Zhao stopped talking as she realized she couldn't even begin to explain. So much of her life had been cloaked in secrecy, that to start explaining it would unravel it all. "You'll just have to take my word for it. I was working on something greater—"

"Greater than family? Greater than basic human decency?" Athena said, laughing bitterly. "Let me guess—in your eyes, you're still the hero of this story."

Zhao shook her head slowly. "There's no such thing as a hero, and no such thing as a villain. These concepts are created to divide us. The world isn't that simple."

Athena didn't reply, looking out at the paddy fields glimmering in the moonlight.

The Land Cruiser hit another pothole, jostling them all from side to side. In the front seat, Gui muttered something under his breath as he wrestled them back onto a straight path.

"Sometimes, to create real change," Zhao continued, her eyes following the swaying truck ahead, "we must be willing to sacrifice everything we hold dear."

The truck's taillights disappeared momentarily as it swung behind a collection of huts. The Land Cruiser followed, and the truck appeared again, taillights glowing blood-red.

"Like watching your daughter die?" Athena's voice was as sharp as a needle. "That's the sort of sacrifice you're talking about?"

"You were getting too close. You would have ruined it all."

"Too close to what?" Athena demanded. "The camps? The people you were torturing. Or was it something else?" She turned and saw Zhao, wholly focused on the truck ahead. "How long have you known about the Lotus Key?"

Zhao's lips tightened, but she said nothing. The truck slowed to navigate around a water buffalo that had wandered onto the road, its massive horns ghostly in the headlights.

"That's it, isn't it?" Athena pressed. "All this time, everything you've done, it all led toward finding this thing. And now what? You're going to use it to, what, make yourself the *leader of the world*?" Athena delivered the final four words in a crazed voice.

"You're not even close to understanding," Zhao said, her voice carrying an edge of steel. "You've never understood, although maybe now it's time you did." The older woman turned as though she'd suddenly realized something. "It's going to be us. We'll do it together."

"We're approaching the great lake, Tonlé Sap," Lavigne said, straining to look out of the window of the Eurocopter as they sped north.

From her usual seat beside Baxter, Eden peered down at a vast expanse of water shining in the moonlight.

Baxter worked the controls, and the chopper dropped in closer to the lake, bringing several floating structures into view.

"What are they?" Eden said, looking at the structures.

"That's one of the floating villages," Lavigne said, his voice loud and clear in the comms system. "These villages have existed for generations. They're just one of the ways people here have adapted to the lake's dramatic seasonal changes. During the monsoon season, the Tonlé Sap expands to several times its dry season size."

As they got closer, Eden saw night fishermen in slender boats weaving between the floating houses.

"The entire community lives on the water," Lavigne continued. "Those larger structures are schools, temples, even small markets—all floating."

Baxter banked the chopper as they reached the lake's far shore. The landscape once again transformed from the shimmering waters of the lake to a patchwork of rice paddies and scattered settlements.

"Landing in two minutes," Baxter announced.

"But O'Smach is still a hundred miles further north," Lavigne said, looking at the map spread across his knees in the glow from a small flashlight.

"The ancients used to say, to move forward, we must first take a step back," Eden said, her tone mysterious.

Lavigne looked up, confused.

"What she means is, we can't approach that region in the chopper," Baxter said. "Northern Cambodia is a secluded and sensitive area. If we go up there in this thing, everyone will know about it before we've even landed."

They crested a small rise and the lights of Siem Reap came into view, sprawling out beneath them like dirty cobwebs. Colonial-era buildings with their distinctive architecture fought for space alongside modern concrete structures, all surrounded by makeshift shacks that seemed ubiquitous across this part of the world.

"If we're not going in the chopper, how are we getting to O'Smach?" Lavigne said, glancing at Eden. "It's a long way on many unpaved roads."

"Don't you worry about that," Eden said, grinning at

Baxter. "I've sorted something, and I think you're going to like it."

"Is it—"

"You said you were ready for whatever it took," Baxter said, interrupting the Frenchman and sharing an amused glance with Eden.

"You'll see," Eden added. "We're landing in two minutes."

As the Eurocopter descended towards the outskirts of Siem Reap, Eden caught sight of their destination—a small yard hidden among a cluster of warehouses and abandoned buildings. Floodlights had been placed around the yard, allowing them to see the clear space to land.

Baxter expertly maneuvered the aircraft, compensating for a sudden gust of wind that threatened to push them off course. They touched down with a jolt, clouds of dust kicking up in all directions.

Through the swirling grit, Eden saw the rusted outlines of old machinery and stacks of weathered shipping containers. As the rotors slowed, she spotted a familiar silhouette emerging from one of the nearby structures, shielding his eyes from the dust.

"I don't understand. What is this place?" Lavigne said, looking anxiously from one decrepit building to the next.

Warehouses flanked the yard on three sides, with piles of scrap metal stacked in front of a chain-link fence on the other. In the distance, the spires of Siem Reap's more tourist-friendly areas were just visible.

Eden unbuckled her harness and shoved open the door.

"I don't think I'm going to like this," Lavigne said, folding his map away and exiting the chopper. "It all looks so filthy."

"Come on, professor," Eden said, helping Lavigne down to the ground. "It's time to meet our ride."

35

EDEN TURNED AND WAVED AT A MAN STRIDING FROM THE shadows.

"Thanks for the landing lights," Eden said. He emerged into the floodlight's beam, arms open wide. "Baxter was worried we might not find you, but we could probably see this from space."

"It's my pleasure," the man called out in a booming Australian accent. "You coming here is big news."

"I hope you kept it quiet; this is supposed to be off the books," Eden replied, closing the distance in two steps and embracing the Australian. "We've been looking for an excuse to come and see you. I'm just sorry we can't stay long." Eden broke off the hug. "Meet Malcolm 'Mac' Ferguson." She made introductions and walked beside Mac as he led them toward one of the warehouses.

"Tell me, how's your father?" Mac said, draping a tattooed arm around Eden's shoulders. "Not seen hide nor hair from him for years."

"Enjoying the quiet life," Eden said, sharing a grin with

Baxter. Quiet was certainly not the way she would describe her father's lifestyle.

"Good old Winslow." Mac paused beside a small rusting door and turned to look at the group. "I hope you're ready for an adventure."

Eden and Baxter nodded.

"What... what... what sort of adventure are we talking about?" Lavigne said, straightening his spectacles and looking as though he might be sick.

Mac's grin widened as he jerked a thumb over his shoulder. "Come and see for yourself." He swung open the door with a theatrical flourish and turned on the lights. Overhead fluorescents buzzed into life, revealing two gleaming off-road motorbikes.

"Your chariots await," Mac said, pointing at the vehicles.

"They are beautiful," Eden said.

"Oh, no. No, no, no," Lavigne stammered, backing away and nearly tripping over his own feet. "This is absolutely out of the question. The number of people who fall ... They're death traps! I can't possibly—"

"These are not deathtraps." Mac paced up to one of the bikes and ran his hand across the saddle. "These are KTM 890 Adventure Rs. Top of the line. Liquid-cooled parallel twin engines, 889cc, pushing out about 105 horsepower."

"They're perfect," Eden said.

"Perfect for killing us all?" Lavigne said, his voice raising an octave. "Do you know how many people die on motorcycles every year? The statistics are—"

"These aren't your average street bikes," Mac interrupted. "Fitted with WP XPLOR suspension, perfect for handling whatever the Cambodian back roads throw at ya. Extra protection on the engine cases, reinforced subframes, upgraded bash plates. Plus," he patted the saddle proudly, "custom seat padding. Your backside will thank me after a few hours on these beauties."

"Hours?" the last bit of color drained from Lavigne's face, his skin taking on the color of old porridge.

"Maybe the professor should stay with you," Eden said, turning to Mac. "You could look after him for a day or so, right?"

"Certainly," Mac said.

"It would, of course, be a shame that he'd potentially miss out on the discovery of a lifetime," Baxter added.

Lavigne's eyes darted from side to side as he clearly struggled with the decision. "No, no, no ... yes ... the discovery of a lifetime." He released a breath as though he was going to deflate.

"That's the spirit, professor," Mac said, clapping Lavigne on the shoulder. "Where's your sense of adventure, mate?"

Lavigne sneezed violently, then rubbed his scarf across his nose. "Do you have any idea how many allergens—"

"Best not to think about it," Mac said, strolling over to a rack which contained biking gear in various sizes. "Get suited up, hold on tight and you'll be there in no time."

The three dressed quickly, with Mac helping select sizes. Once suited and ready to go, Eden slipped on to the saddle and powered up the bike. The machine thrummed hungrily, the noise filling the warehouse. A second engine harmonized with hers as Baxter started his bike.

Eden turned and eyed Lavigne, standing awkwardly in the ill-fitting riding gear. He was wrapped head to toe in what appeared to be every piece of protective gear Mac had in stock—an oversized jacket, pants that ballooned around his legs, and a helmet that made his head look comically large.

"Come on, professor. Stop wasting time and get on." She tapped the seat behind her, grinning.

Lavigne moved like a man walking on the moon and slipped awkwardly onto the saddle. Mac pointed out the pair of specially installed handholds and foot pegs. Once the professor was in place, the Australian swung open the door.

"Stay on the back roads and you'll be there in time for breakfast," Mac said, raising a hand in a wave. "And Eden, tell your old man there's a bottle of scotch here with his name on it."

"Thanks Mac, I'll tell him to stop by." Eden returned the wave and kicked the bike into gear.

"And Lavigne, try not to fall off," the Australian said, his deep belly laugh cutting through the howl of the bikes.

"Falling off, insect bites, allergies—"

Eden revved the engine, cutting off Lavigne's list of potential catastrophes.

"I'm going to die!" Lavigne forgot about the hand holds, looped his arms around Eden's waist and pulled in close.

"We're all going to die, professor," Eden said, accelerating out of the warehouse door, leaving a streak of rubber on the concrete. "But not everyone gets to live."

They swung onto a dusty backstreet, weaving around a pair of tuk-tuks on their sunrise run to Angkor Wat, then sped out onto a larger road. Eden leaned into a turn at an angle that made Lavigne whimper and accelerated out of the city. Within a few minutes, the urban landscape gave way to lush greenery. They bumped onto a narrow unpaved track and wound their way northbound through small villages and verdant rice paddies.

Sometime later, the sun crept up like molten copper behind the palm trees, setting fire to banks of morning mist that clung to the flooded fields. Light spilled like sheets of gold, catching the dew-heavy spider webs that stretched between fence posts and the delicate spirals of steam rising from cooking fires.

A pair of water buffalo waded through the mirror-like paddies, each step sending ripples across the glassy surface. Near a cluster of stilted wooden houses, a farmer in a wide-brimmed hat paused his morning routine, leaning on his hoe to watch the dust-covered riders speed past. Behind one of them, what appeared to be a mummified figure clung to the back of the bike, a green scarf whipping in the wind like a prayer flag.

WITH HER FACE NEARLY PRESSED AGAINST THE GLASS, ATHENA watched as the sun broke across the horizon, spilling gold across the sky. She thought about Eden, Baxter, and the rest of their crew, hoping that they were near. For a moment, she considered whether jumping on top of the crate had been a good idea, but then dismissed the thought. She had long ago learned that questioning your actions in the heat of conflict got you nowhere.

She shot a sideways glance at Zhao, who sat on the other side of the Land Cruiser's rear seat. Despite being just feet from her mother, Athena felt no warmth. This was a woman who had, after all, intended to watch her execution.

Through the glass, a long strand of morning mist swept across the road like a tattered white flag, parting as the flatbed truck lurched through it.

Athena watched as a group of monks in saffron robes

materialized from the gloom at the side of the road. The monks walked in single file along the roadside, their robes swaying in the breeze. One of the young monks at the rear of the line turned to watch the convoy pass.

At that moment, instead of feeling resentful toward her awful excuse for a mother, Athena felt grateful that she had surrounded herself with a surrogate family in the Council. Sure, it wasn't a family with shared biology, but they looked out for and trusted each other.

"We're close," Zhao said, interrupting Athena's thoughts. She picked up the radio and issued instructions to the men in the trucks. "Stop one mile ahead. From there, we'll advance on foot." The radio hissed, followed by an 'affirmative' from the flatbed ahead and the troop carrier behind.

They rumbled around a corner; the road cutting through a small settlement with huts flanking both sides of the road. Athena watched a pair of women sitting outside their huts, stoking their cooking fires, while threads of smoke curled up through the still morning air.

The convoy rounded another bend and Gui eased off the accelerator.

It took Athena a moment to realize why. She leaned to the side and peered out through the windshield. Ahead, a cluster of vehicles lined the roadside. These weren't the battered-up bikes or agricultural vehicles they'd seen since leaving the last town. These were modern 4x4s and what looked like an armored tractor. As they neared, Athena saw that it wasn't, in fact, a tractor, but a vehicle designed for clearing landmines. It had a rotating flail attached to the front, designed to batter the ground and explode any mines lying beneath the soil. A few feet further, warning tape fluttered between wooden stakes, and skull and crossbones signs marked the edge of an unsafe zone.

They bounced on past the vehicles, all still motionless at this early hour, and around another corner.

"Pull in just up here," Zhao said into the radio. "We're close now, as close as we can get on the road."

The flatbed truck slowed and bumped up onto the side of the road, rocking precariously. Gui pulled the Land Cruiser in closer behind and both engines stopped. The troop carrier completed the convoy a few seconds later.

Athena swung open the door and climbed out, stretching after the long drive across unpaved roads.

Zhao rounded the front of the Land Cruiser and spoke to the men already out of the trucks. Despite their lack of sleep, the men were attentive, rifles at the ready.

"Two of you with us," Zhao said, pointing at two men. "The rest of you, secure the Lotus Key."

The guards tasked with staying behind fanned out around the truck. The others stepped away with Zhao and Gui.

"You're coming with us," Zhao said, pointing at Athena.

Athena considered arguing, then saw Gui raise his weapon. She didn't want to give the brute any excuse to use violence, at least not yet.

36

"How are you holding up, Lavigne?" Eden said, her voice coming through the comms system built into the helmets. They swung around a corner, their knees just inches from the dirt.

"I've been better," Lavigne groaned. "I've swallowed so many insects. Not to mention the rash forming on my—"

"Cheer up, Professor," Baxter shouted, pulling up alongside. "Think of the stories you'll have to tell when you get back to Paris."

"Oh Paris," Lavigne said. "How I long for merveilleux Paris."

Eden accelerated, allowing Baxter to drop back behind as the track narrowed. The jungle closed in around them; a troupe of monkeys scampering along the side of the road paused to hiss at the passing bikes. Lavigne whimpered and pulled himself in even closer to Eden.

The sun was high in the sky as they approached a small temple on the outskirts of O'Smach. Sitting between the emerald folds of the forest on one side and a lotus covered lake on the other, it looked as though nature was trying to claim the temple for itself.

Eden slowed her bike, carefully navigating the uneven ground, and came to a stop beside the temple. She removed her helmet, shook out her hair, and looked up at the structure. One wall of the temple had been totally embraced by the roots of a towering tree.

"That wasn't too bad, was it?" Eden said, gazing out across the lake. Water shimmered beneath the lotus flowers; their petals wide open as though worshipping the sun.

A hill, almost the shape of a pyramid, met the lake's far shore, a cliff rising directly out of the water. Creeping plants covered much of the cliff and a waterfall pounded down one part of it, spray rising into the air.

"You can let go now," Eden said, looking at Lavigne, who clung like a baby monkey to its mother.

Lavigne didn't move, his eyes squeezed shut behind well-fogged spectacles. Eventually, his eyelids peeled back, and he looked around, seemingly surprised to find himself still alive.

"Oh, thank heavens," Lavigne gasped, finally prying off the helmet. His hair was plastered to his forehead, soaked in sweat, and his face had the color and texture of a poorly baked pain aux raisin. He dismounted the bike, and toppled sideways, his legs shaking.

Eden reached out and grabbed the professor, holding him until the blood flow returned to his legs. When his composure had partly returned, Lavigne glanced up at the temple.

"Look at this place," he said, as though he was the first person to see it in all history. "This appears to be a lesser-known satellite temple of the Angkor complex. The architectural style suggests late twelfth century, possibly early thirteenth." He approached the wide steps which led into the temple. "The craftsmanship on these lintels is exquisite, even after centuries of neglect."

The doors at the front of the temple creaked open, causing the Frenchman to shriek and scuttle back behind Eden. The door swung wide, and an elderly monk stepped out. He moved out onto the porch and surveyed the lake, the breeze toying with his robes. After a few moments, the monk padded down the steps, his bare feet easily navigating the uneven stone.

"Now's your time to shine, professor," Eden said, pointing at the monk. "Let's see if this guy can help us find what we're looking for."

The monk turned and his gaze settled on the group and their bikes. If he was surprised, or even threatened by their arrival, he didn't show it.

Eden met the old man's stare and smiled. Although his face was deeply lined, his eyes showed the focus of someone very aware of their surroundings.

With an air of a master-showman ready to perform, Lavigne stepped forward. He straightened up to his not-considerable full height and bowed. He clasped his lapels, cleared his throat and addressed the monk in fluent Khmer.

Hearing his native language, the monk smiled and then replied. "Welcome, travelers. It is rare to hear such excellent Khmer from a foreigner. But let's speak in English as I don't get the opportunity to practice much."

"That would be wonderful," Eden said, forcing herself not to laugh.

Lavigne shrunk back, his shoulders dropping.

Eden introduced herself, Baxter, and the professor. She explained that they were seeking a lost temple in an effort to stop a band of unscrupulous thieves. The monk listened closely. He nodded solemnly, his eyes taking on a distant, troubled look.

"Ah, I believe I know the temple you seek," he said in a low, gravelly voice. "You are close, it lies up there." He pointed at the hill which rose out of the lake's far shore. "Prasat Lotus Neak is a place of great mystery and power," the monk said. "It was a royal sanctuary, dedicated to the Naga."

"That's what I said," Lavigne added, his chest puffed up again.

"Naga?" Baxter asked, raising an eyebrow.

"A serpent deity," Lavigne explained, his excitement growing. "Naga plays a crucial role in both Hindu and Buddhist mythology. But a whole temple dedicated to them, hidden away like this? C'est incroyable!"

"The temple is said to be covered in intricate carvings of seven-headed serpents," the monk continued.

"That makes sense," Eden said, her voice hardening. "We'll get there before the others and protect the temple at all costs."

"In ancient times, Prasat Lotus Neak was a place of great spiritual significance." The monk looked up at the hillside, a sadness in his eyes.

"Was?" Baxter said. "Has it been destroyed?"

"Oh no, the temple is still there," the monk said, looking back at each of them in turn. "But it is no longer a place of peace. It is now a place of death."

"That way," Zhao said, pointing up the incline and away from the road. "According to the professor, Prasat Lotus Neak is on the crest of that hill."

"You're putting a lot of trust in that man," Athena said, before the group had the chance to set off. "How do you know he was telling you the truth?"

Zhao spun around and locked eyes with her daughter. "When people face death, they tell the truth," she said. "Move out!"

One of the guards went first, hacking a path through the bushes with a machete. The second guard followed a few steps behind, sweeping his rifle from side to side.

After several minutes and less than one hundred feet of progress, the leading man froze, a fist raised in the air. The small group stopped, listening for danger.

Just two paces behind Athena, Gui un-holstered his weapon and prepared to fire. They all held their breath, looking from side to side. The rustling grew louder, branches snapping and leaves shaking. The guard with the machete dropped into a crouch and raised his rifle.

A band of long-tailed macaques burst through the vegetation. Their gray bodies flowed past like water, mothers clutching infants to their chests, juveniles leaping between bushes. One large male paused to bare his teeth at the group before vanishing into the undergrowth, leaving only swaying branches in his wake.

"You met your match there, boys," Athena said, grinning. "No wonder you were scared."

"It's nothing," Zhao snapped, looking back at the screen of her phone then up at the rise of the hill behind the bushes. "We don't have time for this. Keep moving."

The men continued, cutting their way, inch by inch, toward the temple. As they moved further into the undergrowth, the plants became chest high and then higher still. Flowering bushes, plants and ferns soon blocked Athena's view on all sides. She glanced over her shoulder at Gui, straining on his tiptoes and failing to see over the wall of green.

"Keep moving," Gui grumbled, noticing Athena's smile.

Athena sank into her fighting stance, tempted to at least cause the brute some pain. Then she remembered that even if she could disarm him, Zhao had two armed men ahead and many more waiting back at the truck. For now, it was better to bide her time and wait for her odds to improve.

She turned and reluctantly shuffled on. Although the sound of the leading man hacking the ferns came from somewhere ahead, he was now out of sight. Athena was about to quicken her pace when an explosion roared through the bushes.

The sound hit Athena like a physical blow, followed by a shower of dirt and vegetation. The explosion rolled up the hillside, echoing back seconds later. Birds squawked, leaping into flight, and rocks and clumps of earth thudded back down. Through the ringing in her ears, Athena heard screaming. Gui's hand clamped onto her arm, pulling her down into a crouch.

"Nobody moves!" Zhao shouted from just a few feet ahead. "Don't take a single step."

The screaming continued. Through a gap in the vegetation, Athena saw one of the men lying on the ground.

"It's ... he's been hit," the second guard shouted. It took Athena a moment to realize who the voice belonged to. So far, she'd only heard the men take instructions—an extreme version of the strong and silent type.

"End it," Zhao said, her voice ice cold. "We don't have time for this."

A single shot cracked through the morning air. Then silence, broken only by the soft patter of settling dirt and leaves.

Zhao appeared through the leaves, moving back toward the truck. "Landmines," she said, her voice emotionless. "Back to the truck. Gui, you head back to that de-mining operation. We need their equipment, whatever the cost."

37

THE EXPLOSION ECHOED OUT ACROSS THE LAKE, SENDING ripples across its previously still surface. A flock of birds erupted from the treetops, their panicked cries filling the air as they fled the disturbance.

Eden instinctively dropped into a crouch, her hand reaching for her weapon. Baxter did the same, spinning around and scanning the lake for any sign of incoming danger. Lavigne wailed, covering his face with his hands.

The monk remained eerily calm, his expression one of sorrow rather than surprise.

"That is what I meant by death." He pointed out across the water as a plume of dark smoke rose into the sky, twisting its way into the heavens. The sound of the explosion faded, silence settling over the landscape as though the birds were too stunned to continue their song.

Eden straightened up, watching the rising smoke. "Was that a ...?"

The monk nodded gravely, answering the question before it was complete. "That was a landmine. One of thousands left behind by wars long past. They lie beneath the soil, waiting for an unwary step to awaken them."

"Horrible! This is why I don't leave Paris," Lavigne moaned, his earlier complaints about insects and dust paling into insignificance.

"Many have tried to reach Prasat Lotus Neak," the monk said, nodding toward the hillside. "Some are pilgrims seeking enlightenment, others are treasure hunters seeking personal gain. None have made it there and returned."

"There must be a record of where the mines were laid?" Eden said.

"The placement of the mines was purposefully random, designed to make the area impassable," the monk said. "Plus, after this much time, roots and earth movements will have further shifted them." He pointed out across the lake. "An attempt to reach that temple is a death sentence. It is no longer for humankind."

"Why has no one cleared a path?" Baxter said.

"Look at this area," the monk said, spreading his arms. "Few people live here. De-mining efforts are concentrated near population centers. Even there, the mines are often too numerous to be totally cleared."

"That certainly complicates things," Baxter said, emitting a low whistle.

"But if these people are as determined as you say, they will try regardless."

"We have to beat them there," Eden said, stripping off her bike jacket and trousers. She folded the protective gear and placed it on the saddle. Baxter did the same, pacing toward the lake.

"You ... you want us to go in there?" Lavigne sputtered, a shaking finger pointing across the lake. "You can't be sérieux!"

Eden turned and shot the professor a look. "Stay here if you want, we'll go and find the lost temple without you."

The muscles in Lavigne's face tensed as though the decision was putting a physical strain on his body. His lips twisted one way and the next. "I'm coming, wait!" he shouted, struggling out of his motorbike gear. He stashed the protective gear on the bike and ran after them.

Eden looked out over the water, considering the best way across.

"In the river of life, one must navigate both calm and turbulent waters to reach the shore of understanding," the monk said, his voice quiet but clear.

Eden turned to look at the holy man and offered a smile. The monk lifted his hands together in a gesture of prayer.

Eden returned the gesture and turned back toward the lake. As she turned, she saw something she hadn't noticed before. Behind the twisted roots of a large tree sat a traditional Khmer fishing boat.

She crossed to the tree, scrambled around the roots, and inspected the craft. It was long and narrow, with a raised bow and stern. Although the wood was weathered, allowing it to almost blend in against the thick undergrowth beyond, it looked to be in good condition. She clambered down inside the boat and inspected it for leaks.

"This will get us there," she said, seizing one of the paddles that lay inside. She glanced back toward where the monk had been standing, but the space at the front of the temple was now empty. A cool breeze moved through the trees, rustling the leaves like a whisper.

"At least we're not swimming," Lavigne said, carefully climbing inside. "Small mercies."

Baxter untied the boat, pushed it out into the lake, and then jumped in. Eden settled into the front seat and Baxter took the rear, each grabbing a paddle. Lavigne propped himself up in the middle, looking out at the lake as though he expected something to leap out and bite him.

Eden dipped her paddle in the murky water and made the first stroke. The boat slid smoothly away from the shore and out onto the lake. Navigating through the lotus flowers was difficult, paddles snagging on the thick roots. Eden and Baxter paddled in silence, listening to the gentle splashing of the paddles and the occasional cry of a distant bird.

As they moved further from the shore, the towering cliff and the cascading water came into clearer view. Eden noticed now that, as opposed to falling from the top of the cliff, the water spurted from an opening two-thirds of the way up.

"That waterfall is bigger than I thought," Lavigne said, looking nervously up at the ribbon of white foaming water.

Eden followed the Frenchman's gaze and had to admit that he was correct. The hill, which had seemed modest from the other side, now blocked out the sky. Dense jungle hung over the rocks, creepers and vines dangling all the way down to the lake's surface. The scene was so picturesque, that even one of the theme parks that Eden never saw the point of would struggle to do a better job.

The boat rocked from side to side as they passed the waterfall, each movement eliciting a whimper from Lavigne. After a minute or two of intense paddling, they reached the cliff face, just a few boat lengths beyond the waterfall.

Eden scrambled to the bow and grabbed one of the vines. About the width of her wrist, the vine was certainly strong enough for what she had planned. Even so, she pulled on it, to make sure it was secure. The vine took her weight without giving an inch. She tied the boat to the vine to hold it in position and turned to face Baxter and Lavigne.

She was about to explain their next move when the throb of a powerful engine drifted across the landscape.

"What's that?" Lavigne said, looking up at the cliff.

"I'm not sure," Eden said. "But we'll soon find—"

Another explosion rocked the hillside. The sound swept across the lake and reverberated back from the other side.

"Whatever they're doing, they're getting close," Baxter said.

"We'd better move," Eden said, looking up at the cliff face.

"I'm going to hate it." Lavigne eyed the great wall of rock with disdain.

"Then I won't explain," Eden said, smiling sweetly. "Just pretend you're in Paris, walking around a park or something." She swung off her backpack and removed a length of rope. She made a loop out of one end, passed it to Lavigne, and secured the other end around her waist.

"What's ... what's that for?" Lavigne said, holding the rope up.

"Just tie it like this," Eden said, pointing at the end of the rope she'd tied around herself. "Make it secure and then forget all about it." Without waiting to hear Lavigne's protests, she grabbed the vine and hauled herself out of the boat.

"I'm in Paris, walking around the park," Lavigne said, doing what he'd been told. Then, with the enthusiasm of a death row inmate, he moved toward the cliff face. Looking up at Eden, who was already over twenty feet above, he seized the vine and dragged himself upward.

Baxter waited until Lavigne was well on his way before following. Climbing slowly, he kept his eye on the professor just in case he should be required to play an impromptu game of 'Catch the Frenchman'.

Nearing the halfway point, the rope around Eden's waist pulled taut. Twisting her hand around a vine, she paused and looked down. Lavigne was the very picture of concentration, picking his way up the rock face. She listened intently, catching his repeated mantra: "Don't look down ... ne regarde pas en bas..." murmured alternately in English and French.

Although the climb was arduous, with the vines and rocks slick from the waterfall's spray, the cliff offered plenty of handholds. Also, after the first minute or so, the cliff face had become less steep, allowing them to scramble as opposed to climb.

"We're almost there," Eden shouted, exaggerating their progress for Lavigne's benefit.

Lavigne reached up, grabbed the next section of vine, and froze. The sudden halt sent a shudder up the rope, attracting Eden's attention. She watched the professor, his lips moving like a fish out of water. She noticed what he was looking at, the same moment he managed to form a word.

"Mon Dieu! Mon Dieu!" Lavigne stuttered, looking at the sleek, sinuous form which moved out from the cliff face and wrapped itself around his wrist. His eyes grew to the size of saucers. He shook with fear, his grip on the vines weakening.

"S-s-s..." Lavigne stuttered, his voice barely above a whisper. The thing on his arm moved, and a small, forked tongue flicked out. Then Lavigne screamed.

"Snaaaake! Serpent! Au Secours! Help!"

38

FROM HER POSITION ABOVE, EDEN LOCKED HER HANDS AND feet into the cliff face. She watched as the snake eyed Lavigne curiously. Even from this distance, she recognized it as an Indochinese rat snake—very common in Southeast Asia and well known for making their home in cliffs and forests. The good news was that the rat snake was not venomous. The bad news, however, was that Lavigne was about to throw himself off the cliff with fear.

"Don't move!" Eden yelled. "Stay still! It's not attacking you! You're going to be fine."

Lavigne screeched again, the sound drowning out Eden's reassurance.

"Baxter!" Eden shouted, leaning away from the cliff face to attract Baxter's attention. "We need to get to him now!"

Baxter sprang into action, scrambling up the cliff with the agility of a seasoned climber.

Lavigne squeezed his eyes shut, his mouth flailing in a continuous wail of fear. The snake, disturbed by all the commotion, slithered further up Lavigne's arm.

Although Baxter was closing in on the professor, he still had quite a distance to climb.

"Listen to me," Eden shouted again, hoping to calm Lavigne and buy them time. "It's a rat snake. It's harmless."

As the snake neared Lavigne's upper arm, the professor opened his eyes. He wailed louder now, removing his arm from the cliff and trying to shake the snake off.

Just as it seemed Lavigne might lose his tenuous grip on the vine, Baxter reached him. In one swift motion, he wrapped an arm around Lavigne's waist, securing him against the cliff face. Baxter then gently unwound the creature from Lavigne's arm and released it onto a nearby vine. The snake, seemingly glad to be out of the commotion, quickly disappeared into a crevice.

With Eden pulling on the rope, and Baxter helping him from the side, they half dragged, half shoved Lavigne up the cliff. The professor, still shaking but no longer actively resisting, allowed himself to be guided, inch by painstaking inch.

Eden reached the top first. Wedging her feet against the ledge, she pulled hard on the rope. As the professor neared the top, Eden leaned across the precipice and grabbed him by the arms. She dragged the professor up and over the edge where he collapsed onto his back, chest heaving, and limbs splayed out like a starfish.

"Je suis vivant," Lavigne muttered, "I'm alive."

Eden turned back to the cliff edge, intending to help Baxter up the last few feet, but he had already pulled himself up and over the edge with ease.

"I ... I thought ..." Lavigne gasped, his face pale and slick with sweat.

Eden nodded and placed a hand on the professor's shoulder.

"Let's find this temple and be done with this madness," Lavigne said, forcing himself to his feet and looking out into the forest.

Another explosion roared through the forest behind them. It was closer this time, the sound sharp, and distinct.

Eden turned to face the sound and then paced across to a nearby tree. She scrambled up the trunk, her fingers easily gripping the rough bark. Reaching a sturdy branch near the top, she peered down the hillside toward the explosion. She swung off her pack and dug out a pair of binoculars. Scanning the forest beneath them, she saw movement.

At least a quarter of a mile away, a path cut through the foliage. Several men stood in the cutting, rifles slung casually around their shoulders. A mechanical thrumming, grinding noise started up, drifting up the hillside in rhythmic pulses. She traced the cutting with the binoculars, looking for the source of the sound. At the front of the cutting, she saw a large, armored vehicle battering its way through the thick vegetation. The machine lumbered forward at a walking pace, the apparatus at the front of it whipping the plants out of the way.

"That's a mine-clearing machine," she said to herself, watching the rotating flails churning the earth. As Eden watched, the machine triggered another mine. The explosion kicked up a cloud of dirt and debris, but the armored vehicle didn't even slow.

Eden turned away from Zhao's crew and looked out across the forest. Rising from the canopy nearby, she saw a single stone tower, constructed in the shape of a lotus bud. Adjusting the focus, she picked out intricate carvings, serpentine forms twisting and intertwining beneath moss and grime.

She removed the binoculars, looked at the dense canopy,

then back at the mine-clearing machine. She shimmied down the tree, jumping the last few feet to land between Baxter and Lavigne.

"The temple's right there," she said, slightly out of breath. She pointed through the trees and ran through what she'd seen.

"But how can we possibly get there?" Lavigne said, looking around. "This whole area is covered with land-mines. We could step on one and ... kaboom."

"All we need to do is reach the temple without touching the ground," Eden said, smiling angelically.

"I'm not going to like this," Lavigne replied.

"The trees," Baxter said, pointing upwards. "We use the trees."

"Exactly," Eden said. "The canopy is easily dense enough for us to climb through."

"Bypassing the mines and beating Zhao there," Baxter added.

"You want us to swing through the trees like monkeys?" Lavigne stammered, paling once again.

"It's the trees or the mines," Eden said, shrugging. "I know what I'd choose." Before Lavigne could answer, she climbed up the tree again. Baxter followed, with Lavigne bringing up the rear, muttering prayers under his breath.

They ascended into the canopy, surrounded by the jungle chorus. Birds called out in alarm, monkeys squawked, insects zinged, and behind it all, the de-mining machine howled.

Eden paused on a thick branch to work out the path ahead. The temple's tower was visible through gaps in the foliage, tantalizingly close, but still so far. She took one end of the rope and edged out across the branch of one tree and onto the next. She passed through two more trees and tied the rope onto a sturdy branch.

Baxter tied off the other end, giving Lavigne something to hold on to as he passed from tree to tree. When the professor was across, Baxter untied the rope and scrambled over.

Eden took the other end of the rope and climbed again. She chose her path carefully, staying on sturdy branches, and trying to avoid long stretches between trunks. Once or twice, she paused to find the temple, which was visible only in fleeting glimpses through the foliage.

She tied off the rope again, allowing Lavigne to catch up. While she waited for the professor, she listened to the approaching rumble of the de-mining machine. It sounded as though they were getting closer, although sound carried in strange ways through the jungle.

Once Lavigne was again in position, Eden scrambled through a few more trees and pulled aside a curtain of vines to reveal the temple wall. She reached out and ran her fingers across the stone.

"Prasat Lotus Neak," Lavigne muttered, scrambling through a tree to get a better look. He reached the structure and surveyed the stone. "The craftsmanship, even after all these centuries …"

"What we're looking for isn't out here," Eden said, scanning the wall for a potential entry point. "We need to get inside."

Baxter arrived with the other end of the rope. They secured one end of the rope to the tree and lowered the other down against the temple wall.

Eden scrambled down, using both the rope and the surrounding vines. She dropped onto a ledge that circled the structure a few feet off the ground. Moving aside, she cleared the way for Lavigne and Baxter, who wasted no time following her down. For a moment, all three stood, looking up at the tower, which was now obscured by the trees overhead.

"This way, I think," Eden said, leading them around the structure. She turned the corner and stopped abruptly, with Lavigne almost running into her. Two giant seven-headed stone serpents stood on either side of a doorway.

"Incroyable!" Lavigne whispered, stepping around Eden and approaching the doorway.

He froze and looked up at the effigies, even after all this time, their eyes gleaming with a lifelike intensity.

"Let's get inside," Eden said, stepping into the gloom.

39

Eden led the way inside the temple, the beam of her flashlight cutting through the gloom. With each step, the air grew cooler, and the number of dust motes flying through the flashlight beam increased.

"We could be the first people to see this in decades, if not longer," Lavigne whispered, his voice filled with awe. "It's .... It's truly incroyable." He swung his flashlight across a wall, revealing complex and detailed carvings.

"Wait a second," Baxter said, his attention drawn to a detail in the carving. He stepped closer to Lavigne, his eyes fixed on the vast expanse of intricately worked stone. "This doesn't make any sense, look."

Eden approached to see what they were looking at; three flashlight beams now converging on the wall.

"I can't believe I'm seeing this," Lavigne said, inhaling sharply. "This is the stuff of legend."

"Wait a second—forget the stegosaurus at Ta Prohm. This is something else," Eden said, her voice trembling. She stared at the carving, not quite understanding what she was seeing. In the center of the scene, a giant creature resembling a tyrannosaur charged at an enemy, its powerful jaws protruding from the stone. Behind it, warriors fired arrows from the back of a stegosaurus and a group of soldiers clung to the long neck of a diplodocus as it swept through enemy ranks like a living battering ram.

"That wasn't in my childhood dinosaur book," Baxter said, indicating a creature with six legs and a frill of feathers around its neck.

"And look at the people," Eden said, focusing on a group of human-looking figures with elongated limbs and features of impossible symmetry. "Is someone going to claim the person that carved this just had an off day?"

"This is extraordinary," Lavigne said, removing and replacing his spectacles as though they might be lying to him. "These images ... they're unlike anything I've ever seen in Khmer art."

"They're unlike anything I've ever seen in mainstream history," Baxter added.

"Wait a second." Eden dragged her focus away from the carvings and looked at Lavigne. "Do you think it's possible that this temple was *lost* on purpose?"

Lavigne's gaze tightened in thought. "It's possible, I suppose," he said. "But, by who?"

Eden shrugged and turned her attention back to the carvings.

"Whoever it was didn't want us to know that the builders of this place knew about technology far ahead of their time," Baxter said.

A breeze drifted through the temple, carrying with it the distant grumble of the approaching machine.

"We need to keep moving," Eden said, gazing deeper into the temple. "Zhao and her men aren't far behind."

Eden led them onward, Lavigne narrating the meanings of the carvings as they passed. From his commentary, Eden understood they ranged from depictions of grand battles, celestial events, or strange devices—the purpose of which weren't clear.

They entered the temple's immense central chamber and came to a halt. Eden swept her light across the space, taking in the stepped floor that led to a stone platform with an altar at its center. Her beam settled on an altar and a metallic disc mounted on the top.

"I suspect that's what we're looking for," Eden said, voice now booming with a cathedral-like echo.

"That's it, exactly," Lavigne said, his flashlight beam joining Eden's. "The twin of the one Zhao has." Eager to see the disc up close, the professor rushed into the chamber.

"Wait, it might be a trap," Eden said, recalling their recent trip to a similar chamber buried beneath Egypt's desert sands. She scanned the floor, searching for signs of hidden mechanisms or unseen codes. Constructed with large and uneven flagstones, there was no indication of pressure-sensitive devices, and no markings suggesting which stones were safe and which were not.

"There's no record of the Khmer people utilizing such traps," Lavigne said, striding on and climbing the first stair. The stone held and Lavigne moved his other foot up onto the riser. "You see," he said, holding out his hands as though he had just completed a conjuring trick. "No problem at all."

Lavigne took another step, his eyes locked on the disc on the altar ahead. As his boot pressed down, a muted click sounded. A deep, ominous rumble rang through the chamber, shaking dust from ceiling and sending small pebbles skittering across the ground. Then, grumbling like a waking giant, the slab beneath Lavigne's feet shifted and revealed a hidden pit below. Lavigne teetered backward, then lurched forward, his arms flailing desperately for something to grasp but finding only empty air.

"Lavigne!" Eden shouted, lunging toward the professor.

Lavigne's arms whipped this way and that like a baby bird attempting its first flight. For a moment, it looked as though he might step back on to the previous slab, but his balance was off.

Eden dashed toward him but was too far away. Fortunately, Baxter was closer. With a quick lunge, he reached into the void. His fingers closed tightly around the professor's upper arm. The sudden weight nearly pulled Baxter off balance, but he dug his heels into the stone floor, bracing himself against the edge of the pit.

"I've got you!" Baxter grunted, straining against Lavigne's weight.

Eden grabbed Baxter's belt and together they dragged Lavigne out of the pit and onto solid ground. Baxter and Eden shared a glance at the near miss.

Lavigne swayed on his feet, sucking in deep breaths. He tried to speak, only stammering something inaudible.

"Look at this," Eden said, stepping up to the edge of the pit and pointing her flashlight beam into the chasm. The light revealed a drop of at least a hundred feet with a grim sight at the bottom. Skeletal remains, some still draped in tattered cloth, lay scattered across the pit's stone floor.

"Terrible," Lavigne whispered, stepping as close to the edge as he dared. "We're not the first to fall for this trap."

"I don't think we're the second, or third," Eden said, passing her flashlight beam to another pair of skeletons. "Those men have weapons, look." She focused her beam on rusted weapons and tattered remnants of uniforms.

"They look relatively recent too," Baxter said.

Lavigne leaned forward, squinting to get a better look. His eyes widened in recognition. "You're right. Those uniforms ... they're Khmer Rouge."

"The Khmer Rouge knew about this place?" Eden said, her voice low.

"That explains the landmines," Baxter said.

A groaning sound came from the floor as the slab which had fallen swung back into position.

"That's amazing," Eden said, watching the slab click back into place as though it had never been moved. She looked out at the vast expanse of the chamber. The floor comprised hundreds of slabs, with no way to know which, if any of them, were safe to walk on.

"Masterful work," Lavigne said.

Baxter stepped forward and tested the slab with his toe. "It feels solid. There must be some kind of counterweight system."

"It makes sense that the Khmer Rouge came here," Lavigne said, pushing his spectacles further up his nose. "Whilst they sought to destroy much of Cambodia's cultural heritage, they were also power-hungry. Many believe that they had a secret unit dedicated to finding and exploiting ancient artifacts."

"I'm glad they didn't find this one," Eden said.

"And they met the same fate we almost did," Baxter added.

"You did," Eden said, turning and glaring at Lavigne. "You might be 'king of the classroom', but out here in the real-world things are dangerous."

"You're telling me," Lavigne said, physically shuddering. "I'm never leaving Paris again."

As if to reinforce Eden's claims of impending danger, the grumble of Zhao's machine drifted through the temple.

"It sounds like they're getting closer," Baxter said, turning toward the noise.

"We need to find a way across this chamber," Eden said. "And fast."

40

Eden looked out across the chamber, searching for something that pointed to their safe passage across.

"The craftsmanship, it's just breathtaking," Lavigne muttered, fixated on one of the carvings, yet remaining perfectly still.

"Wait, look at that," Eden said, moving her flashlight beam from one carving to the next. "It looks as though a lot of the figures are pointing towards the ceiling." She craned her neck to look at the ceiling high above them.

"Yes, you're right. That is irregular," Lavigne agreed, looking up at the ceiling too.

For a few seconds, all three of them stood in silence, focusing on the vaulted blocks high above.

"It's a map," Lavigne said, recognizing the lines which spanned from one side of the chamber to the other.

"Do you think ... it couldn't be ..." Eden said, the curvature of the lines above looking familiar. "Could it represent the Mekong River?"

Lavigne inhaled, his eyes darting across the intricate details. "Incroyable," he whispered, his voice filled with awe.

"Tu as raison! That makes sense. The ancient Khmer people ... their entire civilization was built around the rivers."

"It looks like there's an inscription, there in the center," Baxter said, his flashlight beam illuminating a cluster of symbols. "It looks like Khmer script, although I'm no expert."

Lavigne turned his attention to the script, which was carved directly above the disc. He squinted at the text for several seconds, his lips moving as he read.

"No rush," Eden said, the detonation of another mine shaking the hillside.

"It's ... it's a riddle of sorts." Lavigne said, his brow furrowed in concentration. "The sacred waters flow, a path to enlightenment. Follow the river's embrace and find safe passage to the heart of wisdom."

"That makes sense," Eden said.

"It does?" Baxter said, clearly expecting Eden to make a sarcastic comment.

"Yes, thank you very much," Eden said. "Remember, my father told us that the Khmer Empire was constantly under threat from their neighbors. During times of invasion, they used the rivers as a lifeline."

"Quite right," Lavigne said, nodding as though trying to dislodge something. "The Mekong and its tributaries weren't simply trade routes or sources of water; they were paths to safety. The rivers were seen as divine protectors."

"Maybe the builders of this temple used that knowledge as a test of worthiness," Eden said. "I think we have to follow the path of the river across the chamber." She placed one foot on the slab beside her, which was directly beneath the curving river above. She slowly shifted her weight onto the foot, ready to pull back if the slab gave way.

"That would make sense," Lavigne said, still totally

absorbed in the inscriptions above. "It's designed to catch those who don't understand or respect the river."

When the slab didn't move, Eden placed her other foot beside the first. She listened for the grinding noise which had preceded the previous slab's movement. When no sound came, and the slab remained in position, she looked up at the ceiling again. Following the outline of the river, she selected the next slab and stepped across.

Lavigne looked down from the ceiling, and he saw Eden, already several feet out across the floor. "Whoaah, are you sure this is a good idea? I know our calculations seem correct, but it's one thing—"

"Get following, professor," Eden said, throwing him a glance. "We don't have time to wait!"

Reaching the slab, Eden paused and, once again, checked the carving above. Following the river's path, she placed her foot on the next section of the floor. She crossed the slab and looked back up at the carving to check her next move. Tracing the river's path depicted in the design, she carefully chose the next slab and stepped across.

"Even after centuries, the precision of these stones ... it's astounding," Lavigne said, tracing Eden's footsteps exactly. His eyes darted from side to side, no doubt thinking about the chasm below which threatened to swallow them at any moment.

Baxter brought up the rear, stepping precisely from stone to stone.

"We'll admire it once we're across," Eden said, pausing to check the route. "The river forks into two here." She pointed at the carving. "Which way?"

Lavigne studied the ceiling intently, his brow furrowed. After a moment, he pointed to the left branch. "That one," he said, not as confidently as Eden would like. "That's the Tonle Sap, that led to the heart of the Khmer Empire."

"You're sure?" Eden said. "The stakes are pretty—"

"I don't need to be reminded of the danger," Lavigne snapped. "You think I'm here because I want to be? I should be sitting in Le Café Noir, enjoying the quiet, not dodging death traps in some cursed temple."

"Nice of them to name a café after me," Eden said, softening her tone. "You'll be back there soon."

Lavigne scowled, his eyes almost closing.

"The Tonlé Sap." Eden took a deep breath and placed her foot on the slab corresponding to the left fork. She listened closely for the sound of moving stones, only moving her other foot across when the slab held firm.

"Good call, Professor," Eden said, offering Lavigne a smile of encouragement. She pressed on, following the river's winding path toward the center of the chamber. Eventually, and not a moment too soon, she stepped up onto the raised section in the center of the chamber.

A deafening roar tore through the chamber, a vibration so intense it shook the ground beneath their feet. The stone slabs trembled, and clouds of dust rained down from above.

Certain that the slab beneath her was about to give way, Eden darted back to the previous stone and dropped to all fours.

The sound continued for a few seconds, raining dust and debris through the chamber. Then, as quickly as it had begun, it cut out.

"What was that?" Lavigne whispered, looking around wildly.

"I'm not sure," Eden said, climbing to her feet.

"It's Zhao," Baxter said, turning to face the way they'd come. "She's reached the temple entrance."

Then, rising above the silence, they heard muffled voices and heavy footsteps.

"She's here," Eden said.

"There has to be another way out," Lavigne said, looking into the gloom at the rear of the temple. "These places were often built with escape routes."

"First, we get what we came for," Eden said, steadying her nerves and stepping up onto the raised platform in the center of the chamber. She shifted cautiously from one foot to the other, checking for movement. When the surface remained still, she took another step forward.

"Incroyable," Lavigne said, approaching the object which glowed an iridescent gold in the beams of their flashlights. He inched toward the disc and bent over to look closely without touching it.

The rhythmic thud of boots on stone reverberated through the chamber, growing louder with each passing second.

Lavigne removed something from his pocket and rubbed his scarf across it. Then he leaned in and brushed the scarf across the surface of the disc. Starting with the mirrored central section, he worked his way outward.

Eden was about to ask what he was doing when a raised voice bellowed through the chamber.

"You and you, that way," Zhao said, clearly sending her men to check on different parts of the temple. The footsteps diverged, branching off in several directions. Some grew fainter, moving away to explore other parts of the temple, others got louder as they neared.

Eden spun around to look at the entrance. Deep within the gloom, beams of light whipped from side to side.

"It's as though ... it's not of this world," Lavigne said,

completely absorbed by the artifact. He repeated the process with his scarf, cleaning the other side of the disc.

The deafening echo of gunshots boomed through the chamber, followed by the sharp ping of bullets ricocheting from the stone.

"Get down!" Eden shouted, shoving Lavigne behind the altar. Baxter dove for cover alongside them.

41

EDEN AND BAXTER CRAWLED TO OPPOSITE SIDES OF THE ALTAR, slid out their weapons, and laid down some return fire. When the incoming bullets had stopped, Eden peered around the side of the stone block.

One of Zhao's men had been hit in the leg. The rest of the bullets had smashed uselessly into the wall at the back of the chamber.

"Stop your fire!" Zhao shouted, as the men prepared to shoot again. She stepped out of the gloom and into the chamber. Men flanked her on both sides, their guns raised. "Are you going to cower there all day?"

Eden stood up slowly, pointing her weapon at Zhao. Baxter climbed to his feet a moment later.

"Mei-Ling Zhao, I wondered how long it would be until we met," Eden said, striding around the altar in a show of faux-confidence. "I'm going to lower my weapon now, I suggest your meatheads do the same."

Zhao nodded and her men lowered their weapons at the same time as Eden and Baxter did.

"Eden Black." Zhao flashed Eden a look that was so cold

it felt as though the temperature of the chamber had dropped a few degrees. "And this is the acclaimed Captain Baxter, I assume. Have you got someone else lurking back there, too?"

Eden glanced down at Lavigne who was still cowering behind the altar. Realizing he had been spotted, and the game was up, Lavigne climbed shakily to his feet.

"Professor Lavigne," Zhao said, using the tone a psychopath might choose to taunt a trapped animal. "I didn't think we would see each other again so soon. I really should have killed you while I had the chance."

Lavigne whimpered and raised his hands.

Zhao laughed and turned her attention to Eden. "It's a pleasure to finally meet you. I've been a fan of your work for some time."

"Then you'll know what's about to happen," Eden said, flexing her shoulders as though ready for a boxing match.

"Yes. You're about to hand me that disc," Zhao replied, her tone humorless.

"This old thing," Eden said, nodding toward the disc. "You can get ten for five dollars at the market. But if you want this one, no bother." Eden shrugged.

"Why don't you send your guard dogs to come and get it?" Baxter added.

Zhao looked from Eden to Baxter. Clearly confident her scores of armed men gave her the upper hand, she flicked her wrist. The men standing either side of Zhao stepped forward in unison.

Eden stood rooted to the spot, careful not to betray any sign that she knew what was about to unfold. She silently prayed that Lavigne, notorious for blurting out his thoughts the instant they formed, would, for once, manage to keep his mouth shut.

Zhao's lips twisted together, distorting what would have been a pretty face into some kind of horrendous mask. Watching the woman, Eden couldn't see a shred of likeness with her friend, who smiled and joked in even the direst situations.

The men stepped forward again, crossing the invisible boundary. Before anything moved, they took another step forward, leaving the safety of solid ground far behind. For what felt like the longest time, nothing happened. Then, the familiar sound of stones grinding together rose through the chamber. The slab beneath the thugs' feet shifted, causing the men to look around in panic. Their expressions morphed from menace to terror.

As the floor beneath them dropped, they flailed, trying to grab on to something to arrest their fall. A few of Zhao's other men shifted from foot to foot as though waiting for an instruction to rescue their falling comrades. Zhao, watching with grim indifference, offered no such instruction.

With a look of horror, the men plunged into the yawning chasm. Their screams rang out until a crunch silenced them for good.

"Ahh, we forgot to mention that" Eden said, glancing at Baxter.

"Oh yeah, sorry," Baxter said, shrugging.

"A little welcome present from the architects who built this place." Eden pointed at the floor.

The slabs, which had dropped, swung back into place, once again concealing the trap.

"Stop playing games," Zhao spat, a muscle in her temple now visibly pulsing.

"I wouldn't play games when lives are at stake," Eden said, raising her hands in a placating gesture. "This place is a deathtrap, and that is definitely not my fault."

"I heard that you were exasperating," Zhao said, folding her arms. "You won't get away with it with me."

"Challenge accepted," Eden shot back.

"Throw me the disc," Zhao said, unfurling her arms and pointing at the disc.

"This?" Eden said, pointing casually at the disc as though noticing it for the first time. "Actually, now that I've thought about it, I've decided to keep this one for myself. I've grown fond of it."

Zhao's lips twisted in an unnatural manner. "Bring her here," she said, snapping her fingers.

Eden swallowed, bracing herself for the inevitable. Zhao held a card Eden couldn't match.

"Touch me again, and I'll snap your hands off," came a voice Eden recognized immediately. Looking beyond Zhao, she saw more flashlight beams moving in the passageway. Footsteps drummed, the volume increasing with each step. More men appeared, this time dragging a familiar figure with them.

"Nice place you've got here," Athena said, walking into the chamber. She looked around, taking in the carvings on the walls and ceiling. When her eyes met Eden's, she froze. The guards behind her stepped up either side and seized her by the arms.

"I believe you call this young lady Athena," Zhao said, shooting a loveless look at her daughter.

For a moment, Athena remained stationary. Then, realizing the men held her, she dropped her weight, breaking the thugs' grip on her arms. As she fell, she swept her leg in a wide arc, knocking one guard off his feet.

"I told you not to touch me," she said, twisting away from the second guard's grasp.

Eden watched in awe as Athena seized the man's wrist,

twisting it sharply. The man let out a cry of pain, his grip loosening until the gun slipped from his hand and clattered to the floor.

The second thug lunged at her, but Athena pivoted and drove her elbow into his kidney. She grabbed the guard's arm, spun it around, and used his own momentum to slam him into the wall. He crumpled to the ground in a cloud of dust.

Zhao pulled out a handgun and fired, the bullets zinging through the air above Athena's head and smashing the arms off a stone deva frozen mid-dance. Although the shot sailed wide, Zhao's point had been made.

Athena stopped fighting, straightened up, and looked at her mother.

"That's better," Zhao said. She gestured, and two more men stepped up behind Athena. Clearly realizing that she was overpowered, Athena didn't struggle this time.

"You would kill your own daughter for this?" Eden said, looking from Zhao to Athena and back again.

"She should never have been born," Zhao said, her tone flat and emotionless. "I'm certain that you have done your research, so you know that having her was part of my job. I was undercover and her father was the target. He had information, and he wanted a baby. It was my duty to do everything in my power for the mission."

"You're sick," Athena spat, her eyes blazing with fury.

"I should have ended it back then." Zhao looked at Athena, her expression cool and detached. "She's been a thorn in my side since birth."

Eden opened her mouth to say something, but then Zhao continued.

"Let's not waste any more time. We have places to be." She clapped her hands. "Here's what will happen: you either throw me the disc, or I'll have *Athena* go and get it." She pronounced Athena's name as though it were a word in a foreign language. Zhao flicked her wrist, and the men shoved Athena toward the trap.

Eden looked at the position of her friend's feet, now a few inches from the slabs that would collapse under her weight.

"You don't understand what you're asking for," Eden said, injecting a note of desperation into her voice.

"This ... this isn't just an artifact," Lavigne stuttered. "It's a key to something far greater, something that could change the course of history."

"Oh, I understand," Zhao said, arching an eyebrow. "I'm not here to discuss my plans ... certainly not with you."

"Is she always this argumentative?" Eden said, her tone lightening and her gaze turning to Athena.

"Always. You should see it when the whole family gets together. She's a living nightmare." Athena's tone showed Eden that, although captured, she was far from beaten. "But other than the threats of death and violence, we're getting along fine."

"Like a walnut," Eden said. "Once you get through that shell—"

"Silence!" Zhao roared. "For every second you waste my time, my men will shove her an inch forward. Let's see how long you continue with these games." Zhao clicked her fingers. Although keeping their feet firmly planted on the floor, the men shoved Athena toward the unseen precipice.

Eden's eyes darted from Athena to the disc, then on to the treacherous floor.

"Fine," Eden said. "Let her go and then we'll discuss this."

"You are in no position to negotiate." Zhao's lips curled into a cold smile. "Throw the disc to me now, and I will decide what to do with you. You never know, I could use someone like you in my organization." Zhao snapped her fingers again, and the men shoved Athena another inch toward the chasm.

"This is your last chance," Zhao said. "Thow me the disc or your friend here takes an express ride to the bottom of that pit."

Eden frowned and reached for the disc, her hand shaking under the tension.

"Don't do it!" Athena shouted, her voice filling the chamber. "Whatever this thing is, it's too important to—"

Zhao made a gesture, and the men shoved Athena again. Her toes now crossed the line. The mechanism started to groan as Athena rocked forward and back.

"Tick tock, Eden," Zhao said, her voice drenched in false sweetness. "What's it going to be? The disc, or your friend's life?"

Eden met Athena's eyes, hoping to communicate that she would stop Zhao and whatever horrors she had planned.

"You want it so badly? Here, catch!" Baxter lunged forward, snatched up the disc and hurled it at Zhao like a discus.

"What! No!" Athena shouted as the disc arched through the air, spinning end over end.

Zhao looked up at the artifact, her eyes widening and her hands reaching out to rescue it from the fall. Her men looked up at it too, their attention momentarily shifting away from Athena.

Beneath the action, the grinding of old machinery filled the chamber. This time the movement wasn't coming from the floor near Athena, but the slab on which Eden, Baxter, and Lavigne stood.

"Something's happening," Lavigne said, his voice shaking. The large stone altar started to drop, grinding against the other stones as it moved. Clouds of dust fell from the ceiling like fine rain.

With her captors distracted, Athena swung around and elbowed the man on her left, then kicked out the legs of the man on her right. She dodged to the side, avoiding their swings, and darted behind them.

The rumbling noise increased. The stone beneath Eden's feet shook violently.

"I think we're going down," Baxter yelled, dropping into a crouch.

"I don't—" Eden started to say, but right at that moment the ground beneath them swung like a trapdoor, sending them into free fall.

42

As dust billowed through the chamber, Athena charged for the exit. She ducked behind Zhao's guards, all captivated by the scene playing out in the center of the space and sprinted back through the passage.

Pausing for a moment, she glanced over her shoulder as Eden, Baxter, and the professor disappeared into a hole in the chamber floor. She wished her friends well, hoping that no harm would come to them, but knew there was nothing she could do.

"Get out!" Zhao's voice cut through the gloom from somewhere nearby. "We've got what we came for. Move out now!"

Multiple flashlights swung 180 degrees, their beams coming her way like searchlights.

Athena set off back the way they'd come at a full sprint. With the flashlights on her back, her shadow danced against the walls ahead.

"Get her!" Zhao roared. "Don't let her escape!"

Boots thundered against stone as the men gave chase, echoes from the walls disguising their position. A bullet cracked past her head, raining down stone chips from the wall beside her.

"Don't shoot, you idiot," Zhao roared. "I want her alive!"

Athena ducked around a corner, her boots slipping on centuries of accumulated grime, one hand trailing along the wall to keep her balance. She tore around another bend and guard stepped into her path, rifle raised.

She leaped into action and grabbed the barrel, forcing it up as the man pulled the trigger. The weapon discharged, the muzzle flash briefly illuminating the carved faces on the walls. Stone chips rained down from where the bullet struck the ceiling. She drove her knee into the man's stomach with a satisfying crunch. As the man doubled over, gasping, Athena twisted the rifle from his grasp. Without hesitation, she pivoted on her back foot and swung the barrel around, catching the guard on the temple with a dull thwack. The man crumpled to the ground without so much as a whimper.

"Stop her!" Zhao's voice cut through the chaos.

Another guard rushed at her through the haze. He threw a wild swing, the kind of punch thrown by someone used to relying on size rather than skill.

Athena easily sidestepped, the fist sailing past her ear. She caught his extended arm at the wrist and elbow and guided his charge neatly into a thick column. He smashed his nose into the stone and slid to the ground.

Athena rounded a corner and into mottled sunlight streaming through the temple's wide doorway.

Behind her, Zhao barked more orders, followed by the rumble of pursuing footsteps.

She burst out of the temple, blinking against the light, but before she could orient herself, a shadow moved to her left. She spun, but too late—Gui's arm locked around her throat like an iron bar. Her feet left the ground as he hoisted her up with terrifying strength, her boots kicking six inches above the floor.

Athena clawed desperately at his forearm, her nails leaving bloody furrows in his skin, but it was like scratching at a tree trunk. She tried to tuck her chin, to create some space, but his grip was unbreakable. Her lungs burned, screaming for air, as spots danced at the edges of her vision.

She smashed her elbow backward, crunching into the big man's ribs, resulting in nothing more than a hiss. With a surge of desperate energy, she swung her legs up, using Gui's grip as a pivot point. Her boots caught the edge of the temple doorway, rough stone scraping against rubber. She kicked against the stone, throwing all her remaining strength into the movement.

The sudden force caught the big man off guard, sending them both staggering backward. He stumbled, his perfect stranglehold finally breaking as his back slammed into a tree. The impact loosened his grip and Athena twisted like a cat, breaking free and gulping in precious air.

She scrambled to her feet, adrenaline surging through her body, ready to sprint into the jungle. But before she could take a step, the temple entrance filled with movement.

"Run, and my men will shoot," Zhao said, emerging from the gloom. Men stood either side, their weapons trained on Athena.

"Impressive," Zhao said, brushing temple dust from her shoulder. "But ultimately futile." Zhao stepped out of the temple with the disc in her hands. "You're lucky I'm not offended easily."

She beckoned to Gui, who swung off his backpack, accepted the disc and slid it inside a specially designed compartment next to the first one.

Zhao stepped up closer to Athena. "You can fight all you want, but you will lose. I'll do this with you, or against you, although of course I would prefer you to be on my side."

"Never," Athena said. "You're crazy."

At that, Zhao grinned, her eyes softening a tiny bit. "Before you call me crazy, look at what the world considers normal. Normal people pump poison into the air. Normal people pay the wealthy to grow fat as children starve in the streets. Normal people fight wars over imaginary lines on a map. Do you really want to be *normal*?"

Mother and daughter held each other's gaze for a long moment.

"What seems crazier to you?" Zhao continued. "Accepting our broken society as normal, or doing something about it?"

Zhao turned to face her men. Shafts of sunlight pierced the canopy, creating spotlights that illuminated swirling clouds of tiny insects.

"Back to the vehicles," Zhao commanded. "And keep vigilant, they could still be nearby."

The men moved forward, shoving Athena down the path through the minefield.

"Remember," Zhao said, turning to look at Athena as the men pushed her forward. "To be part of the change, all you need to do is accept it."

43

EDEN GROANED, HER HEAD THROBBING AS AWARENESS SLOWLY returned. She blinked, trying to focus in the near-total darkness. The fall had knocked the wind out of her, and for a moment, she struggled to remember where she was.

"Baxter? Lavigne?" she called out. The reverberations of her voice suggested they were now in a much smaller space than the chamber above.

"Yep, I'm about two inches away," Baxter said, his voice very close by. "And now I can add a perforated ear drum to my list of injuries."

"Oui, I'm here too," Lavigne said, from a few feet in the opposite direction.

Eden fumbled around and found her flashlight. She clicked it on, and a dazzling beam revealed their new surroundings. She scrambled to her feet, unsteadily at first. "Seriously, though, everyone okay?" Although aching in several places from the impact, nothing seemed to be broken.

"Other than the eardrum, all good," Baxter said, standing and placing a finger in his ear. He wiggled the finger around as though trying to catch a worm trespassing inside his head.

"Keep going like that and I'll sort the other one ..." Eden said, her voice trailing off as she turned her attention to the place in which they found themselves.

"We're in some kind of antechamber," Lavigne said, climbing to his feet and straightening his spectacles, which had miraculously survived the fall.

The space was perhaps a quarter the size of the chamber above, enclosed on all sides by smooth walls which looked as though they'd been polished to a shine. This chamber lacked the intricate carvings that adorned the upper temple. Instead, a single line swirled and twisted its way across the walls, drawing Eden's attention. She followed the line with the beam of her flashlight and noticed that it glittered as though inlaid with something metallic.

Groping around the floor, Baxter and Lavigne found their lights too. They powered them up, and the three beams crisscrossed the chamber.

"Incroyable," Lavigne murmured, limping towards one of the walls for a closer look. "I've never seen anything quite like this. These patterns ..."

Baxter stepped alongside the professor and ran his hand along one of the inlaid lines.

"As intriguing as this is, we need to find a way out," Eden said. "Zhao and her goons are still up there, with Athena ..." Worry lodged in her throat, forming a physical blockage.

Lavigne leaned in closer to one section of the wall. He pushed his spectacles as close to his eyes as he could, as though they worked like a manual optical focus, and squinted at the markings.

"Wait a moment," he said, his voice pitching up with

excitement. "There's an inscription here. It's in ancient Khmer, but … there's something unusual about it."

Eden and Baxter moved closer, their lights joining Lavigne's.

"You going to tell us what it says, or is this a guessing game?" Eden said, the markings making no sense at all to her.

"As Naga, the celestial serpent, winds through the heavens, so too must you," Lavigne said, tracing the symbols with his fingers.

"Naga is a mythical serpent in Hindu and Buddhist mythology, right?" Eden said.

"Oui and is deeply significant in Khmer culture."

"We followed the river up there," Baxter said, pointing toward the ceiling. The slab they had fallen through had shifted back into place, sealing them inside the chamber.

"The connection between Naga and water in Khmer mythology is profound," Lavigne said, thoughtfully. "Naga is intimately linked with rivers and the cycle of water. I think what this is saying, is that by coming down here, we've moved away from the physical and into the spiritual realm."

"Only metaphorically, I hope." Eden swept her light around the chamber, the line carved into the walls glittering like flowing water.

"Naga was thought to reside in the netherworld, coiled around the base of Mount Meru," Lavigne continued, seizing the opportunity to lecture his literally captive audience. "Meru is the sacred mountain at the center of the universe."

"Can we hurry up and follow Naga's path, then?" Eden said. "Athena is out there with a psychopath."

"Well, that psychopath is her mother," Baxter added.

"That's not reassuring," Eden said, throwing Baxter an

icy look. "With the Lotus Key and both discs, Zhao now has the power to do whatever she's planning."

Lavigne stepped up to the wall, studying it with the maddening slowness of someone accustomed to working with objects that had been dead for centuries.

"It's just..."

"Incroyable?" Eden said, in a mock French accent.

"Yes, how did you know?" Lavigne said, seriously. "They have linked the earthly rivers to the celestial Naga, and ultimately to the stars themselves."

"But where does this celestial serpent lead us?" Baxter said.

"Oui, oui, I'm getting to that. Pass me your knife," Lavigne said, holding out his hand. Eden and Baxter exchanged puzzled glances. "Allez, vite! Time waits for no one."

Eden slid her knife from her ankle sheath and passed it to Lavigne. The professor inspected the blade before placing the tip of the knife inside one of the grooves on the wall. He moved the knife along the wall, tracing the twists and turns of the celestial serpent's body with the blade. The pattern doubled back on itself, winding around the walls, before finally ending on what looked like Naga's head. As the knife reached the final point, a faint click preceded a low rumble.

"Not this again," Eden said, dropping into a crouch. Baxter did the same, preparing for the floor to give way and send them into another freefall. The rumble grew in volume, the noise grinding all around the chamber. They turned one way and the next, searching for the source of the noise.

"Look!" Baxter said, pointing to a section of the wall on the far side of the chamber. "That wall, it's moving!"

Stone ground against stone as the wall slid aside,

revealing a narrow passageway. Cool air wafted into the chamber, carrying with it the scent of wet earth.

"Voilà, our way out of here," Lavigne whispered, his hand extended toward the opening.

Eden glanced at the professor, surprised and impressed to see him uncharacteristically calm. She moved across the chamber, her flashlight cutting through the darkness as she directed its beam into the passageway. The narrow corridor, carved directly into the rock, sloped steeply downward, disappearing into the shadows.

"Let's see where Naga wants to take us," she said, glancing at the men. "Come on, time waits for no one!"

Eden turned and led the way down the narrow passageway. The air grew cooler and damper as they descended, the walls closing in around them.

"I was really hoping I wouldn't see another tunnel like this for a while," she said, peering into the passageway. It had only been a few months since she'd ventured into a similar underground labyrinth on the trail of treasure left by the Templars. She cast a glance over her shoulder at Lavigne and Baxter behind her. At least this time she wasn't doing it alone.

"It's as if we're following Naga's journey through the cosmos and the underworld simultaneously." Lavigne murmured, gazing around the tunnel.

"Watch your step, it's slippery down here," Eden said, calling back to Baxter and Lavigne. "But then I suppose Naga doesn't have to worry about falling over, being a snake and all."

As they ventured deeper, a new sound reached their ears —a low, steady rumble that grew louder with each step.

"Do you hear that?" Baxter said. "Or have you actually ruined my hearing?"

"It sounds like water, fast-flowing water." Eden said.

"Fast ... fast-flowing water?" Lavigne stuttered, his expression of amazement flipping in an instant back to fear. "Haven't we had enough for today?"

As they rounded a bend in the passageway, the source of the sound became clear. The narrow corridor widened into a vast cavern, its roof soaring high above, adorned with glistening stalactites of shimmering minerals. Through the center of the cavern, a swift underground river surged, its torrent ringing against the stone.

"That explains the noise," Eden said, stepping to the water's edge and looking down at the deluge. She turned side to side, tracing the river from a low tunnel on one side of the cavern to another on the opposite side.

"No wonder this temple is connected to Naga," Lavigne said, raising his voice against the torrent. "The ancient builders must have known about this subterranean river system. It's like we've entered the underworld itself!"

Baxter pointed out a narrow ledge on the far bank, barely visible through the mist rising from the churning water. "It looks as though the passageway continues on the other side, but it's too far to jump."

"Definitely too far to jump," Lavigne said, shaking his head frantically. "It must be twenty feet across."

"Look," Baxter said, kneeling beside a series of notches cut into the stone. "These look man-made. There must have been a bridge here at some point."

"If it was made of wood, it would have rotted away centuries ago," Lavigne said.

Eden stared at the rushing water, her mind racing. She swept her flashlight beam across the cavern once more, studying the flow of the river. Suddenly, a realization struck her.

"Wait a minute," she said, her voice rising with excitement. "We don't need to get across."

"What ... what do you mean?" Lavigne said.

Instead of replying, Eden looked at Baxter. Clearly grasping Eden's meaning, Baxter nodded. They turned to look at Lavigne and then at the water.

"Non ... non ... non ... non ... you're crazy!" Lavigne said, his arms outstretched, eyes bulging with terror.

"It's the only way," Eden said, her voice firm, but tinged with urgency. "Let's go."

Before Lavigne could offer any protests, Eden and Baxter rushed forward and each grabbed one of the professor's arms. Lavigne shouted, his body twisting as he tried to break free, but they held him tight.

"Stop! This is madness!" Lavigne cried, his feet scrabbling against stone.

"Take a deep breath!" Eden said when they reached the edge of the platform. With the water roaring in their ears and the spray misting their faces, they jumped.

44

THE SHOCK OF THE COLD HIT EDEN LIKE A PHYSICAL BLOW. The current seized them with a relentless force, dragging them beneath the surface and hurling them downstream at breakneck speed. The water roared in their ears as they tumbled helplessly, their limbs flailing against the powerful surge. They surfaced together, gasping for air, still linked arm in arm. Lavigne yelped as the current dragged them through the darkness, the last glimmers of their dropped flashlights disappearing behind them.

Eden pulled herself in behind Lavigne and used her natural buoyancy to keep his head above the water. The professor sputtered and coughed. The darkness of the tunnel surrounded them completely, the roar of rushing water filling the space.

Eden concentrated on keeping them on the surface of the water and away from the sharp rocks at either side. A tiny pinprick of light suddenly emerged in the distance. Eden swung around, angling them toward the light, knowing what was coming next.

"We're almost there," Eden shouted over the water, her voice almost lost completely. "Hold tight."

Lavigne groaned, clearly aware what was coming next. The light grew brighter and brighter, illuminating the spray-filled air around them. Then they burst out into the fresh air, the world exploding into a dazzling array of colors.

"You know what's coming ..." Eden said, hoping to prepare Lavigne for the fall. She didn't have time. She felt the water accelerate as they neared the cliff. She looked around, seeing the vast expanse of jungle around them and so, so far below, the lotus covered lake.

Lavigne's face tensed, as though he'd bitten into something horrible. Eden pulled the professor in close and grabbed Baxter with the other hand.

For a split second, it felt as though they were suspended at the top of the waterfall, then gravity caught up. They plummeted over the edge, the roar of the waterfall drowning out their cries. The wind whipped at their faces as they fell, water spraying all around them. The lake rushed up to meet them with terrifying speed.

Eden tightened her grip on Lavigne, trying to position herself to take the brunt of the impact. Baxter did the same on the other side. Together they took a deep breath and smashed into the lake with a deafening impact. The world became a confused swirl of bubbles as they plunged deep beneath the surface.

Eden lost her grip on Lavigne and kicked ahead, forcing herself up toward the surface. Her lungs burned, crying out for air. She looked at the light shimmering far above her. She saw Lavigne thrashing around a few feet away. She grabbed hold of him and pulled them both up toward the light.

After what felt like an age, they broke the surface. Eden

gasped for air and blinked water from her eyes. Lavigne gasped, spitting water and howling in a mixture of fear and relief. Baxter appeared nearby and calmly swam their way.

Eden glanced around and saw that the boat they'd used to cross the lake remained tied to the vines. She put her arm around Lavigne's shoulders and dragged him toward it. Baxter held one side of the boat, while Eden scrambled inside. Baxter climbed in next, and then the pair dragged Lavigne out of the water.

Eden slumped into one of the seats and looked up at the torrent of water, throwing itself from the top of the cliff impossibly high overhead.

"You wanted the full Naga experience," Eden said, catching Baxter's eyes. He exhaled slowly, the gesture telling Eden quite how close they had come to a completely different outcome.

Eden sat for a moment, catching her breath and allowing the adrenaline to subside.

Lavigne coughed and spat out a mouthful of water. He sat up slowly, looking around as though he didn't quite understand what he was looking at.

"I am never ever—jamais, au grand jamais—doing that again," he said, holding tightly on to the side of the boat. "I need solid ground, now."

"Coming right up," Eden said, untying the boat and grabbing one of the paddles. Baxter grabbed the other and together they navigated their way back across the lake.

Back on the shore, they tied the boat back into its original position and scrambled out. Eden and Baxter went first, then paused to help Lavigne back onto the bank.

Lavigne dropped into a position of prayer, bent down, and kissed the earth.

"Mon Dieu! Terre bénie!" he said, rocking backward and

forward. Eventually, he climbed to his feet and brushed the dirt from his lips. He straightened his spectacles and looked at Eden and Baxter with a mix of exhaustion and indignation.

"If you ever do that to me again," he said, pointing his finger at Eden and then Baxter, "I'll ... I'll ..." Clearly not able to think of anything suitable, he swung his scarf—which had remarkably remained around his neck throughout the whole ordeal—over his shoulder and marched across to the temple.

Eden and Baxter shared a glance and grinned. They turned and followed Lavigne toward the temple. Approaching the structure, they spotted a familiar figure sitting in the lotus position on the temple steps. The monk remained stationary for over a minute before opening his eyes. He looked at the three wet and disheveled people with a calm and serene expression.

Eden stepped forward and was about to speak, when the monk raised his hand.

"What you found is for you alone." The monk rose to his feet effortlessly and descended the stairs, his robe flowing out behind him. "I am pleased to see Naga has shown you the way," the monk said, looking down at Eden's dripping clothes. He then turned and looked out across the lake. "The lotus flower is seen as an icon of purity, not because it is beautiful, but because it must endure the murky water before it can flourish in the sunlight." He turned and locked eyes with Eden. "Only those who make it through the darkness deserve the light."

A breeze rustled through the trees and the old monk turned towards it.

"Your work is not yet complete. Several vehicles were seen heading south half an hour ago. If you move quickly, you can catch them." He pointed at the dirt bikes beside the temple. Someone had placed two cans of fuel beside them, along with water and food.

"You will need all your strength, because powerful forces are at play here," the monk said, looking from Eden to Baxter and then on to Lavigne. "There is no time to waste."

45

Angkor Wat, Cambodia. The following morning.

SOPHEAP STOOD AT THE RAILING AND LOOKED UP AT ANGKOR Wat's colossal silhouette, backed by the star-studded sky. Moonlight bathed the temple complex in a ghostly glow. Long shadows reached across the moat, as though stretching for something out of grasp.

"Another exciting night in paradise," Ritty, Sopheap's fellow guard, grumbled from his slumped position on a bench.

Sopheap glanced at the other man and saw a cigarette flare, the scent of clove trailing in the smoke.

"Those things will kill you, you know?" Sopheap said, nodding at the cigarette.

Ritty took a deep inhale, then clasped the cigarette between finger and thumb, and pointed it at Sopheap. "Life's a gamble, brother, you gotta play."

"Where did you hear that from, some ancient proverb passed down from your grandmother?" Sopheap said.

"No, that—"

"Let me guess, maybe you read it in one of them books you're always carrying about?"

Ritty shook his head, expelling a cloud of smoke. "That's one of the greatest thinkers of the last hundred years."

"Who?"

"Kenny Rogers." Ritty finished his cigarette, put it out carefully, and slipped the end into his pocket. "He's a clever guy."

"I have no idea where you find this stuff," Sopheap said, looking up at the sky.

Ritty shrugged. "Anything to pass the time. You know what, I'm gonna live dangerously." He immediately set about rolling another cigarette. "It helps keep things interesting."

"You don't find this interesting enough?" Sophead said, looking out across the moat. An eddy of wind skipped across the water, distorting the reflection of the great temple.

Ritty gurgled out a laugh, his voice rough. "This! The same night after night. Protecting this place? From what? Monkeys!"

"Maybe you should stop complaining for a second and look at the—"

Ritty laughed harder this time. "See, that's where you're wrong," he said, pointing at Sopheap with the hand that held the cigarette. "For me, complaining is an art form. You call it moaning, but really, I'm working on my craft."

Now it was Sopheap's turn to laugh. "An art form? Is that what you tell your wife when you're moaning about all the chores you have to do?"

"That's different," Ritty said, his voice softening. "When it comes to complaining, she's like my mentor. She's an expert—"

Ritty stopped speaking in the middle of his sentence and his eyes flared wide.

Sopheap stared at his friend, not understanding what had happened. Ritty gurgled a few words but couldn't form them properly. He fell forward with his face in the dirt. The unlit cigarette rolled across the stone, quickly soaked in a pool of blood.

"What ... I ..." Sopheap said, realizing the danger a moment too late. He spun around and reached for his rifle, standing against the railing a few feet away. He clasped the weapon as two figures stepped out of the gloom. A gun popped and Sopheap fell to the floor beside his friend.

"Excellent work," Zhao said, talking into the comms system from the back of the Sikorsky two miles away. "And you're sure they didn't call for backup?"

"They didn't have the chance," the man replied. "They were gone before they realized what was happening."

"Good," Zhao said. "You have the uniforms, yes? When the next shift arrives, they won't even realize the switch."

The man signaled his understanding and cut the connection.

"Move," Zhao said to the pilot, before turning to look out the window.

The pilot reached up and flipped a line of switches, a low whine filling the cabin as the turbines came to life.

"Just think," Zhao said, turning to Athena who sat beside her, "the fatalities that occur tonight could be the last people ever to die at the hands of another human."

"That's quite a claim," Athena said, glancing at her mother.

"Yes, it is, but that's what we're on the brink of." Zhao turned to look at her daughter, her eyes momentarily narrowing as she thought about her response. "Think of all the technological advancements in the last hundred years." Zhao placed on the headset as the engine noise increased.

Athena took a headset from the hook beside her and placed it on too.

"Take this helicopter as an example," Zhao said, sweeping her hand from right to left. "One hundred years ago, to fly like this simply wasn't possible. We have continued to build, and iterate, and invent, improving life for people all over the planet."

The helicopter lurched slightly as it lifted off the ground. Zhao steadied herself before continuing.

"These technological advances are meaningless if we continue to pollute, to kill, and to fight."

"What do you mean?" Athena said, not quite following Zhao's line of thinking.

"Humans have been squandering their potential for centuries." Zhao said, looking out at the trees. "We will never achieve what we are capable of while people quarrel, to kill each other, or place their own importance above that of the whole."

Athena's brow crinkled in thought. "But what can we do about it? Get people to talk, to understand their differences, to respect one another?"

"Don't you think people have tried that?" Zhao laughed, sounding genuinely amused by the comment. "Some of these disagreements go right to the base of who people are. They are set at the root of their belief systems. To change that would be like a rebirth. It's not possible."

Remembering the crate containing the Lotus Key, which she'd seen Gui attach to the base of the helicopter, it all became suddenly clear to Athena. The blood in her veins turned to ice as the pieces clicked into place. She stared at her mother, really seeing her for the first time—not as the cold-hearted killer she'd always assumed, but as something far more terrifying: a true believer that what she was doing was right. There was a religious fervor in her eyes, a certainty that Athena had somehow missed before.

"You're talking about ..." Athena's voice caught in her throat as the magnitude of it hit her. "You're talking about using the Lotus Key to remove people's free will."

"Exactly," Zhao said, turning to look at her daughter, the lights from the flight controls glimmering in her eyes. "Using the same power the kings of Angkor harnessed for thousands of years, we usher in a new order for humankind. All religion will be gone, all independent thought a thing of the past, self-centered actions an impossibility. People will do what they are told, they will live in order, and the world ..." Zhao paused, clearly affected by her own vision, "... the world will be at peace."

A heavy silence fell over the cabin, broken only by the steady thrum of the rotors. Athena stared at her mother, a look of confusion and unease on her face.

"But that's tyranny," she said, her voice soft. "You can't force your will on others. That's the opposite of freedom. Differences should be celebrated and—"

"Maybe there was a time I would have thought the same," Zhao said, her expression softening. "But then I left America and returned to the land in which my mother was born."

"Xinjiang," Athena said.

"Yes. I knew that I still had relatives in the area, and it

had always been my intention to go back and attempt to get them out."

"The camps," Athena said, thinking of her own experience there, which felt like a lifetime ago.

"Standing there, seeing the camps, I was struck by the awfulness of it all. All those people locked up, their lives wasted, because of ..." Zhao paused, searching for the right word, "... ideological differences."

"Yeah, those people need to be freed—"

"Yes, they do, but not just those people, all people. If everyone could forget the belief structures that make them different, then there would be—"

"But it doesn't work like that!" Athena exploded. "You can't blame the Uyghur people, or any person, for the circumstances of their oppression."

The pair sat in silence as the spires of the Angkor Wat reared up above the trees.

"I don't blame them," Zhao said, sighing. She sounded genuinely exasperated. "I don't blame them in the same way I don't blame a moth for its attraction to the light. But it is their belief structure, and that of the people oppressing them, that is keeping us all trapped in this cycle. Using the Lotus Key, we can break the cycle for all, and order will reign. Not only there, but across the world!"

Athena shook her head, her mind spinning at what her mother had said. "You're talking about erasing cultures, identities, choice, free will ... that's what makes us human. How is that any different from what's happening in Xinjiang?"

Zhao turned back and locked eyes with her daughter. The softness in her gaze had now been replaced by raw fire.

"It's entirely different. What's happening in Xinjiang is targeted oppression. What we're doing is universal liberation. No one group will be singled out because all groups will cease to exist. Don't you see? It's the ultimate equality."

"At the cost of all individualism," Athena whispered, her voice barely audible over the helicopter's rotors.

"One minute out," Gui said, his baritone cutting through the tension.

"Ground team, make your way to the landing site," Zhao said, shaking her head momentarily to return her focus to the mission at hand.

The chopper sped over the moat, sending ripples across the water, then slowed above the temple.

"I know this may be hard to understand," Zhao said, turning to Athena. "But humanity is in chaos, and to save it we must take drastic measures. The Lotus Key isn't simply an artifact; it's the key to a future without suffering, without oppression, without the endless cycle of violence that has plagued us for millennia."

The helicopter started to descend, its rotors whipping the air just feet from the central lotus tower.

"Ground crew ready," came a voice through the comms system. "Lower the crate. Twenty feet."

Athena was about to speak when Zhao raised her finger.

"No more questions now," Zhao said. "You're welcome on this journey with me. But be warned, if I need to sacrifice you to achieve this, that's what will be done."

46

———————

"Time to go," Zhao said, sliding open the helicopter door and attaching the rope to the anchor point. Without looking back, she clipped herself on, swung out, and descended into the temple below.

Athena stood and crossed to the door just in time to see Zhao unclip from the rope and pace across to the crate now sitting a few feet away. She glanced at the temple's famous lotus tower.

"You heard your mother," Gui said, moving up behind Athena. "Get down there now, or you'll have the pleasure of being the last person to die at the hands of another."

Athena turned and looked up at the man, his face an expression of pure disdain. He reached out and shoved Athena on the shoulder, sending her stumbling backwards. A moment before she would have tumbled down out of the chopper, and down to the ground below, she caught a grab handle and steadied herself.

"Touch me again, and it'll be the last thing you do," Athena said, scowling up at the brute.

"What's got you so worked up, princess? Are you scared

of heights? Or having second thoughts about mommy's grand plan?" Gui's snarl morphed into a cruel smirk.

Ignoring the brute's words, Athena leaned out and clipped herself on to the rope. Casting one more contemptuous look at Gui, she swung out into the air and rappelled down into the temple. She landed, unclipped the rope, and moved out of the way.

Zhao strode across to a section of wall, which was tucked away around the side of the tower.

"The opening to the lotus chamber is behind this wall," she said, calling the men across to her. "Keep a record of where each stone came from, as they need to go back in position again once we're through."

The ground team swung bags from their backs and removed rubber-tipped pry bars and other equipment clearly designed to remove the blocks without damaging them. They stepped up to the carvings and worked the bars between the large stones.

Gui thudded down and unclipped himself. He waited while several more men, Athena counted at least ten, rappelled down from the chopper in quick succession. When the last was on the ground, Gui waved at the pilot. The chopper ascended, and sped away, the noise fading as it passed out over the moat.

Once the first stone was an inch out of place, the men removed the tools and worked it loose by hand. Gui joined them at the wall, grabbing the stone in something like a bear hug and dragging the stone out. He and two others manhandled it from the wall and used a wheeled board to move it to the side.

Zhao marched up to the gap and peered inside. Seeing the beam of Zhao's flashlight shine into an empty space behind, Athena's intrigue increased. She stepped up behind and peered through. The space behind the carving extended for about thirty feet, with cobwebs as thick as fingers hanging from one side to the next.

"This place isn't on any of the official surveys," Athena said. She leaned through the gap and looked down into a shaft which descended into pitch black.

Zhao stepped back and indicated that Gui and the men should continue removing the blocks. "This isn't on the official surveys because the people who make them don't want anyone to know about this place. You really think they built this whole structure to serve no tangible purpose?" She raised a hand to indicate the temple.

Now that the first stone had been moved out of position, the men moved the second and third in half the time. Athena noticed that, while the blocks were solid, they were thinner than she'd expected, sometimes only two or three inches from front to back. She remembered what Zhao had said about this wall being positioned to hide the shaft behind and realized that these stones served the purpose of a display, rather than bearing any load.

After the men had removed the fourth stone, Zhao stepped forward and inspected the shaft again.

"We'll go down first," she said, looking at Gui. "Remove as many stones as you need to lower the Lotus Key down the shaft."

"Will you be alright with her?" Gui said, casting a glance at Athena.

Athena shot the brute a look so dirty she felt the immediate need to take a shower.

"My daughter and I will be fine," Zhao said, looking from Gui to Athena. "I think, after all, she'll come around to my way of thinking."

"I wouldn't count on it," Athena said.

"I'll take the discs too," Zhao said, pointing at the bag which was strapped to Gui's back. For a second it looked as though he might challenge the order. Receiving one of Zhao's whip-lash stares, he swung off the bag and passed it across.

"Once Gui is down, seal up the opening," Zhao said, putting on the bag and tightening the straps. "It is important our presence here goes unnoticed, for now. I will contact you if we need anything." Zhao dug a climbing rope from one of the kit bags. She secured the rope to one of the pillars, paced across to the void, and dropped it inside. She pulled out a pair of light sticks, snapped them to start the chemical reaction, and dropped them down too.

"Maybe she should go first," Gui said, pointing at Athena. "You know, as a test of faith."

"Good idea," Zhao said, throwing Athena a head torch. "I'll be right above you, so don't try anything."

"It would be my pleasure," Athena said, acting calm as she stepped toward the opening. "I'm the closest thing you've got to an archaeologist here, anyway."

Athena clipped her harness to the rope and leaned out over the gap. Cobwebs tickled her skin, and she could taste dust on her tongue. She let a few inches of the rope slide through the carabiner and stepped down the wall. The damp air of the underground passage enveloped her as she moved. She leaned further back and peered down. A long way below her the light sticks glowed, just pin pricks of light in the blackness.

She fanned a hand in front of her face to remove a knot of cobwebs and lowered herself another few inches. Growing in confidence, she let out several feet of rope, bounding down the shaft in two kicks. She reminded herself that she'd rappelled down countless cliffs and buildings in the past, and this one was no different.

"I'm coming down." Zhao's voice echoed down the shaft, and Athena felt vibrations move through the rope as she clipped herself on too.

Athena glanced up and saw Zhao—she still refused to think of the woman as her mother—bouncing down the shaft with confidence.

"How's it looking down there?" Zhao said, quickly closing the distance.

"Oh, you know, nothing out of the ordinary. Just like every other hidden shaft beneath a world-famous ancient temple I've come across." Not wanting Zhao to catch up, Athena sped up, bouncing quickly down the rope.

Athena descended another thirty or so feet, before pausing to look down. The light sticks at the bottom of the shaft were now about the same distance as the light from the top. She assumed from the distance she'd descended that the shaft was about two hundred feet deep.

She grabbed the rope and prepared to let out another few feet when her headlamp beam caught something on the wall in front of her. She leaned forward to get a closer look and saw a figure carved into the stone.

"Hold on, there's something here." Athena leaned in to get a better look.

"What is it?" Zhao replied.

"It's a carving, the first one I've seen down here," Athena said, sweeping a knot of cobwebs to the side. "Strange, the rest of the shaft's smooth, except for here."

"Describe it." Zhao stopped descending and the rope hung motionless.

"Oh no," Athena said, her voice low.

"What is it?" Zhao snapped.

"It's Agni, the God of—"

A low rumble filled the shaft, followed by a loud whooshing sound.

"Fire!" Athena shouted. She let go of the rope as a ball of flame burst from the walls all around her. She dropped as fast as she was able, shuffling the rope through the carabiner.

Zhao did the same, dropping through the ball of flame a moment before the shaft became an inferno. Intense heat and blinding light surrounded them on all sides.

Athena slid down the rope as quickly as she could, but within seconds, Zhao caught up.

"Move, before the rope burns through!" Zhao shouted, her feet just inches above Athena's head.

As the heat from the fire began to reduce, Athena slowed her descent and glanced upwards. The fire seemed to spurt from rows of small holes mounted around the shaft, creating a deadly barrier of flame.

"The rope," Zhao said, looking upward. "It'll burn through any second. We need to get—"

The rope dropped a few inches as some of the strands gave way.

Athena looked down. They were still a perilous distance from the shaft bottom, which she expected to be lined with stone. She released the rope in controlled bursts, descending as fast as she dared. The acrid smell of burning fibers filled the air, giving a sensory countdown as the rope burned through.

"Faster!" Zhao urged from above, her usual composure cracking under the pressure.

The bottom of the shaft loomed closer, the light sticks now clearly visible. The rope dropped another inch as more fibers burned through. Realizing they were literally hanging on by a thread, Athena let the rope rush through her fingers, burning her skin. As the ground rushed up to meet her, she applied some pressure to the line, slowing her descent. She hit the ground hard, rolling to absorb the impact.

Zhao followed, her feet touching down half a second later. Without a word, both women rolled away from the shaft as the burning rope plummeted down like a fiery snake.

47

"IT ALL LOOKS QUIET," LAVIGNE SAID, GAZING OUT AT ANGKOR Wat on the other side of the moat. A breeze skipped across the water, rippling the surface like liquid mercury.

The temple's massive silhouette rose before them, its iconic spires little more than shapes against the navy-blue pre-dawn sky. Mist clung to the water's surface, curling this way and that like ghostly fingers.

The first tourists were already gathering along the northern causeway, preparing for the sunrise show. Camera flashes punctuated the night like fireflies, catching the condensation in the air.

"You're sure they would come here?" Eden said, lifting a pair of binoculars to her eyes and sweeping the scene. Everything around the temple looked normal, too normal.

Obscured by the trees, they had watched the temple for almost thirty minutes. Riding straight down from the north, they'd stuck to jungle tracks as much as possible and made the final approach on foot. Now blending in with the daily hordes of travelers who came to witness sunrise at the temple, Eden didn't think anyone would notice their presence.

"Yes, certainly. This is where Zhao found the first mention of the Lotus Key. She said it was hidden inside a wall in the central chamber," Lavigne said, swatting away an insect which had clearly taken a liking to him.

"Hey!" Eden groaned, as Baxter reached across and took the binoculars.

"The security guards are in place as normal," Baxter said, using the binoculars to look at the men lounging beside the causeway. "If Zhao's in there, she somehow got past security without being noticed." He passed the binoculars back to Eden.

Eden glanced down at the water, glittering in the moonlight. "That moat is six hundred feet wide, and they've got the Lotus Key. They're not getting across there without being noticed."

"What's happening then, Miss Know-it-all?" Baxter said.

"As I see it, there are two options," Eden said. "They either got in there without the guards noticing, or—"

"Va-t'en, petit vaurien!" Lavigne barked, wildly flailing his arm from left to right. "Go away, you little scoundrel!"

"I know, professor, I have to put up with her every day," Baxter said.

Eden shot Baxter a filthy look before continuing. "Or we're totally wrong and they're not ..." This time Eden stopped talking without interruption.

"They're not what?" Baxter said, glancing at Eden.

Eden remained silent and unmoving, staring through the binoculars. Her brow furrowed in concentration.

"Earth to Eden," Baxter said. "You were saying?"

"Yes. It might be my eyes playing tricks, and it's really hard to see, but it looks as though there's smoke coming from the temple." She adjusted the binoculars, trying to get a better view through the gloom. Although barely visible against the sky, a cloud rose above the central tower.

"I don't see anything." Baxter squinted, straining his eyes.

"Look at the central tower." Eden reluctantly passed him the binoculars. "Where it meets the sky. It's like ... it's shimmering. Then higher up, the stars are blinking out where it passes."

The hum of approaching tuk-tuks and taxis increased as more tourists arrived at the viewing area.

"See it?" Eden said. "It looks like something's burning inside."

"I don't see how that's ..." Lavigne squinted.

"It's faint, but there's definitely something," Baxter said, nodding.

"That means they're already in there," Eden said, climbing to her feet. "And we don't have time to waste."

"WHAT'S GOING ON DOWN THERE?" GUI'S VOICE BOOMED through the comms system as Athena struggled to her feet. Out of instinct, she turned and held a hand out to Zhao. The older woman accepted the hand and stood, shakily at first.

Without a word they both looked around, taking in the scene for the first time. The chamber was so big that the beams from their head-mounted flashlights barely reached the other side. The ceiling soared at least fifty feet above them, supported by massive columns which were carved like the trunks of trees in some mystical stone forest. Various figures peered down at them from on high, each fresco depicting a battle or a dance with unknown cosmic entities.

"What is this place?" Athena said, her voice filled with awe.

"One of the world's best-kept secrets," Zhao said, pulling off her backpack and digging out a powerful flashlight. She powered up the light and angled it at the ceiling, bringing the incredible detail into view. "This is where the kings of the Khmer Empire would come to broadcast their commands using the Lotus Key."

"I've heard about this place," Athena said, staggering forward in amazement. "But I never knew it was real. If it wasn't built by the Khmer, then who?"

"No one knows for sure," Zhao said, focusing the flashlight on a particular ceiling relief. "But that gives us a clue."

Athena looked where Zhao indicated and gasped. The relief was detailed with inlaid gold, silver, and tiny stones in a whole variety of colors, and showed hundreds of tiny figures climbing into what looked like spacecraft.

"I thought the people who wore tinfoil hats made that stuff up," Athena said, unable to tear her eyes away from the scene.

"That's exactly what those who control the narrative want you to think," Zhao said, swinging the beam back toward the center of the chamber.

"Zhao? Athena? What's going on down there?" Gui's voice came again, this time with a panicked edge to it. "Smoke's pouring out the shaft, and the heat ..." Gui paused to cough. "It's intense."

Zhao tapped the device in her ear, which had thankfully survived the fall, and replied. "We're fine. The shaft has a protection system. I expect there's some kind of timing mechanism, it'll stop soon.

"Understood," Gui replied. "We've almost got the entrance clear now. We'll be ready to lower the Lotus Key soon."

"Excellent," Zhao replied, cutting the connection.

"How does this all work?" Athena said, gazing around the chamber.

"The Lotus Key is powered by sunlight. Without the sun, it's a radioactive hunk of metal ... I say metal, but we don't actually know what it is," Zhao said. "But the problem is, too much sunlight and it has some rather undesirable effects."

Athena remembered the devastation she'd seen on the oil rig.

"But how is the sunlight controlled when we're deep beneath the earth?" Athena said.

"The Lotus Key is placed here," Zhao said, striding toward a long, flat stone in the center of the chamber. When she didn't get swallowed by the ground, or no flaming arrows roared forth, Athena followed. Nearing the stone, Athena noticed an indent in which the Lotus Key would sit. The other side of the stone rose up like a chaise longue for the king, or Zhao, to recline.

"Then this," Zhao said, pointing up towards the ceiling, "is the light well."

Athena leaned back and looked up into another shaft directly above them. The shaft tapered to a point right at the top.

"Turn your light off," Zhao said, killing both her head torch and the handheld flashlight.

Athena did as she was told, and both women craned their necks to look up the shaft.

"Wait a second. That's the sky," Athena said, noticing a tiny dot of starry night sky in the center of the shaft.

"Exactly. That shaft runs directly through the central

lotus tower." Zhao snapped her light on again and shone it skyward. The inside of the shaft was inlaid with something highly reflective.

"So, during the day the sun shines in through the lotus tower. How is that controlled?" Athena asked.

"That's where these come in." With reverence, Zhao slid the first disc from her bag. She crossed the chamber and slotted one into a golden clamp right beneath the tower. She then moved to another clamp and slotted the second into position.

"The center of each disc is a mirror." Zhao pointed at the disc's central section. "With these in place, the king, or whoever, could control exactly how much sunlight reached the Lotus Key."

Athena followed the path the light would take once the sun rose.

"During times of conflict when he may have needed to assert more control over his people, he would keep the key in the sunlight for longer periods. During times of peace, maybe just a few minutes a day would suffice." Zhao folded her arms and strode across to the slab where the Lotus Key would soon sit.

"How do you know how much you'll need?" Athena said, her excitement at the discovery waning as she recalled her mother's tyrannical plans. "Surely it's risky, especially for the person sitting so close to the key."

"As with anything, we'll start slowly," Zhao said. "We start today by controlling people close by. Once that's proved successful, we will increase the exposure day on day, week on week, always measuring the effects. You understand what we're doing here." Zhao turned to look at Athena, her eyes burning with passion. "This is a revolution and will in time sweep the globe, and the best thing—"

"No one will get killed in the process," Athena said.

"Exactly," Zhao said, flashing her daughter a triumphant smile.

"The smoke has cleared," Gui barked down the radio. "We're ready to start moving through the shaft."

"Excellent," Zhao replied, checking her watch. "We've got to move, the sun comes up in thirty minutes."

48

"Why does it always have to involve water," Lavigne groaned as Eden dragged him out of the moat and up the wall onto dry land. "Do you have any idea of the dangers that lurk in these muddy depths?" He pointed back at the moat which glittered with the dazzling reflection of the stars above.

"We've made it so far, haven't we?" Eden said, gripping the professor by the wrist and dragging him up across a patch of open ground and in behind a tree.

She swept back her hair and peered out at the temple's outer wall, now just a few paces away. It appeared as though the smoke had reduced to the occasional wisp.

"First, there's the risk of drowning, obviously," Lavigne continued, counting out the threats to life and limb on his fingers. "But that's just the beginning. Have you heard of snakehead fish? They have teeth so sharp they can slice through flesh. Water snakes too—the most venomous in Southeast Asia."

Baxter silently scrambled up the wall and crawled in

beside the tree. Eden and Baxter shared a sarcastic look at the professor's ramblings.

"Lavigne," Eden said softly, trying to redirect his focus.

"Not forgetting all the parasites, infections, urgh!" Lavigne visibly shuddered, swept his hair back, and twisted it to ring the water out.

"Lavigne!" Eden hissed more forcefully this time. "I get it, you don't like water. Now focus." She swung off her water-proof pack and dug out a tablet computer. She flicked the screen to its dimmest setting and loaded a schematic of the temple. "It looks as though the smoke was coming from around here," Eden said, circling an area. "Does that fit with what Zhao told you about the location of the carving?"

Lavigne removed his spectacles and tried to dry them on his shirt, a fruitless endeavor with water still dripping from it. He grumbled, flicked the spectacles a few times, and placed them back on his nose.

"Yes, that's the central chamber." Lavigne pointed at the tablet. "Zhao told me that the schematic I showed you was hidden behind a carving in the northwest corner." He looked up and squinted into the night sky. "That fits with where the smoke's coming from."

Eden zoomed in on the schematic. "Okay, so we need to get to this central chamber. What's the quickest route?"

Lavigne traced a path with his finger. "There are a series of corridors leading through the south gallery, from there we'll need to climb the stairs and into the central shrine."

A nightjar's eerie cry cut through the stillness and a bat fluttered overhead.

"Alright, let's move," Eden said, stashing the tablet away and rising to her feet. She glanced at Baxter, communicating silently that she would lead, and he should stay back to make sure Lavigne didn't get lost or do anything stupid.

"Why am I always the one babysitting?" Baxter mouthed silently.

Eden shrugged and did a three-sixty to check that no one was in sight. Confident they were alone, she darted across the open space and into the shadow of the temple's vast west wing. She stood with her back against the wall and waited for Lavigne and Baxter to cross. When they were all together, Eden stalked through the shadow toward the entrance.

Reaching the base of the staircase, Eden held up a hand, signaling the others to stop. She peered around the corner, checking for any signs of Zhao's team or the temple's regular security.

"Looks clear," Eden whispered, starting up the staircase.

"Incroyable," Lavigne muttered, staggering in amazement toward one of the walls. "I've seen it many times in photographs, but to be here." He leaned in closely, clearly assessing the detail in the moonlight. "The detail, the skill on display here."

"Not now, professor." Eden grabbed him by the arm and steered him into the temple's shadows.

"But ... But ..." Lavigne stammered, looking longingly back at the carving. "Don't you know that this carving tells the—"

"No professor, we haven't got time for this."

"It's just, to be here alone, it's ..."

"It'll still be here tomorrow, after we've saved the world." Eden dragged Lavigne through the gallery and past a row of massive pillars, their shadows creating two-tone black and blue shadows. Reaching the other side of the gallery, she released Lavigne and approached the doorway. She peered out into the courtyard, searching the shades of silver and blue for movement or concealed observers.

The temple's iconic central tower rose before them, the lotus-bud crown reaching towards the heavens.

"Which way?" she hissed at Lavigne.

The professor scuttled through the gloom and pointed up at the temple's iconic central tower. "The central chamber is up there, surrounding the central tower."

"Can we use those stairs?" Eden said, pointing to what looked like a staircase directly in front of them up the side of the structure.

"Now that's an interesting architectural feature," Lavigne said, shuffling further out to get a better look. "Three of the four staircases serve the purposes of buttresses, holding the incredible weight of the central tower in place. Without them, the thing would have fallen before it was finished. Although they look like staircases, you can see they lead nowhere."

"That's a no then," Eden said. "Which staircase can we use?" She scanned the courtyard again.

"It's on the other side, to the north," Lavigne said, pointing to the right.

"Typical," Eden huffed, shuffling away in the direction Lavigne had indicated. Keeping to the shadows, she led the way around the courtyard. She paused several times, scanning the shadows for movement and listening for noise.

As they neared the staircase, Eden held up her hand again, bringing them to a halt. She crouched low, inching forward to peer around the final corner. Although this staircase looked the same as the others, there was a doorway at the top.

Staring into the dark opening, she caught a glimpse of movement. A figure shifted back and forth in the shadows at the top of the stairs. As he stepped forward, the moonlight glinted off his weapon.

Eden turned and gestured them backward. "There's at least one guard at the top of the stairs," she whispered. "Probably more."

"Can we take them out quietly?" Baxter said.

"Too risky." Eden shook her head. "They'd see us climbing the stairs, and a gunshot is far too loud."

"Plus, one call to Zhao, and Athena's ..." Baxter added, not wanting to finish the sentence. "I've got an idea, although something tells me the professor won't like it." Baxter reached inside his dry bag and pulled out a length of rope and a grappling hook.

"No, no, no, that is not a good idea. This is an ancient site, we must not risk damaging the—" Lavigne protested.

"We'll be careful," Eden said, nodding at Baxter. "It's the only way."

Baxter took the lead, guiding them around the structure until they were safely out of the guard's line of sight. He dashed across the courtyard, stopping at the base of the central structure, then swung the hook into the air. It latched onto something high above, and the rope dangled loosely against the wall. He ducked into the shadow and waited for anyone to register the disturbance. When no one came, he pulled on the rope and scrambled up the side of the structure. Reaching the top with the speed of someone climbing a staircase, he removed the grappling hook and tied the rope securely in position. With a gesture, he signaled for Eden and Lavigne to follow him up.

"When I'm up, tie yourself on," Eden instructed Lavigne. "Then we can help you."

Eden went first, scrambling up the rope at a similar speed to Baxter. In less than a minute, she heaved herself up onto the roof.

She signaled down to Lavigne, who followed her

instructions, tying the rope around his chest beneath his arms. He stepped up to the wall, and half scrambled, half dragged himself up. Although the wall wasn't vertical, it was steep enough to prove difficult, causing the professor to puff and wheeze.

Eden shuffled forward and reached down over the edge. As Lavigne drew near, she grabbed his arm and heaved him up and over the precipice.

"That wasn't too bad, was it?" Eden said, helping the professor to his feet.

Lavigne appeared as though he was going to say something, but then replied with an icy look.

Baxter wound up the rope and stashed it away as the sound of a gruff voice giving instructions drifted through the temple.

Eden pointed toward the noise and together they crossed the rooftop. Nearing the other side, they dropped to their hands and knees and crawled toward the edge. Eden reached the precipice first and peered over into the courtyard below.

A group of at least eight men carried a large crate across the courtyard. The object was clearly heavy, causing the men to huff and groan as they shuffled toward an opening in the temple wall. Several more men stood around in the shadows, watching them work.

Eden gestured silently for Baxter and Lavigne to join her at the edge. As they watched, one of the men—clearly the leader—stepped forward and attached a rope to the crate. The men maneuvered the crate to the edge of what Eden realized was not just an opening, but a shaft descending into the depths of the temple.

"That's the Lotus Key," Eden said, pointing at the crate. "We saw it back in Kompot."

Lavigne nodded. "They're taking it to the chamber."

The leader, who was a foot taller than some of the other men, shouted orders. He stepped away from the opening to let his colleagues move forward with the crate. They placed the crate on the lip of the shaft and backed away. Six men held the rope, while the other two pushed the crate out into the shaft. The rope snapped taut, eliciting a grunt from the men holding it. More men rushed forward to help, seizing the rope to stop it slipping away.

"Whatever's down there, we need to see it," Eden said, turning to look at Lavigne and Baxter.

"I was really afraid you were going to say that," Lavigne said, shivering.

49

"Lowering now," Gui said, his voice distorting through the comms system.

Zhao turned away from the altar and paced back toward the shaft. She stepped out beneath the opening and craned her neck, attempting to see the crate approaching. A bumping, scraping noise drifted down into the chamber, followed by distant grunts as the men lowered the rope.

"I'd stay back from there, just in case," Athena said, remembering the flames that had almost consumed them a couple of minutes ago.

Zhao spun around, momentarily appearing as though she were going to snap at Athena for the instruction, then she smiled. The gesture warmed her face, showing a natural beauty she rarely expressed.

"We're going to change the world this morning," Zhao said, backing away from the shaft as Athena had instructed and placing her palms together in the position of prayer. "Think about it, as people wake up, wherever they are in the world, they'll carry on their hate-filled lives as normal. But slowly, over days and weeks as we increase the power of the

Lotus Key, they will be released from the beliefs which have imprisoned them for so long."

The scraping noise reverberated down the shaft again, followed by a stream of fine dust which skipped through the flashlight beams. The men grunted with effort, Gui's baritone rising above the din as he issued instructions.

"It will be perfect," Zhao continued, taking another step backward. "There will be no great revolution, no overnight change. People will stop caring about the things that once bothered them so much. They'll smile with the neighbor at whom they used to scowl. Ex-partners will be civil, and families will reunite. People will treat each other without the judgement that has plagued our race for so long."

Another scraping noise drifted into the chamber, and another stream of dust ran to the floor.

"Careful up there!" Zhao said, poking the comms device to communicate with Gui. "Don't damage the key."

"We're ... we're doing ..." came Gui's out of breath reply.

Zhao's expression softened again as her thoughts returned to her vision. "There will be no victory march, no banners in the streets, no boundaries re-drawn. Instead, the wars that have plagued us for all this time will just ... stop."

Zhao's tone rose into that of a preacher, spreading an inspiring message to thousands of people. As the only person in earshot, a chill worked its way up Athena's spine as she heard the conviction in her mother's tone.

"Imagine it," Zhao turned and fixed Athena with a stare, "the conflict will fizzle out as the fighters, who were once so adamant in their beliefs, just stop caring."

"But at what cost?" Athena blurted out before realizing she was speaking. "You're talking about erasing people's identities, their cultures, everything that makes them who they are."

Although the stare remained unbroken, the hard edge returned to Zhao's eyes. A moment of silence passed between the two women, backed only by the distant scraping of the Lotus Key making its way down the shaft.

"Tell me," Zhao said, her tone dropping well below freezing point, "what have these cultures, these identities, ever bought us? Right now, today, there are people locked up because of the ethnic group they belong to. Others are forced to leave their homes because they are somehow different to those in power. Crops are spoiled in one land because the rivers are poisoned in another. Why are people dying for something so ..." Zhao's fingers moved through the air as she searched for the words, "... something so ... irrelevant? The Lotus Key offers us a chance to break that cycle once and for all. This is our chance to end the suffering of millions."

"What about the beauty that individualism, culture, faith and belief bring to people?" Athena said, watching her mother closely. "What about hope in times of struggle?"

"There would be far less struggle without division," Zhao replied, her tone as hard as a whip. "Imagine, when the Lotus Key has done its work, the world's defense spending will fund food for the hungry, water for the thirsty, or clothes and healthcare for those who need it. Money once spent on bombs will pay for hospital beds. Developments in science which are now used to kill, will be used to cure. For the first time ever, humanity will stand together." Zhao gestured around the chamber, her arms sweeping to encompass the carvings and the altar where the Lotus Key would soon rest. "Our wars will be against the issues that plague our race—disease and sickness, famine and inequality—not each other."

"But without our free will, and our identities, we are not

a race at all," Athena countered, her voice rising with the same passion as her mother's. "Think about it, pride, and belief, they're responsible for some of humankind's greatest achievements. Look at this very temple, Angkor Wat. This is a testament to human faith and ingenuity. This is a physical manifestation of people's beliefs and aspirations, whoever they were and whenever they lived."

Zhao opened her mouth to interject, but Athena's words now flowed with urgency.

"Throughout history, this sense of love and community has inspired people to push beyond their limits." Athena stepped forward. "It has allowed people to create works of art that touch the soul, to build monuments that stand the test of time. The Sistine Chapel, the Taj Mahal, the Great Pyramids—these weren't built out of hate or division, but out of love, devotion, and a desire to connect with something greater than—"

"No," Zhao snapped, her eyes burning. "All of those places, including this one, were built on the backs of slaves. It's one thing for you to talk about the expressive freedom of the architect, to hold up their creative vision as a beacon of freedom, but what about the forsaken ones whose bodies were disfigured moving those stones into place? How was their freedom considered? Do you think those people *chose* to spend their lives working in the construction of someone else's vision?"

Athena shook her head. "It's not only about the tangible things. Belief brings people, communities, countries or families together and those links provide comfort in times of hardship."

"And tears them apart just as easily," Zhao countered. "How many wars have been fought over whose community owns what? How many people have been persecuted for being on the wrong side of that division? The Lotus Key will end all of that. It will ... *we* will level the playing field."

A loud banging echoed from the shaft above as the crate neared its destination. Small chunks of rock broke off from the shaft wall and tumbled to the floor, forming a growing mound. The pile resembled sand in an hourglass, silently counting down to their final moments.

"By stripping away everything that makes us human," Athena said, raising her voice, "you're talking about erasing the very things that give life—"

"Enough," Zhao roared, her arms sweeping through the air like a scythe. "Privilege has disillusioned your worldview. I feared this would happen, your father being the man he is."

She turned as the crate appeared in the mouth of the shaft. The box swung from side to side, making its final descent to the ground.

"Thirty feet to go," Zhao said, pressing the device in her ear to communicate with Gui.

"Understood," Gui replied, his voice crackling.

The crate inched its way down.

"You say I have been—" Athena said.

"We have no further time to discuss this," Zhao said, cutting her off. All the warmth in her tone was now gone. "You're either with me in shaping this future, or you're one of the people who will be changed once the Lotus Key is in position. Whether you like it or not, sooner or later, you will think like me."

Athena opened her mouth to retort, but her words were cut short by a sudden commotion above. The crate, which had been steadily descending, jerked to a halt about ten feet from the ground. The abrupt stop sent a shower of dust and debris raining down into the chamber.

Shouting echoed down the shaft, followed by several thumps and grunts.

Zhao strode up to the opening, her neck craning upwards. She extended an arm, but the crate was still out of reach.

"What's going on up there?" Zhao barked into her comm device. "Gui, report!"

Only static answered her call.

"Something's wrong," Athena said, stating the obvious, but unable to keep the tremor from her voice.

Zhao tried again, poking the comms device several times. "Gui! Anyone! What's happening?"

The crate containing the Lotus Key fell, bouncing to a stop two feet from the chamber floor. The rope groaned under the strain, swinging from side to side, but holding firm.

The shouting intensified, punctuated by what sounded like gunfire.

50

"MOVE OUT," EDEN SAID, HER VOICE RISING OVER THE PASSING breeze.

"Wait a second," Lavigne said, gripping on to the roof's ridge stones. "You want us to go down—"

He stopped talking as Eden and Baxter slid to the roof's edge. Below, the men worked to lower a rope down the shaft, muscles bulging as they strained against the weight. More men stood around the edge of the courtyard, keeping watch with rifles at the ready.

Eden tried to count the assailants but gave up when she realized that many were hidden in the shadows.

"You wait here until we're clear," she said, turning to face Lavigne who was already making far too much noise.

Lavigne quickly agreed and shuffled out of sight.

"I think—" Baxter started.

"Don't try and talk me out of this," Eden said. "I know it's dangerous, but Athena's down there. Plus, there's no knowing the—"

"I know," Baxter said, placing his hand on Eden's arm. "I

was going to say, let's go in with a bang." Baxter dug out flashbang and held it up.

"I like your thinking," Eden said, flashing him a grin.

Baxter pulled out the pin and hurled the small device across the courtyard. It clattered against the stones and bounced into the recesses of the far gallery not far from three guards.

"Close your eyes and cover your ears," Eden said, turning to Lavigne.

"What?" the professor said, poking his head over the ridge of the rooftop.

"Do this!" Eden said, placing her hands firmly over her ears and clamping her eyes closed.

The flashbang detonated with a thunderous crack. A brilliant white flash turned night into day for a split second. The blast wave rippled through the air, rattling loose tiles and sending dust cascading from the rafters.

The guards near the explosion stumbled backward, crying out as they clawed at their eyes. Rifles clattered against the flagstones as others attempted to cover their ears. Some of the men lowering the rope lost their grip, causing the line to slip through the hands of those who held on. Temporarily blinded and deafened, the guards crashed into each other, shouting instructions no one could hear.

Eden leaped to her feet and ran across the rooftop. Without a second thought, she jumped, sailed through the air, and collided with the two nearest men. She smashed her knee into the first man's back and struck the second with her elbow. Both brutes sprawled to the ground. Landing casually in a crouch, she finished the job by sending the men into oblivion with precisely aimed kicks.

The men at the front regained their senses and hauled

back on the rope just in time. They grunted and groaned with the effort as the rope bit into their hands.

Hearing the report of a rifle, Eden ducked. She turned to see one of the guards taking aim in her direction. Figuring the guard wouldn't risk hitting one of his own, she moved in close to the men holding the rope. Another gunshot reverberated through the temple. This time, when Eden glanced toward the sound, she saw the guard jerk backwards.

Baxter swung down the rope with one hand, a gun raised with the other. He landed, ducked in behind a column, took aim, and fired on another guard before the man could react.

As Eden neared the men holding the rope, one of them let go with one hand and reached for the pistol at his belt. Under the strain of the crate, the man's movement was far too slow, allowing Eden the time to drive her boot into the back of his knee. The man sprawled to the ground, and the rope slipped further, causing the remaining men to stumble.

Eden pulled out her weapon and raised it toward the men holding the rope.

"Do not move," she said, shifting the gun from one man to the next. "I'm in control now. Pull the rope up—"

A heavy force slammed into her from her right, tackling her to the ground. Her gun went flying and landed somewhere in the gloom. Instinctively, she rolled before the attacker could pin her down. A fist the size of a cannon ball sailed her way, cracking the slab where her face had been a second before.

She scrambled backward and got back to her feet, then swung her foot into the side of the man's knee. She then drove her shoulder into the thug's chest, catching him off balance. Looking beyond the assailant, she saw that they were two paces from the shaft's opening. She shoved again, sending the man reeling backwards.

He flailed, grabbing at Eden. She twisted away and shoved him again. The thug's combined weight and momentum sent him tumbling uncontrollably. His boots scraped against the stone and swung out into nothing. He teetered on the edge before falling. A scream echoed through the shaft as he plummeted down.

Realizing they were at a disadvantage while holding the crate, the thug at the front of the pack leaped into action. He seized another length of rope and tied it to one of the columns. He then attached that to the length holding the Lotus Key in place.

With their arms now freed, the remaining men turned their attention to Eden. The man-mountain, who Eden assessed to be the leader, cracked his knuckles as he stepped forward. She looked up at the towering figure, his forearms almost the size of her waist. The other three men stepped to the sides, trying to box her in.

Baxter emerged from the shadows and stalked across the courtyard, his gun raised at the leading man.

"Nice of you to show up," Eden said, taking a step forward to match Baxter's advance.

"My pleasure," Baxter replied. "Which one of these do you want to keep alive?"

"They're not my type to be honest," she said, looking from one man to the next.

"You have a type now, do you?" Baxter said, flashing a smile despite the desperate situation.

"It's definitely not the time for this conversation," Eden said, taking another step forward.

Instead of pressing their clear advantage, the leader grinned. From the shadows at the back of the courtyard a gun howled, forcing Eden and Baxter down. They looked up a second later to see the last of the group seize the rope, jump into the shaft, and rappel out of sight. Baxter fired until his gun clicked empty, but the men were already clear.

Eden raced up to the shaft, with Baxter a step behind. They peered down into the darkness, but the men were already out of sight.

"We need to—" Eden started, her words cut off as an orange glow bloomed in the depths below. The light grew rapidly, accompanied by a rising whoosh that reminded her of a jet engine spooling up.

"Move!" Baxter shouted, grabbing Eden around the waist and yanking her into motion. They sprang away from the shaft as a massive fireball erupted from its mouth, hot enough to singe their clothes.

Eden rolled behind a pillar, shielding her face from the intense heat. The flames licked out of the shaft, sending thick black smoke into the night sky.

51

"GUI, REPORT IMMEDIATELY," ZHAO BARKED DOWN THE comms, getting only static in reply. "Dammit, come in!"

"Eden's here," Athena said, looking up the shaft. "I knew she'd come."

"She'll be too late," Zhao snapped, turning on Athena. Venom now replaced all the passion and excitement that had previously laced her tone. Zhao stepped toward the crate, which hung at waist height above the chamber floor. In a trance-like state, she laid her hand against the side. "There's no way she can stop this now."

Snapping herself into action, Zhao scrambled on the top of the crate, drew out a knife and cut through the rope. The crate slammed down to the ground, booming through the chamber.

"No one can stop this now," Zhao said, turning to look at Athena.

"I don't see how that's true," Athena replied, looking from the crate to the altar on which the key had to rest to work correctly. "How do you plan to move it on your own?"

"I don't," Zhao said, her voice dropping to a whisper. She

climbed down from the crate, took a few steps toward Athena and raised the knife as though ready to attack. "But we will be able to do it together."

"No way," Athena said, folding her arms. "I am not helping you with this crazy scheme."

Zhao lunged, the knife swishing toward Athena's throat.

Seeing the strike coming, Athena parried back and avoided the blade just in time.

Zhao threw the knife down and closed in, targeting Athena with a flurry of precise hits in the stomach and ribs.

Athena doubled over from the strikes but managed to block the next punch, deflecting Zhao's fist with her forearm. She countered with a quick jab to Zhao's face, but the woman was faster than she looked, weaving away from the blow.

"You're good," Zhao said, circling Athena like a predator. "But you're not good enough to stop this." She snapped out a front kick that caught Athena in the kidneys. Before Athena could recover, Zhao followed with a palm strike to the throat.

Athena ducked at the last second, feeling the wind from the strike brush past her ear. Athena grabbed Zhao's extended arm and yanked downward, simultaneously driving her knee up into Zhao's stomach.

Zhao easily absorbed the blow, twisting her trapped arm to break Athena's grip. In the same motion, she hooked her leg behind Athena's ankle and pulled, sweeping her feet out from under her. Athena stumbled, but Zhao caught her before she fell.

"I taught you to fight, remember," Zhao said, holding Athena motionless. "Those hours of training sessions weren't for fun."

"I'll never help you," Athena said, driving her knee up

toward Zhao's midsection. Zhao twisted, grabbed Athena by the arm, and shoved her against the temple wall.

"But it's all gone wrong, you've gotten lazy." Zhao pushed Athena against the wall and placed a forearm across her throat. "I taught you better than this."

"That was always the problem," Athena said, her voice a croak. "You saw motherhood as a competition, and this time you've lost."

"There's only so much pain someone can take," Zhao said, pushing her forearm hard enough to close Athena's throat. "And believe me, causing pain is something I am very good at. Or you could simply accept—"

Athena drove her elbow down hard, breaking Zhao's hold. The older woman ducked and swept Athena's legs out from under her. Athena hit the ground hard, rolling to avoid Zhao's follow-up strike that cracked a stone slab in two.

Athena scrambled to her feet and turned to face her mother as a fist slammed her in the jaw. Stars exploded across her vision, and she stumbled, blood filling her mouth.

Zhao straightened up and looked down at her daughter, like a predator ready for the final kill.

"Once again, you're too slow," Zhao taunted. "It's disappointing. You had so much potential."

"Why are you still talking?" Athena spat blood onto the temple floor. "Although you always did love the sound of your own voice." She straightened up and faced her mother. The taunt hit its mark. Zhao's face twisted into a mask of rage, and she lunged into another attack.

This time Athena was ready; she ducked under the wild punch and drove her shoulder into Zhao's chest. The impact sent them both stumbling, but Athena recovered first, landing two quick jabs. She then wrapped her arm around her mother's throat and pulled her into a chokehold.

"You want to talk about disappointments?" Athena hissed in her ear, rage now overtaking logic. "How about the mother who arranges the death of her own flesh and blood? How's that for a disappointment? You're sick."

Blood clouded Athena's vision as she squeezed, her muscles shaking with the pressure.

Zhao clawed at the arm, croaking noises coming from her open mouth. She stamped down on Athena's feet and sent elbows jarring into her ribs, but Athena remained steadfast.

"But, you know the only thing that disappoints me," Athena spat. "I'm disappointed that I didn't do this all those years ago in the prison. That needle should have been in—"

The gunshot cracked through the chamber like thunder.

Athena flinched, the bullet zipping past her head and striking the rock. She turned, maintaining the pressure on Zhao's throat.

Gui lowered himself down the rope, controlling the descent with his legs as he aimed a gun at Athena and Zhao. He reached the bottom of the rope and dropped, landing on the crate. He jumped down and took a step, the gun remaining fixed on Athena. Three more men followed, landing one after another and drawing out weapons.

"Let her go," Gui said, closing the distance and, as such, diminishing his chances of missing.

Realizing she had little choice, Athena released Zhao and pushed her away.

Zhao dropped into a crawling position, her body trembling as she sucked in several deep breaths. One hand massaged her throat, where angry red marks were already forming from Athena's grip.

She recovered slowly, pressing one palm against the ground and pushing herself up. Her legs shook as she climbed to her feet. Her spine straightened, her shoulders squared, and the mask of control slipped back into place. When she turned to face Athena, her eyes had hardened to obsidian orbs.

"You will help me, whether you want to or not," Zhao said, her tone sharper than ever before. She snapped her fingers and the men, led by Gui, advanced. "My daughter is to have the honor of being the first person to enjoy the effects of the Lotus Key," Zhao said. "Tie her to the altar."

"Don't you—" Athena said, backing away.

Gui closed the distance in two steps and grabbed Athena by the arm. He spun her around and wrenched her arm up behind her back.

Athena struggled, pulling away from her captor. She tried to drop her weight forward, but Gui held her firm. She swung an elbow back, attempting to strike him in the ribs, but hit nothing.

"This will be a lot easier if you stop struggling," Gui said, twisting her arm to its breaking point and dragging her across the chamber.

"I'm not trying to make it easy," Athena said, throwing her head back.

Gui shuffled to the side and looped his other arm around her chest. He dragged her across the chamber and shoved her down against the altar. He crouched and held her in position, his breath warm and disgusting on her cheek.

"The rope," Zhao shouted, pointing at another man. He dug out a length of rope and tied it around Athena's wrists, then looped the rope around the altar, before pulling it tight to secure Athena in place.

Confident that Athena couldn't get up, Gui straightened up and stepped away.

Athena twisted and pulled. The rope bit into her wrists but held her firm.

"Excellent," Zhao said, stepping into Athena's vision. "Like I told you, you will help me whether you want to or not."

52

"You will go down in history," Zhao said, approaching her daughter, the manic grin now back on her face. "It's a privilege—"

"It doesn't feel like it," Athena groaned, pulling on the ropes but getting nowhere. The stone slab on which the Lotus Key would soon rest was cold and hard against her back.

"Actually, saying that you'll go down in history is not strictly true," Zhao said, meeting Athena's stare. "As no one will remember you, except us." Mother and daughter held the stare, then Zhao turned away and marched toward the crate.

"Gentlemen, switch to the red lights." Zhao pressed a button on her flashlight and the beam changed from white to a deep red. Gui and his band of thugs did the same, washing the chamber in a strange kaleidoscopic light.

Zhao paced up to the crate. "We must use this lens color when the Lotus Key is unprotected. The red light's wavelength is too long to power the relic."

Athena remembered what Liang had said about the

crew of the rig going wild, clawing at their own skin. Panic growing, she pulled at the ropes.

"Open it," Zhao snapped, pointing at the crate.

Two of the men laid down their weapons and dug out pry bars. First, they removed the crate's lid and then the sides. As they carried the protective panels away, Athena stopped struggling and looked at the relic that was the center of this whole sorry mess. The object was about four feet from end to end, with lotus shaped buds and petals on the top. Even in the low light, it glimmered with an other-worldly intensity.

"We left the old sarcophagus behind," Zhao said, casually pointing at the object which Athena couldn't seem to look away from. "Although that casket was quality engineering eight hundred years ago, it weighed a ton." Zhao pointed to the stone riser to which Athena was tied. "This way."

Each of the men took a corner of the relic and lifted it out of the specially made base. Working together, they shuffled across the chamber.

Athena watched, almost hypnotized, as the Lotus Key drew closer. Its surface glimmered mysteriously as the red beams of light swirled and danced around.

Zhao paced beneath the shaft which ran up inside the temple's world-famous lotus tower. She peered up at the small patch of sky high above them.

"Not long now," she said, looking at Athena. "As soon as the sun passes the horizon, we will be ready."

The men passed Athena and slid the Lotus Key on to the riser behind her. As the relic dropped into position, the hairs on the back of her neck stood up on end. A tingling sensation, like a shiver but without feeling cold, worked its way across her skin. She tugged again on the ropes, managing to get enough slack to look over her shoulder. The key sat a few inches from her back, perfectly fitting into a recess on the stone. Zhao crossed the chamber and slid onto the riser on the other side of the key.

"Sunrise in one minute," Gui said.

"Think about it," Zhao said, drawing her hands up across her stomach as though she was going to do a meditation. "The kings of the Khmer Empire would sit here, in this very spot, just like I am ..."

"You've got to stop this," Athena shouted, pulling at the bindings. "You'll kill us all."

"It's quite alright, everything's safe," Zhao said, her tone now low and meditative.

Athena strained to one side and managed to catch a glimpse of Zhao, lying in the groove worn by the backs of the power-hungry people who had lain there before.

"Gui, get ready to align the discs when the first rays of sun are visible," Zhao said.

Gui crossed the chamber and stood beneath the sun shaft.

"It'll kill us!" Athena roared, once again tugging at the ropes.

"Thirty seconds," Gui said, using a pair of levers to make minor adjustments to the mirrors.

"No, it won't," Zhao said, her voice calm. "The early dawn rays have such little power that the effects will be minor. This first experiment will only affect someone within a few feet of the Lotus Key. In other words, it will only affect you."

"You're crazy!" Athena shouted.

"That is one thing I am not. I am the opposite of crazy," Zhao replied, her voice now like the murmurings of a monk. "I am helping you see the error of your ways. You will soon understand how foolish it is for people to fight like nean-derthals—"

"I won't! You can't!" Athena shouted, pulling with renewed energy. "You have no idea what damage that'll do!"

Athena frantically yanked against the ropes, wearing the skin from her wrists.

"Fighting is crazy," Zhao continued. "Families torn apart by conflict is crazy. What we will achieve today is divine. This is the perfect solution. And what better way to test it than to bring a mother and daughter back together again?"

"Five seconds," Gui called out.

Athena strained her neck and looked up the sun shaft. A soft orange glow now radiated from the sky as the sun peeked over the horizon. Her heart hammered against her ribs as she made one final desperate attempt to loosen the ropes.

"Don't struggle," Zhao said. "This is your destiny. This is our destiny. Together, we are about to make history."

"Three ... two ... one."

As though responding to Gui's command, the first ray of dawn light lanced down the shaft and into the chamber. Channeled by the shape of the lotus tower and the inlaid reflective metal, it cast a laser-like beam on the first disc which was mounted directly beneath it.

Gui made another minor adjustment to the disc, locking the beam on the second disc across the chamber.

"Yes," Zhao breathed, her face transformed with almost religious fervor. "It's beginning."

Gui jogged across the room and adjusted the second disc. He worked the levers on the base of the mount and an inch-thick bar of golden light swept across the room. The beam crept closer to the Lotus Key, the brightness intensi-fying with each passing second.

"You're about to become part of something far greater than you can ever imagine," Zhao said, the beam inching closer to the key's surface. "Something greater than all of us."

The beam moved closer, turning dust into golden sparkles.

"What if you're wrong?" Athena said through gritted teeth. She struggled from side to side, the ropes slicing through her skin. "What if the Lotus Key has been damaged—"

Athena's voice died in her throat. A low vibration moved through her body. Even though she couldn't see what was happening behind her, she knew the beam of light had reached the Lotus Key and her time was up.

"Yes!" Zhao said, her voice trembling. "It's awakening!"

"Turn. It. Off!" Athena said, her back arched and her jaw set. The tingling sensation on the back of her neck increased until it felt like a warm draft. "You can't ... you can't!"

"Oh, I can," Zhao said. "And what's more, I must. Humankind needs this. It is my duty."

53

Eden and Baxter edged toward the opening, shielding their eyes against the heat and smoke. Still a few feet from the opening, they had to turn back, running out of the smoke, and coughing.

"We haven't got long," Eden said, looking up into the sky where the sun had emerged. Stars were fading one by one, and the great lotus tower was washed in a honey-gold hue.

"Someone will see this." Baxter pointed up at the smoke pouring upwards. "The guards will come and check it out soon."

"Unless the guards are working for Zhao," Eden said, looking back at the shaft. "That would explain how she got the Lotus Key in here unnoticed."

Hearing a bumping, crashing noise, Eden and Baxter spun around, ready to attack.

Lavigne clattered across the rooftop, huffing and puffing. He reached the edge and used the rope to laboriously climb down into the courtyard.

"That was incroyable!" he said, patting down his clothes and straightening out his scarf. "The way you dealt with those men, bouf, bouf!" He delivered a few cartoon style punches.

One of the unconscious men groaned in his slumber, eliciting a cry from Lavigne who rushed across to Eden and Baxter like his tail was on fire.

"With moves like that, you could have come to help," Eden said.

"Oh, I ..."

"They always say that surprise is one of the greatest strategies," Baxter said. "And I'd certainly be surprised if you ran at me."

Lavigne looked up at Baxter, not quite knowing how to take the comment.

Hiding a smirk, Eden turned to the opening from which the smoke poured.

"What can you tell us about this?" she said, glancing at Lavigne.

"It's certainly an interesting feature," Lavigne said, with the casualness of someone discussing a research paper. He adjusted his spectacles and peered at the smoke. "I have read about temples being equipped with defensive mechanisms, but nothing quite like this. The engineering required—"

"My fault," Eden interrupted. "That question was far too vague. Allow me to rephrase, how do we shut this off?"

Lavigne pursed his lips and rubbed a hand across his face. "Although constructed many centuries ago, this is based around the same idea of a modern alarm system. Its purpose is a deterrent, rather than to seal the chamber closed."

"The smoke does look like it's thinning already," Baxter said, peering up into the sky.

"There'll be some kind of system that shuts it off after a

set time," Lavigne said. "You see, the temple builders would have needed to—"

"How long until we can get down there?" Eden said.

"Again, you want the answers." Lavigne sighed, glancing at his watch. "I don't think this will last more than a few more minutes." He squinted at the shaft. "The ancients were brilliant engineers, but even they couldn't create an infinite fuel source. The intensity of each burst should decrease as the pressure—"

A ball of smoke burst out of the opening, before thinning to little more than a trickle.

"You see?" Lavigne said, gesturing excitedly. "It's already less powerful. The system likely operates on a combination of trapped gases and mechanical triggers. Similar to what we found in the temples near—"

"How sure are you that it's not going to start up again?" Eden said.

"Well ... I can't be, you know, certain."

"That's good enough for me," Eden said, retrieving the rope they'd used to climb into the temple and stepping up to the opening.

"I really think we should wait another thirty minutes at least," Lavigne said, frantically looking from his watch to the smoke. "The shaft walls will retain heat long after the flames stop. They're likely hot enough to cause third-degree burns on contact. And, as I said, I can't be certain that the fire won't restart."

"We need to get down there." Eden glanced up at the sky where dawn was now coming in fast. "There's no telling what ..." Eden stopped talking, not wanting to finish the sentence.

She secured the rope to the column beside the charred

remains of the rope which Zhao's thugs had used to rappel down the shaft.

"I'm ... I'm really not sure this is a good idea," Lavigne said, his head swiveling like a meerkat on the lookout. "I never was very good at climbing the rope."

"Yet again, professor, you're welcome to stay up here if you want." Eden pulled on the rope to test that it was securely fastened and glanced up at the lightening sky again.

"Who wants to see a chamber beneath the world-famous Angkor Wat, anyway?" Baxter added, stepping alongside Eden.

Eden pulled three harnesses from the bag. She passed one to Lavigne, one to Baxter, and slipped the last on herself.

"It's impossible to fall with this on," Eden said, tugging at the carabiner now hanging from her waist.

"Impossible?" Lavigne said, adjusting the straps. "I assure you, nothing is impossible."

"With that positive thought, let's get going." Eden fed the rope through the clip and backed into the smoke. Although tendrils continued to rise from the shaft, and heat prickled her face, it now seemed bearable.

"Lavigne, you're next," she said, standing on the edge and leaning back over the void. "Baxter, you're last. See you down there." She stepped back and walked down the shaft walls, lowering herself with the rope.

After about fifteen feet, she glanced up and saw Lavigne nervously back into the shaft. He released the rope and walked down the wall, his movements jerky.

About halfway down she spotted an elaborately carved section of wall encircling the entire shaft. The centerpiece was the image of a man holding a flaming torch. Flames surrounded the figure too.

"Agni," Eden whispered, looking closely at the figure. Above the figure she saw wisps of smoke rising from a series of holes. She jumped into the center of the shaft and let several feet of the rope go in one swift movement. She fell down the shaft, totally avoiding touching any of the carved stones. Hitting the wall again, she froze, waiting to see if any flames roared forth. When they didn't, she exhaled and set off again toward whatever lay beneath.

"I think I've found the trigger for the alarm system," she whispered. "Don't touch any of the carved stones."

"No problem," Lavigne said, clearly tense as he lowered himself another few feet.

With the sides of the shaft now cool, Eden covered the distance as quickly as possible. As she neared, a dull golden glow radiated toward her. She slowed her process and listened.

"It is done," came Zhao's voice, carrying a note of triumph that made Eden's skin crawl. "Untie her now. The Lotus Key has done its job."

Eden quickened her pace, a sickening feeling rising in her stomach.

The golden light intensified as she descended, casting strange shadows up the shaft walls.

"This is remarkable," Zhao said, her voice laced with awe. "Bring my daughter to me."

Eden paused, listening to the movement that followed. She focused on the sound, trying to work out what was going on, but with each sound echoing several times it was impossible to tell.

"My daughter, this is a wonderful day," Zhao said. "Together we are going to make history."

Impatience turning into desperation, Eden released another length of rope. She looked down and saw that the shaft opened into a chamber a few feet below. She released the rope slowly, tightened it around her waist, and turned upside down. She lowered herself inch by inch until she could look into the chamber while remaining mostly out of sight.

She emerged into a vast rectangular chamber. Lit only by red flashlights and a subtle golden light, she couldn't see exactly how big the place was. A stone block sat in the center of the chamber, lit in the strange golden light, and on top of the riser was an object that Eden immediately, instinctively, recognized.

"The Lotus Key," she said, no louder than an exhale.

One of the beams of golden light panned to the side, momentarily illuminating a figure sat beside the riser.

"Athena," Eden hissed.

One of the figures carrying the red flashlights moved across to Athena and worked at the knots which tied her in position.

Athena's head was slumped forward, and she looked almost lifeless. As the knots came loose, her hands dropped into her lap. The man lifted her shakily to her feet and supported her for a few moments before letting her stand on her own.

"It would have been much easier if you had agreed with me in the first place," Zhao said, stepping toward Athena. Eden watched as the woman took Athena's head in her hands, sweeping her hair aside. "I hate to do this to you, but you must see the error of your ways."

Athena leaned into Zhao's shoulder, as though in a trance. When she spoke, her voice was deep and emotionless. "Yes, mother."

54

EDEN WATCHED FOR SEVERAL SECONDS, UNABLE TO TEAR HER eyes away as mother and daughter embraced. Washed in the red flashlight beams and golden pulsing light from the Lotus Key, the whole scene was strangely hypnotic.

Movements on the rope above her pulled Eden's focus back to the present. She took a moment to check out the chamber's layout, noting that the corners and the far side were completely cloaked in shadow. The ceiling where she now hung was probably also invisible, unless a flashlight beam came her way. Glancing down at the floor beneath them, she figured they could probably get down there unseen, providing they were quick and quiet.

Eden righted herself and started down the rope, letting it pass through the carabiner as quietly as possible. She glanced anxiously up at Lavigne, moving somewhere in the shaft above her. Although the professor was many things, stealthy wasn't one of them. Right now, communicating with him was far too risky, she just had to hope he kept quiet.

She had almost reached the ground when the rope swayed and jerked, indicating that Lavigne was out of the shaft. Looking up, she could see him, swinging back and forth. She winced as Lavigne's carabiner squealed against the rope. She held her breath, but no one seemed to notice.

"This is the start of something ... something wonderful ..." Zhao said, still holding Athena in her arms.

Clearly hearing Zhao's voice, Lavigne turned around and saw the chamber for the first time.

Eden watched as a ripple of pure amazement moved through his body. Then, he did the unimaginable. He opened his mouth and ...

"Incroyable!" Lavigne said, speaking before assessing the danger.

Zhao spun around, turning toward the noise. "Who's there?" she said, sweeping her red flashlight through the chamber. "Cover the Lotus Key, get some light in here."

One of the men dragged a thick blanket across the Lotus Key and powered up a standard flashlight. The dazzling beam swept through the chamber, followed a moment later by three more. The beams rounded the walls, before focusing on Lavigne hanging in the mouth of the shaft. One of the beams then moved down the rope and illuminated Eden. The men drew guns, some leveled at Lavigne, others at Eden.

A smile spread across Zhao's face. It wasn't a smile of surprise, but of satisfaction. "Perfect," she said, one hand locked on Athena's shoulder. "This is exactly the test we require. Gui, get them down."

Gui marched across the chamber and seized Eden by the ankle. She considered scrambling back up the rope, but with Lavigne in the way and at least thirty feet of rope to climb before the safety of the shaft, she'd be Swiss cheese before she got there. That didn't mean she had to go easily.

She swung on the rope, using Gui's grip as a pivot point,

and rammed her other boot into his jaw. Gui's head snapped back, but his grip remained iron tight.

Eden released the rope and hit the ground, rolling with the impact. She bounced up almost immediately, ready to fight.

"We have no time for games," Zhao said, her voice deadly calm.

Eden turned and saw Zhao with a gun pointed directly at her.

"If you give me any more trouble, I'll put a bullet through your skull," Zhao said. "Do you understand?"

Eden held Zhao's stare for a long moment and nodded once.

"Good," Zhao said, signaling to Gui. The brute stepped away from Eden and raised his weapon. The pistol looked almost small in his meaty hand, but his aim was steady, the barrel targeting Eden's forehead.

Zhao turned her attention to Lavigne. "It's remarkable that our paths continue to cross in this way, professor. Maybe the universe is trying to tell you that we should work together after all."

"I ... well ..." Lavigne stuttered, gasping in panic.

"No need to explain how you feel," Zhao said, her tone once again that of a master predator. "Come down here and join the party."

Lavigne let the rope go, jerkily bouncing toward the floor. He landed in a heap, huffing and puffing.

Zhao snapped her fingers and another of her men seized Lavigne, marched him across the chamber, and stood him beside Eden.

"I would be surprised if the brave Captain Baxter isn't up there too," Zhao said, in a pantomime stage whisper. She snapped her fingers and another of the men positioned himself at the base of the shaft, his gun pointed skyward.

Clearly realizing he couldn't climb faster than a bullet, Baxter lowered himself down into the chamber. Reaching the floor, he unclipped the rope and let Zhao's man guide him across to where Lavigne and Eden waited.

"I must say, my daughter would be incredibly humbled to know that you've attempted to save her," Zhao said, pointing toward Athena, who stood motionless, her eyes unfocused. "Although, unfortunately, for you, you've arrived too late."

Eden looked at Athena, searching for an indication of her friend in the motionless body. When she saw none of the spark she knew and loved, grief flooded her body.

"Although I must admit, I'm disappointed in you, professor," Zhao said, pointing at Lavigne. "You're an educated man. I thought you understood the historical significance of what we're doing here."

"Historical significance?" Lavigne pushed his spectacles up his nose and adjusted his scarf, as though trying to gather what remained of his dignity. "What you're planning is an abomination! The key was never meant to—"

"The key was meant for exactly this." Zhao cut him off sharply. "And I'm not planning it. The time for planning is past. Now is the time for action." Zhao squeezed Athena's shoulder. "And thanks to my daughter's ... reluctant assistance, we're about to witness its true potential."

"What have you done to her?" Eden inched forward, fighting her instinct to attack Zhao right there and then.

Gui tracked her movements, his trigger finger relaxed but ready.

Athena remained motionless. Dark circles shadowed her

eyes, and her skin looked almost translucent in the flash-light beams.

"Done to her?" Zhao's laugh was as sharp as broken glass. "I've opened her mind." She stroked Athena's hair in a manner that made Eden's skin crawl. "She's free. Liberated from all the wants and desires humankind has been plagued by for eternity. I know she'll understand, and soon you will too." Zhao looked at Athena with pride, then turned to Eden.

"No! I won't let you do this!" Eden shouted.

Zhao's grin spread slowly, like oil across water. She shook her head, the gesture almost pitying. "You have no choice," she said, flatly. "The time for fighting is over. In fact, now that I have the Lotus Key, fighting is over, forever."

"What do you mean?" Eden said, her eyes narrowing. "People will always fight for what they believe in."

"Yes, but that's it," Zhao said. "Starting today, people won't believe in anything. Love, belief, choice, individuality, they're now all things of the past."

"You're insane," Eden breathed, the implications of Zhao's plan finally hitting her. "You're talking about wiping out human consciousness. Turning everyone into ... into ..."

"Into perfect beings," Zhao finished. "No more war. No more suffering. No more of the petty divisions that have plagued humanity since we first crawled from the mud. The ancients understood. They knew that consciousness itself was the problem. Free will, individual thought—these are the sources of all human misery."

Eden glanced at Athena, searching for any sign of the brilliant, passionate woman she knew. But Athena's eyes remained vacant.

"You won't ... There's no way ..." Eden snarled.

"Oh, I will, and I can, but I have another purpose for

you. This will be the first test of the Lotus Key's power."
Zhao snapped her fingers, and the men backed away from
Eden, Lavigne and Baxter.

Eden watched them go, her unease increasing tenfold.

Zhao stepped forward and raised her gun in the air. She
squeezed the trigger three times in quick succession. The
gunshots were deafening in the enclosed space, each crack
like a thunderclap. Bullets smashed into the rock above,
sending ancient stone chips raining down.

"That's a demonstration to show you that we're using
live rounds. There are no last chances here." She lowered
the gun, examining it almost lovingly before holding it out
to Athena. "Take this."

Athena reached out and took the weapon. Her fingers
wrapped around the grip with mechanical precision.

"Now," Zhao said, looking from her daughter to her new
captives. "Your first task is to kill Eden Black."

55

Eden watched, her mouth open in disbelief, as Athena stepped toward her. She held the gun in front of her with perfect form—one hand wrapped around the grip, the other cupped beneath the barrel.

"This will be the true test of the Lotus Key's power," Zhao said, her voice more excited than ever before. "What better test is there than killing a loved one in cold blood?"

Athena's face remained expressionless, her eyes glazed and distant. She took another step, the barrel aligned with Eden's chest.

Gui giggled, as though what Zhao had said was truly amusing. He grinned, his eyes following the scene with a sick enjoyment.

"Athena, this isn't you!" Eden said, trying and failing to remain calm. "It's Eden, we're like sisters. Or at least, you're the closest thing I've ever had to a sister."

The chamber fell into an unnatural silence as Athena closed the distance.

Lavigne whimpered.

"Athena, listen!" Baxter said, stepping forward. He

inched in front of Eden in preparation to take the bullet himself. "Stop this madness. I know you can hear us!"

Athena took another mechanical step forward. Reaching the point where she was close enough to guarantee a hit, she stopped and slipped her finger across the trigger. With robot like precision, she made some minor adjustments to the gun's position.

"Perfect," Zhao whispered, her voice carrying in the stillness. "This is better than I had hoped. Exposure to the key purifies the mind and strips away all emotional weakness."

Gui chuckled again, his fists clenched in pure joy.

"Athena, I need you to listen to me," Eden said, her jaw clenched. "You can beat this, I know you can. Whatever she's done to you, you're stronger than this."

Athena looked up slowly, the hair falling away from her face. She locked eyes with Eden. Her friend's typically warm gaze was now hard and focused.

"Take the shot," Zhao commanded, her tone ice cold.

Athena's finger tensed around the trigger. A bead of sweat rolled down her temple, catching the light like a tear.

Then, almost like a dream, Eden saw Athena's lips moving. She leaned forward, trying to hear her friend's voice. Athena was chanting something, a delusional rhythm perhaps.

"Savasanasavasanaavasana," Athena said, her voice rising into something of a war chant.

"Do it now," Zhao snapped, her hands balled and her expression furious.

"SavasanaSavasanaSavasana," Athena chanted louder, the gun still locked on Eden's chest.

"Do it," Zhao said again, pointing at Eden.

"Savasana, Savasana, Savasana," Athena said.

The memory hit Eden like a brick to the face. The yoga on the beach in Sok San.

"Savasana," Athena said one more time.

"Lie on the ground!" Eden shouted, dragging Baxter and Lavigne down. The professor let out a startled yelp as they hit the stone.

Athena fired. The gun cracked, its report deafening in the enclosed chamber.

The first bullet screamed past where Eden had been a split second before, sparking off the wall behind them. Stone fragments exploded as the round ricocheted, whining off into the gloom.

Her eyes now sharp and focused, Athena spun on her heel and fired twice more. The two guards nearest the Lotus Key never had a chance to react. They stood frozen, still captivated by what they thought was their triumph. The bullets caught them in their chests; the impacts throwing them backward. Athena dropped to her knee and took aim. The other guards, now wise to her intentions, dove for cover.

"No!" Zhao screamed, as Gui tackled her around the waist and dragged her down behind the Lotus Key's riser.

Using the moment of confusion to level the score, Eden sprinted across to one of the fallen guards. She snagged up his rifle, his sidearm, and a couple of spare magazines.

Gui leaned out from behind the riser and fired, missing Eden by inches. She flattened herself behind the fallen guard, who was fortunately bigger than her. She returned fire, forcing Gui back behind the stone, and raced across the chamber. She leaped in behind the stone blocks where one of the discs was positioned.

A guard leaned out from behind his cover in an alcove at the back of the chamber and fired. The bullet slammed into the rock, forcing Eden, Baxter, Athena, and Lavigne to take cover.

Athena rolled out, risking a hit, and fired. The first shot went wide, but the second caught the shooter in the shoulder. He staggered, but didn't fall.

Eden passed the handgun to Baxter, who immediately leveled it at one column behind which the guards took cover.

Without a weapon, Lavigne worked on the levers that controlled the position of the disc. Just as one man popped out to take a shot, Lavigne dazzled him with a bright beam of light.

Eden and Athena fired, two bullets finding their mark. The guard staggered back, slumping into the wall.

Baxter leaned the other way, keeping his attention on the riser behind which Zhao and Gui sheltered. Seeing movement, he fired. His first two shots chipped the stone and then the gun clicked empty. He rolled back into cover.

In the half-second of silence that followed, boots scraped against stone and then the air erupted with gunfire. Clearly encouraged by the sound of Baxter's empty gun, a volley of bullets slammed into their position, smashing the ancient stonework into shards. The volley continued for far longer than necessary, forcing them to cower behind the stone.

The moment the firing stopped, Eden rolled from their cover and brought up the rifle to return fire.

This was exactly what Gui had been waiting for. Having used his ally's gunfire to close the distance, he slammed into Eden with crushing force.

Eden fell backwards, shoved off balance by Gui's bulk and momentum. Her rifle spun across the stone, uselessly out of reach. Another strafe of bullets zipped through the chamber as the last remaining guard charged toward them.

"Athena! Three o'clock," Baxter yelled.

Athena, who had been trying to get a clear shot on Gui, swung around and dropped the final guard before he was close enough to aim. Looking beyond the fallen guard, Athena saw Zhao dashing through the shadows at the back of the chamber.

Athena fired several times, emptying the magazine. Unsure whether Zhao had taken a hit, or was still moving through the gloom, Athena glanced back at Eden, crushed beneath Gui's vast body. Making a snap decision, she leaped at Gui.

Athena hit Gui like a missile, her shoulder driving into his kidney. The impact threw him off balance and Eden slipped free.

Baxter leaped in and attempted to kick the brute, but Gui rolled away. Gui climbed to his feet and charged again, this time swinging for Athena. As Athena ducked the blow, Baxter backed away, spun, and charged for a fallen rifle.

As Athena back stepped, Eden bobbed forward and drove her knee into the big man's guts. He grunted, but didn't go down.

"Eden!" Baxter shouted, kicking the gun across the floor.

Gui reacted first and lunged for the weapon.

Eden jumped too, the pair moving through the air at the same time.

Gui hit the ground first and swept his hand toward the weapon. As Eden reached out, Gui's hand closed around the gun and swung it around. Eden backed up, now focused on getting out of the way of any bullets he sent her way. She was too late, the business end of the rifle leveled with her chest.

Silence descended on the chamber as Gui struggled to his feet, the weapon locked on Eden. The brute grinned through bloodied teeth, moving the gun from Eden to Baxter and on to Athena.

"Time's up," Gui said, his finger on the trigger. "I've been looking forward to this."

The gunshot rang out.

Gui's expression shifted from triumph to confusion. He looked down at a red stain spreading across his chest, then turned toward the source of the shot.

Lavigne rose from his crouched position, his hands trembling around a pistol. His spectacles were askew, and his usually immaculate clothes were covered in dust.

"Que Dieu me pardonne," Lavigne muttered, dropping the gun as though it were infected, and then staring at his hands.

Gui took one stumbling step forward. He clawed at his chest with a mixture of shock and pain. Then his legs gave out, and he crashed down like a fallen tree. This time, though, he didn't get up.

"Professor," Eden said, turning to look at the Frenchman. "I didn't know you could shoot."

"I can't," Lavigne replied. "That was supposed to be a warning shot."

"Don't worry, we won't tell." Athena rushed across the chamber, seized Lavigne, and planted a kiss on his cheek.

"Will ... je dis ... that's totally not ..." Lavigne stuttered, flushing a beetroot red.

"Hold on a minute," Eden said, looking from Athena and across at the Lotus Key, which was still obscured by the blanket. "You were faking that whole time?"

"I figured that was my only way out," Athena said. "If I could make Zhao think she had control over me, then—"

"Inspiré, inspiré," Lavigne said, straightening his spectacles.

"But that means the Lotus Key didn't work," Eden said.

"I guess so," Athena said, shrugging.

"That's no surprise really, it was at the bottom of the sea for almost a thousand years," Baxter said.

"That's too simple." Eden's face tensed with concentration. "Remember the power and destruction it caused on the rig? The only answer is—"

"Someone tampered with it?" Athena said.

Slowly, as realization dawned, Eden, Baxter and Athena turned to look at Lavigne.

"You were the only person outside of Zhao's team to see both discs," Eden said, pointing at the professor.

"I might have played a petite, little, trick," Lavigne said, holding his finger and thumb a minute distance apart.

This time, both Eden and Athena rushed at the professor and pulled him into a hug. Baxter limited himself to a slap on the shoulder, eliciting a wince from the Frenchman.

"What did you do?" Eden said.

"Well, it's quite simple, really," Lavigne said, buying himself dramatic time by adjusting his spectacles. "As you noted, I had the chance to examine both discs. While doing so, I applied a fine coating of sunscreen to the glass."

"Sunscreen?" Eden said incredulously. "You saved the human race with sunscreen?"

"That makes sense, sunburn is a real danger," Athena said.

"Factor fifty, of course." Lavigne nodded, clearly enjoying himself. "You see, when one says that the Lotus Key is powered by sunlight, that's a very general term. It's actually powered by ultraviolet light. I suspected that even the smallest impurity would disrupt the energy transfer."

"How did you get access to sunscreen?" Athena asked. "I didn't think Zhao's hospitality would stretch to such things."

"This is a tropical climate!" Lavigne shouted, aghast. "I have sensitive skin and can't be expected to work in a tropical climate without the necessary protection!"

"He can be annoyingly persuasive," Eden quipped.

"Of course, with my sensitive needs, I required a specialist sunscreen containing a high level of zinc oxide. Fortunately, Zhao was obliging enough to have one of her men fetch some. The zinc oxide reflects the light, scattering the UV rays away from the glass." Lavigne chuckled at his own amusement. "The higher the intensity of light, the more it was scattered away from where Zhao wanted it to go. The more Zhao tried to focus the beams—"

"The less focused they became," Athena finished, shaking her head in amazement.

"Exactement," Lavigne said. "Sometimes the simple solutions are the best."

"I don't mean to break up the party," Baxter said, clicking on another flashlight and sweeping it through the chamber. "But where's mother dearest?"

56

MEI-LING ZHAO HAULED HERSELF UP THE ROPE, HER ARMS burning with each pull. After what felt like an age, she reached out and gripped the top of the shaft. With one last pull, and a grunt of effort, she hauled herself up and over the edge. She lay on the cool stone and took a moment to fill her lungs with air.

After two restorative breaths, Zhao rolled over and stood. Dawn now washed the temple in shades of gold, the first rays of sun catching the ancient stones and setting them ablaze.

Ignoring the majestic temple, she looked back down the shaft and silently cursed Eden and her friends. What exactly had gone wrong with the Lotus Key, she didn't know. She'd followed the diagram in the hidden carving to the letter. Perhaps she'd got something wrong. Perhaps Professor Lavigne wasn't as good as she thought, or perhaps the whole thing was a myth after all.

Right now, Zhao concluded, all that mattered was getting out of here alive and free. Once she was out of sight, she could work out what went wrong and plan her next move. She drew out a knife and cut through the rope.

"At least you're not coming after me," she said, holding the rope out over the shaft. She released her grip, and the rope whispered down into the darkness.

Zhao turned away from the shaft and broke into a sprint. Above her, rose-gold stained the eastern sky. She ducked through the central temple and paused at the top of the steep staircase. The vast complex spread out below her—morning mist sweeping through the lower galleries like a silken scarf. She turned one way and saw hordes of tourists still watching the sunrise, totally unaware of the drama that had played out so close by.

For now, Zhao thought, the masses would continue with their pointless lives. Looking out across the great moat which glowed like molten copper in the sunlight, she saw smoke rising from a small cluster of buildings. She knew these shacks to be one of the villages that survived on tourist traffic to the temples.

Zhao charged down the steps and scrambled out through a window. Soon this place would be crawling with guards and police. Before that happened, she needed to be a long way away.

She ran full pelt into the moat and swam across, staying out of sight as much as possible. Dragging herself out of the muddy water, she ducked in behind a tree. Taking efforts to remain out of sight, she moved from tree to tree until she reached the outskirts of the village.

The smell of cooking fires filled the air. A rooster crowed nearby, and the sound of children's laughter drifted from one of the huts. Two local men walked past, speaking rapid Khmer. Zhao pressed herself against the tree, remaining out of sight. The men walked on, their footsteps soon fading into the noise of the city.

Within a minute or two, she heard the sound she was searching for—the *putt-putt* of a motorcycle struggling to life. The bike protested with a series of angry coughs and rattles, clearly well past its prime. The sound grew louder, accompanied by the crunch of tires on the dirt track. Through a gap in the buildings, Zhao caught glimpses of a beaten-up Honda coming her way.

The bike pulled level and Zhao exploded from the shadows. Her shoulder caught the unsuspecting man squarely in the ribs, shoving him sideways from the bike. She vaulted on to the saddle as the rider sprawled into the pile of empty rice sacks, and wrenched back on the throttle, the rear wheel spinning as she accelerated away.

57

"First, that woman is not my mother," Athena snapped in return, her arms folded.

"Technically, she is," Eden corrected.

"Second, there's only one way out of this place, so she must have ..." Athena's voice died in her throat as she looked over and saw the rope coiled on the ground.

"Oh, no ... no, no ..." Lavigne said, his lips quivering. "That's not good at all."

Eden and Athena rushed across the chamber and peered up the shaft. Far above them, the golden light of the morning seeped down.

"Hello, anyone up there?" Athena shouted, hands cupped around her mouth.

"No one will be inside the temple complex for hours yet," Eden said, folding her arms. "By then, Zhao will be miles away. We'll have lost her." She pulled out her phone. "No signal."

Baxter did the same and found the same result.

"Why didn't one of us wait outside?" Eden groaned,

looking up at the shaft again, painfully out of reach without the help of someone outside.

"I wish I'd done that," Lavigne muttered. "But curiosity got the better of me. Never again." His shoulders slumped and he looked down at the floor, dejected.

"There's got to be another way out of here," Baxter said, looking around at the walls. "There's always an escape route, right Lavigne?" He placed a hand on Lavigne's shoulder.

Lavigne made a nebulous gesture that was halfway between a nod and a shake.

"It's possible that there is," Eden said. "In fact, I'd say it was quite likely, but we'll lose time figuring it out. There's got to be a better way." She turned and looked at the blanket that still covered the Lotus Key.

"Hold on a second, professor, you said that the Lotus Key didn't work because of a layer of sunscreen on the mirrors?"

"Yes, just a fine layer applied by this scarf," Lavigne said, lifting the end of the garment, which had remained surprisingly in place throughout his entire ordeal.

"So, we could wipe the sunscreen away and power up the Lotus Key?" Eden said.

"And then use that to get someone to come and help us!" Athena said. "That's genius."

"It's incredibly dangerous," Baxter said, arms folded. "We've no idea the power this thing has. It could cause serious damage."

"It's fine. The professor here can regulate the power carefully using the discs, right?" Eden said.

"I guess so. Why not?" Lavigne said, turning to look at the discs which had fortunately remained undamaged. He adjusted his spectacles and leaned in close. "It's actually a remarkably complex system, but I think I've got the gist of it.

It's what you might call a primitive laser array. You see, the shaft isn't—"

"Excellent," Eden said, pacing toward the riser on which the Khmer king once would have lain to force his wishes on his empire. "We'll use it to get one of the guards to come here and help. Once we're out, we'll kill the power." She ran her hand across the stone, feeling the human shape worn into it.

"It doesn't look very comfortable. I bet the king had cushions," Eden said, lifting one leg on to the riser, and preparing to slide into place.

"No wait," Athena said. Her voice was quiet but firm.

Eden turned to face her friend.

"I'll do it. My m ... that woman got us into this mess. Plus, I've already been exposed to it. If it turns out there are aftereffects, there's no point in us both suffering."

Eden and Athena shared a long gaze. "Fine, if you're sure," Eden placed her feet back on the floor. "Be careful."

Athena slid onto the riser and adopted the exact position she'd seen Zhao in a few minutes before. She placed her head against the block, which was raised at one end, allowing her to see back across the chamber. Trying to relax, she placed her hands across her stomach.

Lavigne slipped the first disc from its clamp and cleaned the glass with his scarf.

"When this is all over, I'm buying you a new scarf," Eden said, noticing how bedraggled and stained the garment now was.

"Non, merci. No thank you. I'm quite attached to this one," Lavigne replied, slotting the disc back into the clamp and pushing it until it clicked. "The quality of construction here really is incredible," he muttered, moving across to the second disc.

"Switch to red lights, then I'll remove the blanket," Athena said. "You all stay back, just in case."

Eden and Baxter moved around the room, turning off the flashlights that had been dropped by Zhao and her men. Eden picked up one of the red ones and backed away from the riser.

With everyone as far back as possible, Athena sat up and yanked the blanket away from the Lotus Key.

Seeing the object for the first time, Eden gasped. Square at the base, it rose into a lotus shape, and in the dull light of the chamber, it glowed ethereally. Unsure if it was her mind playing tricks, she felt a surge of electricity course through her, as though the relic was tempting them all with its power.

"Ready?" Lavigne called out, slotting the second disc back into place and examining the controls.

"Ready as I'll ever be," Athena said, lying back.

Lavigne crossed back to the first disc and worked the controls. A narrow, golden beam of light swept through the chamber, bouncing from the first disc to the second. He moved back to the second disc and worked that into position, muttering to himself in French as he did so.

"Try not to melt my face off," Athena said, her tone suggesting she was only half joking.

"The alignment has to be correct," Lavigne said, licking his lips as he worked the controls. The beam panned side to side, working its way closer to the Lotus Key.

Eden peered up the sun shaft, the walls glowing.

Finally, the beam of light struck the Lotus Key's surface.

Lavigne stepped away, sweat running down his face. He mopped his brow and turned his attention to the relic.

Now bathed in the bright yellow light, the Lotus Key hummed, a vibration moving through the chamber.

Athena gripped on to the riser as the tremors worked their way through her. Unsure of exactly what to do, she attempted to clear her mind and think about the guards stationed outside.

"Is it supposed to sound like that?" Eden said, turning to Lavigne. "Are you sure you haven't given it too much power?"

"Certain," Lavigne said. "Remember, this is the first time it's been used in almost one thousand years." Lavigne stared at the glowing relic, a smile of pure enjoyment lighting his face.

The Lotus Key's hum intensified, vibrating through Athena's bones. Her teeth chattered, and her vision began to blur at the edges. The chamber pulsed with an energy that felt electric, like the moment before a lightning strike.

The sensation of pins and needles spread from her fingertips, up her arms, then across her chest. Her heart raced, threatening to pound right out of her chest.

"Is everything okay?" Eden said from across the chamber, her voice sounding distant.

The stone at Athena's back no longer felt solid—it rippled and flowed like water, moving at one with her body.

"Something ... something's happening," came a voice. Athena realized a moment later that the sound was her own voice, except now it sounded like it was coming from someone else.

"Stop ... we should stop it ..." Eden shouted.

"No ... it's ..." the voice Athena thought was her own replied. Then colors shifted around her—the red flashlight beams stretching into strange, elongated halos.

The carved figures on the walls appeared to dance in her peripheral vision, though she couldn't catch them moving when she looked directly at them. A pressure built inside her skull. Memories flickered through her mind like a film on fast forward: her childhood, her training, her mother's betrayal, all bleeding together into a kaleidoscope of sensations. She tried to focus on the guards outside, but her thoughts kept slipping away like water through her fingers.

"Eden," she gasped, gripping the edges of the riser until her knuckles went white. "I can't ... everything's ..." The words dissolved in her mouth before she could form them. The chamber spun around her, the ceiling and floor trading places with dizzying speed. Through it all, the key's hum grew louder, filling not just her ears but her entire consciousness.

Then, all at once, something changed. She was no longer sitting in the chamber, shaken to the bone, she was moving weightlessly up through the lotus tower.

Stones blurred past her like water, their carved surfaces rippling with energy. Galleries and corridors twisted, as though the temple was folding in on itself. The normally rigid geometry of the architecture bent and flowed like smoke. Carved Apsaras danced, as though welcoming a traveler after a long absence. She drifted through the temple, not treading on the stone, but moving effortlessly through the air.

Athena looked down at herself but couldn't see her body. She was moving through space and time, untethered from physical form.

Within what seemed like mere moments, she reached a pair of temple guards standing by the eastern gate. Their forms seemed to be both solid and transparent, but Athena somehow knew they were there. Without speaking to them, she made some kind of connection.

Without a moment's hesitation, the men swung around and broke into a sprint.

58

EDEN WATCHED IN SHOCK AS VIBRATIONS MOVED THROUGH Athena's body. At first, she lay on the riser with her muscles tensed. Then her back arched and her face locked into an expression of pain, before slumping back unconscious.

Moving on instinct, Eden ran forward, planning to drag her friend to safety.

"Stay back," Baxter said, seizing Eden around the wrist. "We've got to leave her."

"Like the kings of old, she's now entering the trance," Lavigne said, his face washed in the golden light. "This is where she will take on the key's power. To pull her out now could be dangerous."

Eden froze, her gaze locked on Athena's slumped and peaceful figure. Lying on the riser, with the Lotus Key glowing at her feet, it looked as though she was asleep.

"I'm out, commands given," Athena shouted, the volume of her voice at odds with her position. "Guards are on their way."

"Shut it down!" Eden roared, pulling away from Baxter.

"She's done she what she went there to do. We need to get her out."

"Wait!" Athena's voice cut through the chamber, her tone carrying a deeper, more menacing edge. "I have one more task."

ZHAO SPED UP AWAY FROM THE TEMPLE COMPLEX. SHE PULLED back on the throttle, sending the old engine into a high-pitched scream. Blue smoke belched from the exhaust and the back tire kicked up a cloud of dust.

She shot past a row of ramshackle huts, their corrugated iron roofs flashing in the morning sun. A pair of chickens exploded into panicked flight, feathers scattering in her wake. A woman stepped out of a doorway, a basket of rice balanced on her hip, directly into Zhao's path. Zhao stabbed the horn, its weak bleat almost lost in the engine noise, and wrenched the handlebars hard right.

The bike's rear wheel lost traction, sending it into a side-ways slide. Zhao's boot scraped the ground as she fought for control. She plowed through the remains of a cooking fire, scattering embers in a violent spray of orange sparks. The hot coals pinged off the bike's metal frame and Zhao's arms like angry fireflies.

The bike fishtailed wildly, its chain shrieking as Zhao muscled it back under control. The woman's startled cry faded behind her, replaced by the angry barking of village dogs.

Her route now clear, Zhao accelerated again. She powered past a pair of goats tied to a tree; the animals rearing back in panic, their ropes pulling taut. The tires threw up a spray of pebbles and red dust as she barreled around a sharp corner, taking it far too fast. The rear wheel kicked out, sending the bike into a heart-stopping slide. Zhao's knee nearly scraped the ground as she leaned into the skid, her muscles straining against the handlebars.

A group of monks sauntered out into her path, their orange robes swirling. With the holy men taking up the whole path, Zhao had no choice. She pulled the throttle to its max and aimed for the center of the group. If the monks didn't move, she'd hit them with enough force to smash them out of the way.

One monk turned and saw the approaching threat. His lips moved, but no sound came out. He frantically tapped his nearest brother on the shoulder and pointed at Zhao, racing toward them. The monks scattered, leaping out of the way not a moment too soon as Zhao roared past in a cloud of smoke and dust.

She weaved around a pair of low-hanging banyan trees and powered toward the main road. The wide expanse of asphalt designed for tourists' buses and executive cars, promised Zhao's quickest escape from the temple complex. Picturing the map of Cambodia, Zhao estimated that within an hour she could be in the rural areas, and out of the country by lunchtime. She approached the road at full speed, the front wheel hitting the tarmac with a crack. A shockwave jarred up through the front forks, threatening to knock her from the bike. The Honda reared up, but she countered, gripping the saddle with her thighs. The bike bounced twice and barreled to the left, leaving thick streaks of rubber on the asphalt.

Emboldened by the open road stretching out before her, Zhao allowed herself a moment of relief. Sure, things hadn't gone to plan, but all was not lost. The Lotus Key would now be recovered and transported to some vault or museum. With few people knowing what power it held, Zhao assumed security wouldn't be high on the agenda. She would have ample opportunity to quietly steal it back from right under their noses.

She kicked up a gear and reapplied pressure to the throttle. The bike's rear wheel howled, burning rubber and pinging grit and gravel across the road. A battered Isuzu cargo truck bumped right into Zhao's path. She hit the brakes and swung wide, missing the truck by inches.

"Learn to drive, dammit!" Zhao snapped, scowling at the driver. The truck's faded blue paint, scraped down to the primer, suggested that driving like an idiot was this guy's modus operandi.

Zhao swerved further into the center of the road and flicked the driver an obscene gesture. Pulling level with the Isuzu's hood, she heard the truck's engine roar as the driver hit the gas. The Isuzu sped up, now matching Zhao's speed.

"What is this joker's problem?" Zhao groaned, working the throttle in an attempt to wring more speed from the bike's pathetic engine. She slid forward, winning another few inches, only for the truck to accelerate again.

Ahead, the horn of a tuk-tuk coming in the opposite direction howled for Zhao to get out of the way. She pulled in closer to the truck's side, the peeling paint now close enough to touch. Then, unexpectedly, the tuk-tuk, in fact a pair of tuk-tuks driving nose to tail, hit the brakes. The small vehicles pulled a one-eighty, two wheels leaving the asphalt. They accelerated again, pulling in alongside Zhao in a neat line.

"What is wrong with these people?" Zhao hissed through clenched teeth, searching for an escape route.

The truck swung in closer, looming inches from her left shoulder. She eyed the vehicle and got several return stares from numerous chickens in the cages on the truck's flatbed.

She turned back to the road and saw a tourist bus hit the brakes. The bus slowed to a crawl right in the center of the road, just ahead.

Acting in sync, as though commanded by some unseen force, both tuk-tuks and the truck hit the brakes. As the rear of the bus loomed up ahead, its taillights strobing, Zhao had no choice but to slow as well. She glanced over her shoulder and saw that one of the tuk-tuk drivers had dropped in behind her, preventing her from doubling back. The truck shuffled further in, now an inch from her handlebars.

Before the vehicles could completely box her in, Zhao jumped off the bike. The Honda clattered to the tarmac, its engine still running. She landed in a crouch, spun on the ball of her foot and sprinted through a narrow gap between the bus and the leading tuk-tuk.

The tuk-tuk driver darted from his seat, reaching for her.

Zhao wheeled sideways, avoiding the man's grip by less than an inch. As the other drivers jumped into the fray, she sprinted across the road. As she reached the other side of the road, a pair of vendors leaped out to block her path.

"These people are mad," Zhao groaned, sidestepping, then vaulting a fruit stall. Her foot clipped the table, sending a stack of mangos and lychees skittering in all directions.

Zhao landed and broke immediately into a run. She'd not covered ten feet when two temple guards turned and charged at her. She veered the other way, once again only just missing their outstretched hands. She swung around and saw the edge of the forest a few paces away. In that moment of frantic escape, she figured if she could get into the forest, she could pick her way through the undergrowth unseen.

She sprinted for the trees, her feet slipping over loose earth and her hands pumping at her sides. When she was a few paces away, a pair of tour guides stepped out, blocking her way.

Zhao dodged left, but this time the men were too close. She launched into an attack, raising her fists. Before she could throw a single punch, a hand closed around her wrist. An arm locked around her shoulders, jarring her to a stop.

She glanced over her shoulder and saw the street vendor who had kept pace with her all the way from the road. Several more people closed in from behind, from the sides, and in front.

Zhao struggled as more hands grabbed at her arms, shoulders, back and legs. She worked one free and drove an elbow backward, attempting to strike one of her captors, but a firm hand stopped her motion as more people pressed in. She glanced around at the faces of her countless captors— market vendors, tourists, hotel workers, tours guides, drivers. Then, working together, as though of a united mind, the group forced Zhao down onto her knees and onto the ground.

As a police siren wailed in the distance, Zhao succumbed to the pinning weight of countless people. Lying in the dust, she cursed silently to herself.

EPILOGUE

The *Balonia*, Gulf of Thailand. One week later.

ATHENA LEANED ON THE RAILING OF THE *BALONIA'S* BACK DECK and rubbed at her temples. Even a week after controlling the Lotus Key, she felt echoes of the strange sensation ripple through her mind. It was like a hangover, an unsteady perception, clinging there at the edges of her thoughts. Looking out at the horizon, she felt the world around her steady.

"I'm sure it'll get easier," Alexander Winslow said, joining Athena at the railing. "You went through a stressful situation."

Eden sauntered across the deck and stood at the railing on Athena's other side.

"I know, that's what people keep telling me," Athena said, clamping her eyes shut, then opening them again. "That's not really the ..." Her voice trailed off as she stopped herself saying whatever she had in her mind.

"The world is a safer place because of what you've done," Eden said. "The Lotus Key is now locked away in one of our deepest vaults, surrounded by more security than Fort Knox."

"And the discs?" Athena asked.

"Stored separately," Eden replied. "Different facilities, different continents. No one person knows the location of all three pieces."

"In short, no one will be able to reach it," Winslow said.

"And ..." Athena paused, pulling the courage to ask the question. "And Zhao? What's happening to her?"

"She's opted for extradition to China," Eden said. "We're monitoring the situation and will intervene if necessary."

"She's connected. She'll get out," Athena said.

"Not necessarily," Eden said, flashing a knowing smile. "But either way, you don't need to worry."

"I get that, I know that," Athena said. "But that's not what I'm worried about."

"What is it then?" Winslow said, gripping the railing and looking out at the gently rippling water.

"And don't you dare say it's nothing," Eden added, her tone sharper than she intended. "I mean, I've always been able to see through your secrets." She turned from Athena to Winslow. "And he's got a ridiculous ability to sense when someone's not being honest."

Athena exhaled and then looked at father and daughter on either side. "Okay, this sounds crazy."

"I very much doubt it'll be the craziest thing you've said," Eden said.

"I can't stop thinking about the feeling of being connected to the key in that way," Athena pushed her fingers against her temples. "It's as though I felt its power and understood its ability. It felt like some kind of—"

"Addiction?" Eden finished her friend's sentence.

Athena turned and looked at her. "Exactly like that. It

felt as though in that moment I was so alive. I was weight-less, powerful, invincible. It was like a dream. Now that I've experienced that, the world seems so cold."

Eden wrapped her arm around her friend and pulled her in close.

"That makes sense," Winslow said, his eyes fixed on the horizon. "There are suggestions that the kings who used the Lotus Key suffered with paranoia, violent outbursts and even hallucinations. What you're experiencing could explain that. In fact, I suspect that's why Indravarman decided the Lotus Key was too dangerous. He saw how it affected his father, turning him from a powerful ruler into a wreck in those final years."

"I understand that," Athena said, her head drooping into her chest. "But I feel that this is worse, somehow sinister. It's as though I crossed a line I shouldn't have."

"What do you mean?" Winslow turned, looking at Athena with genuine concern.

"There was a time there," Athena said, her voice so quiet that the others had to lean in to hear her, "when I under-stood what Zhao was trying to do. I had the ability to reach into people's minds and unite them for a single purpose. I used that power to get us out of the chamber, and capture Zhao ..."

"You did what was required to save humanity as we know it," Winslow said.

"A humanity where people kill each other, hate one another, see the differences rather than the similarities," Athena snapped.

"Yes, but that's the cost of free will," Winslow said.

"Everything has a cost, right?" Eden said. "It's those differences, those beliefs, cultures, and individual thoughts that make us who we are. Of course, that comes with challenges, but that's—"

"But the cost is so great!" Athena said, her voice suddenly hard. "Like Zhao, I saw the people in those detention camps. I talked with those who had lost relatives with no explanation. How can that be justified?"

"Because," Eden said, her voice level, "the alternative is—"

"The alternative would be even worse," Athena said, letting out a breath that was so deep it seemed to drain her of energy. "But that's what scares me. When I was connected to the key, it all made perfect sense. I could see exactly how to fix everything, how to make people stop fighting, stop hating. The power was right there."

"And that's precisely why you were the right person to have faced this challenge," Winslow said, planting a hand on Athena's shoulder. "Because you're questioning it even now."

"Am I though?" Athena's voice cracked. "Because part of me, right down here," she pushed a fist against her stomach, "wonders if Zhao was right. I don't agree with her methods, but this is a fundamental problem. We keep saying we're protecting humanity's right to be different, but, by the same token, we're protecting people's ability to be hateful."

"The key here is in the *choice*," Winslow said. "Of course, we must encourage people to do the right thing. But ultimately, if there's no choice, then doing the right thing has no value."

"Actually, we met this old monk at the temple that said something about this," Eden said. "He spoke in riddles the whole time, but one thing he said sort of made sense. Something about—"

"The lotus flower is an icon of purity, not because it is beautiful, but because it must endure the murky water before it can flourish in the sunlight," boomed a voice from behind them. The three turned around to see Lavigne stride bombastically onto the deck. "Only those who make it through the darkness deserve the light!" he announced, his arms spread wide.

"That memory of yours is astounding," Eden said, catching the professor's eyes.

"Stick with it," Winslow whispered in Athena's ear. "Trust you did the right thing, and it will get easier." Winslow slipped out his phone and fired off a text message. "Ready for a demonstration of humanity's ability to choose for itself?" he said so quietly that only Athena could hear.

Athena nodded once and turned to Eden. "By the way, I heard what you said in the chamber when you thought I was under the influence of the key," Athena said, looking at Eden and then Winslow.

"Yeah, that thing about you being like my sister," Eden said, grinning wolfishly. "It was a high-pressure situation. I didn't know what I was saying."

"Whatever," Athena said, clamping one arm around Eden's shoulder and the other around Winslow. "You guys are my family, whether you like it or not. Plus, now we get to do yoga together."

"What do you mean?" Eden said, turning to look at her friend.

"You said that if you ever needed yoga skills to fight off a psychopath threatening the human race, then you would take it seriously," Athena said, folding her arms.

"You did actually say that," Lavigne said. "And you can't argue with my memory."

Eden spun around, pointing her finger at Lavigne. "Hold on professor, you weren't even there at that time!"

Lavigne shrugged, grinned, and sauntered away.

"Answer this question: did your knowledge of yoga save your life, and as such humanity, or not?" Athena said, grinning.

"I ... um ..." Eden frowned, knowing she was beaten.

"You have to see this!" Baxter said, sprinting out on to the rear deck. "Something's been found, its—"

"Is he your family too?" Eden said, nodding at Baxter.

"What?" Baxter said.

"Yes. Everyone needs an annoying little brother," Athena said, stepping forward and driving a fist into Baxter's shoulder. "Come on, bro, what have you got to show us?"

Baxter led the group inside. He ran to the computer and tapped on the keyboard. The image of an ancient temple appeared on the screen, barely visible beneath the forest.

"This temple's been discovered in a remote area of Laos," Baxter said. "It's totally unmapped. The authorities want a team there ASAP before it's crawling with tourists."

"You know what," Winslow said, glancing theatrically at his watch. "I've not got much scheduled in the next few days. I think I'll suggest that Beaumont, DeLuca and I head up there. It's been a while since I really put the old brain cells to work. What do you think, professor?"

"Non merci," Lavigne said, spinning around and presenting Winslow with the palm of his hand. "I have no desire to see another jungle as long as I live. But, if you want to send me the photographs, I will gladly help you with the translation when I'm back at home in Paris."

"Oh, merveilleux Paris!" Athena said, slipping into an uncanny French accent and soliciting a laugh from the others.

"Let me guess," Eden said, "bugs, diseases—"

"Sunburn," Baxter added.

"Although these temples do look incredible," Lavigne said, stepping up to the screen as Baxter cycled through the images.

"You do have plenty of sunscreen left over," Eden said. "Oh, speaking of ancient relics that should probably stay lost in time, I have something for you." She crossed the office and slid something from a drawer.

The professor adjusted his spectacles with poorly concealed excitement and accepted the package. "You didn't have to—"

"See what it is before you thank me," Eden said, holding up a hand.

Lavigne opened the bag and slipped his hand inside. "My scarf!" he said, pulling out the green and yellow silken scarf which they'd forcibly removed from him on their arrival back at the *Balonia*.

"I took it to the best laundry in the Gulf of Thailand," Eden said, looking at the garment which, although bedraggled, had retained some of its color.

Lavigne shot to his feet, swung the scarf around his neck, and paced across the office. "Once again, I feel ready for the streets of Paris ... although ..." he said, his attention caught by one of the images Baxter was cycling through on the screen.

"Paris will still be there in two weeks," Winslow said, sharing a wry smile with the rest of the team.

"Look at those markings," Lavigne said, stepping forward in awe. "They're ...

The group prepared themselves to utter his next word.

"They're ... Do you realize that this could predate the Khmer Empire?" Lavigne said, spinning around and looking at Winslow. "Think of the historical implications!"

"What about the snake implications?" Baxter muttered.

"And the spider implications," Eden added.

"Bah!" Lavigne waved away their concerns. "Where's your sense of adventure? I've always loved to be around the natural world. How soon can we be there?"

Now everyone in the office laughed and then glanced at each other.

"Incroyable!" they shouted as one.

The seventh book in the Eden Black Archaeological
Thriller Series will be out toward the end of 2025.

Pre-order it now to be one of the first people to read it.

Follow the link below or search your local Amazon store for
'Eden Black book 7'

https://www.lukerichardsonauthor.com/edenblack7

AUTHOR'S NOTE

And there we are, Eden's sixth adventure comes to an end. Thank you so much for joining me. It's wonderful to be able to share my stories with you!

Completing a book is always a time for reflection and a chance to look forward to the next adventure. As I write this in December 2024, it's just a few weeks shy of six years since I started to write my first book—the story that ultimately became Kathmandu Killers.

I was working as a high school English teacher at the time, and frustrated with the lack of creativity and freedom the job offered me. When I started writing, all those years ago, I never imagined that this would turn into a job that I deeply love. By buying, reading and reviewing (hopefully!) this book, you're helping me sustain that, so thank you very much.

As with all my stories, I aim to weave something from the setting into the narrative. Mrs. R and I visited Cambodia in July 2024 as research for this book and absolutely loved it. It's a beautiful country with mountains, beaches and incredible temples—we'll return for sure. At the start of our trip, we spent several days visiting the temples in the Angkor region—including the world-famous Angkor Wat. While the Lotus Key, the discs, and the hidden carving are figments of my imagination, there are large parts of this book that could be true or are my interpretation of actual events and places.

Angkor Wat, and the city of Angkor Thom are vast places, expanses of which are still covered by jungle. Scans from helicopters and even from space have shown how big the civilization was—the biggest in the world at that time. I'm certain that many secrets still lie hidden, with undiscovered sites yet to be revealed. The carvings adorning the temple walls also surely hold layers of meaning—like the great works of western writers do—but what those meanings might be is left to the imagination. Although there's no evidence that these carvings point toward a lost and powerful relic, it's a possibility, right?

The Ta Prohm Stegosaurus exists as discussed by the characters in this book. Of course, lots of people say it looks like a wild boar, or a cow with a funny-looking face, while others claim it was added later as a joke. Although these possibilities might be true, I think it's much more fun to let the imagination take over. I'm not suggesting that dinosaurs roamed the planet in the twelfth century, but tales of extinct beasts could have been handed down through the generations to people at that time. Compare this, if you will, to our modern myths surrounding dragons. We're all pretty certain that dragons don't exist right now, but creatures that looked a bit like them might have roamed the planet at some point, or they're an amalgamation of several creatures combined. Either way, to say that it's a wild boar that's not up to the standard of the rest of the carvings, is missing the fun.

The chamber beneath Angkor Wat's central lotus tower

exists and is documented. It's neither as vast, nor as grand as the one I've described in this story. The light well running down the center of the tower is there too. It's designed with such precision that during the equinoxes, when the sun is directly overhead, a shaft of light shines directly into the chamber.

Some suggest this chamber was a mausoleum for King Jayavarman VII, who built the temple, although his remains aren't there. Of course, his remains could have been removed in the intervening years, but the existence of the place raises some interesting questions for me, which I had fun exploring in this story.

To add further intrigue, Chinese diplomat Zhou Daguan who visited Angkor in 1296, described temple vaults overflowing with royal treasures. Yet today, these fabled treasure chambers are either empty, or more excitingly, undiscovered. The treasure could have been looted by invading armies, moved by the Khmer kings themselves, or (my favorite theory) could lie somewhere undiscovered.

Much of what we know about Angkor during this time is thanks to Zhao Daguan, who spent nearly a year in the city and documented his observations. His account provides an invaluable glimpse into Khmer life, the architectural marvels, and the society that thrived there. Daguan was awestruck by Angkor Wat and described its grandeur as surpassing anything he had seen. He noted the intricate carvings, vast reservoirs, and impressive city planning. Beyond the temples, his writings shed light on the daily lives of the people, their social hierarchy, customs, clothing, and agriculture. His, remains one of the best accounts of life at the time.

Daguan vividly described the king's divine status, the elaborate court rituals, and the bustling markets filled with goods from across the region. It was actually Daguan who reported that the Khmer king visited a golden tower at night to commune with a spirit. This spirit was believed to be the true source of the kingdom's power, and if the king should miss this meeting, disaster would strike. Daguan reports that if the spirit failed to show up even once, it was an omen of the king's imminent death. If the king himself missed the appointment, there was a national disaster coming. Some claim that Daguan made this up, or misunderstood what was going on, which could of course be true. Either way, this provided me with the idea for the Lotus Key, and how the king might use the relic's power to communicate his wishes to the people. The truth behind what the Khmer King actually did every night in this golden tower we'll never know, but we can imagine!

Even by the standards of today's sprawling cities, the vastness of Angkor is awe-inspiring. Much of it is thanks to Suryavarman II, who expanded the empire to its greatest extent and then Jayavarman VII, who rebuilt the empire after the Cham invasion and constructed iconic temples like Bayon, Ta Prohm, and Preah Khan. We meet Jayavarman VII at the start of this book, on his deathbed, ready to pass the reins over to his son Indravarman II. Although Indravarman ruled for over twenty years, there is very little recorded information about him—it's almost as though he's been erased from history.

Historians think that his successor, Jayavarman VIII, systematically destroyed records of Indravarman's reign in something of a coverup. In fact, only a single inscription survives to tell us he died in 1243, leaving everything else a mystery. Indravarman II's "disappearance" from history might be linked to something deeper than royal rivalry. As a devoted Buddhist ruler following his father's footsteps, he faced a kingdom increasingly pulling back toward Hinduism. When Jayavarman VIII took power, he led an aggressive Hindu restoration, potentially explaining his attempt to erase his Buddhist predecessors from memory.

Although Indravarman's reign was peaceful, the empire was now in decline. The Khmer grip on Champa slipped away, and the rising Sukhothai kingdom carved off western territories. The rest, as they say, is lost to history. Or maybe he took the Lotus Key out of the temple and without that power, the empire disintegrated. It fits, doesn't it?

After a week in Siem Reap, which is the modern city closest to Angkor Wat, Mrs. R and I traveled to the capital city, Phnom Penh. A thriving, vast and noisy place, Phnom Penh is currently in the midst of incredible growth. I expect that within ten years, with all the foreign investment it's receiving, it'll rival Bangkok or Singapore as an international hub.

Preferring less chaotic places, we quickly moved on to the island of Koh Rong. Although we initially planned to spend only a few days on the island, we were so captivated by its charm that we ended up staying for nearly two weeks. We made our temporary home in a secluded beach hut, two hundred yards from a bar that served cold beer and barbeque food late into the night. Our only company was a family of monkeys that lived in the trees. If there's a better place to spend a few days, I've not yet found it. It was there that I decided, in some small way, Eden should visit the island. Although Koh Rong isn't central to the story, it was important to me that it got an honorary mention in the early pages of this book.

Not far from Koh Rong, lies the Bokor Hill Station where Mei-Ling Zhao based her nefarious operations. As described in the story, Bokor was built by French colonists in the 1920s. The site was envisioned as a luxury retreat to escape the sweltering heat of the lowlands. The centerpiece, the grand Bokor Palace Hotel & Casino, which once hosted Cambodia's elite in art deco splendor, is now an empty ruin. An abandoned church stands nearby and the old post office, police station, and royal apartments are also frozen in time. The whole area was deserted during Cambodia's wars and the Khmer Rouge insurgency in the late 20th century. The eerie, mist-shrouded ruins have since drawn tourists, artists, and filmmakers. Unfortunately, we didn't make it here on this trip, but next time it's top of the list.

As you may know, I share a lot of the facts and legends that go into my stories on social media. Whilst I love creating these, and get loads of positive comments, I also get a few negative ones too.

Here are a three that caught my eye this week:

This is utterly stupid and is frankly offensive. Try promoting real history and archaeology instead of fantasy and nonsense.

Whenever i tell myself to try to be nicer on the internet someone posts something as stupid as this and then i see the insanely stupid people in the comments saying it's a stegosaurs.

Welcome to idiotville Who's excuse investment! As alexa says, you've been exiled here for some kinda punishment! Since someone put a symbol in front of your creations you've been Imprisoned ever since. Funding others amusement!

(I've left the spelling mistakes to illustrate the level of madness we're dealing with here!)

I want to say now, to let it be known, I am not a historian, archaeologist, or scientist—I'm a storyteller. I tell tales about things that interest me, and I hope they'll interest you too. Sometimes the subjects of my books pose interesting questions by contradicting the mainstream narrative. If someone's offended by this, or takes this too seriously, then that's on them. These negative comments make me want to work harder to reach more people who are interested in the things I have to say.

I don't promise that my stories are true, instead I strive to make them fun, exciting and bring joy to those who are open to them. Life can be challenging so if you—or anyone —finds a moment of escape within the pages of my adventures, then it's all been worthwhile. I also love my books to ask questions, like:

"Where do we draw the line between free will and peace?"

Or:

"How did a civilization with only primitive tools build a structure as vast and grand as Angkor Wat?"

Or:

"Is it possible that we don't have everything worked out yet?"

It's also important to me that my writing sheds light on things which I don't think should be ignored. The so-called re-education camps in China's Xinjiang region that are mentioned in this book, for example. Although we didn't visit this place on screen—I was compelled to highlight this issue in the background.

The Uyghur people are a predominantly Muslim ethnic group who live primarily in the Xinjiang Uyghur Autonomous Region in northwestern China. In recent years, reports have surfaced of mass detention and surveillance targeting Uyghurs in Xinjiang. Human rights organizations estimate that over one million Uyghurs, along with other Muslim minorities, have been detained in so-called 're-education camps.' Officially, the Chinese government refers to these facilities as vocational training centers aimed at combating extremism and fostering economic opportunities. However, leaked documents, survivor testimonies, and satellite imagery reveals a different reality.

The international community has responded with sanctions, calls for investigations, and increased awareness campaigns. However, China's significant global influence complicates efforts to address these human rights abuses, leaving the Uyghur people in a precarious situation.

I also wanted to raise awareness of Cambodia's stolen works of art. While walking through the temples today, it's sadly all too common to see the feet of statues remaining, with the rest having been hacked off and sold. While the country suffered under a brutal dictatorship, carvings and ceremonial artifacts were taken from sacred sites across the region and are now in private collections or museums around the world.

Cambodia is now fighting back with a national campaign to recover and repatriate these relics. A team of archaeologists, investigators, and legal experts are working to trace, document and repatriate the country's stolen treasures. Many major museums and private collectors are being forced to confront the provenance of their acquisitions, and several have already returned artifacts to their rightful homes.

These stolen artifacts are not the only haunting remnant of the conflict that once tore the country apart. Even after decades of peace, Cambodia remains one of the most heavily landmine-infested countries in the world. For many

Cambodians, parts of their villages remain off limits for fear of unexploded devices.

The densest concentration of mines exists in the north-western regions near the Thai border (where Eden and her crew visit) with significant numbers around temple complexes that once served as military strongholds. Brave men and women painstakingly clear the ground inch by inch using metal detectors, trained animals, and mechanical de-mining machines, saving lives and restoring safety to communities.

While in Cambodia, we visited an exhibition on how this continues to plague the poorest communities. Inspired by what we saw, we will support the Landmine Relief Fund in 2025. Although there are several charities who do great work in this area, this is the one who runs the museum we visited. In addition to removing the mines, they work with an organization that has built nearly 50 schools on or near old minefields. This means that a small percentage of the money you paid for this book and my other books will end up improving lives of people in the area that inspired this story. Should you be interested you can see the work the Landmine Relief Fund do on their website: https://www. landmine-relief-fund.com/

Although Eden remains the protagonist in the book, I enjoyed exploring Athena's character a little more within these pages. It was fun to dig through her past and have Mei-Ling Zhao arrive on the scene. Throughout the series, I'm enjoying exploring various characters and their relationships with each other.

As I write this, looking into 2025, I'm thinking about the next adventure both for me and Eden. I'm going to take a short break from this series and work on a couple of new projects in the first months of the new year. Don't worry,

Eden Black and the rest of the crew will return toward the end of 2025. What that adventure will look like, we'll all have to wait and see!

Once again, thank you for your company and I can't wait for our next adventure together.

Luke

December 2024.

CAN A PRICELESS PAINTING VANISH INTO THIN AIR?

Eden Black meets Ernest Dempsey's Adriana Villa

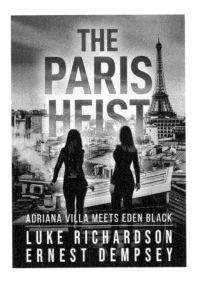

Ten years ago, Bernard Moreau baffled police by stealing a Picasso from the Modern Art Museum. He was arrested and imprisoned, but the painting was never found.

Now, back on the streets, all eyes are on Moreau. But he's a skilled thief and isn't going to make it easy.

EDEN BLACK can't stand corruption and the theft of priceless art. This case reeks of them both. Heading to Paris, she vows to return the Picasso to its rightful home as soon as possible.

ADRIANA VILLA works alone, always, that's the rule. So, when she sees another woman following her mark, things get heated.

To find the painting before a dirty police inspector with a score to settle, the pair must put their egos aside and work together. What they discover shows that nothing is as simple as it first seems.

THE PARIS HEIST is an up-tempo novella which will keep you pinned to the pages until the very end. If you like the sound of a race against the clock, action packed, adventure thriller, set amongst the blissful Parisian streets, you'll love THE PARIS HEIST.

Read The Paris Heist for FREE today!
https://www.lukerichardsonauthor.com/paris

FREE BONUS SCENES

Prose is architecture, not interior decoration.
Ernest Hemingway.

I discover the story as I'm writing it. Although I know the general direction, I don't know exactly how we're going to get there. As such, sometimes I write scenes that don't make it in to the final cut.

It's often in the editing process that I realize I've written a scene that isn't necessary in the final story. And as Hemingway so beautifully writes, if a scene doesn't add to the story, if it doesn't get us closer to the finale, then it shouldn't be there. In The Lotus Key, there were two scenes that didn't make it to the final cut.

Should you want to read them, they're available via the link below. You'll need to enter your email address and will be added to my spam-free email list, the Adventurers' Guild. Of course, you're welcome to leave at any time, although I hope you don't.

Tap here to read the bonus scenes for FREE
Or visit: www.lukerichardsonauthor.com/lotusbonus

THANK YOU!

Books are difficult to write.

Not a month goes by where I don't think it's "too hard," or "not worth it." Every time this happens — as though by magic — I get an email from a reader like you.

Some are simple messages of encouragement, others are heartfelt, each one shows me that I'm not doing this alone. Those connections have kept me going when all seemed lost, and given me purpose when I didn't see it myself.

A special heartfelt thank you to those who support me on Patreon. These people support me with a few dollars, pounds or euros a month. In exchange it's my pleasure to share my travels with them through postcards and other random gifts from the road.

Some Patreon supporters even get the opportunity to read my books early. If that resonates with you, check out my Patreon here:

https://www.patreon.com/lukerichardson

Don't feel obliged, the fact you are here is more than enough.

Thanks goes to (in alphabetical order):

Allison Valentine and The Haemocromatois Society

Anja Peerdeman

Chris Oldfield author of 'The Less Years' series

David Berens (for the cover)

Fritzi Redgrave

James Colby Slater

Jan Galloway

JazzLauri

Jim Howie

Ken Preston

Kirsty 'Wisey' Wiseman

Mark Fearn from the Bookmark Facebook Group

Martha Richardson (Mrs. R)

Marti Panikkar

Melody Highman

Ray Braun

Rosemary Kenny

Sue Laughton

Tim Birmingham

Toulla Corti (www.toullacreative.com)

Valerie Richardson

HAVE YOU READ MY INTERNATIONAL DETECTIVE SERIES?

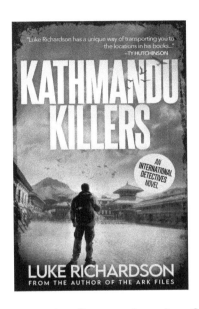

You visit a restaurant in a far-away city, only to find you're on the menu.

Leo Keane is sent abroad to track down Allissa, a politician's daughter who vanished two years ago in Kathmandu. But with a storm on the horizon and intrigue at every turn, Leo's mission may be more dangerous than he bargained for... A propulsive international thriller!

READ TODAY

https://www.lukerichardsonauthor.com/kathmandu

HI, I'M LUKE...

...and I'm applying for the job as your next favorite author!

As an Amazon bestselling author, I've had the honor of sharing my stories with readers around the world. My books are a passport to adventure, blending history, intrigue, and suspense into gripping tales that transport you my favourite places around the world.

From the sun-baked Pyramids of Giza to the glittering skyscrapers of Hong Kong, and from the shadowy back-streets of Kathmandu to the depths of the Atlantic Ocean, my stories will take you somewhere new and exciting. But it's not just about the destinations; you'll meet fascinating characters, encounter unexpected twists, and experience edge-of-your-seat action along the way.

My love for storytelling was ignited during my first trip

to India. As my taxi wove through the streets of Mumbai at dawn, I watched the city unfold like a story. The sight of people going about their daily lives—washing, playing, tending to animals—sparked a desire to capture and share these vivid experiences through writing.

When I'm not globetrotting in search of my next story, you'll find me in Nottingham, England, where I call home. Before embarking on my writing career, I spent years as a high school English teacher, and a nightclub DJ.

Nothing brings me more joy than hearing that my stories have transported someone to a new place or kept them up all night. Whether you're drawn to the lovable characters, intricate plots, or fast-paced storytelling, I'm always working hard to bring you even more thrilling adventures.

So, if you're a history buff, a travel addict, or simply in search of your next literary escape, you're in the right place. I appreciate you being here, now let's hit the road.

Luke :D